Cassie was back.

Her cheeks were pink from the cold, and as Jake adjusted to the shock of finding her on his front steps, he finally noticed what she was holding.

A baby.

Wrapped toe to neck in some kind of zip-up covering, all Jake could see of the child were big blue eyes—just like his own.

A jolt of emotions shot through him so hard he gripped the doorknob tight to keep from falling over in shock.

"What the hell?"

"Jake," Cassie said, "meet your son. Luke."

"My *son*?" Silently, Jake congratulated himself on the control keeping his voice from raging with the fury erupting inside him.

He couldn't believe this. For a year and a half, this woman had haunted him, waking and sleeping. Hell, he'd hardly known her and shouldn't have given her another thought once she was gone. But he had.

He'd even fantasized a couple times about seeing her here again.

He just had never imagined her carrying his child along with her.

His child. He had a son.

The

Pow

THE COWBOY'S PRIDE AND JOY

BY
MAUREEN CHILD

Published in Great Britain 2014
by Mills & Boon, an imprint of Harlequin (UK) Limited,
Eton House, 18-24 Paradise Road, Richmond, Surrey, TW9 1SR

© 2014 Maureen Child

ISBN: 978-0-263-91485-6

51-1114

Harlequin (UK) Limited's policy is to use papers that are natural, renewable and recyclable products and made from wood grown in sustainable forests. The logging and manufacturing processes conform to the legal environmental regulations of the country of origin.

Printed and bound in Spain
by CPI, Barcelona

Maureen Child writes for the Mills & Boon® Desire™ line and can't imagine a better job. Being able to indulge your love for romance, as well as being able to spin stories just the way you want them told, is—in a word—perfect.

A seven-time finalist for the prestigious Romance Writers of America RITA® Award, Maureen is the author of more than one hundred romance novels. Her books regularly appear on the bestseller lists and have won several awards, including a Prism, a National Readers' Choice Award, a Colorado Romance Writers Award of Excellence and a Golden Quill.

One of her books, *The Soul Collector,* was made into a CBS TV movie starring Melissa Gilbert, Bruce Greenwood and Ossie Davis. If you look closely, in the last five minutes of the movie, you'll spot Maureen, who was an extra in the last scene.

Maureen believes that laughter goes hand in hand with love, so her stories are always filled with humor. The many letters she receives assure her that her readers love to laugh as much as she does.

Maureen Child is a native Californian, but has recently moved to the mountains of Utah. She loves a new adventure, though the thought of having to deal with snow for the first time is a little intimidating.

This book is dedicated to my grand-dog, Bristow. Funny, sweet, loyal, Bristow loves with his whole heart and we're so glad to have him in our family.

One

"When Boston comes to Montana, it's never a good thing." Jake Hunter frowned into the distance.

"You always were too hard on your mother."

Jake turned his head to look at the older man standing beside him. At seventy-five years old, Ben Hawkins didn't stand as straight and tall as he once had. But he still had a full head of snow-white hair, piercing blue eyes, and a face weathered and tanned from years of working in the sun.

"And you were always too soft on her."

Ben shrugged that away with a half smile. "She's my daughter."

"There is that." Jake nodded. "Anyway, if it all goes as promised, this will be the last time Boston comes calling for anything but a family visit."

"I've got to ask. Are you sure about this?" Ben

pulled the collar of his coat up higher around his neck against the cold autumn wind. "I mean, what you're planning can't be changed. You're signing away your rights to the business your family built."

"Oh," Jake assured him, "I'm sure. This has been a long time coming, Pop." Jake shook his head. "Hunter Media has nothing I want. Never has."

And he knew how much that fact irritated his mother. She had always planned on Jake taking over the day-to-day running of the company built by her husband's family. The fact that Jake had never been interested really hadn't bothered her any. Elise Hawkins Hunter was nothing if not determined.

Ben snorted a laugh. "You always were more stubborn than anything else."

"Not stubborn." Jake took a deep breath, relishing the sharp, cold sting that hit his lungs. "I just know what I want. Always have."

Now he glanced around at the ranch he loved. The place that had been his solace and comfort when he'd come here during the summer as a kid—and when he'd returned here after leaving the military.

October in the mountains of Montana was spectacular. As though God was putting on a show just before the winter cold settled in. The trees were turning brilliant shades of gold, orange and red. Dark clouds scudded across a sky so wide and blue it almost hurt your eyes to look at it. From the corral and barn came the sounds of horses and the men working with them. And spilling out in front of and below the huge ranch house he'd built was Whitefish Lake, sapphire water surrounded by tall pines that dipped and swayed with the wind.

The view soothed the dark places inside him, just as it had from the first time he'd seen it as a kid. Jake had known even then that *this* was his place. Not Boston, where he was born and where his family created and ruled a dynasty. But here on the mountain where his grandfather had carved out a way of life that spoke to Jake's soul in a way that nothing else ever had.

"No," he murmured, gaze still locked on the lake below. "Boston has nothing to offer me that can compete with this place."

"Have to say I agree," Ben mused. "Though your mother never did feel the bone-deep connection to the land that you and I do."

That simple statement made Jake smile. Maybe a love of the land skipped generations, he thought. This ranch had been in Ben's family for more than a hundred years, always falling to the oldest child to maintain the legacy the Hawkinses had built since the first settler stumbled into Montana and staked a claim to the land. Until, Jake thought, his mother.

Elise Hawkins Hunter hadn't felt the pull of the ranch. His mother had been born and raised here, and she had escaped as soon as she was able. Going to college in Boston, she'd met and married Jake's father there and settled into the kind of life she'd dreamed of. No early mornings to take care of animals. No quiet stillness. No solitude when the ranch was snowed in.

She'd made plenty of trips to the ranch to visit her parents and sent Jake and his sister out here for a few weeks every summer, but Boston was her home as the ranch had never been.

Elise was still puzzled by her son's decision to walk away from moneyed sophistication in favor of hard work and empty spaces. But Jake had his own money—a fortune he'd built through good investments and well-chosen risks. He didn't need to enslave himself to a desk to get his share of Hunter Media.

His mother might not ever understand his decision, but she had at least, finally, accepted it.

"So when's your mother's assistant due to arrive?"

Jake glanced at his grandfather. "Sometime today, and with any luck, by tomorrow she'll be on her way back to Boston."

"Shame she had to fly all the way here to have you sign papers you could have faxed in."

"You know Mom. A stickler for details." Jake shook his head and hopped off the fence, his battered brown boots sinking into the soft dirt of the corral. "She wants the papers notarized and the assistant's a notary."

"Handy," Ben said. "But then, your mom's always been a thorough one."

Thorough. And stubborn. There was a part of Jake that still didn't believe his mother had given up on luring him back to Boston. But whether she had or not didn't really matter, did it? He wasn't going anywhere. Montana was his home. His sanctuary. Damned if he'd give it up.

Cassidy Moore's hands hurt after an hour of gripping the steering wheel tightly enough to make her knuckles white. Driving up a mountain was more harrowing than she would have thought. Maybe if the narrow road had been straight rather than curved with the occasional sharp right-angle turn, it wouldn't have been so bad. But those curves were there and so was the steep drop off the left side.

If she had known the kind of drive she was letting herself in for, she would have tried to rent a tank at the airport in Kalispell rather than the four-wheel-drive sedan she was currently driving.

"But then," she told herself, "a tank never would have fit on this road."

Seriously. The people who built the darn road couldn't have made it a *little* wider? Every time another car came toward her, she winced in anticipation of a horrific crash. The only good thing about this drive was that it wasn't the dead of winter. "Imagine dealing with this road in snow!"

Just the thought of that gave her cold chills. Ordinarily, she probably would have enjoyed this drive through the mountains, with the bright splashes of fall color on either side of her. But the threat of imminent death sort of took the fun out of it.

Cassidy was out of her element and she knew it. Born and raised in Boston, she had never been west of the Massachusetts border. She was used to busy highways, crowded streets and stoplights every block. In her world, tall buildings created shadowy canyons in the city and the sound of honking horns ensured there was never any quiet to be found. Still, she'd be fine. She was only here for the night, and tomorrow she'd be flying back to Boston with the signed paperwork her boss needed.

She pulled off the narrow road and followed a graveled drive up a sharp incline. When she came out from beneath the arch of trees, she simply stopped the car, turned off the engine and stared.

My son refuses to leave his little ranch, her boss had said. *So you'll have to go to him and get these papers signed.*

Little ranch.

Shaking her head, Cassidy got out of the car, her heels shifting precariously on the gravel beneath her feet. She did a slow turn in place, letting her gaze sweep across her surroundings before finally coming back to land on the "little ranch." There was nothing little about it. Granted, the only experience Cassidy had with ranches was what she'd seen on late-night movies. But this was no ordinary place. Jake Hunter's home was a mountain palace.

Two stories tall, the main house was wood and glass, with floor-to-ceiling windows on each story that would provide a wide view of the lake below. Pine trees huddled close to the house, so that it looked as though it was actually a part of the landscape rather than an intrusion. There were other, smaller houses scattered across the property, no doubt for the employees who worked here. *Lucky them,* Cassidy thought, since she couldn't imagine driving up and down that mountain every day for her commute. "Hello, young lady."

Surprised at the deep voice coming from directly behind her, Cassidy spun around so quickly, one of her heels caught on the gravel and her balance went wobbly. The older man snapped one hand out to take her arm to steady her.

"Didn't mean to startle you," he said, giving her a slow smile.

He was in his seventies, but his eyes were sharp and clear and his skin was like old leather from years spent in the sun. His smile was warm and the chuckle beneath his words was kind.

"Sorry," she said, holding one hand out. "I didn't hear you come up. I'm Cassidy Moore."

He took her hand in his and gave it a firm shake. "You're Elise's new assistant." Nodding, he added, "I'm her father, Ben Hawkins."

"She has your eyes."

His smile got wider. "My eyes, but thankfully she got everything else from her mother, God rest her." He took a step back and said, "You're here to see my grandson."

"Yes," she said, grateful for the quick change of subject. "I've got some papers for him to look over and sign…"

"My daughter's a fiend for paperwork," he said, then waved one hand. "Come along with me, I'll take you to Jake."

She glanced at her car, thinking about her purse lying on the front seat, but then she realized that this wasn't Boston and a purse snatcher wasn't going to reach in and grab anything. So she followed Ben Hawkins, taking careful steps that didn't come close to matching his long, even strides.

Cassidy had dressed to impress and now that it was too late, she was rethinking that. She wore black slacks, a white dress shirt and a cardinal-red waist-length jacket. Her black heels added an extra three inches to her measly five-foot-four frame, and in the city that gave her extra confidence. Here, walking on gravel, she could only wish for the sneakers tucked into the bottom of her bag.

But first impressions counted, and she'd wanted to

come across as sleek and professional to her boss's son. So she'd find a way to maneuver over tricky ground and make it look good while she was doing it.

"It's a beautiful place," she said.

"It is that," the older man agreed, slowing his steps a bit. "I lived my whole life here, but in the few years Jake's been in charge he's made so many changes sometimes I look around and can't believe what he's done in so short a time."

She looked at him. "You sound pleased by that."

"Oh, I am." He winked at her. "I know most old men don't care much for change. But far as I'm concerned, if you're not changing, you're dead. So when Jake came to Montana for good, I turned over the ranch to him and said, 'Do what you want.'" Chuckling again, he added, "He took me up on it."

Smiling, she decided she liked Ben Hawkins.

"He started right out building the new ranch house," Ben said, waving one hand at the spectacular building on their left. "Designed it himself and even did a lot of the construction on his own, too."

"It's beautiful," she said, throwing another glance at the gorgeous house.

"It is," he agreed. "Too much house for a man on his own, though."

"On his own?" She frowned a little. "Don't you live there, too?"

Ben laughed. "No, I live there."

He pointed at one of the smaller buildings, and she noted that it did look older, somehow more *settled,* than the newer structures around it.

"It's the original ranch house and for me, it's home."

They approached a corral and Ben took her elbow

to steady her as she stepped off the gravel onto soft dirt. Her heels sank and she grimaced, but her gaze was caught on the cowboy riding a big black horse around the interior of the corral.

The cowboy looked as comfortable in the saddle as she was in a desk chair. Animal and man moved as one and Cassidy stepped closer to the rail fence, mesmerized as she watched their progress. There was a cold wind blowing, yet she hardly noticed the chill as she kept her gaze fixed on the man on the horse.

"That's my grandson, Jake," Ben told her. "I'll let him know you're here."

Ben walked off but Cassidy didn't see him go. Instead, she studied the cowboy even more closely. And she realized why it was that her boss hadn't been able to convince her son to move to the city. A man that at home on a horse would never be happy in a city of concrete and cars. Even from a distance there was a wildness to him that intrigued her even as her mind whispered for caution. After all, she wasn't here to admire her boss's son. This visit was not only going to be brief, but strictly business as well. Which didn't mean, she assured herself silently, that she couldn't admire the view.

Ben whistled, sharp and short. Jake looked up, then looked to Cassidy when his grandfather pointed her out. She saw his features tighten and she told herself it didn't matter. But as he rode closer to her, she took a single step back from the corral fence.

Were all horses that big?

Jake Hunter swung down and leaned his forearm on the top rail of the fence even as he rested the toe of one battered boot on the bottom rung. Cassidy swallowed hard. Close up, he was even more intriguing.

Black hair, mostly hidden beneath his hat, curled over the collar of his brown leather jacket. His eyes were so blue and so hard, they looked like chips of ice. Black beard stubble covered his jaws and his mouth was thinned into a straight line. His jeans were faded and worn, and over them, he wore a pair of soft, light brown chaps that seemed to hug what looked like *very* long, muscular legs.

A swirl of something warm and intimate rushed through her and Cassidy took a deep, deliberate breath of the cold mountain air, hoping it would help. It really didn't.

"You're not what I was expecting," he said and his voice was a low rumble.

She could have said, *yeah, same to you.* But she didn't. This was ridiculous. She was here to do a job. This was her boss's *son* for heaven's sake, and standing there ogling him like an idiot was so not the kind of impression she had planned to make.

"Well, I'm pleased to meet you anyway," she finally said and held out one hand.

He glanced at her outstretched palm for a long second or two, then reached through the fence and took her hand in his. An instant zing of electricity shot up her arm to settle in her chest and send her heartbeat into a wild, hard gallop. *Oh my. Only here for ten minutes and I am using horse metaphors.*

Releasing her, Jake took off his hat and speared his fingers through his hair. Which only made things a little worse for Cassidy because really, did he have to have such beautiful, thick, shiny hair?

"Mike!" His shout jolted her out of her thoughts, thank heaven. When another man answered, Jake called out, "Take care of Midnight, will you? I've got some business to see to."

"Sure thing, boss," the man said.

"Midnight's your horse?"

"That's right," Jake told her just before he climbed over the corral fence to jump to the ground right beside her.

There went that little warm bubble of something dangerous, she thought and tried to get a grip. She was not the kind of woman to idly daydream about a gorgeous man. Usually. Jake Hunter seemed to be an exception. He was so tall, she felt dwarfed as he loomed over her, even counting her heels, which were now slipping farther and farther into the dirt.

Frowning, he looked down, then met her eyes and asked, "You wore high heels? To a ranch?"

"Is that a problem?"

"Not for me." A ghost of a smile curved his mouth so briefly, she couldn't be sure it had actually been there at all. Then he turned and headed to the house.

She watched him go, those long legs of his striding purposefully across the graveled drive. He never looked back. Didn't bother to help her as his grandfather had. She opened her mouth to shout after him, but snapped it shut before she could. Fuming silently, Cassidy drew first one heel then the other out of the dirt and started clumsily to the ranch house. Her first impression had gone fabulously badly. Now he thought she was an idiot for not dressing appropriately.

Well, that was fine, because she thought he was a troll for walking off and leaving her when he knew darn well that walking across that gravel in heels was practically a competitive sport. *So much for those warm, intimate thoughts,* she told herself. For a woman to have a decent fantasy going, the hero of said fantasy had to at least be civil.

Which seemed like too much to expect from Jake Hunter.

Jake headed straight for the great room and the wet bar. Usually it would be too early to have a drink, but today was different. Today, he had looked into a pair of cool fog-gray eyes and felt a stirring of something he hadn't even thought about in more than two years. Hell, if he'd had his way he *never* would have felt that deep-down heated tickle of anticipation again.

The only other time he'd ever experienced anything like it had led to a marriage made in hell.

"Good times," he muttered, and tossed his hat to the nearest chair. He shot a quick look out the wide front windows to the sprawl of gravel and grass beyond the glass. Damn woman was still coming, heading to the house with short, wobbly steps that almost made him feel guilty for leaving her to manage on her own.

Almost. Yeah, he could've helped her across the uneven ground, but he would have had to touch her and that buzz of something hot and complicated was still fresh enough in his mind that he didn't want to risk repeating it.

"I didn't ask her to come here," he whispered and poured a shot of Irish whiskey into a crystal tumbler. Lifting the glass, he drank that shot down in one gulp and let the fire in its wake burn away whatever he might have felt if he were any other man.

His gaze fixed on her through the window. Behind her, the wide sky was filling with heavy gray clouds that could bring rain or snow. You just never knew in Montana. Wind lifted her dark blond hair off her shoulders and threw it into a wild halo around her head. Her short red jacket clung to impressive breasts and stopped right at her narrow waist. Her black slacks whipped in the wind, outlining her legs—short but definitely curvy—and those stupid high heels wobbled with every step.

A city girl. Just like the last woman he'd allowed into his life. And even as his body felt interest surge, his mind shrieked for some semblance of sanity. Why in the hell would he let himself be interested in the same kind of woman who had carved out a chunk of his soul not so long ago?

He thought about pouring another drink, then decided against it as his mother's gofer finally made her way onto the porch steps and followed him into the house.

"Mr. Hunter?"

"In here." He heard those heels first, tapping against the bamboo flooring, and as those relentless taps came closer, he stepped out from behind the oak bar to meet her.

She paused in the open, arched doorway and he watched as her gaze swept the room. He saw the pleasure and the approval in her eyes and felt a quick jolt of pride. When he moved to the ranch permanently, he'd wanted to build a new, bigger ranch house. Something that would house the whole family when they came to visit. Something that would mark the land as *his.* He wanted this place stamped as his, and Jake's grandfather had given him free rein.

He'd done a good job on this house. He'd designed it himself, working with an architect to build just the right place—something that would look as though it had always been standing here, in the forest. He had wanted to bring the outdoors in and he had been pleased with the results.

The support beams had been built to look like tree trunks. The windows between those beams showcased the lake below them and the miles of open country, forest and sky that made Montana the best place in the world to live. Dark brown leather couches and chairs were arranged around the huge open space, and a riverstone fireplace stood on the far wall, flames inside the hearth dancing and snapping as a sharp wind chased across the top of the chimney.

"Wow," she said, stepping slowly into the room. "Just…wow."

"Thanks." He smiled in spite of everything, enjoying her reaction to the home he loved. "Pretty great, I admit."

"Oh," she said, shaking her head as she turned in place, taking in everything, "it's better than great. It's so gorgeous I'm even going to forgive you for being a jerk and leaving me out there to make it into the house on my own."

Surprised, he snorted a laugh. "Jerk? Is that the way to talk to your boss's son?"

Cool gray eyes slid over him. "I have a feeling she wouldn't blame me."

He thought about it, imagining his mother's reaction to how he'd left her assistant standing in the yard, and had to wince. "No. Probably not."

"Is there some reason in particular that you're not happy to see me?" she asked. "Or is it women in general you disapprove of?"

One corner of Jake's mouth quirked. "Let's answer that with another question. Are you always this forthright?"

"Usually," she said, nodding. "But I probably shouldn't be. So maybe we should consider ourselves on even ground and start over. Deal?"

He looked at her for a long moment and tried not to notice that her eyes were the very color of the fog that lifted off the surface of the lake. Or that her hair looked soft and tumbled, as if she'd just rolled out of bed. Damn, it really had been too long since he'd had a woman.

"All right," he agreed, to end his train of thought before it went even more astray of the subject at hand. "Deal. Now, you've got some papers for me to look over and sign, correct?"

"Yes. They're in my bag in the car."

She actually turned as if to go lurching out across the gravel again to retrieve her bags. Jake stopped her by saying, "One of the guys will bring your stuff in. You're probably beat from the flying and the drive up the mountain…"

"Actually," she admitted, "I would love a shower and change of clothes."

Oh, he wasn't going to think about her in the shower. He'd been prepared for her to spend the night, though. It was a two-hour drive from the airport, and by the time he finished going over the papers before signing them it would be too dark for her to safely drive down the mountain. So she'd be here overnight and gone in the morning. The earlier the better.

"My housekeeper has your room ready for you," he said abruptly. Leading her across the room, he pointed to the staircase directly opposite the front door. "At the top of the stairs, turn right. Third door on your left."

"Okay," she said, already heading for the stairs. "And thanks."

"Dinner's at seven," he told her. "So come down whenever you're ready."

She laid one hand on the heavily carved banister and turned her head to spear him with one long look. "I'll see you in an hour. We can go over the paperwork before dinner."

"Fine." Good idea. Remember that this was all business. His mother hadn't sent him a woman to warm his bed. She'd sent her assistant here to finally give Jake what he'd wanted for years. Freedom from the Hunter family conglomerate.

Freedom to live his life the way he wanted.

The fact that his mother's messenger was more than he'd expected…well, that wouldn't matter once she was gone.

Two

A few minutes later, Cassidy was trying to relax in a bedroom fit for a queen. She was tired, and she wanted a shower and something to eat. But first, she grabbed her cell phone and checked for coverage. Not surprising to find that she was good to go. Heck, Jake Hunter probably built his own cell tower on the mountain.

Shaking her head, she hit speed dial and listened to the phone ring until her sister answered. "Hey, Claudia," Cassidy said, smiling. "Just wanted to let you know I got here safely."

Her younger sister laughed. "Yeah, Montana's not on the far side of the moon, so I figured you were okay when I didn't hear any news about a plane crash."

"Ouch." Cassidy plopped onto the edge of the bed and let her gaze wander around the bedroom she'd been given for the night.

As spectacular as the rest of the house, the room was as large as her entire studio apartment back in Boston. And furnished better, she added silently. Again, there were floor-to-ceiling windows offering that tremendous view of water surrounded by pines bending and twisting in the wind. There were colorful rugs strewn across the gleaming wood floor, a fire burning cheerfully in the hearth and two overstuffed chairs pulled up in front of it, looking cozy enough to be on a Christmas card. On a narrow table against the wall sat a crystal decanter of what was probably brandy, considering the two bulbous glasses beside it. But there were also two bottles of wine. Red and white and accompanying glasses—which she would so take advantage of as soon as she was off the phone.

The bed she sat on was huge and covered in a silky quilt in varying shades of green that made her think of the forest beyond the house. The mattress was so soft and welcoming, it practically *begged* to be napped on.

"So how did your test go this morning?"

"Aced it," Claudia retorted quickly and then laughed with glee. "I'm going to be the best damn doctor in the country by the time I'm done!"

"You will. And so humble, too," Cassidy said, smiling at her sister's enthusiasm. Since she was a child, Claudia had wanted to be a doctor, and now that she was taking premed at college, she was just unstoppable. Thanks to scholarships and the hefty salary Elise Hunter paid Cassidy, they wouldn't have to worry about college expenses and Claudia could pursue her longtime dream.

"So what's it like in the Wild West?"

Cassidy chuckled. "No stagecoach holdup if that's

what you mean. It really is gorgeous even though Elise's son is kind of…" Hmm. How to explain that rush of attraction combined with the troll attitude?

"Ooh," her sister said, "I sense intrigue. Cass is interested in an actual living, breathing *male.*"

"I'm not interested." Okay, that was a lie, but she wouldn't admit to it. Besides, interest and attraction were two different things, right? Interest would imply that she was looking at Jake Hunter as more than simply a great-looking man with a crappy attitude. Attraction was an involuntary biological imperative for the survival of the species and—oh for heaven's sake, she sounded like one of Claudia's professors.

To her sister, she said, "I'm just here to get him to sign some papers and then first thing tomorrow I'm on a plane home again."

"Uh-huh. First thing tomorrow means you've still got all night tonight."

Yes, she did. Funny, but the thought of spending the night at the ranch hadn't bothered her at all until she'd gotten her first look at Jake. Now, it was different. That buzz of sensation she'd felt just shaking his hand left her feeling oddly off-balance and she didn't really enjoy that at all. Not that she would tell Claudia any of this, of course.

"Is there some reason my baby sister is trying to shove me at a man she's never even met?" Cassidy scooted off the edge of the bed and walked across the room to the window.

"Because my big sister has been living like a nun for way too long," Claudia countered. "You haven't been on a date in like forever. Do you even remember what *fun* is?"

Stung, Cassidy dropped onto the window seat, leaned against the cold glass and said, "I have fun all the time."

"Doing what?"

"I like my job—"

"Work is not fun."

"Fine. Well, I went to the movies just..." She had to think about that, and when she realized how long ago it had actually been, her scowl deepened. "Fun is overrated."

"Uh-huh." An all-too-familiar sigh of exaggerated patience sifted through the phone. "I'm all grown up now, Cass. You can stop throwing yourself on the altar of substitute motherhood."

Her gaze locked on that amazing view, Cassidy let her sister's words rocket around her mind for a second or two before she said, "Claud, I never thought of it like that."

"Oh sweetie, I know." Claudia sighed again. "Cass, you've been great. You've always been there for me but I'm grown now—"

"Yes," Cassidy interrupted wryly, "nineteen is practically aged."

"—and I'm in college," Claudia went on as if her sister hadn't said a word, "and you should really start concentrating on your own life."

"I have a life, thanks."

"You have work," Claudia corrected. "And you have me. And Dave. But our brother's married with kids of his own now."

True. It had been the three of them for so long, it was hard to realize that her younger brother and sister were grown and didn't need her hovering all the time as they used to. Especially Claudia. She had been only ten years old when their mother decided to follow her current "soul mate" into the sunset. So at nineteen, Cassidy had taken over. She'd been both mother and father—since their illustrious sperm donor parent had disappeared shortly after Claudia's birth—and if she had to say so herself, Cassidy had done a great job of parenting. Maybe that was why it was so hard to *stop*.

"Fine," she said. "I promise I'll find a life. Once I get home."

"Why wait? No time like the present to get started," Claudia argued. "You're on a ranch with a cowboy, for heaven's sake. That's a classic fantasy. Is he cute?"

Cute? No. Jake Hunter was way too manly to be classified as merely "cute." He was gorgeous. Or rugged. Or strong, masculine, gruff and all sorts of other really good words, but *cute* wasn't one of them.

"I didn't notice," she lied.

"Sure." Her sister laughed. "Anyway, my point is, relax a little. Enjoy yourself. Flirt. Consider it practice for when you get back home and I badger you into doing this for real."

Flirt? With Jake Hunter? Oh, Cassidy didn't think so. First of all, he was her boss's *son*. No way would she risk a great-paying job for a short-term fling— even if he were interested, which he probably wasn't, considering the way he'd talked to her so far. But more than that, Cass wasn't a one-night-stand kind of girl. She'd be uncomfortable and feeling all slutty so she wouldn't even enjoy herself anyway, so what would be the point?

God. Had Jake actually called her forthright? Her

mind was spinning like an out-of-control carnival ride. And suddenly, she was done thinking about this.

"Don't you have another test this afternoon?"

"See?" Claudia laughed. "You're way too focused on *my* life. Time to find your own, Cass! Love you!"

When her little sister hung up, Cassidy just stared down at her phone and thought about that brief yet involved conversation. Yes, maybe Claudia had a point, but in her own defense, Cass hadn't exactly been shown the most shining examples of relationships in her life.

Cass's father had abandoned the family when Claudia was born, saying only that three kids were just too many. Her mother had moved from man to man always looking for her "prince." But there were no princes, only frogs she continued to kiss in the hopes there would be a miraculous change.

So instead of following in her mother's footsteps, Cassidy worked, put herself through city college and made sure her siblings stayed in school. Eventually it had all paid off, of course. Dave was now a successful contractor with a wife and six-month-old twin boys. And Claudia was going to be the doctor she should be.

But, Cass thought as she shifted her gaze back to the view outside her window, maybe she *had* allowed work and worry to completely envelop her. And maybe Claudia was right that it was time Cass found out if there really was more to life than work.

Not that she would find that out *now,* she assured herself. "Good times do not start with a crabby cowboy no matter how gorgeous he is," she said out loud for emphasis. "Besides, as you told yourself earlier, he's your boss's *son*."

Well, that should be enough to tamp down whatever lingering flickers of attraction were still burning inside her. She couldn't afford to risk her job by giving in to a momentary flash of heat that might or might not mean she was really attracted to the grumpy man downstairs. Not that her boss, Elise, had ever been that much of a tyrant or anything, but why take chances?

"Now that that's settled," she murmured, tossing her phone onto the deep green velvet window seat, "time to take a quick shower and maybe a little nap before I go downstairs and tend to business."

She walked to the bed, unzipped her suitcase and got out the things she'd need before stepping through a connecting door and coming to a dead stop. This house kept staggering her.

The bathroom was huge and opulent. Again, green was the main color here, but every possible shade of that color was represented in the tiles on the floor, the backsplash, the acre or so of granite countertops, the walk-in shower with six showerheads, and most spectacularly of all, in the gigantic Jacuzzi tub that was tucked beneath a bay window continuing the view of the lake and the wide sweep of sky outside.

There were lovely bottles and jars of soaps, lotions, shampoos and even, she thought with an inward sigh, bubble bath. Cassie had always loved lounging in a hot bath, but normally, who had the time? She glanced at that shower, then looked again at the tub that seemed to be calling to her. No reason her new acceptance of "fun" in her life couldn't start here.

"Okay," she whispered, picking up one of the thick white towels to lay on the wide ledge of the tub, "no shower for you, girl. Bath it is."

* * *

Jake tugged the collar of his jacket higher on his neck and tossed a wary glance at the darkening sky above him. A cold wind pushed at him, but he ignored that and strode toward the barn. Best thing to do was go about his business. Put Cassidy Moore out of his mind and focus on what was real. What was important.

And a woman who would be here on the ranch for less than twenty-four hours was *not* important.

The combined scents of hay and horses greeted him as he walked into the cavernous building. It was lined with stalls on either side, and some of the horses had their heads stuck out the doors, watching the cowboys at work, hoping for treats. Instantly, his mind shifted from thoughts of a very temporary woman to focus on the life he'd built for himself.

An hour of hard work, setting out feed and water and clearing stalls, made him feel better. Sure, he didn't have to do the dirty work himself, but concentrating on a task had always been the best way to soothe his mind. Of course, once the work was done his brain had too much free time.

"That's a pretty girl."

Rolling his eyes, Jake snorted. He didn't bother to turn and look at his grandfather. "She's not a girl, Pop. She's a woman."

"So you *did* notice."

You could say that. Slanting the older man a hard look, he said, "Yeah. Hard not to, what with her stumbling around on those high heels of hers."

"If that's all you noticed," Ben said, "then I worry about you, boy."

Jamming his hat down onto his head, Jake headed

outside. "No need to worry then. I'm not blind." He glanced back over his shoulder. "I'm also not interested."

All right, that wasn't entirely true. His body was *more* than interested. It was just his mind that was keeping things rational here. He'd been down this road before. Letting his desire for a pretty woman blind him to reality. And even as he thought that, he realized there was no point. The woman in question would be leaving in the morning and with any luck, he wouldn't see her again.

"Let it go, Pop." Jake kept walking, sure without looking that his grandfather was right behind him. "She works for Mom and she's not staying. Two very good reasons for you to keep your imagination in check."

"Pretty woman shows up on your mountain and you want to ignore her." A snort of derision followed that statement. "Youth really is wasted on the young."

At that, Jake stopped and looked back at the older man. "I'm not that young."

He didn't feel young, anyway. At thirty-four, he'd done too much, seen too much. After two tours of service in the Marines and surviving a marriage that never should have happened, hell, sometimes he felt as old as time.

Ben walked up to him and slapped one work-worn hand onto Jake's shoulder. "I know you've been through some rough times. But that's past, boy, and you've got to move on. The problem is, you're just too much inside your own head, Jake. Always have been. Spend a little less time thinking and a little *more* looking at pretty girls, might improve your attitude."

Jake laughed shortly. "My attitude's fine, Pop."

"Whatever you say, boy." Ben gave his shoulder another friendly slap then headed off toward his place. "All I'm telling you is that if I was you, I wouldn't be spending my time in the stable taking care of horses when I could be talking to that pretty girl."

Shifting his gaze to the main house, Jake thought briefly about the woman waiting inside for him. He was probably making more of this than there was. A buzz of sensation when he shook her hand didn't mean a damn thing. A flash of heat could dissipate as easily as it fired. This was simply a momentary blip. He'd reacted to her so strongly because he hadn't been down off the mountain in months. Enforced celibacy could make a man edgy. Hell, all he really needed was a woman. *Any* woman. That's why his mother's assistant had hit him as hard as she had.

Once she was gone, he'd head into town, find a woman and take care of his "distraction" problem.

Two hours later he was in his study when he heard Cassidy Moore heading downstairs. About time, he told himself and half wondered if she was always late for an appointment or if she wasn't looking forward to this meeting any more than he was. He could leave her to wander the house looking for him, he supposed. But then that felt a little too cowardly. So he stood up, walked to the doorway and looked down the hall.

One glance at her was all it took to reignite the buzz of interest his body seemed to be focusing on. She had changed clothes after her shower. Gone were the slick black slacks and killer red jacket. Instead, she wore jeans that looked faded and comfortable along with a dark blue button-down shirt and a pair of tennis shoes.

Her dark blond hair was soft and loose, hanging over her shoulders in thick waves. He watched her as she let her gaze slide across her surroundings and he smiled to himself at the appreciative gleam in those fog-gray eyes of hers.

"No more high heels?" he asked and his deep voice seemed to reverberate in the empty stillness.

She snapped her head around, her gaze locking onto his. "You startled me."

"Sorry." Though he wasn't. He'd enjoyed having a good long look at her without her being aware of his presence.

"It's okay." She brushed his apology aside with the wave of one hand. Glancing down at her outfit, she shrugged and added, "As for the heels, I just couldn't put them back on. First impression is over anyway, so I went for comfort."

"First impressions are that important?"

"Of course." She started walking toward him. "I represent your mother and Hunter Media, and even though you're her son, I have to be professional."

"I didn't realize my mother was such a tyrant," he said, amused.

"Oh, she's *not,*" Cassidy said quickly. "That's not what I meant at all. I just take my job seriously and—"

"Relax." He interrupted her because he could see from the frantic gleam in her eye that she was probably worried about what he might say to his mother about her. "I was kidding."

"Oh." She took a breath and blew it out. "Okay. That's good. I really like my job."

"I'm sure. So. You have papers for me to sign?"

"I do." She held up one hand to show him the manila

envelope she'd brought downstairs with her. "Sorry I'm later than I thought I would be. But I lay down on that wonderful bed and fell asleep. Guess I was more tired than I thought. But I've got everything right here. Your mother said that she'd sent a copy to your lawyer to have him look them over."

"Yeah." Not that he was worried about his mother trying to cheat him. Although he wouldn't have put it past her to work in a clause somewhere that he would now have to visit Boston five or six times a year. "Everything's set so might as well get it done."

He walked back into his study and heard her footsteps on the floor as she followed.

Jake took a seat behind his desk and waited for her to sit down opposite him. When she did, she handed over the envelope and as he opened it to take the sheaf of papers out, she looked around the room, her gaze finally settling on the window behind him and the view so beautifully displayed.

"How do you get any work done?" she wondered absently. "If it were me, I'd be staring out that window all the time."

"One reason why it's behind me," he said as he flipped through the pages. Deliberately, he avoided looking at either the view *or* her.

"Sure, but you still know it's there."

He knew she was there, too, and that knowledge was far more distracting than even the sweeping view of the mountains that he loved. Jake picked up a pen and held on to it with a grip that should have been tight enough to shatter the steel barrel. What was it about this woman that was getting to him so completely and so quickly?

She stood up to move around the room, and Jake lifted his gaze just enough to see her. He zeroed in on her as she paused to examine the paintings hanging on the walls, the books in the bookcases and even the photographs on the mantel over the hearth where a fire burned against the chill of the day.

When she turned back to face him, his gaze dropped to the papers on his desk.

"This house is really amazing," she said. "You've got those same braces in here—the beams or whatever, that are made to look like tree trunks."

That had him smiling. Those support beams were a favorite of his. It had felt like bringing the forest inside the house, though the builder hadn't been thrilled with the extra work it had required.

Giving up on the illusion of examining the papers, he looked up at her and watched as she continued her inspection of his study. It was a big room, with plenty of heavy, dark brown leather furniture, and rugs in muted colors dotted the wood floors. Jake spent a lot of his time in here, so he'd wanted it to be comfortable.

"It's a big house for one man," she said softly.

"I like a lot of space."

"I can see that. But it would be a little creepy for me to have this big a house and be all by myself."

"Creepy how?" Intrigued in spite of himself, he leaned back in his chair and watched her.

She threw him a smile over her shoulder as she bent lower to inspect the books on the bookshelf. His gaze settled on the curve of her behind in that faded, worn, soft denim and a flash of heat shot through him with the swiftness of a lightning bolt.

"I'd always be expecting someone to break in," she said.

Frowning, he tore his gaze from her butt. "This isn't Boston."

"Oh, it's really not." She straightened, walked the perimeter of the room slowly and finally sat down opposite him again in one of two matching leather chairs. Resting her elbows on the arms of the chair, she folded her hands across her middle, tipped her head to one side and said, "Your mother really wants you back in Boston, you know."

"Yeah," he said, a reluctant smile curving his mouth. "She really hasn't kept that a big secret."

"She talks about you a lot. I think she misses you."

A ping of guilt stabbed at him, but he fought it down. Guilt didn't fix anything. Didn't change anything. Frowning now, Jake asked, "You're her personal assistant, right?"

"That's right. Why?"

"Aren't assistants supposed to be sworn to secrecy and discretion?"

She shrugged. "You're her son, and it's not like you don't already know everything I'm saying."

True. But he didn't enjoy having someone remind him that his mother missed him. He knew she did. But he saw her and his sister, Beth, and her family whenever they visited the ranch. That was enough. Jake wouldn't go back to the city again if he could help it. The closest he wanted to come to a city was downtown Kalispell, and that was only when he couldn't avoid it.

"So why are you so anti-Boston?" she asked quietly.

His gaze narrowed on her. "I know my mom didn't put you up to that question."

"No, that's just me. Being curious."

"Polite word for nosy."

"Guilty. You don't have to answer."

"Yeah," he said. "I know."

"But you will," she countered with an easy smile as she sat back more comfortably in the chair.

"What makes you think so?"

"Because you'll want to defend your position."

"Ah," he said, leaning back in his own chair. "But why would I care what you think of me?"

"Oh, you don't," she said. "But you can defend yourself to *you,* by explaining it to me."

Irritation warred with intrigue inside him. He'd known her only a few hours and she was already playing him. Were women *born* knowing how to maneuver a man into doing exactly what they wanted him to do?

"It's none of your business," he finally ground out.

"Ah." She nodded sagely. "The best defense is a good offense."

Surprised, he laughed. "You know football?"

She shrugged. "My younger brother played in high school and college. I went to a *lot* of games. And you changed the subject. Well done."

Shaking his head, Jake studied her for a long minute and found her gray gaze steady and filled with interest. "Okay. I grew up in the city. But this ranch always felt like home to me."

"And…"

"And, after college and the Corps, I couldn't settle in the city. Too much noise. Too many people. Too many things crowding in on me." He stood up, unable to stay behind the desk. Walking to the fire, he picked up a poker and stabbed at the smoldering logs until flames hissed and jumped to life again.

Funny, he hadn't thought about any of this for a long time, and remembering coming home from his last tour of duty and being surrounded by the crazed noises and crowds of the city brought it all back. That itchy, unsettled feeling that resulted in a cold, deep chill that had skimmed over his heart and soul, making him feel as if he were slowly freezing to death.

Grinding his teeth together, he swallowed hard, reminded himself that he'd left that old life behind and said, "I didn't belong there anymore. I needed space. Room to breathe. Couldn't find that in the city."

She was watching him. He didn't have to see it to feel her gaze on him. He knew she was wondering what the hell he was talking about. Considering him nuts for turning his back on Hunter Media and all that entailed. But he didn't face her; instead he simply stared into the flames and let himself be mesmerized.

Until she spoke and shattered the quiet.

"Really, I sympathize with your mother, but I can't see you living in Boston at all."

He lifted his head and shifted a look at her. He didn't see sympathy or concern or amusement on her features, and for that he was grateful. "Is that right? Why?"

She laughed a little and the sound was soft. "Well, first off, I do understand everything you just said. Sometimes the crowds downtown make me feel like I can't draw a breath."

He nodded.

"But secondly... Please. You wear boots and jeans

and a hat that you can pull down deliberately low enough to keep people from seeing your eyes."

A frown tugged at the corners of his mouth. Observant, wasn't she?

"I just can't see you sitting in on board meetings wearing a three-piece suit and sipping espresso."

He snorted at the idea. "Yeah, that was never going to happen."

"I think your mom gets that now," Cassidy said. "She's still disappointed, but she's accepted that you're never moving back to the city."

"Good. Took long enough," he mused. His mother had clung to the idea of Jake returning to the city to take his rightful place as the head of Hunter Media for far too long. It had been a bone of contention between them for years, even though he'd pointed out repeatedly that his younger sister Beth was right there, more than capable and *eager* for the job.

"But I'm curious."

His thoughts came to a dead stop as he looked at her. "*More* curiosity?"

"You never find out anything if you don't ask."

"Ask what?"

"Why the lonely cowboy on top of a mountain?" Her gray gaze locked on his, she watched him as if she could read his answer on his features. "You walked away from a dynasty in the city to come here. Why here? This mountain? This place?"

"Forthright again," he muttered.

"Not really. Nosy again."

He laughed shortly at the admission. "At least you're honest."

"I try to be."

Jake had once thought his ex was an honest woman, too. Turned out she was like most people. Honest only until it served her not to be. But what the hell, he'd give her an answer.

"When we were kids, Beth and I used to come here every summer to see our grandparents." His mind turned back, flipping through memories like a card-sharp about to deal a hand filled with images. "It was so different here. Bigger, of course. But more than that. Pop used to take me fishing and out with him when he was working the cattle. In Boston, I was a kid, told to watch out for cars, not to talk to strangers, and wasn't allowed to ride the damn T without an escort."

"Really? You couldn't ride public transit alone?"

He shrugged at that memory. "My parents were cautious. Always said that rich kids might get kidnapped. So Beth and I were watched constantly." Shaking his head, he continued. "Here, we were free. We ran wild all over the ranch with no one to hold us back. Went swimming in the lake, hiked all over the forest. It was a different world for both of us. But for me, it was the world I wanted." Grudgingly, he added, "When I got out of the Marines, I came straight here. I needed this place after that and—"

He stopped talking suddenly, surprised as hell that he'd told her all of that. Hell, he hadn't talked about his past in—well, ever. He didn't like looking back. He didn't believe in looking into the future, either. For Jake, the present was all that mattered. The here and now was all he could control, so that's where he put his focus.

"I can understand that," she said softly.

Jake straightened, set the poker in its stand and

walked back to sit behind the desk. Gathering up the papers, he began to read, skimming his gaze through the lawyer-speak with ease. He was a Hunter, after all, and he'd grown up knowing the ins and outs of deal making. "I didn't ask for your understanding," he muttered.

"Too bad," she told him. "You have it anyway."

He shot her a frown that she completely ignored.

"Just because you're a recluse doesn't mean you have to be crabby, too."

She made it sound like he was a damn hermit. He wasn't. He went into town. Just not lately. "Who says I'm a recluse?"

"Your sister."

Jake rolled his eyes. "Beth thinks five minutes of silence is some sort of torture."

Cassidy laughed and he found he liked the sound of it. "With her kids, I'm guessing she doesn't have to worry about silence most of the time."

He looked at her. "You sure seem to know a lot about my family."

"That's part of my job," she said with a shrug. "As your mother's assistant, I try to make her life easier—work and family. Luckily, I really enjoy your sister. And your mother is a brilliant woman. I'm learning a lot from her."

She jumped to her feet, came around the desk and leaned over his shoulder to point at something on the front page of the papers. "I almost forgot. Talking about your mother reminded me. She said you should be sure to read this clause especially well. Once you sign, it's irrevocable."

Jake tried to focus on what she was pointing to. Instead, though, the scent of her wrapped itself around him. Something cool and clean, like the forest after a rain. She smelled like springtime, and drawing it into his lungs made his brain fuzz out even as his body tightened. Damn, this wasn't going to work.

"Yeah. I see it. Thanks." He turned his head to look at her and found her mouth only a breath away from his. She met his gaze and looked away briefly before meeting his eyes again. Then she licked her lips nervously and the tightening inside Jake went into overdrive.

Blinking frantically, Cassidy moved back slightly and kept her voice brisk as she said, "Once you sign this, you're giving up any chance to come back and run Hunter Media. Basically, your signature is agreeing to accept Beth as the heir to the throne, so to speak."

"It's what I've wanted for years," he told her, grateful that she'd stepped far enough back that he could draw a breath without drowning in her scent.

"But it's permanent, so your mother wanted to make sure that you understood this can't be undone. She doesn't want Hunter Media's board to be unsettled."

"Permanent. Good." Jake nodded, and let his gaze drop to the sheaf of papers again. Much safer than staring into foggy eyes that held shadows and light and… damn it. He needed to keep his mind on business, but he wouldn't be able to do that right now. Not with her so close. "I'll sign these after dinner. Why don't we go see what my housekeeper left for us?"

Getting out of the study was a good idea. The kitchen was good. A huge room. Brightly lit. No cozy corners or any reason at all for Cassidy Moore to lean into him.

"Okay, I'm starved."

So was he.

But whatever they might find to eat, Jake didn't think it would ease the kind of hunger he was feeling.

Three

Dinner was good, if tense.

Just like the rest of the house, the kitchen was a room pulled right off the pages of some glossy magazine. Acres of pale wood cabinets, a heavy round pedestal table at one end of the long room, plum-colored walls and miles of black granite so shiny it glinted in the overhead lights. The appliances were stainless steel and the effect of it all was cozy and intimate in spite of its size.

The two of them sat at the table silently eating a hearty stew and crusty homemade bread left for them by Jake's housekeeper, Anna. Cass would have enjoyed the meal except for the fact that her host had pulled into himself and completely shut her out.

Amazing that only a few minutes ago they'd been chatting easily, and now, he'd become the recluse his sister called him. She had to wonder what had changed. What had suddenly made him close off to the point of ignoring that she was even in the room? Naturally, Cass couldn't take the silence for long.

"You *really* don't like having company, do you?" she asked.

His head came up and his eyes locked on hers. Cass felt the slam of that gaze punch into her with a kind of electric awareness that set off tiny ripples of anticipation over every square inch of her skin. Maybe she shouldn't have said anything. Maybe it would have been better to leave things as they were, with the silence humming between them. But it was too late now.

"What makes you say that?"

Cass shook her head and waved her spoon at him. "Please. You're sitting there like a statue—except for the glare you're shooting at me right now. You haven't said a word since we sat down to eat, and if body language is a real thing, at the moment, yours is saying *don't talk to me.*"

He frowned at her.

"See? My point exactly."

"Fine," he muttered, reaching for the glass of red wine in front of him. "I don't get a lot of company here."

"Not surprising since you're at the top of a mountain and the road to get here is a death-defying thrill ride," she noted with a little shudder as she remembered her drive.

That frown flickered across his face again. "There's nothing wrong with the road—"

"—that a few more feet on either side couldn't cure," she interrupted. "Anyway, now that you *do* have company, however short-lived, you could try to be…*nice."*

"Nice." He said the word as if he was speaking a foreign language.

Cass gave him a slow smile. "Would you like me to define that for you?"

"Thanks, I think I've got it." Though his tone was sarcastic, a twitch of his lips told her he might even be amused.

"Excellent." She took a sip of her wine. "So, let's try conversation. I'll start. This dinner is wonderful. Your housekeeper's a great cook."

"She is," he agreed.

"Two words. Not much, but it's a start," she said, enjoying the flash of irritation that shot across his eyes. "I know I keep saying this, but your house is just amazing. Every room I see makes it more so. But this kitchen, it's so big and there's only you to cook for. Seems a shame, somehow."

"Not to me." He pulled off a piece of bread from the slice in front of him and popped it into his mouth. "Besides, whatever Anna cooks here, she takes most of it back to her house for her and her husband. And then when there's something big going on, she cooks for the whole ranch."

Cass took a bite of her bread. "Something big?"

He shrugged. "Anything that keeps the ranch hands from getting back to their cabins to do for themselves. Could be a storm, or a fire on the mountain that we're helping to put out. Or even just a horse auction when we've got potential customers gathered. Cowboys have to eat and if you feed them well, they work harder."

Cass watched him as he spoke. For a recluse, he

could really get going when he wanted to. Of course, all it took was to ask him questions about the ranch he so obviously loved. Then his features were animated, there was a gleam in his eyes, and every word he spoke was flavored with enthusiasm.

She felt an inner sigh that she was grateful he couldn't hear or sense. Jake Hunter really was gorgeous. It wasn't fair that she could be so attracted to a man who should remain untouchable. Boss's son. Recluse. Geographically undesirable.

And yet…as she watched him, she felt a swirl of something hot begin to unfold deep inside her. His smile kicked her heart into an odd little lurch and the pit of her stomach felt as if there were a million or so butterflies lodged there. Not to mention the tingles of expectation that were settling in a little lower.

It had been a long time since she'd felt an instant attraction for a man, and she'd *never* felt one this strong.

And *why* did she keep hearing Claudia's voice whispering, *Go for it! Flirt! Live!* She couldn't do that, could she?

No. Absolutely not. Just thinking about doing what she was thinking about after knowing the man for only a few pitiful hours probably qualified her for Skank of the Century.

"Oh, God…"

"Are you okay?" He was looking at her.

"Yes, why? Did I say that out loud?" she asked.

"Yeah. So what's wrong? You feeling all right?"

"Fine, fine." Astonishing how much easier she was finding it to lie. Maybe she should be worried about that. "I was, um, thinking about the paperwork and making a mental note not to forget to get you to sign it."

Oh, that didn't sound pathetic at all.

"Okay, let's go get that done right now then," he said and carried his dirty dishes to the sink. He rinsed them out, then took hers and rinsed those as well.

"I like a man who cleans up after himself."

"Yeah, well, we didn't have a lot of maids in the Marines," he said wryly.

He turned off the kitchen light and darkness swallowed the room as they left it behind. Cass hadn't even been aware of how much time had passed, but apparently, it got dark early up in the mountains. She shivered a little as they walked down the hall and the world beyond the window glass looked black as pitch. There were no outside lights on, so it was impossible to see anything but their reflections in the glass as they walked.

Looking away from the dark, she shifted her gaze to the man striding down the hall in front of her. His boot heels clacked hard against the wood floor, and her own sneakers whispered accompaniment. Her gaze swept him up and down, from his hair, curling over the collar of his white long-sleeved shirt, down to the tight way his jeans clung to his behind. The man had a great butt.

Oh boy. Another rush of heat swamped her and Cass was forced to shake her head in an effort to dislodge the thoughts that came rushing to the surface of her mind. Desperate for conversation, she asked, "How long were you in the Marines?"

He glanced over his shoulder at her. "Four years."

"Do you miss it?"

MAUREEN CHILD   49

"Sometimes," he admitted, and looked surprised at his own statement. "Things were *clear* in the military in a way they can't always be in the civilian world."

"I guess I can see that," she said, pleased to have something to focus on besides how good the man looked in a pair of jeans. "But I don't think I'd be very good at following orders."

He turned into the study, sparing her another look over his shoulder. "Odd, because my mother's always been great at issuing orders."

"True," she admitted, walking behind him to the desk on the far wall. The lights were on in the study, so the outside world remained just a mirror image of the inside, with darkness outlining the two people framed in the glass. "But she also listens to suggestions, and I'm guessing superior officers in the military aren't real big on that."

He laughed and nodded. "You'd be right."

But she could see him as a marine. Tall, handsome, probably gorgeous in his uniform. And there was the attitude, too. Sure of himself, confident in a way that most men simply weren't. Jake was the kind of man women daydreamed over, and if she wasn't careful she was going to fall into that trap easily.

Sliding into his desk chair, he skimmed the papers again and though it looked fast, Cass knew it was also thorough. Plus, his lawyer had already gone over them, so when he scrawled his name across the signature line in a wide, generous hand, it was almost anticlimactic.

"Done," he said and sounded satisfied.

"I hope you don't regret it someday," she said when he handed the papers over to her. It really wasn't any of her business, but he was signing over his heritage.

Any interest he might have had in Hunter Media was now gone and she hoped he'd considered this from every angle.

"I won't. This has been a long time coming."

Cass knew he meant that, but a part of her simply didn't understand it. He was severing ties to his family. Okay, not emotional ties, financial ones. But they were still *ties*. Family was something Cass never took for granted because she'd fought so hard to hold on to the pieces of her family that she had left. She couldn't imagine a time ever coming when she would want space from Claudia or Dave. She had spent years holding tight to the threads that kept her and her brother and sister together, and the fact that Jake could so easily walk away from even one part of his family mystified her.

"Your mother is hurt by this, you know."

His features tightened and Cass thought she had probably stepped over a line. But there was no going back now that the words had been said.

"That forthright business can be annoying."

"I know, but that doesn't change the truth."

"She'll get over it," he said simply and stood up.

His physical presence was so overwhelming, she almost took an instinctive step backward. Instead though, she stayed just as she was—though it cost her a jangle of nerves. "You're her son and you're turning down what she and your father worked to build."

He blew out a breath and looked down at her. His eyes were shadowed, his thick hair fell across his forehead, and she could see the shadow of stubble on his jaw with a clarity that made her want to know if it felt as rough as it looked. Then her brain took that thought and ran with it, providing her with images of that stubble rubbing against her skin as he moved down her body, lavishing her with kisses.

Whoops.

Instantly, she dialed back the hormone rush and tried to focus on what he was saying.

"My parents built the dream they wanted. I'm doing the same thing. My mother gets it—" he gave her a brief, wry smile "—even if she wants to pretend she doesn't. And if you're worried about Hunter Media, don't be. My sister Beth is the right person for the job of running the company."

"Maybe," she said and wondered why she was saying all of this. Elise hadn't asked Cass to intervene on her behalf and would probably be horrified if she knew that Cass was haranguing her son over a decision that had been made months ago. But Cass couldn't seem to stop herself from continuing. "But your mother hates that you're so far away. Hates that you don't want to be a part of their daily lives."

Frowning, he eased down until one hip rested on the edge of his desk and their eyes were leveled on each other. "Why are you trying so hard? What does any of this matter to you?"

"Because it's not about the business. Though," she added as an aside, "most people would kill to be a part of Hunter Media. It's about family, and for me, that's important."

Even in the shadows, she saw his features tighten again and she wondered if *she* was the only one who could irritate him so easily.

"And you think my family's not important to me."

"I didn't *say* that."

"Didn't have to." His blue eyes darkened. "I don't know why I'm even bothering to talk to you about this. You've only been here a few hours. You don't know me, yet you think you can tell me what my life and my family should mean to me."

Cass winced, knowing she had that coming.

"I'm going to say this flat out. Listen close because I won't be repeating it. I love my family. That doesn't mean I'm willing to live in a crowded, noisy city to prove it. This is my life. This ranch. This mountain. Loving them doesn't mean I'm willing to give up on my own dreams. And since I was a kid, my dreams were centered *here*."

His voice was rough and low, and carried a passion she had already noticed appeared only when he was talking about the home he'd built here. He was defending his choices to her when he really didn't owe her any explanation at all. And she wondered why he was telling her this rather than stalking out of the room.

"You're right," she said. "I don't know you and it's none of my business what you do. I was just—"

"Doesn't matter," he said and picked up the sheaf of papers from the top of his desk. Handing them over to her, he said, "It's done now."

Cass hated being interrupted, but it was clear that he was finished with this conversation and completely uninterested in any kind of apology she might make. His hand brushed hers as Cass took the papers and she felt that same zing of electricity that she'd experienced before. Worse, she was sure he felt it too, because his eyes narrowed and darkened—which told her he was no happier about it than she was.

The room seemed smaller all of a sudden. As if the

walls had shrunk to encapsulate the two of them in a space that now felt…intimate, somehow.

"I should probably head out to the barn," he said, voice hard and low. "Check on the horses."

"Right," she agreed. "And I should go upstairs. I have to leave early in the morning to catch my flight back to Boston."

"Yeah," he murmured, bending his head toward her. "Good idea."

"I can catch up on some work before going to bed," she whispered, though work had never been further from her mind. She could feel the heat of his body reaching out to her and she leaned in, tipping her head back to watch his face as he came closer and closer.

"That'd be best," he said, gaze moving over her face before coming back to her eyes.

He didn't have to say a word for her to know what he was thinking—mainly because she was thinking the same thing. Lust was alive and well and eagerly jumping up and down in the corner of the room. An electrical field seemed to be snapping and sizzling between them, heightening every breath, every feeling, every desire.

"This would be a really bad idea," Cass said, licking her lips in anticipation of the kiss she knew was a breath away.

"No doubt," he agreed and took her mouth with his.

Heat exploded inside her. Cass's brain shut down with a nearly audible thud as her body, her wants and needs, took over. She dropped the signed papers and reached up to encircle his neck. He pulled her in close, his arms firm bands around her midsection as he held her in place, pressed tightly to him.

Her mouth opened under his and the first swipe of his tongue stole what was left of her breath. She groaned a little as she gave herself up to the amazing response quickening inside her. Cass had been kissed before, of course, but nothing she'd ever experienced could have prepared her for what she felt now.

It was as if she were lit up from the inside. Sparks of reaction sizzled in her bloodstream, and her heart-beat was loud enough to be deafening. Her stomach pitched and swirled and a heavy, throbbing ache began at the core of her. Need clawed at the base of her throat and she went with it.

Threading her fingers through his thick, soft hair, she held his head to hers and responded to his kiss with everything she had. Their tongues tangled together in a dance of passion that could lead to only one place. One place she suddenly wanted to go more than anything.

It didn't matter that she hardly knew him. Didn't matter that she would only be in his house one night. Didn't matter that she could hear "Skank Alarms" ringing distantly in her mind. All that *did* matter was the next moment. The next touch.

His hands swept up and down her back while his mouth plundered hers hungrily. She felt his touch as bolts of heat driven down into her bones, and still she wanted more. There was a desperation between them. A raw, pulsing need that clamored to be answered.

When he shifted his hold on her and covered one of her breasts with his palm, Cass broke free of his kiss to gasp in renewed pleasure. His thumb stroked across her hardened nipple and even through the fabric of her shirt and her bra, the heat of his caress jolted her.

"This is a mistake," he whispered as he quickly undid the buttons lining the front of her shirt.

"Absolutely," she agreed, and turned so he wouldn't have to reach too far to get to his goal.

"We should definitely stop before this gets out of control."

She opened her eyes, stared into his and asked, "What's *control?*"

He laughed shortly. "Good point."

Then her shirt was opened, his hand was over the lacy cup of her bra, and her already-hard nipple seemed to strain to punch its way through the delicate fabric just to reach him.

Cass moaned softly and shifted her gaze past him as she focused only on what he was making her feel. Making her *want*. That's when she became alert enough to notice and remember that there was a wall of windows right behind them and that if anyone happened by this side of the house they were going to get quite the show.

"Oh, God!" She jerked in his arms and turned her back to the glass.

"What is it?"

"Windows," she muttered. "The whole world's watching…"

He laughed and Cass scowled at him. "Not funny."

"Also not an issue," he told her, turning her back around to face him. "When the house was built I had all of the glass treated. We can see out but no one can see in."

Relief coursed through her as she looked up into his eyes. "Really?"

"Really." He stroked the tip of one finger down the

center of her chest and she shivered. "Remember me? The recluse? The guy who likes privacy?"

"Privacy's good…"

With the edges of her shirt still hanging open, it was easy for him to flick open the front clasp of her bra, baring her breasts to him. The kiss of the cool air on her skin gave her a chill, but the heat of his touch followed so quickly after, Cass hardly noticed.

Now that she knew no one could see them, there was almost a thrill to standing in front of those windows while he touched her. She could see their reflection in the glass and was mesmerized as his hands covered her breasts. His thumbs moved over her erect nipples, stroking, pulling, teasing, and everything in her lit up in reaction. Her heartbeat sped up, that throbbing ache between her thighs became more insistent, and her breath puffed in and out of her lungs in short, sharp gasps.

Then he bent his head and took one of her nipples into his mouth and what was left of the slippery threads of her control disappeared. All there was, was this moment. This man. His incredibly talented mouth.

Crazy or not, she was really going to do this. She was going to have sex with her boss's son and she wasn't going to regret it later, either. "Jake…"

"Yeah." He lifted his head only long enough to take her mouth again in a brief, hard kiss. "We should move this upstairs and—"

In the distance, the front door slammed and they both jolted.

"Jake?" A man's shout, echoing throughout the house.

"Damn it," Jake muttered, "that's my foreman, Charlie. Something must be wrong."

"Go," she whispered frantically, "go."

He did, stalking from the room and down the hall. His boot heels sounded fainter and fainter the farther away he got. Fingers shaking, head still a little buzzed from sensation overload, Cass quickly hooked her bra and then did up the buttons on her shirt. Running her hands through her hair, she took a breath and nearly groaned as reality came crashing down on her.

For those few wonderful, amazing stolen moments, she'd forgotten about everything but what it had felt like to be touched by Jake. But now the chill of the room was overtaking the residual heat inside her, and clarity was also rearing up its ugly head.

That skank alarm she'd heard so distantly was now clanging like church bells, reverberating through her brain. What had she been thinking? Well, that answer was easy enough. She hadn't been. Not at all. She'd given in to what she was feeling without a single thought for what would inevitably come after.

Now, with a few moments to actually have a thought and recognize it, she knew that what they'd almost done would have been a colossal mistake. She was here for *one night*. What if Elise found out? Her boss had sent her out here on business, not to jump into bed with her son. Oh God, this was just so humiliating.

Before she had time to really revel in what an idiot she was, Cass heard Jake coming back to the study. The man's boots pounded against the floor in obviously hurried strides. She couldn't be standing here waiting to be ravished when he arrived, either. Cass bent down, scooped up the signed papers from the floor and clutched them to her chest like a medieval shield.

She would have to let him down nicely. Tell him that she'd done some thinking—*finally*—and that it would be better if they both forgot about what had happened.

"That's it. Easy," she whispered and hoped when she talked to Jake she sounded more confident. Because even *she* didn't believe her.

He stopped in the open doorway and the shadows hid most of his expression. All she could really see was the grim slash of his mouth as he stared at her.

"Look," he said tightly. "I'm needed out in the barn, so I can't be in here with you."

Disappointment and regret bubbled up inside her in spite of the fact that she'd been about to give him nearly the same speech. He was cutting her off before she could do the same to him. Why that bothered her, she couldn't have said. "Is there a problem?"

He walked farther into the room and now she could see his eyes. They were flat and cool, and absolutely none of the passion she'd seen moments ago was visible now. He stood stiffly, shoulders squared, like the marine he had been. It was as if he'd already distanced himself from her and was now only going through the physical motions.

"Yeah," he said. "There is. One of the mares is in labor. Not going well. The vet's on her way here now."

Each word was bitten off as if he resented having to be here at all, explaining himself.

"Okay," she said, clutching the paperwork even more tightly to her. "That's probably best anyway."

"Probably," he agreed and turned for the door. Before he left, though, he took another long look at her over his shoulder. That's when Cass knew the heat they'd shared wasn't gone.

It was being ignored.

Jake was tired as hell and still wound so tight from tangling with Cass that he could hardly walk without wincing in pain. Hell, he hadn't been this hard and achy for a woman in longer than he cared to remember.

He'd had a lucky break last night, getting called away before he could give in to the desire that had been eating away at him for hours. The taste of her had haunted him all night. The images of her face, her body, swam through his mind like a movie on constant repeat. He remembered every touch and how her skin—silky, smooth—had felt beneath his calloused hands.

And he'd told himself, in spite of all of that, that it was a good thing they'd been interrupted. One-night stands were bad enough, but with his mother's personal assistant? That was asking for grief he didn't need. Besides, he'd already tried being involved with a woman who didn't understand his need to be here on the mountain. Damned if he'd go through that again.

He'd built the life he loved. Cass didn't have a place in it. No woman did. He'd never let another one get close—no matter how much he wanted her.

So the next few days were going to be uncomfortable, to say the least. Because his lucky break was over and he was about to get tossed into the flames.

He heard her coming downstairs and walked to the front of the house to meet her. She looked pretty in those sleek black slacks, a deep green shirt and that bright red blazer. She was even wearing her heels again. He had thought that seeing her in those city clothes, back in her professional assistant role, would ease some of the fire inside him. He was wrong.

She smiled and said, "I just came down for some coffee before I head to the airport."

"You're not going to the airport today," he told her.

"What?" Frowning, she came down the last few steps to stand beside him. "Of course I am. My flight leaves in two hours."

He took her hand, drew her to the front door and threw it wide. "It's going to leave without you, Cass. There's no way to get down the mountain."

She stared at the yard and he watched her eyes widen and her jaw drop. He knew how she felt, and the snow wasn't even a surprise to him. He'd still been in the barn dealing with the mare when the early storm rolled in. And in the hours since, the steel-gray clouds overhead had dropped at least eight inches of fresh snow and it was still falling.

A cold wind sighed into the house, wrapping itself around the two people standing in the doorway. The walkways hadn't been plowed yet, so the whole yard looked magical and untouched.

"It's only October," she murmured.

"Welcome to Montana," he said, giving her hand a squeeze before releasing her. "The roads to and from the ranch are closed. It'll be a few days before the plows get up this high, so you're not going anywhere."

"But—" She tore her gaze from the white world spilling out in front of her to look up at him.

He met her gaze and felt as if he were sealing his own fate as he said, "Looks like we're stuck with each other."

Four

"It's been two days," Ben said, "and you've spent most of that time as far away from that woman as possible."

Jake glared at his grandfather. "What's your point?"

Ben leaned one arm on the top board of the stall gate and got comfy. "My point is, whether you like it or not, this storm has stranded Cassidy here and you owe it to your guest to make her feel welcome."

Jake continued rubbing down his horse. They'd spent the last two hours riding through the heavy snow, checking on the small herd of prize cattle the Hunter ranch held. It was cold and wet and miserable and pretty much summed up Jake's mood. And still it was better than hanging around the ranch house, smelling Cassidy's presence in every room.

"She's not a guest," he argued. "She's trapped here."

"A reluctant guest is still a guest," Ben countered, then crossed his arms on the fence slat, propped his chin on his arms and asked, "What is it about her that has you hiding out?"

That statement brought a snort of derision. "I don't *hide.* I've got work to do. Don't have time to babysit a bored woman with nothing to do. Besides," he added, "I saw her last night. She was on her laptop doing some work for Mom on the internet. I figure that's what she's still doing. And she doesn't need my help with that."

Of course, he couldn't be sure what she was up to because Jake had left the house at dawn that morning with most of the ranch hands. Hard enough trying to sleep just down the hall from her room; seeing her wasn't going to help the situation any. Besides, he had work to do. And if that work kept him away from Cassidy Moore, well, he considered that a bonus.

Normally, Jake didn't mind an early snowstorm closing off the mountain from visitors. Kept things quiet. But this storm was damned inconvenient.

"Think you've got her all figured out, do you?"

Jake slanted a hard look at his grandfather. When the hell had the older man become so damn nosy? But even as he thought it, Jake realized that Ben was always keeping his hand in what went on at the ranch—the difference now was, with Cassidy here, Ben had something beyond ranch business to be interested in.

Problem was, Jake was interested in her, too, though far differently from his grandfather. Not in a forever kind of way, though. He would never try that again. But he had a hell of a lot of interest in one night with Cassidy—whether it was a good idea or not. And it really was not a good idea.

"I do have her figured out." Jake ran the brush across his horse's back in long, even strokes that practically had the big animal purring. When he spoke again it wasn't just to his grandfather. He needed to hear it all said out loud, too.

"She's from the city, Pop. When it snows in Boston, there are snowplows out making the streets navigable. Sidewalks are swept off and my guess is she wouldn't know what to do with herself any more than Lisa did when the snow's up to your thigh and just walking across the yard is more aerobic exercise than most people get in a year."

"Always comes back to Lisa, doesn't it?"

Jake stopped brushing the horse and looked at his grandfather. "Why wouldn't it? She was my wife."

"*Was* being the operative word here."

Jake sighed. "You're the one who told me if you're going to make mistakes, don't make the same one over and over again. Remember?"

Scowling, Ben said, "I remember. But I don't see Lisa around here anywhere, so—"

"Maybe she's not here in person, but Lisa was as attached to her computer as Cassidy seems to be. They're both from the city. And I'm willing to bet that neither of them knows anything about ranch life or how to do anything more strenuous than hitting a keyboard without breaking a nail."

Shaking his head, Ben Hawkins blew out a breath and said, "You remind me of that old saying about the guy who got cheated by a Frenchman and then swore that *all* of the French were thieves."

"I didn't—"

"That's just stupid thinking if you ask me. You lump

all women together and you'll never notice when the right one shows up."

Jake stared at the other man for a long moment. "Where've you been, Pop? I'm not looking for the 'right' one. As far as I'm concerned that mythical woman doesn't exist." But, he added silently, Cassidy Moore would make a great "right now" woman. He gave his horse one last pat before easing out of the stall and latching the gate closed behind him. Brushing past his grandfather, he said, "If it'll make you happy I'll go to the house now and check on her. Okay?"

Ben smirked. "If you want to check on Cassidy, then you should come with me."

Frowning, Jake followed after his grandfather as the old man walked the length of the barn before pushing open one of the double doors. Holding it open with one hand, he used his free hand to signal Jake in a come-here motion. Still frowning, Jake looked out and couldn't believe what he was seeing.

There was Cass, wielding a snow shovel alongside Jim Hatton, clearing the sidewalks and porches of the cottages and bunkhouse. The two of them were laughing and talking, tossing shovels full of snow at each other and in general acting like they were the best of friends.

"She's shoveling?"

"Been at it for hours, too," Ben told him with a note of satisfaction in his voice. "You took most of the hands out with you, so that left Jim to do the clearing while I saw to the horses."

"Yeah…" No big deal. The ranch had an ATV with a snow blade attachment. All Jim had to do was drive the damn thing around the yard, clearing paths and around the barns. Nobody had asked him to clear side-walks and porches, too. That could have waited.

"Cass came out, said she wanted to help." Ben grinned when Jake shot him a look. "She had Jim show her how to drive the ATV, then they took turns. After that, Cass went in to help Anna fix dinner for everyone and when she was finished, she came back out to help Jim clear the sidewalks and porches."

"Been busy around here."

"Yeah," Ben said wryly. "And I never did see her laptop today…"

"Funny. Real funny."

"She's a nice girl. Helpful. Seems to know how to enjoy herself, too." Ben paused. "Maybe she could teach you."

Jake didn't know about that, but there was plenty he'd like to teach her. He shifted his gaze back to her in time to see Cass slip on some ice and fall over into a drift of knee-high snow. Her laughter pealed out into the cold, still air and something inside Jake ignited. Then that heat became a blistering fire as he watched Jim reach one hand down to pull Cass up and then turn her around to brush the snow off her back and butt.

A rumble of disquiet rolled through Jake, though he couldn't have put a name to the feeling. It cost him, but he ignored Jim's presence and focused on Cassidy. She was wearing a jacket that was too big for her, and a borrowed knit snow hat in blazing orange that boasted a pom-pom on top of her head. Heavy leather gloves covered her hands, and her jeans were stuffed into knee-high boots. Her cheeks were red from the cold; her hair, dusted with snow, hung down around her shoulders, and even at a distance he saw the joy on her face and knew her smoke-gray eyes would be sparkling.

She was having fun.

Working.

Outside.

Hell, Lisa had never left the confines of the house until all snow had been brushed aside for her. She had never taken the time to get to know the men who worked on the ranch, either—let alone work alongside them. All right, maybe Jake had judged Cassidy too harshly. But wasn't that the safest way to handle her? Knowing how she made his body react, keeping her at arm's length seemed the wisest decision.

"Not much like Lisa at all if you ask me," Ben mused.

Jake slanted his grandfather an impatient glance. Hearing his own thoughts voiced aloud wasn't helping. "Nobody asked you."

Ben only chuckled, which had Jake gritting his teeth. A hell of a thing, for a man to be thirty-four years old and still have his grandfather see through him so easily. He turned his back on the view of Cass and headed back into the barn. "How's the new foal doing?"

Another snort of laughter. "Nice change of subject."

"You know as well as I do we've got to watch a late foal—winter's a hard time for a horse that young."

"We'll get her through." Ben rubbed one hand across the back of his neck. "She's got a warm stall, plenty of feed and her mama to keep her safe."

"Think I'll take a look at her just the same."

"Thought you might."

Jake stopped dead and looked over his shoulder at

his grandfather. "This has nothing to do with avoiding Cassidy. This is about work. Responsibility."

"Real handy then that it also gives you a reason to stay put rather than face that laughing woman out there."

Jake scowled but didn't bother answering, mostly because he couldn't argue with truth. So instead, he walked along the length of the barn. Most of the stalls were empty as the cowboys hadn't come down off the mountain yet. But there were a few horses tucked away from the winter storm.

He took the time to stop and check all of them, starting with the stallion that was his prize stud. People paid big money to have their mares impregnated by Blackthorn. The big horse huffed out a breath in welcome, then nosed at Jake's pockets, looking for treats. "I've got nothing for you right now, but I'll be back with an apple later, all right?"

Jake would swear that the horse understood him when he talked, and the stallion gave him a disappointed shove with his big head as if to underscore that. "Okay," Jake said, laughing a little. "Two apples."

He locked the stall behind him and walked on, stopping to check on a mare with a strained foreleg. She was healing well, but Jake wanted to see it for himself. The horse continued to eat as he pulled up a stool, plunked down on it and began to unwrap the binding around her leg. This was what he needed to do. Focus his thoughts, his energies, on the animals who needed him. On the ranch that had become his world.

"Looks like your days of relaxation and pampering are about over," he told the horse and smiled to himself when the animal whickered gently as if arguing with him.

"You've got it easy, don't you?" he asked, comfortable with talking to the horse. It was a good time to gather his thoughts, to ease his mind. Talking to animals who couldn't answer back was better than therapy. He should know. He'd had plenty of that when he got back from his last tour of duty.

It was the nightmares that had gotten him a one-way ticket to a shrink's couch. Memories that he couldn't or wouldn't deal with when awake managed to slip into his dreams and drive him mad, as if he were still in a battle for his life. Images, sounds, smells, chased him in his dreams, hurtling him from sleep with a jolt, night after night.

But the therapist and all of her *face your fear, remember and embrace what you lost,* hadn't helped a damn. How the hell could he be expected to embrace a damn thing? What was lost was gone forever. What he had left was this place. *That's* what had saved him. Coming home. To the ranch that smoothed every rough edge on his soul until he was finally, he thought, nearly whole again.

And now his dreams were back to being haunted. Haunted not by the sights and sounds of war, but by a visceral need that had him wound so tight he could hardly walk without pain. There was probably something ironic in there somewhere but damned if he could see it.

The mare shifted impatiently as if telling him to get out of his own head and on to more important things. He couldn't agree more.

"Another day or two," he murmured as he ran his

palm up and down her foreleg. "Then you'll be good to go."

"Is she hurt?"

Jake's head snapped up to see Cassidy watching him from just outside the gate. Where'd a man have to go these days to get some time to himself? "What're you doing here?"

"I'm happy to see you, too." She smiled in spite of his less-than-warm welcome. "Your grandfather said if I came in here, you'd show me the baby horse."

"Foal," he corrected, then muttered more quietly, "Of course he did." Jake wished Ben would find a new hobby.

"So, is this horse all right?"

Concentrating on the task at hand, Jake checked again for swelling and smiled to himself when he couldn't find any. "It's just a muscle strain," he said, "and she's nearly back to normal."

Quickly, efficiently, he rewrapped the animal's leg, gave her a pat, then stepped out of the stall, forcing Cassidy to move out of the way. Good. Distance was key. And even with that thought, he caught a whiff of her scent, instinctively dragging it deep inside him. His gaze swept her up and down. His old jacket swamped her much smaller body and fell down nearly to her knees. She had snow dusting her hair, on that silly hat and caked on an old pair of Anna's boots, and she looked…happy. When his gaze settled on her face, he saw her cheeks were red from the cold, her gray eyes were dancing, and there was a half smile on her face. "You should go into the house. You're probably freezing."

"I'm cold but not frozen yet," she said, giving him another grin.

"Yeah. I saw you out there with Jim."

"I was helping," she said with a shrug, then winced and rolled her shoulders.

He gave her a knowing look. "You think your muscles ache now? Wait awhile."

"It was worth it," she said. "It felt good to get outside in the cold air."

"Can't argue with that," he said, walking past her toward the last couple of stalls. He understood the need to be outside, doing something, feeling the slap of the wind against your cheeks. He just wouldn't have thought that *she* would understand it.

The gelding he looked in on next had his head hanging out the stall door in anticipation of a good rub between his eyes. So Jake obliged while Cassidy walked up behind him and said, "Look at him. It's like he's a puppy getting a belly rub."

Jake had to smile. "Rocky always wants you to give him a pat or a scratch. If he could figure out how to do it, he'd be a lap-horse."

She laughed at the idea, and the sound of that laughter reached right inside to twist and tangle him into even more knots. The woman was dangerous.

"His name's Rocky?"

"Yeah, short for Rocking Chair."

"What kind of name is that?" She reached out to smooth her hand down the length of Rocky's nose and the horse moved into her, silently asking for more.

"He's lazy," Jake said with affection. "Even as a colt, he would rather walk than run and rather roll in a shady spot of grass than walk. So. Rocking Chair.

He's not a stud. No one wants the lazy gene passed on. And the only people who'd enjoy riding him are little kids for a slow walk around the corral."

Cass tipped her head to one side and looked at him, measuring. "Yet you keep him here."

Jake's gaze flashed to hers.

"The horses are your business and Rocky is, despite being a sweetie, not really a part of that business, but you keep him anyway."

Frowning, Jake muttered, "Who'd buy him?"

Cass only smiled and stayed right behind Jake. "Your grandfather says you have to take extra care with a horse born this close to winter."

"He would be right." He tossed a glance at her over his shoulder. "They're too young to withstand really cold temps, so we have to ensure they stay warm and well fed."

"Ben says you understand horses better than anyone he's ever seen."

"Sounds like my grandfather's talking your ear off." And apparently had plenty to say.

"I like him."

He looked at her, saw that she meant it and nodded in approval. Lisa and his grandfather had never gotten along. Not that it mattered any that Ben and Cass clearly did. "He likes you, too."

"That's nice to hear." She leaned on the stall door after he went through. "Oh, isn't she sweet?"

The foal was a charmer, all long legs and big eyes with flirty eyelashes. Still a little wobbly, the foal came close to the stall door and let Cass lean over to pet her head. The mare, of course, was keeping a close eye on everything, but Sadie was a good-natured animal and Jake wasn't worried. He went on, checking out the mare, giving her some extra attention, then made sure there was plenty of feed in the stall before slipping out the door again and latching it behind him.

Obviously reluctant to leave the tiny horse, still standing close enough to be petted, Cassidy spoke softly. "Your mother says the one thing she really misses about the ranch is the horses. I can see why."

He moved in closer than he should have, reached over the stall gate and grazed his palm across the foal's head. "Know a lot about horses, do you?"

She looked up at him with a grin. "Not a thing. But they're beautiful. And *big*. Except for this little guy—girl."

"They are beautiful," he agreed, and silently added, *so are you*. That smile of hers was deadly accurate. It lit up his insides like a fireworks explosion and he didn't need that. Didn't want that. So he forced himself to move away from her, from temptation. "They're a lot of work too, so I'd better get busy."

"Oh. Sure. Me, too. I guess I'll head back to the house."

"More internet work?"

"No. I promised Anna I'd help set out the meal and serve the hands when they got back, so I should get to the kitchen."

He frowned to himself as she started to walk away. She puzzled him. Intrigued him. Attracted him in a way no other woman ever had, and that was damned irritating. "You don't have to do this, you know."

She stopped and turned to face him. "Do what?"

He threw both hands out. "Help. Work. Cook with Anna. Shovel with Jim. It's not your job to do any of it."

Tipping her head to one side, she stared at him for a long moment. "This bothers you?"

"It confuses me," he admitted and could hardly believe he'd said it out loud.

She smiled at him and shook her head. "I don't know why. I'm here. There are things to be done—I'm helping do them. Simple."

"Why do I think there's nothing simple about you?" His gaze was locked on her. Snow fell behind her, twisting and dancing in the cold wind. Horses whickered softly in their stalls. Standing there in the coat and work boots and that silly hat, she looked as if she belonged. But he knew she didn't, despite appearances, and that stiffened his resolve even as she took the few steps back to stand directly in front of him.

"I think that may be the nicest thing anyone's ever said to me," she told him.

Then before he could think of a damn thing to say, she went up on her toes, reached for the back of his neck and pulled his head down to hers. She kissed him and he knew he should set her back, pull away from the tantalizing taste of her.

Just as he knew he wouldn't.

In an instant, he'd snatched her up close, pulling her into him until their bodies were pressed so tightly together, he could feel the heavy drum of her heart. She opened her mouth to him and Jake moved in, taking what he'd hungered for the last couple of days. Surrounded by her heat, her scent, her taste, he lost himself in the glory of it and shoved away all thoughts of caution.

Something raw and powerful rose up inside him and he rode the crest of that raging need, taking Cassidy with him. She moved in even closer, threading her arms around his neck and holding on as if he was the only stable point in her universe. He knew that feeling as the world around him rocked and swayed unsteadily.

In the back of his mind, a voice sounded, whispering, insisting that he stop now before he lost his grip on the last tattered remains of his self-control. And he fought the voice because he didn't want control. He wanted *this. Her.* He didn't know why she had hit him as hard as she had, but there was no denying the spark between them, the heat engulfing them.

The question was, did he surrender to the flames or snuff them out? Before he could make a call, the decision was made for him as shouts and conversation and bursts of laughter reached them from outside. His cowboys were back, headed to the barn.

Jake tore his mouth from hers and quickly pulled her arms from around his neck. She swayed a little and damned if he could blame her. But in a couple of quick seconds, she was steady again and he envied it. For him, the world was still slightly tilted and the pain in his groin was like a throbbing toothache.

"I should go. Help Anna."

"Yeah." He yanked off his hat, speared his fingers through his hair and sucked in a long, deep gulp of icy air. It didn't change a thing. "We'll all be inside soon."

Nodding, she backed up, her gaze locked on his. He couldn't look away either, because whether he wanted to admit it or not, he was done avoiding her. Done pretending that the need clamoring in his gut was going away. He needed her. Wanted her. And she wanted him back. Tonight, damn it, they'd have at each other and put the passion to rest.

She reached the door and had to squeeze past the cowboys and their horses. A few of them spoke to her, and she answered, but Jake hardly heard any of it. All he could think was, night couldn't come soon enough for him.

It was like a big, noisy family, Cass thought as she carried platter after platter of fried chicken, potatoes and corn to the table set up at one end of the massive kitchen. She was still amazed that the long table had folded out from the wall. It easily sat twenty, and could be folded down and tucked away when not in use. The house kept amazing her at every turn.

Of course, so did the man who had designed it all. Her gaze slid to where he sat at the head of the table, laughing at something his foreman and Anna's husband, Charlie, was saying. Cass's heart gave a little lurch in her chest. Jake Hunter scowling was enough to make a woman drool. Jake Hunter *smiling* made her want to climb right up all six feet four inches of him and settle in for a long visit.

Tingles of anticipation, flavored by memory, whipped through her bloodstream as she chatted and laughed with the cowboys. Anna had a good system here. Cook up a mountain of food and just keep it coming. The laughter, the good-natured teasing, the shouts, the bets on football games, it was…cozy, somehow. With the snow outside and the fire in the kitchen hearth snapping and crackling, this room was like sunlight.

Cass had always loved the idea of a big, boisterous family and now here she was, smack in the middle of one. She wondered if Jake even knew that his employees were his family. He was so determined to be alone, to have no connections, that he probably hadn't even realized that he was never really alone. Everyone here was important in his life.

And for right now anyway, Cass was a part of it all.

Her gaze landed on Jake again and he looked up, as if sensing her staring at him. His blue eyes darkened and a muscle in his jaw twitched. He was remembering their kiss in the barn. Remembering how they'd nearly set fire to each other with the heat between them. Heck, she hadn't been able to think of anything else for the last two hours. Several times, Anna had caught Cass daydreaming when she was supposed to be cooking and Cass didn't even have a good excuse to give.

"Cass, Anna says you made these chocolate cookies."

Shaken out of her thoughts, she turned to Lenny and nodded. "I did."

"Well that settles it, you'll have to marry me."

Everyone laughed, even Lenny's wife, sitting beside him.

"I'll run away with you as soon as Evelyn says you can go," Cass promised.

"Ready to toss me over for a cookie?" Evelyn gave her husband a slap on the shoulder.

"Really good cookies," he insisted and popped a piece of one into Evelyn's mouth.

She groaned, looked at Cass and said, "Forget Lenny, marry *me*."

The people around this table were family. Mostly single men, who lived in the bunkhouses; only the ranch foreman, Charlie, and the head horse wrangler,

Lenny, lived in cabins with their wives. More laughter, more fun, and then Cass was looking into Jake's eyes again and the humor died away, burning in the flames she read there.

She wanted him bad, and if she didn't get off this mountain soon, she didn't know what she was going to do. Already, she'd kissed him. Twice. And sadly, she was forced to admit, only to herself of course, that if the cowboys hadn't returned to the ranch when they had—oh, better not to think about that.

The man had great hands. And an incredible mouth. Not to mention that truly fabulous butt. He was the whole package, plus—fantasy bonus—a cowboy. Claudia was right, Cass told herself as she took a seat as far from Jake as she could manage, it had been way too long since Cass had had a man in her life. Those stolen moments with Jake told her it was time to change all of that. Oh, not now. Not Jake. Yes, she had kissed him first this time, but that had clearly been out of character. She couldn't do that again, and he would probably keep avoiding her until it was time for her to leave the ranch....

But when she got back to Boston, she'd look for a guy who could do to her what Jake was able to. Surely there had to be more than one man in the world who could send skyrockets flashing through her bloodstream.

Determined, she nodded at the thought, glad to have a plan. She picked up a piece of chicken, bit in and chewed, her gaze shifting unerringly to Jake again. He lifted his beer for a sip and she watched the muscles in his throat move. She licked her lips, sighed a little and told herself grimly that there was absolutely no man anywhere who could compare to Jake Hunter.

Finding a cowboy in Boston would be as easy as finding a stockbroker in Montana. No, when she went home, she'd be leaving the fantasy behind. The question was, would she go home with a smile on her face? Or regret in her heart?

Five

Once the work was done, what was she supposed to do?

Cass wandered the big, silent house and wished she could sleep. But that wasn't going to happen. She'd taken a hot bath to ease her sore muscles, tried to read a book and even flipped through a few dozen TV channels. Nothing had worked.

Now she was so unsettled, she couldn't even sit still. So she walked, her bare feet soundless on the wood floors. She paused to look at framed photos of the Montana countryside hanging on the walls. She ran her fingertips across the spines of leather-bound books on shelves. She stared out the windows at the dark night beyond the glass, then went on, moving into the great room, where a fire lay slowly dying in the hearth. The soft hiss and sizzle of flames looking for a meal on the charred wood was the only sound as she finally stopped her wandering and eased onto an overstuffed chaise covered in a blue-and-white flowered fabric that hinted of spring and promised comfort.

Taking a breath, she let it slide from her lungs and stared unseeing out the window. Her own reflection wavered in the glass, highlighted by the last of the firelight, and behind her lay the empty room. And then *he* was there.

As if conjured from the racing thoughts in her mind, Jake appeared out of the shadows and stood right behind her. His reflection joined hers and as he looked at their mirrored selves, he asked quietly, "Why're you sitting here in the dark?"

"There's firelight still," she said softly, gaze locked on the man in the glass. She could feel him behind her, and yet, the wavering figure in front of her had all of her attention. "Did I wake you?"

He shook his head. "Couldn't sleep."

She wondered why. Was he feeling what she was? The restlessness that seemed to nibble at her insides? When he closed his eyes, did he see *her?* Did he feel that kiss they'd shared in the stable? Did he remember that flash of anticipation, expectation, that had jolted between them?

Even now, her body was tingling, and staring into his eyes, dark in the glass, made her feel that tingle light up and sing. Cass had been over this and over this in her mind. She'd gone through the whole "boss's son" thing and she could admit, at least to herself, that she no longer cared. After all, it wasn't as if she would run home to Boston and announce that she'd had sex with Elise's son. No one had to know. This wasn't forever.

This was—she looked at him again and felt everything inside her turn over—*necessary.*

Silence stretched out between them, taut, humming with so much tension, it nearly burned the air.

"I like whatever it is you're thinking," he said.

"Not surprising, since I believe you're thinking the same thing." Her voice didn't sound the least bit breathy and desperate. Good for her.

He came around the edge of the chaise, held out one hand to her and, when she took it, pulled her to her feet. He didn't let go, but ran his thumb back and forth across her skin, sending shivers up and down her arms.

Cass looked up into his eyes and watched as they darkened, filled with the same need that she knew glittered in her own.

"I've been thinking it since the first time I saw you."

A swirl of something hot and lovely spun in her center and Cass took a long, deep breath, reveling in the sensation.

"Me, too." She couldn't believe she'd just admitted that to him. But then, not really a secret, was it? Each time they'd kissed, they'd set off so many internal explosions it had left her rattled for hours after.

"You should know—" He looked at her, hunger shining in his eyes, mouth tantalizingly close. "I didn't *want* to feel it."

She had to smile, how could she not? She'd been going through the same thing for days now. Good to know she hadn't been alone. "Now who's being forthright?"

"It's time, don't you think?" A small smile curved his mouth briefly as he pulled her closer. When he spoke again, though, all trace of amusement was gone from his features. His blue eyes were dark, serious and fixed on her as if she were the only person in the world. "I want you and I'm done waiting."

"Oh." She blew out a breath. "Okay. Good."

Time seemed to pause. Her mind raced with so many thoughts, and yet each one somehow allowed itself to be acknowledged before the next one rushed forward.

She liked him. A lot, really. Before she came to Montana, Jake's mother and sister had both told Cass about him. She'd listened to the stories and heard both their pride in and exasperation with him. She'd known before she came here that he kept his emotions on a short leash, that he didn't like company and that loyalty was important to him.

She'd heard about his short-lived marriage, his tours of duty and his love for this ranch. Once she got here, his grandfather had shared more stories until she felt as though she'd always known him. Yes, he was closed off and hard to know, but Cass had seen his gentleness with the horses. Seen him smile at his housekeeper and laugh with his grandfather. She remembered him with Rocky, the lazy horse.

Cass smiled to herself at the memory. He could tell himself that Rocky was only here under sufferance, because there was no way to get rid of the animal. But she knew the truth. She'd seen it in his eyes. He loved that horse and that's the only reason he kept him.

There was kindness beneath Jake's gruff exterior. And caring. And a capacity for love that he was denying himself. She had to wonder why. He intrigued her, attracted her and touched something deep inside her that had never before been awakened.

There was more to Jake Hunter than it appeared. And Cass wanted him so much the sensation was overwhelming. She'd never felt anything close to this need, this rush to touch and be touched before.

All of these thoughts and more swam through her mind. It seemed to take forever and yet she knew, logically, that only a handful of seconds passed.

Cass stared up at him and wondered how they'd come to this moment. Finding this…connection, with Jake Hunter wasn't something she'd expected. But now, it seemed inevitable that she step into the heat sliding from his body. That she keep her gaze locked on his as he spoke again.

"Good?" He smiled again and the way that curve of his lips lit up his eyes was simply staggering.

"Yes," she said, knowing exactly what she was saying yes to. She moved in eagerly as his arms locked around her and pulled her in.

"Glad to hear it," he whispered, then he bent his head to take her mouth.

That first brush of his lips against hers turned a key in a lock that was so deep inside her she hadn't even realized it was there. Every time he kissed her, she'd felt a buzz of rightness. A sense that it had been meant to happen. But this time, knowing that the kiss was leading to something more opened every door in her heart and mind.

She parted her lips for him and tangled her tongue with his. Breathing fast and hot, they gave and took and shared until her heartbeat thundered in her chest. She felt the same reaction in him as his arms tightened around her, holding her to him so that nothing separated them but the layers of fabric they wore.

And suddenly that was too much. He tore his mouth from hers, stared down into her eyes and said, "Up-stairs. Now."

"Oh, yes."

He took her hand and led her from the room, and Cass was forced to run to keep up with his much longer strides. Her breathing was staggered, her pulse pounding, and when they hit the stairs, she was just a step behind him. Which was apparently too slow for Jake.

Stopping, he turned, swung her into his arms and took the rest of the oak staircase two steps at a time. "Wow. When you say now, you're not kidding."

He grinned down at her and Cass's heart tumbled in her chest. "No point in wasting time once the decision's made, is there?"

"No point at all." She hooked her arms around his neck and let herself enjoy being swept—literally—away. It was romantic, a gorgeous, muscular guy carrying her up a grand staircase to a bed that was— "That is the biggest bed I've ever seen."

Jake gave her another smile and said, "Custom made. Big enough for me to stretch out."

"With a dozen of your closest friends," Cass whispered as he walked up to what had to be a king and a half mattress.

His room was as beautiful as the rest of the place, in a purely masculine fashion. Not that she had a lot of time to look around, but in a fast glance, she caught the dark red duvet on the mattress, and black leather chairs pulled up in front of a stone hearth where a fire burned brightly. The windows were bare, providing what would in daytime be a sweeping view of the ranch and the lake far below. There were bookcases, tables, and an adjoining door that probably led to the attached bath.

But most of her concentration was fixed on that bed. Especially when he laid her down onto the mattress and loomed over her.

"You're thinking," he accused warily. "Not changing your mind, are you?"

"Not a chance."

"Good to know," he said, lying down beside her and gathering her into his arms with a strength that sent chills racing along her spine.

His kiss woke every nerve ending in her body, leaving them all screaming for more. Her mouth opened under his and his kiss deepened until all she could think about was the next taste of him. This was what she had wanted. The mind-numbing passion that had eluded her for her entire life. Here, in his arms, she was thrown headfirst into a tumult of emotions and sensations that were too many, and coming too fast, to even identify them all.

And it didn't matter. Nothing mattered but having his hands on her. She felt him tug at her shirt and she moved to help him strip it off. The cool, slick feel of the duvet chilled her skin even as his touch heated her through. He tore his mouth from hers as if desperately in need of air, but then shifted to drag his mouth down the line of her throat, his lips and tongue leaving a line of fire in their wake.

She gasped and arched into him when his fingers undid the clasp at the front of her bra and spilled her breasts into his palms. At his first touch, she half lifted off the bed, moving into him as his fingers and thumbs tweaked and tugged at her nipples, pleasure darting through her at every action.

Her breath came in short, hard gasps when he took first one hardened nipple then the other into his mouth. His tongue did amazing things to her skin, his hot breath brushing her flesh with more heat than she thought she could bear.

"Beautiful," he whispered, his voice a tight groan in the firelit night. He lifted his head and looked at her. In his eyes, she read more passion than she had ever seen before. "Cassie, I want you badly enough that I can't promise to go slow."

Cassie. No one in her life called her Cassie and she liked it. It spoke of intimacy, a connection beyond the physical that only added to what she was feeling already. Hunger pumped through her. A need to lose herself in the feel of him.

"Who needs slow?" she answered softly and her words were swallowed by the cavernous room.

He grinned at her and her heart responded with that wild tumble again. What did he do to her? How did he do it? Days she'd known him and yet, to Cassidy, it felt as if somehow she'd *always* known him.

His hands were everywhere; she felt him. Every touch, every slice of heat that speared through her, driven by his caress. She moved and writhed on the bed, drowning in the feelings overtaking her. Too many, yet not nearly enough.

He dragged his mouth down the length of her body, stopping only when he came to the waistband of her jeans. Then his fingers quickly undid them and slid them down her legs and off. Her fingers fumbled with his clothes, too, and he let her have her way.

She skimmed her palms up and across his hard, muscled chest, loving how the hard planes of bronzed skin heated her hands.

Again and again, she touched him as if she couldn't get enough, and his response was immediate.

He jumped off the bed, practically growled, "Be right back," then stalked across the room to disappear through a doorway. Vaguely she heard a drawer open, then snap closed. Suddenly he was there again, before her body had time to cool at his absence.

Watching her, he stood by the side of the bed, stripping out of the rest of his clothes, then tearing open the condom he'd gone to the bathroom to get. He sheathed himself as she watched, her gaze locked on the hard length of him. He was as big there as he was everywhere else, and the anticipation inside her thrummed into overdrive.

"Been waiting days for this," he muttered, coming down on top of her as she parted her legs to draw him in. "Feels like years."

"It does," she agreed breathlessly. Oh, the heavy, solid feel of him covering her body was so right. So tantalizing. And then he slid inside her in one glorious thrust.

Cass gasped and moved with him as he took her over completely. He filled her to the point where she thought she would never feel empty again, with or without him in her life. She knew his imprint would remain long after this night was over—that thought squeezed her heart painfully, so she dismissed it and focused on what he was doing to her now. There would be time enough later for regrets, for pain.

He moved in her, his body sliding in and out in a

frenzied dance of need and passion. Her hands moved up and down his back, along his thighs, felt the power in his leanly muscled body and gloried in it. She lifted her legs to wrap them around his hips, pulling him in higher, deeper, and still it wasn't enough. It might never be enough.

Tension coiled inside her, tightening with his every thrust until she was gasping, lungs heaving for air that couldn't get past the knot lodged in her throat. And still she pushed him forward.

His whispered words, his kisses, all drove her toward the peak. She moved with him, around him, their flesh fused together by heat and passion. Cass groaned, called his name and reached for that dazzling light hanging in front of her. She had to have it. Had never known such bone-deep need, such desperation…

"Take it, Cassie. Take me," he whispered. "Let it go and grab for it."

"With you," she insisted, shaking her head against the duvet that now felt like a silky pool of fire beneath her. Shadows twisted, firelight danced in his eyes as she stared into their depths and gasped, "We go together."

He smiled, buried his face in the crook of her neck, and nibbled at her throat as he reached down between their bodies to flick his thumb across the hard swollen bud at her core. When she splintered in his arms, she heard him murmur, "You first."

Power slammed into her, shuddering through her body as she clung to him, soaring higher than she'd ever been before as he continued to move inside her, pushing her ever higher. The last of her climax was still rippling through her when she heard him groan her name. As his body rocked with completion, she held on to him, wondering how she was ever going to let him go.

What she'd just experienced would never happen with a different man. She knew it. It was Jake who had gotten past every one of her hesitations, her worries, and made her forget her reluctance to get involved with the one man she shouldn't.

And now she knew why she'd instinctively tried to hold herself back from him. It had nothing to do with worry over her boss or even the fact that she would be leaving and going back to Boston. No, this was more elemental than that. Somewhere, she had known that this man was the one who could reach her heart.

Jake Hunter was the one man in the world who could make her want to let go of old doubts and mistrusts.

To risk falling in love.

Jake rolled to one side and as he lay there beside her, Cass could practically *feel* him pulling away. She knew that right then, he was trying to find a way to let her down easy. To tell her that this didn't mean anything. That it had been a mistake and wouldn't be repeated.

But it *would* be repeated if she had anything to say about it. For the time she was in Montana, she wanted him with her, in her, over her. She wanted to wrap herself around him and luxuriate in the feeling of his skin along hers.

Because she knew, when she left, it would be over.

Oh, she hadn't counted on this. Hadn't expected to find…*him*. Now that she had, though, she also had to accept that she was going to lose him. Her heart pinged with an ache she realized would be with her for the rest of her life. But she hadn't asked for forever and he hadn't offered. Judging by the expression on his face and the shutters across his eyes, that offer wasn't about to be made, either.

So Cass would keep this light and never let him know that she was already more than halfway in love with him.

Turning her head to look at the man beside her, she noted his forearm tossed across his eyes, his chest moving with long, deep breaths and the *wall* he was already erecting between them.

As she watched him, he went up on one elbow and turned to look at her. She could read on his expression that he was about to start the whole this-was-a-mistake-and-I've-got-to-get-out-of-here speech. So she spoke fast, saying the first thing that came to mind. Something she'd wondered about since arriving at the ranch.

"Why don't you have a dog?"

His mouth snapped shut and he stared at her as if she were speaking Urdu. "What?"

"A dog." She stretched comfortably and smiled. "Cowboys. Dogs. They kind of go together, but you don't have one. I was wondering why."

Shaking his head a little, confusion shining in his eyes, he said, "That's what you want to talk about? *Now?*"

Cass forced a casual shrug she really wasn't feeling. "What would you rather talk about? How you're a loner and this was a mistake and how you don't want me to get my heart broken or anything—" She broke off and deepened her voice into an overly dramatic drawl. "I'm not the kind of man you need and you should just forget about all of this and realize that I'm not interested in forever?"

That confused look in his eyes was now tangled up with the first flares of irritation. She'd been right, of course. That's exactly what he had been about to say. Apparently having her say it for him didn't sit very well with Jake Hunter. Well, too bad.

Seconds passed in silence but for the log in the hearth that cracked in the heat and dropped to the grate below with a muffled crash.

"The 'talk' is unnecessary," she assured him, ignoring that tiny ache in her heart. "So why not ask about the dog situation?"

He huffed out a breath and frowned. "I don't know what to make of you."

"Forthright, remember?" Internally, she scoffed at that. If she were really forthright, she'd be telling him that she was almost in love with him and all it would take was a tiny push from him to complete the fall. But that would be like yelling "fire!" He'd be out of this room so fast, her hair would lift in the wind.

His gaze narrowed on her. "Right." Another second or two passed before he said, "I've got enough animals here that I have to care for. Don't really need a dog, so I've never gotten one."

She nodded. "I understand, but the horses and the cattle are business, aren't they? A dog would be more company than anything else."

"Who says I need company?" he challenged. "I've got twenty hands who work and live here—two of them with their wives—I've got my grandfather across the yard and plenty of clients who come and go. Not like I've got the time or the leisure to get lonely."

Though his words were firm and it was clear that he believed them, Cass thought she'd never met a lonelier person in her life. True, Jake was surrounded by all the people he'd just named, but he never let them in. According to his grandfather, even *he* had to fight to maintain any level of closeness, and she knew Jake loved the older man.

"Cassie," Jake said and the calm, patient tone of his voice caught her attention. "We really should talk about this."

Cass didn't want to. She didn't want to see him pull away, didn't want to hear words that had no meaning because she already knew there was no future here for her. So she rolled into him and slid one arm around his waist. "No," she said, looking up into his eyes. "We really don't. I'm a big girl, Jake. I'm in your bed because I want to be here. You don't owe me anything."

Emotions too varied to read darted across his face before he reached for her and pulled her in tightly enough so that Cass could feel his desire stirring to life again.

"You puzzle me," he admitted. "You never do or say what I expect you to."

Her heart tumbled in her chest at the heat in his eyes. "That's good," she said, brushing her mouth across his. "I would really hate to be predictable."

One corner of his mouth tipped up and he shook his head. "No worries there," he assured her.

"Jake, there's nothing we have to say to each other right now, okay?" She moved so that she could slide her fingers through his thick hair, each strand moving against her skin like a caress. "Let's just take tonight and not dissect it."

He seemed to think about it for a long minute. Then he said, "Storm's over, you know. The road out should be cleared in a day or two."

Another sharp stab of pain, regret, poked at her insides, but she ignored it. "Then in a day or two, I'll be gone and we can both go back to our lives. Good enough?"

His arm around her tightened, and for one heart-beat, Cass thought that he didn't like the idea of her leaving. She'd like to tell herself that he wanted her to stay. But the moment passed and she grimly reminded herself not to build illusions that would only shatter her later. Take what's here, she thought. Take it and treasure it, then let it go. It was the only way.

"I think we've talked enough," was all he said and then he dipped his head to take one pebbled nipple into his mouth.

Cass groaned and sighed all at once. Satisfaction and need curled together into a tangled knot until she didn't know which was the stronger. She held his head to her breast, sliding her fingers through his hair as his mouth tormented her with gentle torture designed to have her quivering into a puddle of goo.

Take it. Treasure it.
Then let it go.

A few hours later, Jake lay quietly in the dark with Cass curled up into his side. She slept, her breathing deep and even, her arm draped across his chest, her legs entwined with his.

His body was, for the moment, at peace. But his mind wouldn't shut off. The plain and simple truth was, he'd had his world rocked and he still wasn't sure how he'd allowed it to happen.

She was in his bed. Nestled up next to him. And he should be jumping to his feet and making tracks. Yet instead, he stayed here, next to her, feeling her breath brush across his chest. Inhaling the scent of her, drawing it deep inside him. He felt her heartbeat, soft against him, and felt invisible manacles snap closed around his wrists.

Well, *that* mental image got him moving.

Carefully, he eased out from under her. She whispered in her sleep, then curled up in the warmth his body had left behind on the sheets. In the moonlight drifting through the windows, he looked at her, that soft spill of dark blond hair, her creamy smooth skin, the rise and fall of her breasts beneath the quilt they'd been sharing. And the view shook him to his bones.

Deliberately, he turned his back on the bed and the woman in it and stalked to the adjoining bathroom. He hit the wall switch and winced as the lights jumped to life. Black and white tiles, black granite and black sinks gleamed in the harsh light, but when he looked in the mirror, Jake saw a man on the edge.

He curled his fingers around the end of that cold granite and leaned into the mirror. "What the hell?"

He'd wanted her for days and had assumed, naturally, that the minute he'd had Cass, the need for her would wane. It always had before. Every woman who'd come through his life—including his *ex-wife*—had left absolutely zero impression on him. If they were there, he was with them, but when they were gone, he didn't miss them. Hell, even when Lisa left him while he was still serving overseas, he'd been more pissed than hurt.

And when he'd come home, he'd easily gone on with his life without her.

Jake had always assumed that the lack was his. That there was just something missing within him that kept him from forming any kind of attachment to the women he encountered. But maybe, he thought now, it wasn't him. Maybe it was the women he'd chosen in the past.

Because he had new evidence. Cass was asleep in his bed.

And he wanted her all over again.

He turned from the mirror and the questions he saw in his own eyes. Walking into the shower, he turned the faucets and purposely stood beneath a fall of icy water. He didn't need more heat. Hell, he felt as if his blood were still boiling.

What he needed was cold. And distance. And some damn logic.

Lathering up the soap, he scrubbed his skin as if he could wash away her scent, but even as he tried, he had the feeling that he'd never be able to accomplish that. Cassidy Moore was a complication he hadn't figured on. He had to mitigate the danger to himself by getting her off his mountain and back to Boston as fast as he could manage it.

Just because he'd taken her into his bed for the night didn't mean that there was room in his life for her.

He was better off alone.

Six

Fourteen months later...

Cass's world was imploding and all she could do was stand there and watch it go.

But then ever since she left Montana, her life had been nothing but one shock after another, she told herself, so really...what was one more?

Leaving Jake had been harder than she would have thought. That last morning on the ranch, he'd kept his distance until it was time for her to leave. Then, he'd waved her off with a casual air—no kiss, no hint of regret to see her go—as if what they'd shared had meant nothing to him, and the pain of that memory traveled with her. And still, when she was first home in Boston, Cass had actually expected Jake to call her. To admit that he missed her. Naturally, he didn't. Stubborn man.

Then, two months after returning to Boston, Cass discovered that condoms weren't foolproof. She smiled at the memory of her shock and the thin thread of panic that had shot through her. Despite all of that, though, she had been thrilled to find out she was carrying Jake's baby. She'd always wanted a family of her own, and knowing that she would always have a piece of Jake with her had made missing him a little easier.

But the pregnancy had also meant she had to quit her job, because she couldn't continue working with Elise and not tell her about the baby—her grandchild.

Just as Cass couldn't tell Jake. Oh, her conscience had driven her nuts for weeks over that decision, but in the end, Cass knew it was for the best. Jake wanted to be alone and it was hard to be alone with a newborn in the house. And keeping her pregnancy from Elise wasn't easy, but if the woman knew the truth, she would tell her son and then…oh, it was a vicious circle. So in the end, Cass had kept her secrets, given up her job and built a life for herself and her child.

Sure it was scary, being a single mother, but it was worth it. Her son was her world and until today, she would have said that everything was going great.

Of course, that was before her brother and sister had shown themselves to be traitors.

Panic nibbled at her insides and every breath was a victory because it had made it past the knot lodged in her throat. Her heartbeat was loud and heavy in her ears and chills raced along her spine as she tried to come to grips with the worst-case scenario playing out in front of her eyes.

"I still can't believe you did this."

Cass needed to move. To get up and walk. Maybe

run. Problem was, there was nowhere to go. It was early December in Boston and even here, the snow was deep enough to make going for a walk less than pleasant.

So she settled for jumping up from the chair by her front window and stalking the three short steps to the opposite wall and back again. Pacing was less than helpful when the confines were so small.

Ordinarily she had no problem with her tiny one-bedroom apartment. But today, with her family gathered, she could feel those walls shrinking. While she stalked angrily, she sent Claudia another hard glare. "You had no right." Swinging her gaze to her brother, she added, "*Either* of you."

Claudia was unbowed and unrepentant. Her long blond hair was done in a single braid with strands of plastic holly berries woven through it. She wore a green and red sweater that read Santa Knows How to Deliver and her dark blue jeans were tucked into knee-high black boots. "Somebody had to," she said. "Dave and I talked about it and we decided—"

Cass turned her furious gaze on her younger brother. Dave's blond hair was cut short and he kept stabbing his fingers through it as if remembering when he was a teenager and wore it to his shoulders. His brown leather jacket was worn, his jeans and steel-toed work boots looked battered, and his features clearly said he wished he were anywhere but there.

"How do you two get to make a decision about *me?*"

He growled a little, shot a hard look at their youngest sister and then looked back to Cass. He followed her as she moved back to her chair and dropped into it.

"We *all* talked about it. Me, Emma and Claud, and we agreed this was the best way to handle it."

If she were any more furious Cassidy figured the top of her head might blow off and shoot right through the ceiling and the roof.

"You and your wife and our sister decided the best way to handle *me?* Since when have I needed to be 'handled'?"

"Since you started acting as stubborn as a sack of rocks," Claudia told her.

Another wave of rage swept through her and Cass had to fight to drag air into her lungs. "You had no right. Any of you. This is *my* life."

"Yeah, it is," Dave said and dropped to his haunches beside her. Looking up into her eyes, he said, "You spent a lot of years working to take care of me and Claud. We don't think it's fair that you have to do this by yourself. And more than not fair, Cass," Dave added quietly, his gaze locked with hers, "it's not right. He deserves to know."

He deserves to know.

Hadn't that sentence been repeating over and over again in her mind for the last year or more? Cass glanced across the room to where her infant son lay sleeping, completely oblivious to the family battle going on within feet of him.

Jake's son.

A child he knew nothing about.

Oh, she'd had an internal war over telling him or not ever since the pregnancy test read positive. She knew she should tell him, but at the same time, he'd made it more than clear that family wasn't important to him.

Besides, during their time together, they'd agreed that their situation was temporary. A baby wasn't temporary.

But it was more than that and she knew it. Though she had wanted to tell Jake about his son, she hadn't because she hadn't wanted to risk her baby's heart.

What if Jake got involved and then eventually pulled back? What if Luke was old enough to feel *his* father's rejection as brutally as she had felt her own dad's absence? No. She wouldn't do that to her child.

Although now, she might not have a choice.

"Why now?" she demanded, looking from one to the other of them in turn. "Why not six months ago? Or six months from now?"

"Because it's Christmas," Claud said in a huff. "It's past time he knew, Cass. And with the holidays and all..."

"Damn it Cass," Dave put in, "we're not going to feel guilty about this. You need the help and he needs to know he's a father."

"It was my decision," she argued. "Jake didn't want kids, so I didn't tell him."

"Yeah, that was before you got pregnant. It's easy enough to dismiss having children when it's theoretical. But when it's real, that's different." Dave's voice tightened. "He'd change his mind damn quick if he knew he had a son."

Her gaze shifted to him. "You don't know that."

"I'm a father. I *know.*"

"And even if he doesn't change his mind," Claudia added, "so what? The least he can do is help support Luke so it all doesn't fall on you."

Shaking her head, Cass said, "I don't want his money."

"Maybe not, but you need it," her stubborn sister countered. "Ever since you quit your job with Hunter Media, you've been scrambling."

"Claud's right," Dave said. "There's no need for you to kill yourself like this, Cass."

"You know darn well money's been tight whether you want to admit it or not," Claudia put in.

"I have plenty of clients," Cass argued, getting more defensive by the moment. Yes, she missed that healthy paycheck from Hunter Media, but she'd had to quit that job when she found out she was pregnant. How could she have kept on working for her son's grandmother and not *tell* the woman? But if she had told Elise, then Elise would have told her son and then Jake would have felt trapped into doing whatever the heck he considered the right thing and who needed any of that?

"Your clients are all great, but they're small-time and they don't pay you enough."

True, she was forced to admit—albeit silently, since she didn't want to give her siblings any more ammo to use against her. Her at-home billing business hadn't grown as quickly as she'd hoped, but it would.

"I can work from home on my laptop and that means I can be here with Luke. Whatever's missing from my old paycheck is saved by not needing day care."

"Uh-huh." Dave spoke again and Cass swung her gaze back to him. "But you'll need a bigger apartment soon and hopefully in a better neighborhood. That takes money, and there's no reason Jake can't help support his son."

God, she felt as if she were being attacked from all sides by the people who loved her best. She knew they were doing it because they cared, but what they'd done could change everything. Ruin everything.

"You don't get it." Cass stood up, unfolded the letter she had already read in disbelief a dozen times and shook it until the heavy paper rattled like dead leaves. "Claudia told Elise about Luke and now Elise is threatening to take him away from me."

Dave didn't bother reading the letter. He didn't have to. When Cass had called this emergency family meeting, she'd read the letter over the phone to both of her siblings.

"She can't do that."

"Of course she can," Cass snapped. "She's rich. I'm not. Luke is her grandson."

"She can but she won't," Claudia said, kicking back on the love seat and crossing her booted feet at the ankles.

It was extremely infuriating that her little sister looked neither contrite nor worried. "Oh really. And why not?"

"Because it would seriously piss off her son and she doesn't want to do that."

"I should take your word for it because you're such an expert on Elise Hunter?"

"No, you shouldn't take my word for it." Claudia sat straight up and met Cass's gaze with a fierce stare. "You should call Jake and tell him what his mother's up to."

Cass just blinked at her. As if she'd gone momentarily deaf, she shook her head to clear it and said, "Call Jake? I've been avoiding calling Jake since I found out I was pregnant."

"Which I didn't agree with," Dave put in.

Cass sneered at him, then faced her sister again. "I can't believe *you* haven't called Jake. You called his mother—betrayed your big sister and practically handed your nephew over. Traitors. You're both traitors."

Snorting, Claudia briefly inspected her fingernails, then pushed to her feet. "You've really become a drama queen since having a baby. I wanted to call Jake, believe me. And I would have, but I didn't have his number. I did call Elise because I figured *she'd* call Jake. I didn't think she'd make a play for Luke on her own."

Cass sighed and rubbed her forehead. Elise hadn't called her son. Cass knew that for a fact because if she had, Jake Hunter would no doubt be standing on her doorstep right now demanding answers. Why Elise hadn't told him was a mystery. But the meaning behind her letter was clear. She wanted her grandson and if Cass didn't find a way to fight her old boss, the woman would find a way to get custody of Luke.

Her pounding temper was turning into a pounding headache. Taking a breath, she focused inward, trying to find a solution to this jumbled-up mess her life had become.

What if she was wrong and Jake did want his son? Would he try to take Luke from her? Would she go to him for help only to find herself fighting two custody suits instead? And what if everything went great? What then? She'd been solely responsible for Luke from the start. What would it be like to suddenly have to share him?

There had been so many times over the course of her son's life that she had wished for Jake to be there with her. To be able to share the joyful moments along with the scary ones. And in spite of the worry shooting through her at the moment, a part of her yearned for the closeness with her son's father.

"Cass, we didn't mean to hurt you," Dave was saying.

"We were trying to help," Claudia added. "You've worked so hard your whole life. You took care of me single-handedly—practically raised Dave, too. It's not right that you have to do all the worrying and work alone again."

Cass sighed. "I know you meant well."

They loved her. They had been trying to help. Instead they'd created a tangled mess that Cass would have to solve. But she would solve it. This battle she couldn't afford to lose.

She walked across the room to stare down at her sleeping son. He had thick black hair and big blue eyes, just like his father. And like his daddy, Luke's smile melted her heart. Five months old and he was her entire world. Until he had come into her life, she'd had no idea you could love so deeply, so completely. She couldn't risk losing him. Which meant she really had only one option.

Jake.

This was going to be Luke's first Christmas and she'd wanted to make it special. Well, it didn't get much more special than meeting your father for the first time. Worry curled in the pit of her stomach. What would it be like to see Jake again? Her pulse skipped into a quick beat. So many times she had dreamed of being with him again. Now, it seemed, her wishes were about to be granted.

"Montana," she whispered, more to herself than her siblings, "here we come."

* * *

The last storm ended four days ago, but Jake knew there was another one coming in, fast. December in Montana meant snow. Lots of it. They were prepared as much as they could be, though. Generators at the house, barn and cabins were at the ready in case the power went out. There was enough firewood cut and stacked to last everyone a month and food storage was plentiful. They were ready for whatever Mother Nature tossed at them.

And still, he was restless.

"Probably Christmas getting to me," he muttered, standing at the kitchen counter staring out over the yard and the acres of white that seemed to fill the landscape. Every pine tree was draped in a solid cape of snow, and every oak and maple and aspen stood naked but for the lacy snow covering each of the bare branches and twigs.

He'd already made his traditional trip out to the forest to cut a Christmas tree for his grandfather, and then he'd had the traditional argument over why *he* didn't want one for the main house. Jake didn't do Christmas. Hadn't in years. In fact, the last holiday season he had "celebrated" had been on his first tour of duty in a war zone.

The guys in his company had built a "tree" out of whatever they could find—mostly discarded enemy weapons—and decorated it with string and bullets and paper "snow" torn out of padded envelopes sent from home. Missing their families, they'd all sung some carols, built a fire and pretended they were home. Until the enemy mortar fire exploded into camp, destroying the makeshift tree and killing two of Jake's friends.

He hadn't bothered celebrating since. For Jake, December was just a month to get through. Get past.

"Just as I'll get through this one."

"You say something?"

He turned to look at Anna as she hustled into the room and went straight to the stove where a huge pot of beef and barley soup was bubbling and sending out aromas designed to bring a hungry man to his knees.

"No," he said, pushing old memories aside to focus on the here and now.

"Fine then." She gave the pot a stir, then turned and braced both hands at her hips. Anna was in her fifties with graying blond hair, a thick waist and a no-nonsense attitude that Jake appreciated. "Charlie's back from town. He's just pulling into the front drive now."

"Good." Jake set his coffee cup down onto the counter. "I'll go meet him." His foreman had left the ranch in the four-wheel-drive Jeep more than an hour ago, without a word of explanation. And since Jake needed to talk to him about getting some hay out to the cattle before the next snow hit, he was anxious to find out what the hell had been important enough to drag him away from ranch business. He started across the room, then stopped. "Did he tell you why he went into town?"

Anna's eyebrows lifted as she gave him a cool, hard glare. "He did."

What was she mad about? "And?"

"*And,*" she repeated, tapping the toe of one boot against the floor, "you should go and see for yourself."

Anna was usually a reasonable woman, Jake thought, but at the moment, she looked angry enough to come at him with the spoon she still clutched in one hand.

Maybe Christmas was getting to everybody.

"Fine, I'm going." Shaking his head, he headed out of the kitchen and down the long hall toward the front of the house. Maybe Charlie knew what the hell was going on with his wife. Muttering darkly, Jake snatched his coat off the newel post at the foot of the stairs and shrugged into it. Then he tugged on his hat, grabbed the doorknob, yanked on it and almost plowed right into Cassie, standing on his front porch.

Her smoke-gray eyes shone with surprise, and her dark blond hair streamed down her shoulders from beneath a knit purple hat. She wore a heavy black coat and knee-high boots. Her cheeks were pink from the cold and as he adjusted to the shock of finding her on his front steps, he finally noticed what she was holding.

A baby.

Wrapped toe to neck in some kind of zip-up covering, all Jake could see of the child were big blue eyes— just like his own. A jolt of emotion shot through him so hard, he gripped the doorknob tight, to keep from falling over in shock.

"What the hell?"

"Jake," Cassie said, "meet your son. Luke."

Seven

"**My** *son?*" Silently, Jake congratulated himself on the self-control that kept his voice from raging with the fury erupting inside him. He looked into those soft gray eyes, read her defiance, and that damn near pushed him over the edge.

He couldn't believe this. For nearly a year and a half, this woman had haunted him, waking and sleeping. Hell, he'd hardly known her and shouldn't have given her another thought once she was gone. But he had. He'd missed her body and the soft, slick feel of her skin beneath his palms. The sound of her voice. Her laughter. The smoke-gray eyes that betrayed everything she was thinking, feeling. He'd missed the feel of her in his arms, the sighs as he entered her and the gasping groans when they each found their release.

Jake had even fantasized a couple times about seeing her here again.

He just had never imagined her carrying his child along with her.

His child.

He had a son.

She'd been keeping the truth from him for a year and a half and he *still* felt that rush of desire he hadn't found with anyone else. He looked at her and his body tightened, his heart banged against his rib cage, and his hands itched to touch her.

Didn't matter, it seemed, what she'd kept from him. He wanted her.

Grimly, he pushed those needs aside in favor of facing her down with the hard truth currently smiling up at him from a drooly face.

"What the hell, Cassie?" The words were ground from his throat as sharp and cold as pieces of broken glass.

"Don't swear in front of the baby," she muttered and pushed right past him into the house. Then she stopped, looking up at him. "We have to talk."

"Yeah," he said, torn between dumbfounded shock and pure fury. "I'd say so."

Anna came hurrying down the hall, glared at Jake and clucked her tongue at him so fast, it sounded like machine-gun fire. Then she dropped one arm around Cassie, enveloping her and the baby she carried, and steered them off to the great room.

"You come on in here and get warm by the fire," his turncoat housekeeper was saying. "And you give me a peek at that little darling, too…"

Jake shook his head and snatched off his hat, crumpling the brim in one tight fist. The wind rushing through the still-open front door sliced through his coat with icy knives, but he hardly felt it. Mind racing, emotions churning, his gaze landed on Charlie, standing in the yard staring at him.

"Sorry, boss. Cass called Ben from the airport and Ben sent me to fetch her."

Why the hell hadn't Ben said anything to Jake? Warned him? That was a thought for later. Right now, he looked at his foreman and said, "It's fine."

"I'll bring in the baby's car seat and Cass's bags," Charlie said, wincing a little at the words.

"Her bags? Of course she has bags." Seemed that she had plans to stay. Well, good, because she wasn't going anywhere until Jake had answers to all of the questions racing through his mind. Gritting his teeth, he said, "Take them up to the room she had last time she was here. After I talk to Cassie, I'll see you at the barn."

As soon as he could breathe again. As soon as he had some answers from the woman who had walked into the great room as if she belonged here. As if she hadn't been gone more than a year and given birth to his *son*.

Cassie had called Ben for help. And Ben had sent Charlie to the airport without a damn word to Jake. His own grandfather was a part of this. Then he had to wonder if Ben had known about the baby all along. Had he been a part of keeping Jake's child from him? Betrayal stung and fury roared fresh and new through his bloodstream. The anger churning inside nearly stole his breath.

Anna had known about Cassie flying in, because

Charlie had. How long had she known? Was she also in on the baby secret? She hadn't seemed surprised by it. How long had Ben known? Was his whole ranch in on this? Was everyone calling him a fool behind his back? Laughing at the man who was so clueless he had no idea he was a damn *father?*

Tossing his hat to the nearest table, he shrugged out of his jacket and dropped it onto a chair as he marched into the great room. Anna and Cassie were talking together, huddled around the baby, peeling his little snowsuit off while he jabbered and made nonsense noises. Jake stopped dead and watched the little boy from a distance.

His feet wanted to take him closer, but his mind was keeping him in place. Before he let himself be distracted by the child, he needed some answers from the boy's mother. As if the women could sense him watching them, they both turned around to face him. They'd stripped that cold weather covering off of the boy. Anna was holding the baby now and the infant—in a pair of tiny jeans, a flannel shirt and baby-size cowboy boots—gave Jake a grin that displayed four or five teeth.

Jake's heart fisted painfully in his chest. His throat closed up with emotions too thick and too many to name. A child. He could see the resemblance. Hell, there was no denying this boy was his son—even if Jake wanted to, which he didn't.

How was it possible to feel so much so quickly? Jake's instincts were kicking in with a force that shocked him. He suddenly knew that he would do anything to protect a child he hadn't known existed an hour ago. That boy was a part of him and no one would keep Jake from him. He'd already missed too much. Damned if he'd miss another minute. But for now, he needed some answers. Keeping his gaze fixed on the baby, he said quietly, "Anna, take him into the kitchen. Give him a cookie or something."

"You don't give a baby a cookie, Jake Hunter," she snapped. "But I think a banana would be welcome if that's all right with his mama."

"Oh, Luke loves bananas. Thank you, Anna," Cassie said, dropping a quick kiss on the baby's head.

His son loved bananas. *Good to know,* Jake told himself, still looking at the boy who had him hypnotized. His heart did another sharp squeeze in his chest as the kid laughed and clapped his tiny hands together.

Anna smiled at Cassie, then narrowed her eyes on Jake. "Anyway, I know how to take care of a baby without your advice, Jake Hunter," she grumbled and took the diaper bag from Cassie. "Don't you worry, honey, I raised four of my own. The boy will be fine with me. You come on in and have some tea once you're done with *him.*" She shot Jake a death glare as she swept past him, carrying his son.

Astonished, he looked after his supposedly loyal housekeeper for a long minute. This was nuts. Suddenly *he* was the bad guy here? How did that make sense?

"What the hell did I do?" he demanded of no one in particular. "I didn't know I had a kid, did I?"

Anna kept walking, her quick steps sounding like gunshots in the stillness. He turned away abruptly and his gaze swung to Cassie, standing there staring at him. Jake had the satisfaction of seeing her features tighten and her lips go bloodless.

"I know you want an explanation and I'll tell you whatever you want to know," she said in a rush, as she slid out of her heavy jacket to reveal a red sweater that reached to her thighs, and black jeans tucked into knee-high boots. She shoved the sleeves of her sweater up to her elbows.

Damn, she looked good. Having a baby had ripened her curves, made her even more desirable than she had been, and that was saying a lot.

Not the point.

"Start with why you called my grandfather to arrange a ride here from the airport. Why didn't you call me? Hell, while we're on it, why didn't you call me when you found out you were pregnant? When you had the baby?"

"I called Ben this morning because I didn't want to explain all of this to you over the phone." She pushed her hair back from her face and took a breath. "And I didn't want you to meet your son in the airport."

"That takes care of today," he ground out, crossing his arms over his chest. "Now explain the last fourteen months."

She took a breath and blew it out. "That'll take time. And there's something you have to know, first. The reason I'm here."

"You mean," he cut in, "the reason you're finally telling me about my *son.*"

"Yes." She reached into her bag, pulled a piece of paper out and crossed the room. Thrusting the page at him, she ordered, "Read that."

It only took a second or two and in that time, the temper he'd thought was as high as it could go burst past the breaking point. "My mother is going to sue you for custody of *my son?*"

Cass wrung her hands, tugging at her fingers, then started pacing back and forth across the huge room. While she walked, she threw glances at him. "My sister Claudia told your mom about Luke, and two days later, I got *that* in the mail. She'll do it, Jake. Elise Hunter will take my baby if you don't stop her."

"No one's going to take your baby from you," he muttered, gaze running over the few sharp and to-the-point sentences on the heavy stationery his mother preferred. "No judge would allow it."

"She's rich," Cass muttered. "I'm not. She can hire a fleet of lawyers and I can't." She stopped in front of him, tipped her head back and stared up into his eyes. "I won't lose my son. You have to do something."

Those fog-gray depths were filled with pain and worry, tugging at something inside him, awakening a protective streak he hadn't felt since he'd left the military. Back then, you watched your buddies' backs. You looked out for them all like family. Risked your own life to save theirs and never gave it another thought. Back home, he'd felt that same sense of loyalty to his grandfather, mother and sister—but with Cassie, that urge to defend came roaring through his blood like a battle cry.

Crumpling the paper in one hand, he walked to the phone on a side table near the couch. He grabbed the receiver out of its cradle, stabbed in a few numbers and waited for his mother to answer her private line. When she did, Jake didn't waste time on niceties.

"What's this bull about you trying to take Cassie's baby from her?"

"Well hello, Jake. So nice to hear from you. I'm very well, thanks for asking. And you?"

Cool, her voice had that dismissive tone he knew she used on business rivals. "I'm great," he ground out, gaze flashing to Cassie. "I just found out I'm a father and that my mother's trying to take my kid. How's your day going?"

Cassie's face flushed but her gray eyes were still clouded by worry.

"I won't have my grandson raised by a woman who can't afford to take care of him properly," his mother said tightly.

"He's my son and you're not taking him from his mother," Jake told her. "Hell, what made you think I'd allow that?"

"You've turned your back on your family, Jake," his mother said and he thought he heard a note of hurt coloring her words. "You cut me and your sister out of your life. How was I to know you'd feel differently about your son?"

"I didn't cut you out, mother. I cut the company out of my life. There's a difference."

"Not to me," she insisted. "You've locked yourself away on the mountain, Jake, and you worry me. You're so closed off, so self-contained, you don't need any of us. Well, that baby is a Hunter and if you won't do the right thing by him, then I will."

Furious now, his gaze firmly locked on the woman staring at him helplessly, he reminded his mother, "I wasn't given the chance to do the right thing. Nobody told me about that baby. Until five minutes ago I didn't know he existed."

"Well," his mother said softly, "now that you do know, what're you going to do about it?"

That was the question, wasn't it? He didn't have an answer. How the hell could he know what to do when the world as he'd known it had been upended in his face? Could he have five damn seconds to think?

"I'll let you know," he snapped and hung up. Tossing the phone onto the couch before he could smash the damn thing in his fist, he faced Cassie. "That's done. She won't be making a grab for the baby again."

"You don't know that," she whispered and he heard fear in her voice.

"I'll make sure of it."

A part of him wanted to go to her, pull her into his arms and hold her. Soothe her fears. Ease the worry shimmering around her like a stormy aura the color of her eyes. But a greater part of him was aching from betrayal.

From the fact that this woman had kept his son from him. Had kept his son's existence a secret.

"You should have told me."

She paled. "Maybe."

"Maybe?" He stalked toward her and inwardly cringed when he saw her dart backward a couple of steps. He wasn't trying to scare her, for God's sake. He only wanted answers. Explanations. But maybe he was too furious right now to hear them. Stopping in his tracks, he snorted a harsh laugh. "You really think I'd hurt you?"

"No, of course not." She shook her head and once again shoved both hands through her hair. It had grown, hanging down now to the middle of her back. With her jerky movements, long ropes of that dark blond silk fell over her shoulders to lay against her breasts. Rubbing her fingertips across her forehead, she murmured, "It's just been a long day. Luke didn't like the airplane ride. The passengers didn't like a crying baby. Then they couldn't find my luggage and the ride up the mountain road was terrifying and I just feel like…"

The tightness in his chest eased a little watching her. She'd had as rough a day as he was having. "Nice day, huh?"

Her head whipped up, her gaze locked on his, and whatever she saw there had her shoulders relaxing and a glint of humor sparking her eyes. "I've had better."

"Me, too." He still wanted to know. *Needed* to know. Everything. But there were things he had to do and he had to have some time to think. "Come on. I'll walk you to the kitchen."

Surprised, she asked, "We're not going to talk?"

"Later. Storm coming. Have to get the animals ready for it."

A strangled laugh slipped from her. "And we're back to cowboy-speak. That hasn't changed, anyway."

"Plenty else has," he said just as shortly, stopping only long enough to grab his hat and jacket. "And I'm gonna want to hear it all."

In the kitchen, Anna was seated at the table, holding the baby on her lap. On the floor, a big yellow Lab sat beside her, his nose on the baby's legs. The dog winced every time the baby patted his head, but otherwise, didn't move.

"A dog?" Cassie said. "You got a dog?"

The Lab pushed to his feet and came across the room to welcome Cassie with a snuffle and a few dozen licks. While Cassie heaped praise on the dog, scrubbing his ears, Jake could only think how much he wanted her hands on *him*.

"When did you get a dog?" she was asking.

Before he could answer, Anna did. "He got him right after you left the last time. Hardly a week before we had a puppy running around the house."

Jake glared at his housekeeper, but she paid him no mind at all.

He'd once told Cassie he didn't have a dog because he had enough animals to care for. But the truth was, after she left a year and a half ago, the damn house had been too quiet. Too…empty.

So he bought a dog for company. What was the big deal?

The baby shouted a babbled greeting and lifted his arms for his mother. Jake scowled, tugged his hat on and buttoned his jacket as he headed for the back door. "Come on, Boston. Work."

"Boston?" Cassie echoed the dog's name and Jake flinched as embarrassment swept through him.

Grinding his teeth, he managed, "I'm from Boston, too." When she didn't say anything to that, he added, "We'll talk later." He waited for the dog to join him, then opened the door to the blowing wind and snow.

There were heavy ropes strung between the back door of the house all the way across the yard to the barn. Ropes also hung between cabins and between the main house and his grandfather's place. When the predicted blizzard hit, the wind-driven snow would be so thick, flying so fast, a person could get lost between the house and the outbuildings. Without that rope to cling to, you could wander off track and freeze to death before anyone had a chance to find you.

But for now, the wind was light and the only snow blowing was lifting off the drifts and mounds already on the frozen ground. Jake hunched into his jacket and headed for the barn and stables. Beside him, Boston's tags jingled like music as the big dog jumped from snow pile to snow pile.

Inside the barn, warmth engulfed him and the scents of hay and horses welcomed him. Here was the peace he'd built for himself. Here was where his world made sense. Boston ran the length of the center aisle and dropped to the ground beside Jake's grandfather, standing at one of the stalls.

A jolt of anger shook Jake. He stalked across the distance separating them and finally stopped alongside the older man.

Ben didn't even look at him. "Charlie tells me the boy looks just like you. Can't wait to see him."

"You knew." Betrayal was a living, breathing pain in his chest. This old man had been one of the centers of Jake's life. When he'd come home from war, he'd come to this ranch—as much for the steadiness of this man as for the peace of the mountains. "You knew and didn't say a damn word."

Ben scrubbed a hand over the back of his neck and squinted up at Jake. "I knew when your mother found out. Couple days is all."

"It's more warning than I've had." Jake gritted his teeth. "You should have told me."

"Thought about it."

"Doesn't count."

"Your mother thought this way was best."

"My *mother* wants to take that baby away from his mother."

Ben snorted. "Your mother wants *you* to step up for that baby."

Stunned and insulted, Jake stared at him. Did his family really think so little of him? Did they actually believe that he wouldn't do the right thing by his own blood?

"I didn't know about him. Hard to step up for something when you have no idea it exists."

"Well, now you know." Ben's still sharp eyes narrowed on him. "What're you gonna do about it?"

"Wish to hell people would stop asking me that," Jake muttered.

Cass was still feeling jumpy hours later.

Sure, thanks to Jake she didn't have to worry about any plans his mother might have to try to take Luke from her. But now she had to deal with Jake.

"How'd he take it?" Claudia asked.

"Stunned. Shocked." *Angry,* she added silently. Clutching the phone a little tighter to her ear, Cass kept her voice low, since Luke was sleeping in a crib beside her. "He wasn't happy, let's put it that way."

"But after you explained…"

"I didn't get the chance," Cass admitted with a sigh as she dropped onto the window seat and stared out at the view she'd been dreaming about for months. "After he called his mother, he walked out. He hasn't been back to the house since."

"So, drama queen meets drama king," Claudia mused. "A match made in, well, okay. Maybe not heaven."

Rolling her eyes, Cass countered, "Easy enough for you to take this so lightly. It's not your life."

"I'm not taking it lightly," Claud argued. "But Cass, you couldn't just go on forever not telling him. And you know it."

"Maybe," she admitted. Far off in the distance, dark clouds roiled, twisting in the wind, moving ever closer. "But I don't like being pushed into it, either."

"Look on the bright side," her sister said. "Hard part's over. He knows about Luke. Now you just have to work it out between you."

"That *is* the hard part. He's not even talking to me, Claudia. He's—" She broke off and stared as Jake and his dog emerged from the barn and headed for the house. The big yellow dog jumped and rolled in the snow drifts like a clown and Jake looked fierce. Seemed his mood hadn't improved any in the hours since she'd seen him last.

"He's what?"

"He's coming," Cass told her sister. "I've got to go."

"Okay, good luck!"

She was going to need it. Over the last few hours, Cass had been settling into the room she'd used when she was here the last time—at least the room that had been hers until she'd begun staying in Jake's bedroom. Of course, that wasn't going to happen this time. She hadn't come back here for sex.

Her body tingled and she frowned.

Just thinking about sex with Jake was enough to make her body hum and her brain shut down. But she needed to be able to think rationally. To talk to Jake and make him understand why she'd done what she'd done. To tell him what her plans were for their son.

And then, she had to get out of Montana. This time for good.

Downstairs, she heard the kitchen door slam and shivered. He was inside now and probably headed for her. So she stood up, squared her shoulders and lifted her chin. A quick glance into the crib had her smiling. Sleeping soundly, her son was in his favorite position, sprawled spread-eagle, much like his father. As she watched, Luke reached for a tuft of his own black hair and rubbed it between his fingertips.

Her heart filled to bursting and her spine straightened. There was nothing she wouldn't do for this baby. No one she wouldn't face. Nothing she wouldn't dare.

Cass *felt* Jake before she heard him. The man still moved like a ghost, and she wondered if that came naturally to him or if it was a holdover from his time in the military. Either way, it didn't matter once she turned her head to look at him, framed in the open doorway. The yellow Lab slipped past him and went first to Cass, his nails clicking on the hardwood. After she'd given him a pat, the dog stuck his nose between the rails of the crib, snuffled, then lay down right beside it, as if taking up guard duty for the tiny boy inside.

Jake, though, didn't come in, just looked at her, then shifted his gaze to the crib and the sleeping baby. "Where'd you find the crib?"

His voice, though low, was rough and harsh.

"Anna had Charlie bring it down from your attic. She said your grandfather stored the family stuff up there and that you wouldn't mind Luke using your old crib."

"It's fine." His features tightened and a muscle in his jaw clenched. "You should have told me."

Cass flushed and she felt the heat of it sting her cheeks. She could give him excuses, tell him the rationalizations that she'd run through in her mind over and over during the time they'd been apart. Heck, she'd even rehearsed exactly what she would say on the plane ride out here. But now that it was time... now that she was looking into his lake-blue eyes, she couldn't do it.

The simple truth was, he was right. She should have told him from the first. Should have shared the miracle of their son right from the beginning. It had been wrong not to. Her brother and sister had tried to convince her of that, but her own fears had kept her from realizing it.

For so long now, she'd been on her own with Luke, seeing his first smile, his first tooth, and not being able to share it with the one other person who should have been there. There really was no excuse for not telling him—there was only her fears.

"I know."

Surprise flickered in his eyes. "Didn't expect that."

The light was going, sun setting, and with any luck, Luke would sleep through till morning. He'd had a very long day with no nap and too many changes in his routine.

Cass knew the talk she and Jake were about to have was long overdue, but she didn't want to have it here, where they might wake up their son. She gave a look to where the dog lay prone beside the crib, then glanced at Jake. "Is it all right for the dog to stay here?"

"Looks like he already figures Luke is his," Jake told her. "Boston."

The dog lifted his head from his paws.

"Stay."

That heavy yellow tail thumped twice on the floor and then Boston closed his eyes for a nap.

"Good boy." Cass bent down to pet the dog again and then stood to walk to where Jake waited. There was no more putting it off. It was well past time they said what had to be said.

Jake turned in the doorway so she could pass him and as she did, her breasts brushed against his chest. Sparks of awareness, of need, lit up her insides and she had to take a deep breath to steady herself. God, it had been so long since she'd felt that quickening of her pulse. The hot rush of desire churning through her insides.

She looked up at him and knew he'd felt that same electrical jolt—and he didn't look any happier about it than she felt at the moment. "Jake—"

"Not here." He took her elbow in one palm and led her to the next door down the hall, to his room. Once inside, he closed the door partially, leaving it open just wide enough that they would be able to hear the baby if he stirred.

Strangely, that small action caused her heart to ping with tenderness. Then the moment was past and she was watching him stride across the master bedroom toward the wall of windows that overlooked a wide, snow-covered forest and Whitefish Lake, its sapphire-blue surface covered in snow and ice. "Explain."

"Jake—"

He turned to face her, his features grim, his luscious mouth tight and firm. "Explain to me why you never bothered to use a damn phone. Why you thought

I wouldn't want to know that you were carrying my son."

Cass winced under that blow, but a part of her knew she deserved it. She looked at him and didn't see only the righteous anger she'd been prepared for, but she also saw pain. Pain she'd caused because she'd been too much of a coward to face him with the truth.

And while she could admit to all of that, in her defense, he'd made no secret of the fact that he wasn't interested in family. Was it wrong that she'd taken him at his word?

"You're the one who told me you were a loner. You didn't want family around."

"I didn't say I wouldn't want my *son,*" he said, each word dropping like an ice cube between them.

"No, you didn't," she agreed, walking farther into the room. She tried not to look at that wide bed where they'd spent so many hours tangled together. Because the memories were already so rich, they were cluttering her mind, making it difficult to think straight. "But we agreed that what we had was temporary, Jake."

"It was. Luke isn't."

"No, he's not. He's precious and wonderful and I don't want him to be a burden you're forced to pick up and carry because you're an honorable man." And she couldn't risk having her son grow to count on his father, depend on him, only to be shattered if Jake suddenly decided that he wasn't interested in a family anymore.

"So you get to decide for me? Is that it?" He turned his face from hers briefly, staring out at the sky and the blustering wind.

"I thought it would be easier. On all of us."

He whipped his head around to glare at her. "You thought wrong."

"Yeah. I can see that." She walked past the bed and didn't stop until she was standing right in front of him. "If you want to know your son, that's great. But I'm not expecting anything from you, Jake."

"Well, I'm expecting plenty." His eyes were on fire with emotions. She felt his body nearly vibrating with everything that he was keeping locked down, locked away.

The room was filled with shadows. The last of the sun had faded as they talked. A half moon was rising, fighting to shine in spite of the dark storm clouds rushing across the sky. Wind rattled the windows as Jake demanded, "What's his name? His *last* name."

Cass frowned, prepared for battle. He wouldn't like this, but it had been her decision to make, after all.

"Moore." Before he could speak, she said, "You're listed on his birth certificate as his father, but I thought it would be easier if my son and I had the same last name."

"Agreed," he said, reaching out for her and pulling her tightly to him. "Only difference is, that last name is going to be Hunter."

Shocked nearly speechless, it took Cass a moment to recover before she blurted, "Excuse me?"

"Welcome home, Mrs. Hunter."

Eight

Jake's belly clenched as soon as he said the words.

Hell, who could blame him? The last time he'd asked a woman to marry him, it had turned into a major disaster. Jake had vowed to never repeat that mistake. To keep to himself. To never risk letting someone get too close again.

Yet what choice did he have? His son was sleeping in the other room. He'd made a child and now it was time to do the right thing. Marry that child's mother.

Even as he considered the situation, he reassured himself that this proposal wasn't about love. He still wouldn't be letting Cassie get under his skin. *On* his skin was something else. And that consideration eased the skittering panic in his brain. Sex with Cassie was amazing. Hadn't he been missing it for nearly a year and a half?

Marrying her would ensure that he could have her all the damn time and that was a huge plus.

Not to mention his son would be *here* on the ranch, where he belonged. Through the confused thoughts came one image, that of his little boy, racing across the ranch yard, with Boston at his heels. Damned if that didn't bring a smile to his face. Until Cassie started talking again.

"Are you crazy?"

Not the reaction most men got with a proposal.

"No."

"That's it? Just 'no'?"

She stared at him for a long minute or two, neither of them speaking as shadows crept from the corners of the room like thieves, stealing the last of the light.

Jake studied her in the dimness and felt more than his belly clench. His groin was hard and aching and everything in him yearned to hold her tighter, closer. Yeah, he wanted her. In spite of the anger over her keeping his son from him. In spite of everything, he wanted her. Would *always* want her. But damned if he'd admit that to her.

When she pulled free of his grasp, he let her go. Only so far, though.

"I'm not going to marry you, Jake."

He crossed his arms over his chest and planted his feet wide apart in a "ready for a fight" stance. "Don't see a way around it."

"None of that cowboy-speak, either. Use full sentences."

"Fine," he said, moving in on her. "You want lots of words? Here are a few for you. You kept my son from me. You kept his existence a secret. You think

I'm just going to say thanks for dropping by so I could get a look at him? Not a chance. That boy's a Hunter and he stays here. Where he belongs."

She blinked and shook her head. "He belongs with me."

"There you go." He waved one hand. "That's why the marriage. He's going to have a mother and a father."

"I told you I didn't want Luke to be the burden of honor that you picked up because it was the right thing to do," she countered, moving in on him now, poking him dead center of the chest with the tip of her index finger to emphasize each word. "Well, I won't be your duty, either. I know you don't want a family and I'm not going to sign on to be your wife out of obligation. No thanks."

Anger erupted. Not surprising since it had been there, deep inside him, bubbling, churning, demanding release, since she'd first walked into his house carrying that baby. Emotions he'd thought long buried were swimming to the surface, but he didn't want to look at them now. There were too many of them and he was in no position to try to sort through every feeling that was knocking around his heart demanding to be recognized.

He couldn't let the anger or the emotions guide him right now. Instead, he grabbed for a single, slender thread of logic and clung to it.

His gaze fixed on hers, and he willed her to hear. To understand. "You say 'duty' like it's a dirty word. It's not. Duty means you accept responsibility for what you've done. It's making a personal vow to do what's right. What's necessary. It's an obligation to face what others can't or won't. Duty means something to me, Cassie, and I can't change that. Even for you."

"I don't expect you to change," she argued, looking up at him, her emotions churning in the fog of her eyes. "I'm not asking you to. Just as I'm not going to marry a man who thinks of me as an obligation."

He snorted. "Not an obligation, Cassie," he said, "a thorn. An attractive thorn that I wouldn't mind tossing onto my bed about now, but still a thorn."

She had been just that right from the start. A thorn jabbed into his skin, painful and irritating until he pulled it out and still felt the ache. Cassie had wedged herself into his life, made him nuts while she was here on the ranch, and then made him full-on crazy once she left. Now she was back and he couldn't make sense of anything he was feeling, thinking.

The only thing he knew for sure was that he wanted her. Bad. His desire for her hadn't waned a damn bit while they were apart and he knew now it never would.

"Wow. Be still my heart." Shaking her head slowly, she said, "That's even less incentive to marry you, Jake."

"You want incentive? What about our son?" God, that felt weird to say. Weird to know that he was a *father.* "What does he deserve?"

"He deserves to be loved," Cassie said quickly, decisively. "And cared for. And not thought of as a cross to bear."

That flash of anger burned a little brighter. Did she really think him so small that he couldn't love his own child? No, he hadn't planned on having a family, trusting fate to keep them safe so he wouldn't have his heart ripped out, but now that the choice had been made for him, he wouldn't wish it away.

"You don't get to say that to me, Cassie. How old is he?"

"Almost five months."

Jake gritted his teeth. "You've had him five months and knew about him for nine before that. You've had the chance to love him. I've barely caught a glimpse of him. So don't be telling me that I won't love my son."

"I don't want you to *have* to love him. Don't you see the difference?"

"If you had told me about him from the jump there wouldn't be any worries about 'having' to love him, would there?"

She threw her hands in the air. "How do I know that? How do *you?* If I had called you when I first found out, would you have wanted the baby?"

He swallowed hard past the knot of emotion clogging his throat. Cassie latched onto that moment of hesitation.

"See? You don't even know how you would've reacted, and I couldn't take the chance. Not with my baby's future happiness at stake."

"I deserved to know," he finally said, not bothering to counter her arguments because at the heart of it, he was right and she was wrong and he had a feeling she knew that as well as he did.

All of the fight went out of her like air sliding from a balloon. "You did. You really did. And I'm sorry."

Nodding, he looked down at her and felt resolution settle into his soul. He wouldn't say he loved her because how the hell did he know what love was? But he could admire her. Respect her. Desire her. She'd been a single mom and she'd done a good job. Luke looked healthy and happy and that was due to her. He had no idea what her life had been like over the last fourteen months, but he knew what his had been. Enduring endless nights, where he cursed the solitude he used to crave. Spending the days doing what he always had, never once guessing that a piece of him was living and growing without him.

She had been strong and he could appreciate that. But now things had changed. Now she was here, and he wasn't letting her go again. There was only one way this was going to end. *His* way.

"Yeah, well, I'm sorry too, Cassie."

She flicked him a sideways look, wary and suspicious. "Sorry for what?"

Jake cupped her chin in his fingers and felt that buzz of connection that he'd felt the very first time he touched her. He held her so that she was forced to meet his gaze, forced to see in his eyes that he meant everything he said next. "You don't have to worry about my mother anymore. But I'll tell you this. You either marry me, or I'll sue you for custody myself."

Cass pulled out of his touch and the tips of his fingers still felt warm from the contact with her skin.

Eyes wide, breath hitching in her chest, she said, "You wouldn't do that."

"Watch me," he promised, even as he acknowledged objectively that the Hunters were a damned vindictive family. Even him. She'd wanted him to save her from his mother and now she was finding out that the price for that favor was surrendering to him. He wouldn't have thought himself capable of threatening a woman—especially *this* woman—but it seemed the surprises of the day were still coming.

"I won't lose my son."

She choked out a laugh, lifted one hand to cover her mouth as if she could push the sound back inside, then looked up at him. "You realize I came to you for help?"

"Ironic," he acknowledged.

Cass walked away from him and dropped down to sit on the edge of his bed. Seeing her there again brought back all the memories he'd been trying to ignore for months. The scent of her on his pillows. The image of her hair, spilling across the sheets. The gleam in her eyes when he filled her with his body and the soft sigh of completion that always touched something deep inside him.

All of those memories and more came crowding back until he nearly choked on them. He'd been fine with his world before she came here and got trapped for a week. And after she left, he worked damned hard to be fine again. Hadn't really happened, but he'd been moving toward some sort of peace until she showed up again.

When she looked at him, she said softly, "So basically, I went from the frying pan into the fire?"

"Yeah."

She laughed shortly and shook her head. "One word. Typical."

Sighing, Jake let the anger within dissipate. He'd learned long ago to accept what had already happened because he couldn't change it. He'd lost so much time with his son that he'd never get back, but that was done.

All he could do now was ensure that he wouldn't lose any more of his child's life.

He walked over, sat down beside her and took a breath, dragging her scent into his lungs. "Were you ever going to tell me about Luke?"

Her hands twisted in her lap as she admitted, "I don't know."

Nodding, he briefly shifted his gaze to the window and the night. "What happened to forthright?"

Cass looked at him. "If lies will protect my son, then that's what I'll do."

"You think he needs to be protected? From me?" Insult stabbed at him.

"It's my job to make sure Luke is happy. Safe. Loved," she said, not really answering the question.

The room was dark so that he could hardly see her, and maybe that was best. If he read fear or worry or anything remotely like that in her eyes, he might soften. Might relent. And he couldn't.

He wasn't going to lose his son, so Cassie had best make up her mind to be his wife.

"We'll do that. Together."

"I'm not going to marry you, Jake."

"Your choice," he said softly. "But you're not going anywhere, Cassie."

"I'm not a prisoner," she countered. "You can't make me stay here if I want to go, Jake."

"Oh, I could. Make no mistake. As it turns out though, I won't have to." He pointed at the wall of windows and the dark winter beyond the glass. "There's a severe storm warning for this area for the next five days. A blizzard's going to hit and it's gonna be a big one. So settle in, Cassie. You and Luke are going nowhere."

* * *

The wind screamed for hours.

Like the shriek of lost souls, it wound itself around the house, as if frustrated at not being able to find a way in. Just as Cassie couldn't find a way out.

Physically, she was good and trapped here. Once the snow started falling, she knew she could never risk traveling on that terrifying mountain road. It would be one thing to risk her own safety, but no way would she strap her son into a car and hope for the best.

But emotionally, she was trapped even more neatly. For almost a year and a half, she'd done her best to forget about Jake. To put him on a shelf in her mind so that she wasn't constantly tormented by the memories of the week she'd had with him. But with Luke looking more and more like his father every day, forgetting wasn't easy.

She'd even begun to question if she really wanted to forget. Cass had wondered constantly if she'd done the right thing in keeping Luke a secret from his father—though there was no changing that decision. Now she was back with a man who was both furious and determined to get her to marry him.

How could she do that, though? Marry a man who didn't love her? Wasn't marriage a risk even *with* love?

Cass had seen her parents' marriage erode into rubble and she still had the emotional scars to prove it. She couldn't set her own child up for the kind of hurt she'd once known. Sure, Jake was positive he wanted her and Luke here now. But what about a year from now? Five years? What if he one day decided he'd had enough and sent them away?

How could she live with herself knowing that she'd

brought Luke the kind of pain no child should ever know? The pain of knowing that your parent didn't want you.

To make matters worse, she couldn't *sleep.*

Luke wasn't the problem. He'd been sleeping through the night since he was two months old, bless him. No, it was her own mind that was keeping her awake. Thoughts of Jake refused to quiet down and go away.

This was not how she had expected her trip to Montana to go. Cass had been prepared for Jake's anger, but the thought that *he* might now want to take custody of Lucas had never occurred to her. As for the proposal, that hadn't been real and they both knew it. He was just angry—he had a right, she could admit that—but he didn't want *her,* he wanted his son.

He couldn't have Luke.

Even sharing her son was going to be hard at first. After all, since Luke's birth, Cass had been on her own, doing everything herself. Yes, that was her own doing, but the fact remained that things were going to be changing now.

Remembering the last of their conversation hours before, she cringed.

"I know you believe that proposing to me is the right thing to do," she said, struggling to keep a calmness she wasn't feeling in her voice, *"and I appreciate the thought. But this isn't the 1950s and I don't need you to step in and save my reputation. Luke and I are doing fine on our own."*

"But you're not on your own anymore, Cassie," he said, voice as dark as the shadows crouched in his eyes. *"There's me to contend with, too. And I don't*

*give a flying damn about some fifties ideal. I asked
you to marry me because you're the mother of my son
and I figured you'd rather be where he is."*

"I will be. In Boston."

"Montana. Get used to it."

How was she supposed to get used to an ultimatum?
She flipped onto her side, facing the crib and the
wall of windows, and punched at her pillow. It wouldn't
help her sleep, but it took care of a little of the frustration clawing at her.

How could you argue with a man who spoke in
two-word sentences?

But he'd had more to say today, hadn't he? And
then the proposal? Her stomach swam with nerves
and…pleasure?

Oh, God. She slapped one hand to her forehead.
How could she even pretend to enjoy that dogmatic demand for marriage? She had to be as crazy as he was.

Desire was one thing, she told herself firmly—letting it get out of hand was something else. She had
to remember what was important here. Luke. That's
why she'd come back to Montana. Keeping her son
safe had been the goal.

Though now she had to worry about Jake's trying to
get custody, so had she really ensured Luke's safety?

When the door to her bedroom opened quietly, a
spear of light from the hallway slanted across her bed,
lighting up the darkness. She didn't turn to look. She
didn't have to. She could *feel* Jake's presence. What
she didn't know was what he wanted. But she'd had
enough of arguing for the night, so she feigned sleep,
not moving a muscle as he stepped into her room.

The door remained open and the light looked like a

golden slash through the shadows. He moved so softly, all she heard was the whisper of his jean-clad thighs. Holding her breath, she waited to see what he would do. If he came to her, if he kissed her, Cass knew she'd be lost. All of these months without his touch left her vulnerable to his slightest caress.

But he didn't come to her. Instead, he walked to the crib. Cass heard Boston's tail thump against the floor before Jake shushed him with a quiet command. Cass looked at the man in the shadows and watched as he bent low over the crib, reaching down to the sleeping baby. She saw him smooth his work-roughened hand over his son's head and her heart twisted at that gentle action.

"Hello, Luke," Jake whispered in hardly more than an expelled breath. "I'm your father. You don't know me yet. But I promise you will."

Luke snuffled and made the little squeaky sound that always made Cass think he was dreaming.

Jake watched the sleeping boy for what felt like hours. Cass's heart ached for the man and for herself. She was in serious trouble here and she knew it. Because the simple truth was, she loved Jake Hunter—a man determined to keep his heart locked away behind a wall of his own making.

Then finally, as quietly as he'd arrived, he left her room, shutting the door behind him.

By morning, the wind had died down a little and the sky looked as if it had been cast out of molten silver. Huge clouds settled over the mountain, looking as though they might drop right out of the sky any minute. It was cold, too, but Cassie had Luke bundled against the weather, zipped into his baby snow sack. When she carried him outside and stepped off the porch, she gulped in a breath of air that was so cold it felt like icicles being shoved down her throat. She probably should have stayed in the house, but she wanted to talk to Ben, and making an old man come out in the cold seemed mean somehow.

It only took a few seconds to walk across the yard to Ben's cabin, and as she got closer, she noticed that Jake's grandfather had a Christmas tree set up in the front window. The lights on it glowed in the shadowy day, looking cheerful enough to make her smile even after a long, sleepless night.

Ben opened the door before she could knock and swept her and Luke inside. Warmth wrapped itself around her and Cass sighed in appreciation.

"You shouldn't have come out in this cold, Cassie girl," Ben was saying as he adeptly lifted Luke out of her arms.

"I will admit that it's nice to be inside. Even that short walk is really cold."

"Blizzard's coming in fast," he said, with a quick glance out the window at the sky. "Best you two don't stay long and get back to the main house."

"Will you be all right over here by yourself in a blizzard?"

He laughed at that and set the baby more easily on his forearm. "Cassie, I've lived through more Montana blizzards than you could count. Got plenty of food, plenty of firewood, and just in case, I've got the generator. Jake installed a top-of-the-line generator at the main house and every cabin here when he took over. Trust me, we're set." He shrugged. "Besides, I've got a front-row seat and I kinda like watching it when the storm starts getting mean."

Cass smiled. "Jake's a lot like you, isn't he?"

"Only if that's a good thing," Ben replied with a wink. "I know things are rough going between you two right now, Cassie. But Jake's a good man. He'll do the right by you."

"That's the problem," she admitted, her heart sinking at yet more evidence that Jake Hunter would pick up his sack of troubles—Cass and Luke—and carry on stoically. "He'll do the right thing even if he doesn't want to."

"You think he doesn't want to?" Ben laughed, and led the way into the front room, fully expecting her to follow him. "You young people sure are blind sometimes. Wonder if it's on purpose?"

"If what's on purpose?" she asked.

"Nothing, nothing." The older man turned Luke in his arms so he could see the tiny face staring back at him and Ben gave the boy a wide grin. "A great-grandson. Isn't that something, though?"

A ping of guilt hit her hard and Cass told herself she had more people than just Jake to apologize to. She'd kept Luke from his family and she had the distinct feeling that guilt was going to be with her for quite a while. "I'm sorry, Ben. I should have told you and Jake and even Elise a long time ago."

Ben's sharp blue eyes fixed on her. "I expect you had your reasons."

"I did," she admitted as she slipped out of her coat. "They even made sense until I got here and talked to Jake."

Ben chuckled and carried Luke across the front room. "Well, you two will work things out eventually."

He sat down in a big leather recliner, balancing Luke on his lap. Ben's big, work-worn, time-weathered hands held the baby as gently as he might have a wounded bird. The little boy squirmed excitedly until his snowsuit was unzipped and he was freed from captivity. Then he pushed himself up on wobbly legs and braced his small hands against his great-grandfather's chest. Eyes met, smiles were exchanged and in the span of moments, Cass watched as love was born.

It hurt to admit that she'd been cheating her son out of the love that was his due. His right. She'd cheated all of them and didn't have a clue how she could make up for it.

She took a seat nearby and looked at Ben's Christmas tree. It filled the house with a luscious scent and sparkled and shone like a new morning.

Christmas. Luke's first.

"It's a beautiful tree."

"Jake goes out and cuts me down the perfect one, every year."

"But he doesn't get one for himself?"

Frowning, the older man sat Luke on his lap again and gave the boy his pocket watch to play with. "Jake hasn't celebrated Christmas in so long, he might not even know how to anymore."

Now it was her turn to frown. She'd wondered why there hadn't been any sign of Christmas in the ranch house. Of course, a man alone wouldn't do much decorating, but she had been surprised that Anna hadn't put out pine boughs and lights and things. Now she understood the barrenness of the main house. "Do you know why?"

"He never told me."

"Secrets and shadows," she murmured, turning back to the tree where lights burned brightly and strings of silver tinsel caught the reflections of that light and spun it out again. Across the yard, the main house looked dark and forgotten in comparison to the hopeful joy of Ben's tree. "I can't stay with him."

She didn't know why she'd said it. Probably shouldn't have, but Jake's grandfather had been a friend to her before and she desperately needed one now.

"Too early to give up, Cassie."

"Is it?" She looked at her son and then at the older man. "Should I stay and try and then fail? Should I let Luke fall in love with his father and then have his heart broken when we eventually go our separate ways?"

"Why do you young people always think about divorce?"

"I didn't—"

"Seems to me that when you're talking about getting married, then you should be thinking about succeeding, not failing. Why go into *anything* if you believe you'll fail?"

"He doesn't want to marry me, Ben. He only wants his son."

"Can you blame him for that?"

"Of course not, but—"

"I think you two have to find a way to reach common ground," he said, like a diplomat. "But it won't happen if you shut each other out."

She laughed shortly. "He never let me in."

Ben winked at her. "He got a dog, didn't he?"

"What?"

"The dog. Always said he didn't want one," Ben mused. "Said a house dog was too much trouble and too much time. But you hadn't been gone a week when he brought that puppy home."

"That doesn't mean—"

Ben's white eyebrows lifted. "Called him Boston, too."

True, she had thought that maybe he'd named the dog that because of her. But as Jake made a point of telling her, *he* was also originally from Boston.

"That's where he was born," Cass said, shaking her head more firmly. "His family lives there."

"Uh-huh, and he's spent most of his adult life trying to break away from Boston," Ben reminded her. "The only reason I figure he gave the dog the name of a city he can't stand is because of you. Because he couldn't forget you, and more—didn't want to forget."

Hope jumped to life in one small corner of her heart. If Ben was right, maybe there was a chance. Maybe she and Jake could find a way past their own doubts and fears and make this work. *If* Ben was right.

When she left here the last time she had been half in love with him. Seeing him with Luke last night in her room had given her that extra shove she'd needed, though Cass knew that love alone wouldn't be enough. Could she trust him to stay? Could she believe that a happy ending was possible?

"Would you mind looking after Luke for a little while?" Cass stood up and pulled her coat back on.

"Not a bit. What've you got up your sleeve, Cassie?"

She wasn't sure. Heck, she wasn't sure of much

anymore, it seemed. But she did know that she was here now and if she didn't at least try to get through to Jake, she might spend the rest of her life regretting it.

"I'm hoping there's magic up my sleeve."

Nine

Jake was cold to the bone and exhausted.

Several hours out on the land in a driving, icy wind would do that to a man. Of course, the exhaustion probably had a lot to do with the fact that he hadn't gotten any sleep the night before. With Cassie in the room right next door to him, he'd lain awake, tormented by thoughts and images of her.

The anger that had burned so brightly the day before was now just smoldering embers. Yes, he could understand what she'd done and even why—he hadn't exactly shown her the picture of a man interested in family when she was here the last time. But knowing how much of his son's life he'd already missed cut at him harder than any icy wind. What he had to decide was what to do now.

He knew what he wanted. He wanted Cassie. Now more than ever.

And he wanted his son.

But the man he'd become wasn't exactly good material for building a happily ever after.

Jake stabled his horse, gave it a good rubdown and made sure it and the other animals in the barn had plenty of feed and water before heading for the main house.

The blizzard was finally kicking in, Jake thought as he stepped from the shelter of the stable into a wind strong enough to knock a man down. Wrapping his right arm around the rope stretched across the yard, he made his way to the main house. The snow was flying and with every step he took, the flakes came faster, thicker, until even squinting, he could barely see the porch he was aimed for. It was as if the storm had waited for him and the ranch hands to return before cutting itself loose. He finally reached the porch, stomped most of the snow off and gratefully stepped inside.

Warmth reached for him and Jake took a deep breath, then released it on a sigh. Grateful to be out of the cold, it took him a second to realize that the scent of pine permeated the house.

"What the hell?"

He shrugged out of his jacket, tossed his hat and scarf onto a nearby hook, then stomped through the entryway into the main room, looking for the source of that smell.

Everyone on the ranch knew he didn't do Christmas. Didn't do trees. So he knew Anna wouldn't have brought anything into the house. Which left Cassie. Though how she would have managed—

His thoughts broke off. There was no tree in the room, just boughs of pine branches lining the fireplace mantel and stuck behind picture frames. There was a vase filled with pine branches, and the roaring fire heated the scent, saturating the air until it was rich and thick.

"You're back."

His gaze snapped to the woman sitting on the floor in front of the wide windows. Her hair was long and loose around her shoulders and her smile when she looked at him sent heat sliding through him. It had been a long, hard, cold day, but coming home to that smile was something a man could get used to.

Backlit by the growing storm, Cassie looked impossibly young and beautiful as she sat opposite Luke, with Boston sprawled on the floor beside them. As he watched, the baby slapped both hands onto the dog's broad back and rocked unsteadily from side to side, grinning wildly when he'd completed the task. An answering smile of pride touched Jake's mouth briefly. How was it possible that such a tiny human being could turn a man's heart inside out?

Boston's tail thumped in appreciation.

"This is the best dog," Cassie said, her voice breaking the spell holding him in place as she reached out one hand to stroke Boston's head. "He just loves Luke to pieces."

"Yeah, he does." She and the baby were taking over his home, his life. Hell, even his dog had abandoned him in favor of Luke. Jake's gaze swept around the room, taking in the rest of the pine decorations until he spotted a nativity scene on the coffee table. He hadn't seen it since he was a boy. "Where did you find that?"

Cassie pushed herself to her feet, picked Luke up and wandered over as if she had all the time in the world. As if she hadn't noticed the tightness in Jake's voice.

"In the attic," she said with a smile, setting Luke down in front of the hand-carved wooden pieces. Instantly, the little boy picked up a sheep and started gnawing on it. "It was Ben's idea. He said that all of the old family decorations were up there and I should help myself to what I could find."

His own grandfather. Still working against him. Ben liked Cassie, and now that Luke was involved too, the older man was making no secret of the fact that he wanted them to stay. Well hell, so did Jake. But he had more at risk than Ben did, so Jake had to look at the situation from all angles.

He took another pine-scented breath and tried to still the rumblings inside him, his gaze fixed on the long-forgotten nativity. Ben had carved that set himself when Jake's mother was just a girl. When he was a kid, Jake had done the same things that Luke was doing now. Funny, he hadn't thought about that nativity set in years. But then, he didn't spend a lot of time thinking about the past or Christmas in particular.

Still, he watched Luke move the cows and sheep around on the table and he found himself smiling again.

"Good. You don't mind that I set it up. Luke loves it. He's been playing with it all afternoon." Then she looked up at him and seemed to see him for the first time. "You look tired. Are you hungry? Anna left a pot of stew cooking before she went home. She said since the blizzard hadn't hit yet, there was no reason for her to stay."

"Yeah, the men will be out working in this mess tomorrow so Anna will probably spend the next few days cooking here for everyone. So it's good she went home to rest up."

"So many words," Cass said with a smile. "You must be hungry."

"Yeah. Hungry." That was probably the reason his defenses were down enough that he wasn't telling her to take away the pine branches and pack up the nativity. Had to be the reason, he assured himself.

"Come on," she said, scooping up Luke and heading for the kitchen without waiting to see if Jake was following. "You can eat and tell me what it's like out there."

He fell into step behind her and his gaze dropped unerringly to the curve of her behind in her faded jeans. His body tensed and despite the exhaustion pulling at his every cell, he found he might not be *too* tired. Whatever else lay between them, there was passion, bright and burning and damned hard to ignore.

Shaking his head, he walked into the kitchen and stopped her before she could take down a bowl and spoon. "I can serve myself. You don't have to do it."

Cassie set Luke into a high chair—no doubt also rescued from the attic—strapped him in and said, "I don't mind. You've been out in this mess all day." She glanced out the window at the wall of snow getting thicker by the minute and shivered. "Sit down."

He sat beside his son and kept his gaze locked on the boy because he figured that was safer than watching Cassie making herself at home in his kitchen. Memories of Lisa and his failed marriage rushed up to nearly choke him. He didn't remember a single time that Lisa had come to the kitchen to serve herself. His memories of her were more about what others could do for her. At Christmastime especially, it had been about gifts she expected, the more expensive the better. She never would have gone into the attic after an old nativity set. Never would have strung pine branches around the house.

Cassie wasn't like her, he told himself, and yet the mistrust was still there. He was waiting, he knew, for Cassie to fail. To show him that underneath her façade, she was another Lisa. She was another invitation to misery. Cassie had come into his life, turned it upside down and shaken it like a child's snow globe, and then left—only to return with a baby she hadn't bothered to tell him about.

Didn't that prove that she couldn't be trusted?

His heart iced over as he watched her. He couldn't afford to trust again. Couldn't risk making another huge mistake. And yet…there was Luke to consider in all this. His son. Jake wouldn't lose the boy—so that meant finding a way to deal with his mother.

Cassie was humming under her breath as she moved about the room and Jake's instincts went on high alert. She was too damn cheerful. Here she was, trapped at the ranch, and judging by the strength of this storm she wasn't going anywhere for quite a while. Yet she was humming. Acting as though she was happy. Why?

"Ben tells me you went out to lay down hay for the cattle before the storm hit."

"Yeah. Made it back here just in time, too." He

ran one hand through his hair and handed the baby a cracker from the tray on the table. Smiling to himself, he watched as Luke took a big bite and then reached over the edge of the chair to try to share with Boston. Better, he thought, to talk about ranch business, the storm—anything other than what lay between them.

Sighing a little, he explained, "Rather than dig through snow to find grass, cattle will just stand there and starve to death. We laid out hay near a series of caves that will give them shelter if they want it. Best we can do for now." He glanced out the window and hissed in a breath at the sight of a white wall flying horizontally past the glass.

Mid-afternoon and it was dark outside. He couldn't see the lights from Ben's house or the other cabins. The storm was a big one and was bound to get even worse. "After I eat, I'll check the generator again, make sure it's good to go if the power gets knocked out."

"Ben and one of the guys did that earlier while you were gone," she told him as she served up a bowl of stew that smelled like heaven. "They checked every one of them and they're all good. Ben says you bought top-of-the-line generators to make sure everyone would stay warm during a power outage."

Even as pleased as he was at the prospect of a meal, he felt a stab of irritation that she was so at home here. She was close with his grandfather. Had made friends with Anna and the hands who worked on the ranch. He'd seen it for himself the last time she was here. Again, one word echoed in his mind. *Why?*

Pushing all of his doubts aside for the moment, Jake picked up a spoon and dug in, relishing the warmth that spilled through him at the first bite. When he'd eaten half a bowlful, he glanced up at Cassie, who sat opposite him. Time to get a few things clear. Let her know that she couldn't just rearrange his house and life as she wanted.

"Maybe you didn't know this, but I don't celebrate Christmas."

"I know," she said, handing Luke another cracker. "Ben told me."

"Ben's got a lot to say."

"In fairly long sentences, too," she added with a quirk of her lips.

He sighed, then his gaze fixed briefly on her mouth and the memory of the taste of her swamped him. She was the one woman he couldn't forget. The one he couldn't stop wanting. And the one who could make his life the hardest—just by being her.

"If you knew how I felt," he blurted out, "why all the pine?"

"I didn't put up a tree," she pointed out, then reached across to smooth Luke's hair back from his face.

"That's not what I asked."

Shaking her head, she looked at Jake. "This is Luke's first Christmas and my first Christmas away from my brother and sister. Until we can get back to Boston—" the dog looked up hopefully "—I'm going to do what I can here."

Back to Boston.

Those three words wiped out any other argument he might have made about the Christmas decorations. A sinking sensation opened up in his gut. It felt as cold as the storm raging outside the warmth of the house.

The thought of Cassie's leaving wasn't something he was willing to consider. Whether she liked it or not, she was staying. So before anything else was said, they had to get this one thing straight between them.

"You're not going back," he told her, his gaze locked on hers, so he saw the flare of outrage spark in those gray eyes. "At least, no time soon. So you might as well put through a call to whoever you work for and tell them you're gone until at least January."

She stiffened in her chair. "You can't order me around, Jake."

"Just did." He set his spoon in the bowl and though he'd like more of that stew, this conversation had priority. "I want time with the son I just found out I had."

She flinched. Good. Even better if she really thought he was willing to let her leave come January, because it would keep her defenses down. The truth was, he would do whatever he had to do to make sure that she and Luke never left this ranch. He might not be husband and father material, but that didn't matter anymore, did it? Trust each other or not, the two of them were linked by a son they both wanted. For now, that would be enough.

Sighing, Cassie said, "I work for myself. From home. I do billing for several small companies in Boston."

Again, that tail thumped against the floor.

"Good. So you can stay with no worries." He carried his bowl to the sink and rinsed it out. Turning, he braced both hands on the counter behind him and looked at her. Jake had the feeling he could stare at Cassie forever and never tire of the view.

When that thought sailed through his mind, he told himself he should probably be worried. But he wasn't. He might not trust her completely, but he could admit, at least silently, that she tugged at strings inside him he hadn't even known were there. She was thawing a heart that had been cold for so long, it was a wonder it could beat.

Even when her fog-gray eyes were flashing with indignation, as they were now, she was the most beautiful thing he had ever seen in his life. And he wanted her now more than he wanted to go on living. Everything in him itched to take her. To lose himself in her heat and scent.

"I'll stay," she said shortly as she pushed up from her chair and crossed to him. "For now, anyway."

At least they agreed on that much, Jake told himself, looking down into her eyes, feeling himself fall into that smoky fog.

"But this isn't settled, Jake," she whispered.

Giving in to instinct, Jake reached for her, dragged her close and kissed her, hard and deep. His head swam, his blood rushed and his heartbeat pounded so hard it should have sounded like a drum in the stillness of the room.

She yielded to him, bending her body into his, wrapping her arms around his neck and parting her lips for his tongue. Desire sizzled into a blistering arc between them. When he pulled his head back after what felt like an eternity, he stared at her and agreed, "Not settled."

When his phone rang, Ben picked it up, smiling. "Hello, honey."

"Hi, Dad," Elise said. "How's it going on your end?"

Ben looked through his windows at the main house and imagined the three people inside it. Cassie and

Jake were making this so much harder on themselves than it had to be. Ben had seen for himself what was shining in the air between those two. And with the baby they shared, they had the beginnings of something wonderful—if they chose to take the chance.

"It's…interesting," he finally said, settling into his chair. "That baby is a cutie."

"He is, in the pictures Cass's sister showed me." She sighed a little. "Luke looks just like Jake at that age. I can't believe I have a grandson I've never even met. And now, with Cass as angry at me as she is, who knows when I will meet him?"

"You did the right thing, Elise," Ben told his daughter. "Threatening to take the baby. Jake and Cassie both were too stubborn to see what was right in front of them until they were faced with a common enemy."

"That's me," Elise Hunter said with a sigh. "The enemy."

"It'll work out, honey. Now, let me tell you about your grandson…"

The blizzard raged for the next three days.

Cassie had never seen anything like it. Every time the wind died down long enough for the men to get out and run the snowplows across the yard—as soon as they were finished it all began again. Trees were bent with the weight of the snow on their branches. Drifts piled high against the sides of the ranch buildings and the wind howled. It was like living in the middle of a disaster movie.

And yet, in a weird way, the storm forced a closeness that she and Jake might have spent months building between them otherwise. She worked day and night, just as he and the hands did, catching brief naps whenever she could. She brewed coffee by the gallon, made hundreds of sandwiches and oceans of soup. The men came in and out of the house at all hours, looking for food or just a chance to get out of the wind.

Whenever they showed up, she was ready. There was hot soup, cookies, slow-cooker meals. The kitchen stove never cooled off and she was busier than she'd ever been before, and yet Cassie couldn't remember a time when she'd enjoyed herself more. She was needed here, and seeing approval and surprise in Jake's eyes was as good as a medal to her.

She knew he'd half expected her to sit out the storm hiding in her room or concentrating solely on Luke. But as she jumped in to help, she saw that he was grateful. And that made the hard work worth every minute.

Of course, she also found time to torment him, too. She knew he didn't like Christmas, but she didn't know why. And since he wouldn't talk to her, tell her what he was feeling, she went right on, building Christmas piece by piece. Every night, when he came back to the ranch house, there were more decorations spread around. She found old strings of lights in the attic, and hung them around the main room, draping them over the pine branches. With the generator's help, they cast a multicolored glow over the big room.

In the attic she'd also found an abandoned, threadbare quilt that she'd cut up and, in snatches of time when she wasn't cooking, sewn into Christmas stockings. Three of them. She hung them from the mantel and couldn't help but be proud. And today, with what looked like a break in the storm, she'd liberated an old box of ornaments from the attic. They might not have a tree, but she could hang the decorations from the pine boughs, adding to the determinedly cheerful picture she was trying so hard to create.

"What've you got there?"

Cass jumped, startled, and looked up at Jake as he walked into the great room. She was seated in front of the hearth, where a fire snapped and hissed, sending heat out into the room. The box of ornaments was in front of her and she'd already unwrapped several layers of tissue paper to reveal toy soldiers, a miniature fire engine that Luke would love, and a Christmas star.

"I went up to the attic a little while ago and found this."

"That attic must be about empty by now." Shaking his head, he crouched beside her and picked up the fire engine. The ornament looked even smaller on the palm of his big hand, but he stroked the tip of one finger gently across its chipped paint. "I remember this."

Her heart twisted a little at the tenderness in his eyes and the bemused smile on his face. He kept so much of himself locked away that seeing even a small part of him revealed was like opening a Christmas present and finding exactly what you had hoped for.

As she watched, he eased down to sit on the floor beside her, his back to the fireplace. "I was five or six, I guess, and wanted to be a fireman. Mom bought this for me at a store in Whitefish. It was the ornament I always hung on the tree. My sister's was a stupid dancing bear and—"

"This one?" Cass held it out to him and he nodded, taking the little bear standing on her toes in ballet shoes and a ragged tutu.

"Yeah. She wanted to be a dancer." He snorted.

"Beth is so clumsy she trips over her own feet, but she was always trying to dance."

"Dreams are a good thing," Cass said quietly, trying not to shatter the moment.

"Yeah," he said, frowning as he looked at pieces of his past for another long moment before shifting his gaze to her again. She saw emotion crowd his eyes before he shuttered them and asked, "Where's Luke?"

Disappointment curled in the pit of her stomach. The chance for a deeper connection was lost as he stepped back behind the wall he kept between them. Even loving him wouldn't be enough to keep her here, Cass told herself. Not if he couldn't give. Bend. Not if he insisted on maintaining emotional distance from her.

"Sleeping," she said, letting go of the hurt wrapping itself around her heart. "Boston's lying under the crib. I swear that dog's better than a baby monitor. He lets me know instantly when Luke wakes up."

"Good. That's…good." He stared down at the ornaments in his hands and she could tell he was mentally miles away from this room. And her. He didn't want to open up with her, she knew that. But maybe if she pushed a little, at just the right time…

"Why'd you get him? Boston?"

He lifted his eyes to meet hers. A second ticked past. Then two. Then a few more, before he finally answered on a gusty sigh. "Because the house was too damn quiet after you left."

Warmth stole through her like a whispered breath. "You missed me."

Scowling, he set the ornaments back into the box with a gentleness that told her he still treasured those reminders of his past, whether he wanted to admit it or not. "Yeah. Didn't expect to. Wasn't happy about it. But yeah."

"I hoped you might call me, but you didn't."

He sighed. "Thought about it. A lot. I did miss you, though."

"I missed you, too." God, she had missed him. The sound of his taciturn voice. The heat of his body coiled around hers in the middle of the night. She'd missed hearing his boots on the hardwood floors. Missed seeing his hat hanging on a peg by the door. She'd missed the rare, treasured smiles he gave her and the way he fought against the tenderness that was a part of him. She'd missed everything about him.

His smile faded until his features were still and if she hadn't seen the suddenly churning emotions in his eyes, Cass might have thought he hadn't even heard her. "You should have called me, Cassie. About Luke. You should have called."

"I should have," she agreed and leaned closer, drawn to this man as she had never been drawn to another. But was that enough to build a lifetime on? Shared passion? Could she take that risk not only for herself, but for her son?

Jake leaned in, too, and then they were kissing and Cass's body lit up like the flickering lights ringing the room. She felt a blast of awareness sizzle through her system, trailing sparks through her bloodstream. She reached for him, linking her arms around his neck and holding on, as if afraid he would pull away, pull back.

She didn't have to worry about that, though. Jake drew her onto his lap, taking her mouth in deep, hungry gulps, as if he couldn't get enough of her. Their tongues tangled together, breath mingling, heartbeats racing in time as they each explored the other. Hands touched, caressed, pushed past the fabric denying them the feel of hot skin and found what they needed.

Strangling on the heavy beat of her own heart, Cass broke the kiss and gasped for breath as Jake's mouth closed on first one nipple, then the other. She didn't know where her shirt was. Didn't remember taking it off. Didn't care.

In seconds they were both naked and stretched out on the rug before the fire. Shadows danced and leaped on the walls. Outside, it was cold; inside, heat raged, claiming them, enveloping them both in a frantic sea of need and desire that was greater than anything else.

Touching, tasting, stroking, they moved together, skin sliding across skin, their tangled bodies creating more shadows on the walls. Jake swept one hand down to the blond curls at the center of her and when he stroked her hot, damp core, she arched off the floor, pushing into his hand.

"Jake, please," she whispered and heard her voice break unsteadily as she fought for air. It had been a nearly year and a half since he'd touched her, and she was ready to shatter already. Her body was eager to rocket off into the satiated oblivion she remembered so well.

"We've been apart too long," he whispered, dipping his head to kiss her, to run his tongue across her bottom lip. To nibble at her mouth while she whimpered and rocked her hips against him.

"We have. I can't wait. Don't want to wait." Gray eyes locked on blue. "Be in me," she said. "Be with me. Now, Jake."

"Now," he agreed and pushed his body into hers, sheathing himself so deeply that Cass gasped at the strength of his possession. She'd forgotten—or tried to forget—what it was like with Jake. How she lost herself in him. How her body became his. How he could make her want and feel so much more than she ever had before.

And now she had him inside her again and it was so right. So good. She wanted it to never end. She moved with him, and when he rolled over onto his back, she was astride him, taking him even deeper as she moved on him.

She watched the firelight play across his sculpted muscles. Watched her own hands stroke his skin and watched him squirm in response. He clenched his hands at her waist as he urged her into a faster pace. She rocked on him, throwing her head back, feeling like some wild warrior queen with him beneath her. And when her body trembled, letting her know the release was coming, she looked into his eyes, drowning in that deep, lake-blue.

She called his name as her body splintered and heard his hoarse shout moments later as he emptied himself into her.

When it was over, when her body was humming and replete, Cass slumped across Jake's chest and never wanted to move again.

"So," he whispered, waiting until she lifted her head to look at him. "Wrong time to ask, but you wouldn't be on the pill, would you?"

Her forehead hit his chest as the implications of that question slapped her. "No. I'm not."

"Doesn't matter," he said and that got her attention.

"Doesn't— What do you—how can it *not* matter?"

"We've got one kid. Would one more be so bad?"

Her heart hurt at the words. She'd always wanted a big family and in her mind, she could see her and Jake and the crowd of kids they would make living on this ranch. Plenty of room for children to run and they'd have horses and dogs and two parents who— didn't love each other? No. The dream images popped like soap bubbles.

How was it possible for her body to feel so good and her heart and mind to be steeped in misery? Propping herself up on her forearms, she looked down at him and shook her head. "We don't know what's going to happen between us, Jake. We can't go making another baby."

"Too late to worry about that now," he reminded her. "In fact, I hope you *are* pregnant."

Surprised, she blurted, "You can't be serious."

"Damn straight I am." He hooked one arm around her waist and rolled, pinning her beneath him. Looking down into her eyes, he said, "If you are, then this time I'll see my child grow in you. I'll be there when he's born—not hear about it five months later."

"And then what, Jake?" She shook her head slowly. "It wouldn't solve anything. It would just be more… complicated."

Jake's gaze shifted slightly and she wanted desperately to know what he was thinking, feeling. But the wall was up again and she was on the wrong side.

"Maybe," he said quietly, "but you'd have to stay here. With me. That, at least, would be settled."

She stared up at him for what felt like forever before saying, "Instead of just asking me to stay, you'd prefer to trap me. Or order me."

Scowling, he reminded her, "I asked you to marry me."

"You *told* me to marry you. There's a difference."

"You're trying to make this romantic. A love story," he muttered, and idly stroked a lock of her hair back from her face. "It's not, Cassie. It's two people who work well together finding common ground."

She caught his hand in hers and wished it was as easy to take hold of his heart. But looking into his eyes, she saw it was over. For her, it was done.

He wouldn't be what she needed. Wouldn't be the man he could be—just by opening his heart. So she couldn't stay. Couldn't risk him one day walking away as her father had done. Cass wouldn't put herself through that kind of loss again, and Luke would never know what it felt like to have his father turn his back and leave him behind.

She had to say it now, while she had the nerve. While she could force the words from her throat because the threat to her heart was so real. So immediate. "When the road's clear, I'm taking Luke and going back to Boston."

Jake went absolutely still. She felt her words hit him like stones because she saw pain in his eyes before he drew that so familiar shutter over what he was feeling.

"I won't let you go."

"Jake, you can't stop me." She touched his face because she could, her fingers tracing the stubble on his jaw. "I want what you can't give me. I love you, Jake."

He closed his eyes as if that would shut down his

hearing as well, and the pain of his reaction wound through her like barbed wire, tearing at her insides.

"I love you, but you won't love me," she said softly, willing those lake-blue eyes to open again. When they did, she said quietly, "So I can't stay."

"You love me," he said, gaze pinning hers. "But you'll still leave."

"One-sided love isn't going to work." God, did her voice sound as shaky as she felt? Could he hear her heart breaking?

He didn't see the truth. She wondered why, because it was all suddenly so clear to her.

"This, what we have? It's not enough, Jake. Not for me. Not for Luke. Heck, not even for you."

"That's where you're wrong," he said, arms tightening around her as if he could keep her there by sheer force of will. "I'll make it enough."

Ten

It would never be enough. Not with Cassie. Jake knew it. He just couldn't make himself admit it. Not to himself. Not to her.

Knowing she loved him gave him a sense of rightness he hadn't known in way too long. Knowing she was going to leave left him staring at a pool of darkness so complete he thought he would drown in it.

He knew what she wanted. What she needed. But he couldn't bring himself to comply. Doing that would lay everything on the line. Risk the life he'd built for himself. The peace he'd finally found.

Though if he were to be honest, he'd have to acknowledge that the so-called "peace" hadn't been the same since Cassie walked into his life.

He forked some hay into a stall, then moved along the line and did the same for the rest of the horses. It had always soothed him, these ordinary tasks. Usually, he let his mind wander while he did what needed doing as quickly as possible. Now though, he was taking his time because he was in no hurry to go back to the main house.

Yeah, he wanted to see Cassie. Hold her. Kiss her. But he didn't want to see the questions in her eyes. Didn't want to give her the chance to tell him again that she was leaving.

It had been three days since he'd watched her eyes as she told him she wouldn't stay. Three days and three nights and every one of those nights, they'd been together. Him, trying to show her what they could have if she'd back down; her, saying goodbye every time she touched him. He felt her pulling back, distancing herself from him in exactly the same way he had distanced himself from her since the beginning.

And it was damned hard to take.

Leaning on the handle of the pitchfork, he shot a quick look down the center aisle toward the open stable doors. The wind had eased off and it hadn't really snowed since yesterday. A couple more days like today and the roads would be clear and he'd have a hell of a time keeping her here. Where she and Luke belonged. He couldn't lose them. Either of them.

"Where's another damn blizzard when you need one?"

"Talking to yourself is never a good sign, son."

Jake turned to watch his grandfather approach. The older man was bundled up in his heavy coat, with his hat pulled down tight.

"At least when I talk to myself," Jake told him, forking more hay out for the horses, "I know I won't get a fight for my troubles."

"Won't you?" Ben snickered. "Isn't that what you're doing out here? Having a fight with yourself?"

Jake shot the older man a scowl that would have sent any of his employees running for cover. "Why do you have to be so perceptive?"

"The gift of age," Ben told him, leaning one arm on the top rail of a stall door. "Some things get harder, but you see everything around you a lot more clearly."

"Is that right?" Jake didn't want to have this conversation. All he wanted was some time to think. To plan. To find a way through the maze that lay stretched out in front of him.

"Like I can see plain as day that you're in love with Cassie."

Jake flinched, shook his head and tossed extra hay to one of the horses. "Nobody said anything about love."

"And that's a damn shame because if you can't say it, like as not, you'll lose it."

Jake's chest felt tight, as if there were an iron band squeezing his middle until his lungs could hardly draw air. Lose Cassie. He'd already lived without her once and didn't want to go back to the dark emptiness that his life had become in her absence.

But love? Love was dangerous. Love meant opening yourself to pain. Hadn't he had enough damn pain in his life already?

Ben stood there looking at him and Jake caught the sympathy in the older man's gaze. Rolling his shoulders, he shrugged off the pity and told himself he didn't want it. Didn't need it. He was in charge of his life and he wouldn't make apologies for the decisions he made. Even if those decisions cost him the one thing he wanted most.

"I had forty-nine years with your grandmother, Jake," Ben was saying softly, "and I wouldn't trade one moment of that time for all the treasure in the world."

Jake sighed at the reminder. His grandparents had the love story that most people only dreamed of, he knew that. Which was one of the reasons his spectacular failure with Lisa had torn the ground out from under his feet. He had expected the same kind of marriage. But maybe, he thought, he shouldn't have. He'd gone into that relationship too quickly, closing his eyes to who Lisa really was. Because he had *wanted* what his grandparents had shared. What his parents had found together before his father died.

When he didn't get it, Jake admitted silently, he'd shut down, refusing to try again. But who the hell could blame him? Lisa had made everyone's life a misery until she'd done him the supreme favor of leaving him. Hell, he'd take another tour of active duty in a war zone over going through that kind of marriage again.

Defensive, he asked, "Is there a point to this?"

"Yeah," Ben told him with a shake of his head. "The point is, don't be a jackass."

Jake snorted in spite of the thoughts racing through his mind. "Can always count on you to call it like you see it."

Ben sighed heavily and looked at him as if he were a huge disappointment, and Jake flinched under the uncomfortable feeling.

"You're a stubborn one. Always have been."

"Wonder where I got it?" Jake mused.

Snorting, Ben acknowledged, "Came by it naturally, that's for damn sure. Anyway, I'm here to tell you your mother wants to talk to you. She's on the phone in my place."

Jake was in no mood to talk to his mother. Her threat to take his son from Cassie was too fresh in his mind. "I'm busy."

"Jake…"

Stubborn, Jake reminded himself. His whole damn family was stubborn so it was pointless to try to avoid this call. His mother would only call back until she got hold of him. Best to just get it done now.

"Fine." He had a few things to say to her anyway. Maybe he could figure out just what she had been up to by threatening Cassie. That kind of move wasn't like his mother. She wasn't mean or vicious, so why even pretend to be willing to take Luke? There was something his mother wasn't telling him and now was as good a time as any to figure out what that was.

He leaned the pitchfork against the stable wall. "A man can't have five minutes to his damn self around this place. It's dogs and kids and women and grandfathers and now mothers."

Ben chuckled as Jake stomped out of the barn, and hearing that muffled laughter didn't improve Jake's mood any. Love. He wasn't in love. He was madly in *lust*, he knew that much for sure. But love wasn't something he was looking for.

Jake headed toward Ben's place and deliberately avoided looking at the main house. Once inside, Jake savored the warmth and tried to ignore the scent of pine that permeated the rooms. The power was back on and the Christmas tree lights shone brighter than ever, as if now that they were free of the generator, they were determined to light up at least this one small corner of the world.

His gaze drawn inevitably to the main house despite his efforts, he looked through the windows and pictured her inside. He knew that Cassie would have the lights she'd strung around the main room blazing. She was probably playing with Luke or maybe baking more Christmas cookies since he and the hands had eaten all of the batch she'd made the day before.

She'd made herself a part of this place. A part of *him*. And losing her was going to kill him.

Now in a particularly crappy mood, Jake snatched up the phone from beside his grandfather's favorite chair. "What is it, Mom?"

"Well, hello to you too," Elise Hunter said coolly. "And merry Christmas!"

His eyes rolled practically to the back of his head. The whole family knew he didn't do Christmas, yet none of them stopped trying. "Right. Same to you. What's up?"

"Do you think you might be able to speak to me without trying to bite my head off?"

Sighing, Jake yanked off his hat and scraped one hand through his hair. "A week ago, you threatened to take my son from his mother and now you're surprised that I'm a little testy?"

She laughed and the sound was so familiar, it eased some of the heaviness he felt inside.

"Oh, Jake. I was never going to take Luke from Cassie."

"What?" Frowning, he fixed his gaze blindly on his grandfather's tree, spots of bright red and green and blue blurring weirdly into a kaleidoscope of color. "What do you mean? You threatened Cassie. That's why she ran to me in the first place."

"You're welcome."

"What?"

Her laughter faded away and drowned in a sigh of frustration. In his mind, he could see her, sitting at the desk that had once been his father's with a wide window and a view of Boston at her back.

"Jake, I would never take your son. I was only trying to force Cassie's hand. Once her sister told me about Luke, was I supposed to just sit quietly and pretend I didn't know?"

His frown deepened as his fist tightened around the phone.

"Would you rather I'd done nothing?" she prodded, her insistence demanding an answer. "Would you rather not know about Luke at all?"

"No," he said abruptly. The thought of not knowing about Luke's existence hit him hard. Not ever seeing the boy? Never feeling his solid weight in his arms? Not seeing that wide, drooly smile, hearing his crow of laughter?

If Cassie left, Jake wouldn't see his son's first steps. Wouldn't hear his first word. Wouldn't teach him to ride a horse or to make a snow fort. He wouldn't show Luke the best fishing spots on the mountain and he wouldn't be a part of his own son's day-to-day life. He'd miss everything, big and small, and that knowledge tore at him, leaving Jake cringing from the pain.

That emptiness was back inside him again at the thought of not having Luke in his life. And Cassie. Without her, what the hell did he have? An empty house? A lonely ranch? He nearly choked on the thought of another fifty or so years of life spent without her laughter. Without her touch.

"Jake," his mother said softly, "don't let this chance with Cassie slip away."

Is that what he was doing? Was he really going to allow her to leave and try to pretend it didn't matter?

"I know, the hermit on the mountain doesn't want to hear that he's not invincible on his own."

Jake reached out and flicked his finger against a candy cane on the tree, sending it swinging. "I'm not a hermit."

"And you're not invincible," Elise said quietly. "Jake, Cassie loves you. Her sister told me."

"I know," he muttered, gaze fixed on that twist of red and white peppermint as if it meant his life. "I know that."

"I think you care for her, too," his mother continued.

"Of course I care," he told her hotly. "What am I, made of stone?"

"Have you bothered to tell her that?" She waited for him to say something and when he didn't, she sighed again. "Of course you haven't. Jake, I'm your mother and I love you. So I'm going to tell you that if you lose this chance at happiness, you'll never forgive yourself."

He dropped his hat onto Ben's chair, scrubbed one hand across his face and wished he could just hang up. But ending the conversation wouldn't stop any of the thoughts charging through his mind.

"Have you forgotten Lisa?"

She laughed. "That would be hard to do," his mother said. "That woman caused more problems—wait a minute." Her voice went low and hard. "Are you saying

that's why you've shut out your family and any chance
at love? Because you made a mistake with Lisa?"

"Doesn't that make sense?" he demanded, trying
to defend himself and his actions. Though hearing his
mother say it out loud made him sound profoundly
stupid. "I married her, didn't I? My mistake, and it
was a big one."

"Yes, it was." Elise sighed a little and he heard the
love in her voice when she said, "But you learn from
a mistake and move on. Jake, Cassie isn't Lisa, and
you're doing a disservice to both of you if you can't
see that. Cassie deserves better and frankly honey,
so do you."

Well, hell. Oh, he could admit that right from the
beginning, he'd been waiting for Cassie to somehow
morph into Lisa. To become demanding and complain-
ing. But she hadn't. She'd more than proven herself,
yet apparently there was still some small part of him
that didn't believe.

"I know she's not Lisa." He did. Jake had seen that
for himself during the first week she was here, and he'd
seen it again after she showed up with Luke. Cassie
had made a place for herself here. She had friends on
the ranch. She knew how to work and wasn't afraid to
step in and do what needed doing.

Yes, he'd been waiting for her to fail. To prove to
him that she couldn't handle ranch life. But she hadn't.
Not once. She did what was needed and more. And she
did it with a smile. Unlike Lisa, Cassie didn't complain
about the ranch being so far from "civilization." Hell,
she didn't complain about much of anything.

Frowning, he did silent battle with his own feelings.
Want fought against caution. Need scuffled with fear.

Fear?

Jake wasn't a man who admitted to being afraid. Not on the battlefield. Not when he was caught in a blizzard. Nothing shook him—well, nothing *had* until Cassie.

"I knew if I threatened to take Luke from her, Cassie would go to you," Elise was saying, and Jake struggled to focus. "I hoped that you two would find a way to work out what was keeping you apart."

"It's not that easy," he whispered.

"It could be if you let it," his mother argued. "Jake, I love you. But you're a fool if you let this chance at the family you always wanted get away from you."

When his mother hung up, Jake stayed right where he was, thinking. Surrounded by the scents and sights of Christmas, he pulled up mental images of Cassie and lost himself in them. Her, smiling up at him. Her, rising over him in the night, taking him into her body and holding him there. Cassie playing with Luke. Cassie working alongside the men to clear snowdrifts, and still finding the time to pack a few snowballs and get a war started to break up the tedium of the work.

Cassie laughing. Cassie sleeping beside him. Cassie sitting on the floor of the main room, pieces of long past Christmases scattered around her.

His heart ached and his head pounded. Misery settled on his shoulders and he couldn't shake it off. Maybe he didn't deserve to. Maybe Cassie was a gift and because he'd been too stupid to see it, he was destined to lose her and the family they might have made, leaving misery as his only companion.

And if what they had ended, it would be his fault.

Cassie hadn't failed. He had. Through his own re-luctance to try again.

And didn't that make him a coward? Instinctively, he turned from that word, but it was, he told himself, the only one that fit.

He looked out the window again at the house across the yard. Draped in snow, blurred lamplight was the only thing he could see through the treated windows. His woman and his child were in that house.

Was he going to fail them?

Hell no.

"It's not enough, Claudia." Cass sat on the window seat in Jake's bedroom. He was out on the ranch some-where and Luke was downstairs with Anna. They'd let her sleep in today and though she appreciated the thought, she hated sleeping away what little time she had left at the ranch.

"Cass," her sister said quietly, "you've got to stop judging all men by Dad's sterling example."

"Easy to say," Cass murmured, watching the guys plowing paths through the snow. The sky was blue, the wind was still, and she knew that if the weather held, she'd be leaving in a few days.

Her heart ached at the thought, but what choice did she have?

"You've only been there a week, Cass. Are you re-ally ready to give up so easily? I thought you loved him."

Stung, Cass frowned. "I do love him. And I'm not giving up, I'm just accepting reality rather than wait-ing around for it to bite me in the butt."

"Right." Claudia blew out a breath in exasperation.

"You've spent most of my life telling me to stand up for myself. To acknowledge what I want and go after it. To not let anything get in my way."

"Yes, so?"

"So, you want the cowboy!" Claudia's voice went sharp. "And you're not willing to stay and fight for him."

"How can I?" Cass lowered her voice and leaned her forehead against the cold glass pane. Looking down into the yard, she watched the cowboys, all bundled up in their hats and coats, and searched for Jake. She didn't see him out there and she frowned in disappointment.

Even knowing that she was leaving, he clung to the taciturn, stoic cowboy image rather than show her the man he kept locked away. Why wouldn't he let her in before it was too late? And how was she going to live without him in her life?

"Unless he loves me, there's no guarantee he won't one day just walk away."

"There's no guarantee anyway," Claudia pointed out.

"Good pep talk. Thanks."

Claudia laughed a little. "Who knew love could be such a gigantic pain?"

"Wait until it's your turn," Cass warned.

"Please. I'm nineteen. Talk to me when I'm thirty."

"Fine." Cass leaned back against the wall, keeping her gaze on the wide sweep of blue sky and the snow-tipped evergreens standing around the edge of the lake far below. "Look, I just wanted to let you know that once the road clears, I'll be coming home."

"Uh-huh." Claudia huffed out a breath. "Cass, you

said Jake wants you to marry him. To stay there on that ranch you told us about so often you bored us to tears. He wants you to be pregnant again."

That all sounded great in the abstract, Cass thought, wishing her sister could understand. But maybe that was impossible. Claudia had been only ten when their father walked out on them. And because Cass and Dave had been there for her, her life really hadn't been interrupted. It was Cass who remembered the devastation left in her father's wake.

"But he won't—"

"Cass, sweetie," Claudia cut in, "you do realize that *you're* the one walking away, right?"

That one quiet sentence slammed home like a thunderclap. She sat straight up as if jerked into place by invisible strings. Was that what she was doing? Was she running first to keep from being left behind? Had she so little faith that the only way to protect herself was to leave before Jake could?

"Oh my God. You're right."

"That just never gets old," Claudia murmured on a heartfelt sigh.

Cass hardly heard her. Thoughts racing, heart pounding, stomach spinning, she inched off the window seat and started pacing. "Funny, I never saw it like that, Claud. I just want to make sure Luke's protected. Safe."

And me, too, she thought but didn't say aloud. *I want me to be safe, too.* She couldn't bear it if Jake walked away from her. If he turned his back on her and their children. So what had she done instead? She'd given up to avoid being hurt.

"Of course you want to protect Luke," Claudia

agreed. "But maybe you could give his father more of a chance to figure this out? I mean, you've had Luke and the knowledge of him for nearly a year and a half. Jake's had what? A week or so?"

"True." Cass looked out the window and still didn't see Jake. Where was he? She had to talk to him. "I've gotta go find Jake, Claud. I'll call you later."

She dropped the cell phone onto the bed and hurried out of the room and down the long second-story hallway. She didn't notice the rugs on the bamboo flooring or the family photos and paintings dotting the walls. Taking the stairs quickly, she made a turn to go to the kitchen and ask Anna to watch Luke for a little longer, but something in the great room caught her eye and dragged her to a stop.

A Christmas tree.

The biggest, most beautiful tree she'd ever seen sat square in front of the windows, lights bursting from every branch. Heart in her throat, Cass walked hesitantly into the room and then stopped dead again when Jake, with Luke perched on one arm, stepped out from behind the tree and smiled at her.

Jake was nervous.

Hell, he hadn't been nervous since the night he left for boot camp. But he had the warm, solid weight of his son on his arm and the scent of Christmas filling his lungs, so he fought past that flutter of nerves and started talking.

He'd have felt better if Cassie would smile at him, but she looked so dumbfounded, he figured that wasn't going to happen.

"I went out and got us a tree."

Nodding, she whispered, "I see that. It's beautiful."

They were talking like strangers and it was his fault, Jake told himself silently. He'd spent so much damn time keeping her out, that now she wasn't even trying to get in anymore.

But screw that, it couldn't be too late.

"Luke and I decorated it," he said and grinned as his son patted his cheek.

"Nice job. Jake..."

"I went out this morning to get the tree." He glanced at it now, saw its beauty, and wondered why he had avoided this season and the miracle of it for so long. Shifting his gaze back to her, he said, "I cut myself off from a lot of things over the years and it took you and Luke to remind me of all I've been missing."

"Why, Jake?" Her gaze locked with his. "Can you tell me *why* you stopped celebrating Christmas?"

He hitched Luke a little higher, smoothed one hand over the baby's soft hair and took a breath. It wouldn't be easy, but he was through holding back. It was time to take a chance. He told her about that long-ago Christmas Eve on a battlefield and as he did, he relived it himself. The smells, the sounds, the awful silence when the attack was over and his friends lay broken in the sand.

When he looked at her again, he saw tears shining in her eyes, and had to force words past the knot in his throat. "When those guys died, I think something in me did, too."

"Oh Jake, I'm so sorry."

He blew out a breath, looked at the tree, then looked to her again. "I used that night as an excuse to pull back. Just like I used Lisa to keep you at bay. Didn't really see that clearly enough until today. But I see it now. I know what's important. *Who's* important."

Walking toward her, he kept his gaze fixed on hers and kept a tight grip on their son, until Luke leaned out and reached for his mother. As Cassie folded Luke into her arms, Jake stared at the two of them for a long minute. "You two are everything to me, Cassie. *You* are everything to me."

Shaking her head and blinking back tears, she said, "I can't believe you went out in chest-high drifts of snow to get a Christmas tree."

"Yeah, well," he said with a quick grin and a shrug, "you wanted one and Luke deserves one. And me?" He shot a look at the tree over his shoulder and felt years of pain and loneliness and misery slide from him in the soft glow of way too many lights. Looking back at Cassie, he said, "I wanted this tree because this is our first Christmas together. As a family."

"Oh, Jake…"

He reached out and pulled her and Luke into the center of his arms. "And I need you to know that I don't want this to be our *last* Christmas together." Bending his head, he kissed her gently, then dropped a kiss on Luke's forehead.

"I want it all, Cassie," he said, his gaze moving over her features like a caress. "I want kids and dogs and noise and chaos. I want that life we could build together. Marry me, Cassie. Marry me because I love you. Because I'm no damn good without you."

She gasped in a breath and a solitary tear fell and tracked down her cheek.

"Marry me because we deserve to be happy. And we will be. I swear it to you." He looked into fog-gray eyes and saw a future shining there that he never would have believed possible until he'd met her. "Marry me and I swear, every day will be Christmas."

She laughed a little, choking on the tears clogging her throat. How was it possible, Cassie wondered, to be so sad and lonely one minute and have the world offered to you in the next?

Her gaze slid to the massive Christmas tree and she thought about him riding out in the aftermath of the storm just so she wouldn't be disappointed. Just to make her happy. To prove he loved her.

Staring up into his eyes, Cassie knew this man would never walk away from his family. He would always be there for her. He would always come through—even if it meant pushing through eight feet of snow. He was a better man than her father had ever been, and she would never doubt him again.

"You haven't said yes yet," Jake told her, draping one arm around her shoulders and steering her toward their first Christmas tree. "So let me give you your present."

"Present?" Cassie laughed. The man was full of surprises.

Scooping Luke into his arms, Jake handed Cassie a small hand-carved box from under the tree. When she opened it, her heart melted. Nestled inside was an antique ring. Gold with several tiny diamonds and one opal in the center, it was lovely. "Oh, Jake."

"It was my grandmother's," he said, lifting the ring from its nest to slide onto her left ring finger.

"But I can't—"

He kissed her quick and light, then gave her a smile that lit up all the old shadows in his eyes, shattering them forever. "I want you to have it. So does Pop. This ring has a history of a lot of love," he told her. "I want to build on that love with you."

Outside was snow and cold. Inside was firelight, Christmas lights and more warmth than Cassie had ever felt before.

Jake cupped her cheek in his palm. "Tell me you still love me and that the answer is yes. Marry me, Cassie. Don't leave me alone on the mountain."

Her heart was so full it was hard to breathe, and Cassie simply didn't care. If she could freeze this one moment in time she would, because it was perfect and she wanted it to last forever. Yet even as she thought it, she knew their future was going to be just as wonderful and she couldn't wait to get started on it.

"Yes, Jake, always yes. I love you so much."

"Thank God," he whispered, kissing her again before pulling her against him.

And in the soft glow of Christmas, fresh promises were born.

Epilogue

One year later

"Me do it, Daddy!" Luke jumped up and down until his father picked him up and held him high enough that he could put the little fire engine ornament as close to the star at the top of the tree as possible. When he was finished, the little boy turned a wide grin on his father. "Fire truck onna tree!"

"You bet." Jake laughed, gave his son a hug, then set him down to race through the house with Boston—probably headed for the kitchen.

"Oh, Jake, that baby is the cutest thing I've ever seen," his mother said, coming down the stairs from the nursery.

"You mean since me, of course," Jake teased.

"She means, since *me,*" his sister interrupted from

her spot curled up on the couch. Beth, her husband and kids were here for Christmas along with Cassie's sister Claudia and her brother Dave and his family.

It was a full house and Jake was enjoying every minute of it. What a difference a year made, he told himself as he smiled at his grandfather, sitting in a chair by the fire, reading to Beth's youngest.

Not only did Jake have Cassie and two amazing kids, but he had his own family back in his life as well. The mountain wasn't as lonely as it used to be, and he thanked heaven for it every night.

"Cassie asked me to send you upstairs," his mother said as she went up on her toes to kiss his cheek.

"Everything all right?" Instant worry shot through him and he knew that it would always be like that. When a man had a lot in his life—he had a lot to lose.

"Fine, worrier. She's out of baby wipes and she wants you to bring her some from the storage room in the basement."

"Okay. That I can do." He turned toward his mission, but his mother stopped him with one hand on his arm.

"I can't tell you what it means to me to see you so happy."

He kissed her forehead. "You don't have to. Now that I have kids, I finally get it."

"Good." She pushed him away, called out to Beth's husband to pour her some wine and then told Jake, "Go. Don't make your wife wait."

Smiling to himself, Jake went to the basement, got a couple boxes of wipes, then headed back upstairs. As he went, he looked into the great room at his extended family. There were lights and candles and cookies and wreaths and a gigantic tree and damned if it all didn't look perfect.

From the kitchen came the amazing scents of a roasting turkey and the sounds of Anna sneaking Luke an extra cookie that Jake was sure would be shared with Boston. Claudia was in the study on the phone with one of her friends and Dave and his wife were out in the stables while their kids napped upstairs. Anna was in her glory with so many kids to look after, and she kept sending parents out of the room so she could have as much fun as she wanted to.

With the noise of a stereo playing Christmas carols and conversations rising and falling, Jake shook his head and took the stairs two at a time. He went directly to the nursery beside the master bedroom.

Pausing on the threshold just to watch his wife and child, Jake knew he would never get enough of this view. Cassie sat in a flowered rocker, nursing their daughter as snow fell softly outside the window. A small lamp beside the chair threw pale, golden light across his girls. When Cassie heard him, she looked up and smiled and everything inside Jake went completely still.

She was his everything.

"How's our girl doing?" he asked, walking into the room to squat down in front of the rocker.

"Rachel is almost finished with her dinner, aren't you, sweet girl?"

He'd had his wish and spent nine months watching Cassie grow with their child and he'd loved every minute of it. Labor and delivery were tougher than he would have imagined, but he learned again just how strong his wife was. She was already talking about having another one, and Rachel was only three months old. That was fine with Jake, though. They both wanted a big family.

The baby gurgled, gave a milky smile, then reached out and grabbed hold of Jake's finger, curling her tiny fingers around his. His heart squeezed painfully and as he dropped a kiss onto the baby's forehead, he looked up at Cassie. Briefly he remembered his life before the chaos, when peace was all-important and silence ruled his days and nights. He couldn't even understand the man he used to be. He was simply grateful that man was gone.

Looking into fog-gray eyes, he whispered, "Thank you for saving the loner on the mountain."

"Merry Christmas, Jake."

* * * * *

This was what Whitney wanted— to feel normal.

To be normal. To be able to walk into a room and not be concerned with what people thought they knew about her. Instead, Phillip had taken her at face value and made her feel welcome.

And he had a brother who was coming to dinner?

What did Matthew Beaumont look like? More to the point, what did he act like? Brothers could like a lot of the same things, right?

What if Matthew Beaumont looked at her like his brother did, without caring about her past?

What if he talked to her about horses instead of headlines?

What if— What if he wasn't involved with anyone?

Whitney didn't hook up. That part of her life was dead and buried. But…a little Christmas romance between the maid of honor and the best man wouldn't be such a bad thing, would it?

It could even be fun.

* * *

A Beaumont Christmas Wedding
is part of The Beaumont Heirs trilogy:
One Colorado family, limitless scandal!

A BEAUMONT
CHRISTMAS
WEDDING

BY
SARAH M. ANDERSON

MILLS & BOON

Published in Great Britain 2014
by Mills & Boon, an imprint of Harlequin (UK) Limited,
Eton House, 18-24 Paradise Road, Richmond, Surrey, TW9 1SR

© 2014 Sarah M. Anderson

ISBN: 978-0-263-91485-6

51-1114

Harlequin (UK) Limited's policy is to use papers that are natural, renewable and recyclable products and made from wood grown in sustainable forests. The logging and manufacturing processes conform to the legal environmental regulations of the country of origin.

Printed and bound in Spain
by CPI, Barcelona

Award-winning author **Sarah M. Anderson** may live east of the Mississippi River, but her heart lies out West on the Great Plains. With a lifelong love of horses and two history teachers for parents, she had plenty of encouragement to learn everything she could about the tribes of the Great Plains.

When she started writing, it wasn't long before her characters found themselves out in South Dakota among the Lakota Sioux. She loves to put people from two different worlds into new situations and to see how their backgrounds and cultures take them someplace they never thought they'd go.

Sarah's book *A Man of Privilege* won the 2012 RT Reviewers' Choice Award for Best Harlequin Desire.

When not helping out at her son's school or walking her rescue dogs, Sarah spends her days having conversations with imaginary cowboys and American Indians, all of which is surprisingly well tolerated by her wonderful husband. Readers can find out more about Sarah's love of cowboys and Indians at www.sarahmanderson.com.

To Fiona Marsden, Kelli Bruns and Jenn Hoopes—
three of the nicest Twitter friends around.
Thanks, ladies! You guys rock!

One

Matthew Beaumont looked at his email in amazement. The sharks were circling. He'd known they would be, but still, the sheer volume of messages clamoring for more information was impressive. There were emails from *TMZ, Perez Hilton* and PageSix.com, all sent in the past twenty minutes.

They all wanted the same thing. Who on earth was Jo Spears, the lucky woman who was marrying into the Beaumont family and fortune? And why had playboy Phillip Beaumont, Matthew's brother, chosen her—a woman no one had ever heard of before—when he could have had his pick of supermodels and Hollywood starlets?

Matthew rubbed his temples. The truth was actually quite boring—Jo Spears was a horse trainer who'd spent the past ten years training some of the most expensive horses in the world. There wasn't much there that would satisfy the gossip sites.

But if the press dug deeper and made the connection between Jo Spears, horse trainer, and Joanna Spears, they might dig up the news reports about a drunk-driving accident a decade ago in which Joanna was the passenger—and the driver died. They might turn up a lot of people who'd partied with Joanna.

They might turn this wedding into a circus.

His email pinged. *Vanity Fair* had gotten back to him. He scanned the email. Excellent. They would send a photographer if he invited their reporter as a guest.

Matthew knew the only way to keep this Beaumont wedding—planned for Christmas Eve—from becoming a circus was to control the message. He had to fight fire with fire and if that meant embedding the press into the wedding itself, then so be it.

Yes, it was great that Phillip was getting married. For the first time in his life, Matthew was hopeful his brother was going to be all right. But for Matthew, this wedding meant so much more than just the bonds of holy matrimony for his closest brother.

This wedding was the PR opportunity of a lifetime. Matthew had to show the world that the Beaumont family wasn't falling apart or flaming out.

God knew there'd been enough rumors to that effect after Chadwick Beaumont had sold the Beaumont Brewery and married his secretary, which had been about the same time that Phillip had very publically fallen off the wagon and wound up in rehab. And that didn't even include what his stepmothers and half siblings were doing.

It had been common knowledge that the Beaumonts, once the preeminent family of Denver, had fallen so far down that they'd never get back up.

To hell with common knowledge.

This was Matthew's chance to prove himself—not just in the eyes of the press but in his family's eyes, too. He'd show them once and for all that he wasn't the illegitimate child who was too little, too late a Beaumont. He was one of them, and this was his chance to erase the unfortunate circumstances of his birth from everyone's mind.

A perfectly orchestrated wedding and reception would show the world that instead of crumbling, the Beaumonts were stronger than ever. And it was up to Matthew, the former vice president of Public Relations for the Beaumont Brewery and the current chief marketing officer of Percheron Drafts Beer, to make that happen.

Building buzz was what Matthew did best. He was the only one in the family who had the media contacts and the PR savvy to pull this off.

Control the press, control the world—that's how a Beaumont handles it.

Hardwick Beaumont's words came back to him. When Matthew had managed yet another scandal, his father had said that to him. It'd been one of the few times Hardwick had ever complimented his forgotten third son. One of the few times Hardwick had ever made Matthew feel as if he *was* a Beaumont, not the bastard he'd once been.

Controlling the press was something that Matthew had gotten exceptionally good at. And he wasn't about to drop the ball now. This wedding would prove not only that the Beaumonts still had a place in this world but that Matthew had a place in the family.

He could save the Beaumont reputation. He could save the Beaumonts. And in doing so, he could redeem himself.

He'd hired the best wedding planner in Denver. They'd booked the chapel on the Colorado Heights University campus and had invited two hundred guests to the wedding. The reception would be at the Mile High Station, with dinner for six hundred, and a team of Percherons would pull the happy couple in either a carriage or a sleigh, weather depending. They had the menu set, the cake ordered, the favors ready and the photographer on standby. Matthew had his family—all four of his father's ex-wives and all nine of his half brothers and sisters—promising to be on their best behavior.

The only thing he didn't have under his control was the bride and her maid of honor, a woman named Whitney Maddox.

Jo had said that Whitney was a horse breeder who lived

a quiet life in California, so Matthew didn't anticipate too much trouble from her. She was coming two weeks before the wedding and staying at the farm with Jo and Phillip. That way she could do all the maid-of-honor things—dress fittings and bachelorette parties, the lot of it. All of which had been preplanned by Matthew and the wedding planner, of course. There was no room for error.

The wedding had to be perfect. What mattered was showing the world that the Beaumonts were still a family. A *successful* family.

What mattered was Matthew proving that he was a legitimate Beaumont.

He opened a clean document and began to write his press release as if his livelihood depended on it.

Because it did.

Whitney pulled up in front of the building that looked as if it was three different houses stuck together. She would not be nervous about this—not about the two weeks away from her horses, about staying in a stranger's house for said two weeks or about the press that went with being in a Beaumont Christmas wedding. Especially that.

Of course, she knew who Phillip Beaumont was—didn't everyone? He was the handsome face of Beaumont Brewery—or had been, right up until his family had sold out. And Jo Spears was a dear friend—practically the best friend Whitney had. The only friend, really. Jo knew all about Whitney's past and just didn't care. And in exchange for that unconditional friendship, the least Whitney could do was suck it up and be Jo's maid of honor.

In the high-society wedding of the year. With hundreds of guests. And photographers. And the press. And...

Jo came out to greet her.

"You haven't changed a bit!" Whitney called as she shut her door. She shivered. December in Denver was an entirely different beast from December in California. "Except you're not wearing your hat!"

"I didn't wear the hat when we watched movies in your house, did I?" Jo wore a wide smile as she gave Whitney a brief hug. "How was the drive?"

"Long," Whitney admitted. "That's why I didn't bring anyone with me. I thought about bringing the horses, but it's just too cold up here for them to be in a trailer that long, and none of my dogs do well in the car."

She'd desperately wanted to bring Fifi, her retired greyhound, or Gater, the little mutt that was pug and…something. Those two were her indoor dogs, the ones that curled up next to her on the couch or on her lap and kept her company. But Fifi did not travel well and Gater didn't like to leave Fifi.

Animals didn't care who you were. They never read the headlines. It didn't matter to them if you'd accidentally flashed the paparazzi when you were nineteen or how many times you'd been arrested for driving while intoxicated. All that mattered to animals was that you fed them and rubbed their ears.

Besides, Whitney was on vacation. A vacation with a wedding in it, but still. She was going to see the sights in Denver and get her nails done and all sorts of fun things. It didn't seem fair to bring the dogs only to leave them in a bedroom most of the time.

Jo nodded as Whitney got her bags out of the truck. "Who's watching them?"

"Donald—you remember him, right? From the next ranch over?"

"The crusty old fart who doesn't watch TV?"

Jo and Whitney shared a look. In that moment, Whitney was glad she'd come. Jo understood her as no one else did.

Everyone else in the world thought Donald was borderline insane—a holdover hippie from the 1960s who'd done too much acid back in the day. He lived off the grid, talked about animals as if they were his brothers and discussed Mother Earth as if she were coming to dinner next week.

But that meant Donald wasn't tuned in to pop culture. Which also meant he didn't know who Whitney was—who she'd been. Donald just thought Whitney was the neighbor who really should install more solar panels on her barn roof. And if she had to occasionally listen to a lecture on composting toilets, well, that was a trade-off she was willing to make.

She was going to miss her animals, but knowing Donald, he was probably sitting on the ground in the paddock, telling her horses bedtime stories.

Besides, being part of her best friend's wedding was an opportunity even she couldn't pass up. "What's this I hear about you and Phillip Beaumont?"

Jo smiled. "Come on," she said, grabbing one of Whitney's bags. "Dinner will be in about an hour. I'll get you caught up."

She led Whitney inside. The whole house was festooned—there was no other word for it—with red bows and pine boughs. A massive tree, blinking with red-and-white lights, the biggest star Whitney had ever seen perched on top, stood in a bay window. The whole place had such a rustic Christmas charm that Whitney felt herself grinning. This would be a perfect way to spend Christmas, instead of watching *It's a Wonderful Life* on the couch at home.

A small brown animal with extremely long ears clomped up to her and sniffed. "Well, hello again, Betty," Whitney said as she crouched down onto her heels. "You remember me? You spent a few months sitting on my couch last winter."

The miniature donkey sniffed Whitney's hair and brayed before rubbing her head into Whitney's hands.

"If I recall correctly," Jo said, setting down Whitney's bag, "your pups didn't particularly care for a donkey in the house."

"Not particularly," Whitney agreed. Fifi hadn't minded

as long as Betty stayed off her bed, but Gater had taken it as a personal insult that Whitney had allowed a hoofed animal into the house. As far as Gater was concerned, hoofed animals belonged in the barn.

She stood. Betty leaned against her legs so that Whitney could stroke her long ears.

"You're not going to believe this," Jo said as she moved Whitney's other bag, "but Matthew wants her to walk down the aisle. He's rigged up a basket so she can carry the flower petals and it's got a pillow attached on top so she can carry the rings. The flower girl will walk beside her and throw the petals. He says it'll be an amazing visual."

Whitney blinked. "Wait—Matthew? I thought you were marrying Phillip?"

"She is." A blindingly handsome man strode into the room—tall and blond and instantly recognizable. "Hello," he said with a grin as he walked up to Whitney. He leaned forward, his eyes fastened on hers, and stuck out a hand. "I'm Phillip Beaumont."

The Phillip Beaumont. Having formerly been someone famous, Whitney was not prone to getting starstruck. But Phillip was looking at her so intently that for a moment, she forgot her own name.

"And you must be Whitney Maddox," he went on, effortlessly filling the silence. "Jo's told me about the months she spent with you last winter. She said you raise some of the most beautiful Trakehners she's ever worked with."

"Oh. Yes!" Whitney shook her head. Phillip was a famous horseman and her Trakehner horses were a remarkably safe subject. "Joy was mine—Pride and Joy."

"The stallion who took gold in the World Equestrian Games?" Phillip smiled down at her and she realized he still had her hand. "I don't have any Trakehners. Clearly that's something I need to rectify."

She looked at Jo, feeling helpless and more than a little

guilty that Jo's intended was making her blush. But Jo just laughed.

"Too much," Jo said to Phillip as she looped her arm through his. "Whitney's not used to that much charm." She looked at Whitney. "Sorry about that. Phillip, this is Whitney. Whitney, this is Phillip."

Whitney nodded, trying to remember the correct social interaction. "It's a pleasure. Congratulations on getting married."

Phillip grinned at her, but then he thankfully focused that full-wattage smile on Jo. "Thanks."

They stared at each other for a moment, the adoration obvious. Whitney looked away.

It'd been a long time since a man had looked at her like that. And, honestly, she couldn't be sure that Drako Evans had ever looked at her quite like that. Their short-lived engagement hadn't been about love. It had been about pissing off their parents. And it had worked. The headlines had been spectacular. Maybe that was why those headlines still haunted her.

As she rubbed Betty's ears, Whitney noticed the dinner table was set for four. For the first time since she'd arrived, she smelled food cooking. Lasagna and baking bread. Her stomach rumbled.

"So," Phillip said into the silence. His piercing blue eyes turned back to her. "Matthew will be here in about forty minutes for dinner."

Which did nothing to answer the question she'd asked Jo earlier. "Matthew is...who?"

This time, Phillip's grin was a little less charming, a little sharper. "Matthew Beaumont. My best man and younger brother."

Whitney blinked. "Oh?"

"He's organizing the wedding," Phillip went on as if that were no big deal.

"He's convinced that this is the PR event of the year," Jo said. "I told him I'd be happy getting married by a judge—"

"Or running off to Vegas," Phillip added, wrapping his arm around Jo's waist and pulling her into a tight embrace.

"But he insists this big wedding is the Beaumont way. And since I'm going to be a Beaumont now…" Jo sighed. "He's taken control of this and turned it into a spectacle."

Whitney stared at Jo and Phillip, unsure what to say. The Jo she knew wouldn't let anyone steamroll her into a grandiose wedding.

"But," Jo went on, softening into a smile that could almost be described as shy, "it's going to be amazing. The chapel is beautiful and we'll have a team of Percherons pulling a carriage from there to the reception. The photographer is experienced and the dress…" She got a dreamy look in her eyes. "Well, you'll see tomorrow. We have a dress fitting at ten."

"It sounds like it's going to be perfect," Whitney said. And she meant it—a Christmas Eve ceremony? Horse-drawn carriages? Gowns? It had all the trappings of a true storybook wedding.

"It better be." Phillip chuckled.

"Let me show you to your room," Jo said, grabbing a bag.

That sounded good to Whitney. She needed a moment to sort through everything. She lived a quiet life now, one where she didn't have to navigate family relations or PR events masquerading as weddings. As long as she didn't leave her ranch, all she worried about was catching Donald when he was on a soapbox.

Jo led her through the house, pointing out which parts were original, which wasn't much, and which parts had been added later, which was most of it. She showed Whitney the part that Phillip had added, the master suite with a hot tub on the deck.

Then the hall turned again and they were in a different part, built in the 1970s. This was the guest quarters, Jo told her. Whitney had a private bath and was far enough removed from the rest of the house that she wouldn't hear anything else.

Jo opened a door and flipped on the light. Whitney had half expected vintage '70s decor, but the room was done in cozy green-and-red plaids that made it look Christmassy. A bouquet of fresh pine and holly was arranged on the mantel over a small fireplace.

Jo walked over to it and flipped a switch. Flames jumped to life in the grate. "Phillip had automatic switches installed a few years ago," she explained. On the other side of the bed was a dresser. Jo said, "Extra blankets are in there. It's going to be a lot colder here than it is at your ranch."

"Good to know." Whitney set her bag down at the foot of the bed. The only other furniture in the room was a small table with an armchair next to it. The room looked like a great place to spend the winter. She felt herself relax a little bit. "So…you and Phillip?"

"Me and Phillip," Jo agreed, sounding as though she didn't quite believe it herself. "He's—well, you've seen him in action. He has a way of just looking at a woman that's… *suggestive.*"

"So I wasn't imagining that?"

Jo laughed. "Nope. That's just how he is."

This did nothing to explain how, exactly, Jo had wound up with Phillip. Of all the men in the world, Whitney would have put "playboy bachelor" pretty low on the list of possible husbands for Jo. But Whitney had no idea how to ask the question without it coming out wrong.

It could be that the Phillip in the kitchen wasn't the same as the Phillip in the headlines. Maybe things had been twisted and turned until nothing but the name was the same. More than anyone, Whitney knew how that worked.

"He has a horse," Jo explained, looking sheepish. "Sun— Kandar's Golden Sun."

Whitney goggled at her. "Wait—I've heard of that horse. Didn't he sell for seven million dollars?"

"Yup. And he was a hot mess at any price," she added with a chuckle. "Took me a week before he'd just stand still, you know?"

Whitney nodded, trying to picture a horse *that* screwed up. When Jo had come out to Whitney's ranch to deal with Sterling, the horse of hers that had developed an irrational fear of water, it'd taken her only a few hours in the paddock before the horse was rubbing his head against Jo. "A whole week?"

"Any other horse would have died of sheer exhaustion, but that's what makes Sun special. I can take you down to see him after dinner. He's an amazing stud—one to build a stable on."

"So the horse brought you together?"

Jo nodded. "I know Phillip's got a reputation—that's part of why Matthew insists we have this big wedding, to show the world that Phillip's making a commitment. But he's been sober for seven months now. We'll have a sober coach on hand at the reception." A hint of a blush crept over Jo's face. "If you'd like…"

Whitney nodded. She wasn't the only one who was having trouble voicing her concerns. "I don't think there's going to be a problem. I've been clean for almost eleven years." She swallowed. "Does Phillip know who I am?"

"Sure." Jo's eyebrow notched up in challenge. "You're Whitney Maddox, the well-known horse breeder."

"No, not that. I mean—well, you know what I mean."

"He knows," Jo said, giving Whitney the look that she'd seen Jo give Donald the hippie when he gave her a lecture on how she should switch to biodiesel. "But we understand that the past is just that—the past."

"Oh." Air rushed out of her so fast she actually sagged

in relief. "That's good. That's *great*. I just don't want to be a distraction—this is your big day."

"It won't be a problem," Jo said in a reassuring voice. "And you're right—the day will be very big!"

They laughed. It felt good to laugh with Jo again. She hadn't had to stay a whole two months with Whitney last year—Sterling hadn't been that difficult to handle—but the two of them had gotten along because they understood that the past was just that. So Jo had stayed through the slow part of the year and taught Whitney some of her training techniques. It'd been a good two months. For the first time in her adult life, Whitney hadn't felt quite so…alone.

And now she'd get that feeling again for two weeks.

"And you're happy?" That was the important question.

Jo's features softened. "I am. He's a good man who had an interesting life—to say the least. He's learned how to deal with his family with all that charm. He wasn't hitting on you—that's just how he copes with situations that make him nervous."

"Really? He must have an, um, unusual family."

Jo laughed again. "I'll just say this—they're a lot to handle, but on the whole, they're not bad people. Like Matthew. He can be a little controlling, but he really does want what's best for the family and for us." She stood. "I'll let you get freshened up. Matthew should be here in a few."

"Sounds good."

Jo shut the door on her way out, leaving Whitney alone with her thoughts. She was glad she'd come.

This was what she wanted—to feel normal. To *be* normal. To be able to walk into a room and not be concerned with what people thought they knew about her. Instead, to have people, like Phillip, take her at face value and make her feel welcome.

And he had a brother who was coming to dinner.

What did Matthew Beaumont look like? More to the

point, what did he act like? Brothers could like a lot of the same things, right?

What if Matthew Beaumont looked at her the way his brother did, without caring about who she'd been in the past? What if he talked to her about horses instead of headlines? What if—? What if he wasn't involved with anyone?

Whitney didn't hook up. That part of her life was dead and buried. But…a little Christmas romance between the maid of honor and the best man wouldn't be such a bad thing, would it? It could be fun.

She hurried to the bathroom, daring to hope that this Matthew Beaumont was single. He was coming to dinner tonight and it sounded as if he would be involved with a lot of the planned activities. She was here for two weeks. Perhaps the built-in time limit was a good thing. That way, if things didn't go well, she had an out—she could go home.

Although…it had been eleven years since she'd attempted anything involving the opposite sex. Making a pass at the best man might not be the smartest thing she could do.

She washed her face. A potential flirtation with Matthew Beaumont called for eyeliner, at the very least. Whitney made up her face and decided to put on a fresh top. She dug out the black silk before putting it aside. Jo was in jeans and flannel, after all. This was not a fancy dinner. Whitney decided to go with the red V-neck cashmere sweater—soft but not ostentatious. The kind of top that maybe a single, handsome man would accidentally brush with his fingers. Perfect.

Would Matthew be blond, like Phillip? Would he have the same smile, the same blue eyes? She was brushing out her short hair when, from deep inside the house, a bell chimed.

She slicked on a little lip gloss and headed out. She tried to retrace her steps, but she got confused. The house had a bunch of hallways that went in different directions. She tried one set of stairs but found a door that was locked at the bottom. That wasn't right—Jo hadn't led her through a door.

She backtracked, trying not to panic. Hopefully, everyone wasn't downstairs waiting on her.

She found another stairwell, but it didn't seem any more familiar than the first one had. It ended in a darkened room. Whitney decided to go back rather than stumble around in the dark. God, she shouldn't have spent so much time getting ready. She should have gone back down with Jo. Or gotten written directions. Getting lost was embarrassing.

She found her room again, which had to count for something. She went the opposite direction and was relieved when she passed the master suite. Finally. She picked up the pace. Maybe she wasn't too late.

She could hear voices now—Jo's and Phillip's and another voice, deep and strong. Matthew.

She hurried down the steps, then remembered she was trying to make a good impression. It wouldn't do to come rushing in like a tardy teenager. She needed to slow down to make a proper entrance.

She slammed on the brakes in the middle of a step near the bottom and stumbled. Hard. She tripped down the last two steps and all but fell into the living room. She was going down, damn it! She braced for the impact.

It didn't come. Instead of hitting the floor or running into a piece of furniture, she fell into a pair of strong arms and against a firm, warm chest.

"Oof," the voice that went with that chest said.

Whitney looked up into a pair of eyes that were a deep blue. He smiled down at her and this time, she didn't feel as if she were going to forget her own name. She felt as if she'd never forget this moment.

"I've got you."

Not blond, she realized. Auburn hair. A deep red that seemed just right on him. And he did have her. His arms were around her waist and he was lifting her up. She felt secure. The feeling was *wonderful*.

Then, without warning, everything changed. His warm smile froze as his eyes went hard. The strong arms became iron bars around her and the next thing she knew, she was being pushed not up but away.

Matthew Beaumont set her back on her feet and stepped clear of her. With a glare that could only be described as ferocious, he turned to Phillip and Jo.

"What," he said in the meanest voice Whitney had heard in a long time, "is Whitney Wildz doing here?"

Two

Matthew waited for an answer. It'd better be a damn good one, too. What possible explanation could there be for former teen star Whitney Wildz to be in Phillip's house?

"Matthew," Jo said in an icy tone, "I'd like you to meet my maid of honor, Whitney Maddox."

"Try to stop being an ass," Phillip said under his breath.

"Whitney," Jo went on, as if Phillip hadn't spoke, "this is Matthew Beaumont, Phillip's brother and best man."

"Maddox?" He turned back to the woman who looked as though she'd been stepped on by a Percheron. At least they could all agree her first name was Whitney. Maybe there was a mistake? But no. There was no missing that white streak in her hair or those huge pale eyes set against her alabaster skin. "You're Whitney Wildz. I'd recognize you anywhere."

Her eyes closed and her head jerked to the side as if he'd slapped her.

Someone grabbed him. "Try *harder*," Phillip growled in his ear. Then, louder, Phillip said, "Dinner's ready. Whitney, is iced tea all right?"

Whitney Wildz—Matthew had no doubt that was who she was—opened her eyes. A wave of pain washed over him when she looked up at him. Then she drew herself up.

"Thank you," she said in that breathy way of hers. Then she stepped around him.

Memories came back to him. He'd watched her show, *Growing Up Wildz*, all the time with his younger siblings Frances and Byron. Because Matthew was a good brother—the best—he'd watched it with them. He'd even scored VIP tickets to the *Growing Up Wildz* concert tour when it came through Denver and taken the twins, since their father couldn't be bothered to remember that it was their fifteenth birthday. Matthew was a good brother just taking care of his siblings. That was what he told everyone else.

But that wasn't, strictly, the truth.

He'd watched it for Whitney.

And now Whitney was here.

This was *bad*. This was quite possibly the worst thing that could have happened to this wedding—to him. It would have been easier if Phillip were screwing her. That sort of thing was easy to hush up—God knew Matthew had enough practice covering for his father's indiscretions.

But to have Whitney Wildz herself standing up at the altar, in front of the press and the photographers—not to mention the guests?

He tried to remember the last time she'd been in the news. She'd stumbled her way up on stage and then tripped into the podium, knocking it off the dais and into a table. The debate hadn't been about *if* she'd been on something, just *what*—drugs? Alcohol? Both?

And then tonight she'd basically fallen down the stairs and into his arms. He hadn't minded catching a beautiful woman at the time. The force of her fall had pressed her body against his and what had happened to him was some sort of primal response that had taken control of his body before he'd realized it.

Mine, was the only coherent thought he'd managed to produce as he'd kept her on her feet. Hell, yeah, he'd responded. He was a man, after all.

But then he'd recognized her.

What was she on? And what would happen if she stumbled her way down the aisle?

This was a disaster of epic PR proportions. This woman was going to mess up all of his plans. And if he couldn't pull off this wedding, would he ever be able to truly call himself a Beaumont?

Phillip jerked him toward the table. "For the love of everything holy," he hissed in Matthew's ear, "be a gentleman."

Matthew shook him off. He had a few things he'd like to say to his brother and his future sister-in-law. "Why didn't you tell me?" he half whispered back at Phillip. "Do you know what this *means* for the wedding?"

On the other side of the room, Jo was at the fridge, getting the iced tea. Whitney stood next to her, head down and arms tucked around her slender waist.

For a second, he felt bad. Horrible, actually. The woman who stood thirty feet away from where he and Phillip were didn't look much like Whitney Wildz. Yes, she had Whitney's delicate bone structure and sweetheart face and yes, she had the jet-black hair with the telltale white streak in it. But her hair was cut into a neat pixie—no teased perm with blue and pink streaks. Her jeans and sweater fit her well and were quite tasteful—nothing like the ripped jeans and punk-rock T-shirts she'd always worn on the show. And she certainly wasn't acting strung out.

If it hadn't been for her face—and those pale green eyes, like polished jade, and that hair—he might not have recognized her.

But he did. Everything about him did.

"It means," Phillip whispered back, "that Jo's friend is here for the wedding. Whitney Maddox—she's a respected horse breeder. You will knock this crap off now or I'll—"

"You'll *what*? You haven't been able to beat me up since we were eight and you know it." Matthew tensed. He had a scant half inch on Phillip but he'd long ago learned to make the most of it.

Phillip grinned at him. It was not a kind thing on his face. "I'll turn Jo loose on you and trust me, buddy, that's a fate worse than death. Now knock it off and act like a decent human being."

There was something wrong about this. For so long, Matthew had been the one who scolded Phillip to straighten up and fly right. Phillip had been the one who didn't know how to act in polite company, who'd always found the most embarrassing thing to say and then said it. And it'd been Matthew who'd followed behind, cleaning up the messes, dealing with the headlines and soothing the ruffled feathers. That was what he did.

Briefly, Matthew wanted to be proud of his brother. He'd finally grown up.

But as wonderful as that was, it didn't change the fact that Whitney Wildz was not only going to be sitting down for dinner with them tonight, but she was also going to be in the Beaumont wedding.

He would have to rethink his entire strategy.

"Dinner," Jo called out. She sounded unnaturally perky about it. There was something odd about Jo being perky. It did nothing to help his mood.

"I really wish you had some beer in the house," he muttered to Phillip.

"Tough. Welcome to sobriety." Phillip led the way back to the table.

Matthew followed, trying to come up with a new game plan. He had a couple of options that he could see right off the bat. He could go with denial, just as Phillip and Jo seemed to be doing. This was Whitney Maddox. He had no knowledge of Whitney Wildz.

But that wasn't a good plan and he knew it. He'd recognized her, after all. Someone else was bound to do the same and the moment that someone did, it'd be all over. Yes, the list of celebrities who were attending this wedding was long but someone as scandalous as Whitney Wildz would create a stir no matter what she did.

He could go on the offensive. Send out a press release announcing that Whitney Wildz was the maid of honor. Hit the criticism head-on. If he did it early enough, he might defuse the situation—make it a nonissue by the big day. It could work.

Or it could blow up in his face. This wedding was about showing the world that the Beaumonts were above scandal—that they were stronger than ever. How was that going to happen now? Everything Whitney Wildz did was a scandal.

He took his seat. Whitney sat to his left, Phillip to his right. Jo's ridiculous little donkey sat on the floor in between him and Whitney. Good. Fine. At least he didn't have to look at Whitney, he reasoned. Just at Jo.

Who was not exactly thrilled with him. Phillip was right—Matthew was in no mood to have Jo turned loose on him. So he forced his best fake smile—the one he used when he was defusing some ticking time bomb created by one of his siblings. It always worked when he was talking to reporters.

He glanced at Phillip and then at Jo. Damn. The smile wasn't working on them.

He could *feel* Whitney sitting next to him. He didn't like that. He didn't want to be aware of her like that. He wasn't some teenager anymore, crushing in secret. He was a grown man with real problems.

Her.

But Phillip was staring daggers at him, and Jo looked as though she was going to stab him with the butter knife. So Matthew dug deep. He could be a gentleman. He could put on the Beaumont face no matter what. Being able to talk to a woman was part of the Beaumont legacy—a legacy he'd worked too hard to make his own. He wasn't about to let an unexpected blast from his past undermine everything he'd worked for. This wedding was about proving his legitimacy and that was that.

Phillip glared at him. Right. The wedding was about Phillip and Jo, too. And now their maid of honor.

God, what a mess.

"So, Whitney," Matthew began. She flinched when he said her name. He kept his voice pleasant and level. "What are you doing these days?"

Jo notched an eyebrow at him as she served the lasagna. *Hey*, he wanted to tell her. *I'm trying.*

Whitney smiled, but it didn't reach her eyes. "I raise horses." She took a piece of bread and passed the basket to him. She made sure not to touch him when she did it.

"Ah." That wasn't exactly a lot to go on, but it did explain how she and Jo knew each other, he guessed.

When Whitney didn't offer any other information, he asked, "What kind of horses?"

"Trakehners."

Matthew waited, but she didn't elaborate.

"One of her horses won gold in the World Equestrian Games," Phillip said. He followed up this observation with a swift kick to Matthew's shin.

Ow. Matthew grunted in pain but he managed not to curse out loud. "That's interesting."

"It's amazing," Phillip said. "Not even Dad could breed or buy a horse that took home gold." He leaned forward, turned on the Beaumont smile and aimed it squarely at Whitney.

Something flared in Matthew. He didn't like it when Phillip smiled at her like that.

"Trust me," Phillip continued, "he tried. Not winning

gold was one of his few failures as a horseman. That and not winning a Triple Crown."

Whitney cut Matthew a look out of the corner of her eye that hit him funny. Then she turned her attention to Phillip. "No one's perfect, right?"

"Not even Hardwick Beaumont," he agreed with a twinkle in his eye. "It turns out there are just some things money can't buy."

Whitney grinned. Suddenly, Matthew wanted to punch his brother—hard. This was normal enough—this was how Phillip talked to women. But seeing Whitney warm to him?

Phillip glanced at Matthew. *Be a gentleman*, he seemed to be saying. "Whitney's Trakehners are beautiful, highly trained animals. She's quite well-known in horse circles."

Whitney Wildz was well-known in horse circles? Matthew didn't remember any mention of that from the last article he'd read about her. Only that she'd made a spectacle of herself.

"How long have you been raising horses?"

"I bought my ranch eleven years ago." She focused her attention on her food. "After I left Hollywood."

So she really was Whitney Wildz. But…eleven years? That didn't seem right. It couldn't have been more than two years since the last headline.

"Where is your ranch?"

If Matthew had known who she really was, he would have done more digging. Be Prepared wasn't just a good Boy Scout motto—it was vital to succeeding in public relations.

One thing was abundantly clear. Matthew was not prepared for Whitney, whatever her last name was.

"Not too far from Bakersfield. It's very…quiet there."

Then she gazed up at him again. The look in her eyes stunned him—desperate for approval. He knew that look—he saw it in the mirror every morning.

Why would she want his approval? She was Whitney

Wildz, for crying out loud. She'd always done what she wanted, when she wanted—consequences be damned.

Except…nothing about her said she was out of control—except for the way she'd fallen into his arms.

His first instinct had been to hold her—to protect her. To claim her as his. What if…?

No.

There was no "what if" about this. His first duty was to his family—to making sure this wedding went off without a hitch. To making sure everyone knew that the Beaumonts were still in a position of power. To making sure he proved himself worthy of his father's legacy.

At the very least, he could be a gentleman about it.

"That's beautiful country," he said. Compliments were an important part of setting a woman at ease. If he were smart, he would have remembered that in the first place. "Your ranch must be lovely."

A touch of color brightened her cheeks. His stomach tensed. *She* was beautiful, he realized. Not the punk-rock hot she'd been back when he'd watched her show, but something delicate and ethereal.

Mine.

The word kept popping up in his head, completely unbidden. Which was ridiculous because the only thing Whitney was to him was a roadblock.

Phillip kicked him again. *Stop staring*, he mouthed at Matthew.

Matthew shook his head. He hadn't realized he was staring.

"Matthew, maybe we should discuss some of the wedding plans?" Jo said it nicely enough but there was no mistaking that question for an order.

"Of course," he agreed. The wedding. He needed to stay on track here. "We have an appointment with the seamstress tomorrow at ten. Jo, it's your final fitting. Whitney, we ordered your dress according to the measurements you sent in, but we've blocked out some additional time in case it requires additional fittings."

"That sounds fine," she said in a voice that almost sounded casual.

"Saturday night is the bachelorette party. I have a list of places that would be an appropriate location for you to choose from."

"I see," she said. She brushed her hand through her hair.

He fought the urge to do the same.

What was wrong with him? Seriously—*what* was wrong with him? He went from attracted to her to furious at everyone in the room and now he wanted to, what—stroke her hair? Claim her? Jesus, these were exactly the sort of impulses he'd always figured had ruled Phillip. The ones that had ruled their father. See a beautiful woman, act on the urge to sweep her off her feet. To hell with anything else.

Matthew needed to regain control of the situation—of himself—and fast.

"We'll need to get the shoes and jewelry squared away. We need to get you in to the stylist before then to decide how to deal with your hair, so we'll do that after the dress fitting." He waited, but she didn't say anything.

So he went on. "The rehearsal dinner is Tuesday night. Then the wedding is Christmas Eve, of course." A week and a half—that didn't leave him much time to deal with the disruption of Whitney Wildz. "The ladies will get manicures that morning before they get their hair done. Then we'll start with the photographs."

Whitney cleared her throat—but she still didn't meet his gaze. "Who else is in the wedding party?"

He wanted her to look at him—he wanted to get lost in her eyes. "Our older brother Chadwick will be walking with his wife, Serena. Frances and Byron will be walking together—they're twins, five years younger than I am." For a second,

Matthew had almost said *we*—as in he and Phillip. Because he and Phillip were only six months apart.

But he didn't want to bring his father's infidelity into this conversation, because that meant Whitney would know that he was the second choice, the child his father had never really loved. Or even acknowledged, for that matter. So he said *I*.

"That just leaves the two of us," he added, suddenly very interested in his plate. How was he going to keep this primal urge to haul her off under control if they were paired up for the wedding?

He could not let her distract him from his goals, no matter how much he wanted to. He had to pull this off—to prove that he was a legitimate Beaumont. Ravishing the maid of honor did not fall anywhere on his to-do list.

"Ah." He looked up when he heard her chair scrape against the floor. She stood and, without looking at him, said, "I'm a little tired from the drive. If you'll excuse me." Jo started to stand, but Whitney waved her off. "I think I can find my way."

Then she was gone, walking in a way that he could only describe as graceful. She didn't stumble and she didn't fall. She walked in a straight line for the stairs.

Several moments passed after she disappeared up the stairs. No one seemed willing to break the tense silence. Finally, Matthew couldn't take it anymore.

"What the *hell*? Why is Whitney Wildz your maid of honor and why didn't either of you see fit to tell me in advance? Jesus, if I'd known, I would have done things differently. Do you have any idea what the press will do when they find out?"

It was easier to focus on how this was going to screw up the wedding than on how his desire was on the verge of driving him mad.

"Gosh, I don't know. You think they'll make a big deal out of stuff that happened years ago and make Whitney feel like crap?" Phillip shot back. "You're right. That would really suck."

"Hey—this is not my fault. You guys sprung this on me."

"I believe," Jo said in a voice so icy it brought the temperature of the room down several degrees, "I told you I was asking Whitney Maddox to be my maid of honor. Whitney Wildz is a fictional character in a show that was canceled almost thirteen years ago. If you can't tell the difference between a real woman and a fictional teenager, then that's *your* problem, not hers."

"It *is* my problem," he got out through gritted teeth. "You can't tell me that's all in the past. What about the headlines?"

Phillip rolled his eyes. "Because everything the press prints is one hundred percent accurate, huh? I thought you, of all people, would know how the headlines can be manipulated."

"She's a normal person," Jo said. Instead of icy, though, she was almost pleading. "I retrained one of her horses and we got to spend time together last winter. She's a little bit of a klutz when she gets nervous but that's it. She's going to be fine."

"If *you* can treat her like a normal person," Phillip added. "Man—I thought you were this expert at reading people and telling them what they wanted to hear. What happened? Hit your head this morning or something?"

Matthew sat there, feeling stupid. Hell, he wasn't just feeling stupid—he *was* stupid. His first instinct had been to protect her. He should have stuck with it. He could do that without giving in to his desire to claim her, right?

Right. He was in control of his emotions. He could keep up a wall between the rest of the world and himself. He was good at it.

Then he made the mistake of glancing at that silly donkey, who gave him a baleful look of reproach. Great. Even the donkey was mad at him.

"I should apologize to her."

Phillip snorted. "You think?"

Damn it, he felt like a jerk. It didn't come naturally to him. Chadwick was the one who could be a royal pain simply because he wasn't clued in to the fact that most people had actual feelings. Phillip used to be an ass all the time because he was constantly drunk and horny. Matthew was the one who smoothed ruffled feathers and calmed everyone down.

Phillip was right. Matthew hadn't been reading the woman next to him. He'd been too busy thinking about old headlines and new lust to realize that she might want his approval.

"Which room is she in?"

Jo and Phillip shared a look before Phillip said, "Yours."

Three

Whitney found her room on the first try and shut the door behind her.

Well. So much for her little fantasy about a Christmas romance. She doubted that Matthew would have been less happy to see her if she'd thrown up on his shoes.

She flopped down on her bed and decided that she would not cry. Even though it was really tempting, she wouldn't. She'd learned long ago this was how it went, after all. People would treat her just fine until they recognized her and then? All bets were off. Once she'd been outed as Whitney Wildz, she might as well give up on normal. There was no going back.

She'd thought for a moment there she might get to do something ordinary—have a little Christmas romance between the maid of honor and the best man. But every time she got it in her foolish little head that she could be whoever she wanted to be…well, this was what would happen.

The thing was, she didn't even blame Matthew. Since he recognized her so quickly, that could only mean that he'd read some of the more recent headlines. Like the last time she'd tried to redeem Whitney Wildz by lending her notoriety to the Bakersfield Animal Shelter's annual fund-raising gala dinner. She'd been the keynote speaker—or would have been if she hadn't gotten the fancy Stuart Weitzman shoes she'd bought just for the occasion tangled up in the microphone cords on her way up to the podium.

The headlines had been unforgiving.

Whitney shivered. Boy, this was going to be a long, *cold* two weeks.

As she was getting up to turn her fireplace back on, she heard it—a firm knock.

Her brain diverted all energy from her legs to the question of who was on the other side of that door—Jo or a Beaumont?—and she tripped into the door with an audible *whump*.

Oh, for the love of everything holy. Just once—once!—she'd like to be able to walk and chew gum at the same time. She could sing and play the guitar simultaneously. She could do complicated dressage moves on the back of a one-ton animal. Why couldn't she put one foot in front of the other?

She forced herself to take a deep breath just as a male voice on the other side of the door said, "Is everything all right in there, Miss...uh...Ms. Maddox?"

Matthew. Great. How could this get worse? Let her count the ways. Had he come to ask her to drop out of the wedding? Or just threaten her to be on her best behavior?

She decided she would not cower. Jo had asked her to be in the wedding. If Jo asked her to drop out, she would. Otherwise, she was in. She collected her thoughts and opened the door a crack. "Yes, fine. Thanks."

Then she made the mistake of looking at him. God, it wasn't fair. It just *wasn't*.

Matthew Beaumont was, physically, the perfect man to have a Christmas romance with. He had to be about six foot one, broad chested, and that chin? Those eyes? Even his deep red hair made him look distinctive. Striking.

Gorgeous.

Too darned bad he was an ass.

"Can I help you?" she asked, determined to be polite if it killed her. She would not throw a diva fit and prove him right. Even if there would be a certain amount of satisfaction in slamming the door in his face.

He gave her a grin that walked the fine line between awkward and cute. He might be even better-looking than his brother, but he appeared to possess none of the charm. "Look, Ms. Maddox—"

"Whitney."

"Oh. Okay. Whitney. We got off on the wrong foot and—"

She winced.

He paused. "*I* got off on the wrong foot. And I want to apologize to you." His voice was strong, exuding confidence. It made everything about him that much sexier.

She blinked at him. "What?"

"I jumped to conclusions when I realized who you were and I apologize for that." He waited for her to say something but she had nothing.

Was he serious? He looked serious. He wasn't biting back laughter or— She glanced down at his hands. They were tucked into the pockets of his gray wool trousers. No, he wasn't about to snap an awful photo of her to post online, either.

He pulled his hands from his pockets and held them at waist level, open palms up, as if he knew what she was thinking. "It's just that this wedding is incredibly important for rebuilding the public image of the Beaumont family and it's my job to make sure everyone stays on message."

"The…public image?" She leaned against the door, staring up at him. Maybe he wasn't a real man—far too handsome to be one. And he was certainly talking like a space alien. "I thought this was about Jo and Phillip getting married."

"That, too," he hurried to agree. This time, his smile was a little more charming, like something a politician might pull out when he needed to win an argument. "I just— Look. I just want to make sure that we don't make headlines for the wrong reason."

Embarrassment flamed down the back of her neck. She looked away. He was trying to be nice by saying *we* but they both knew that he meant *her*.

"I know you don't believe this, but I have absolutely no desire to make headlines. At all. Ever. If no one else recognized me for the rest of my life, that'd be super."

There was a moment of silence that was in danger of becoming painful. "Whitney..."

The way he said her name—soft and tender and almost reverent—dragged her eyes up to his. The look in his eyes hit her like a bolt out of, well, the blue. He had the most amazing eyes...

For that sparkling moment, it almost felt as if...as if he was going to say something that could be construed as romantic. Something that didn't make her feel as though the weight of this entire event were being carried on her shoulders.

She wanted to hear something that made her feel like Whitney Maddox—that being Whitney Maddox was a good thing. A great thing. And she wanted to hear that something come out of Matthew's mouth, in that voice that could melt away the chilly winter air. Desire seemed to fill the space between them.

She leaned toward him. She couldn't help it. At the same time, his mouth opened as one of his hands moved. Then, just as soon as the motion had started, it stopped. His mouth closed and he appeared to shake himself. "I'll meet you at the dress fitting tomorrow. To make sure everything's—"

"On message?"

He notched up an eyebrow. She couldn't tell if she'd offended him or amused him. Or both. "Perfect," he corrected. "I just want it to be perfect."

"Right." There would be no sweet words. If there was one thing she wasn't, it was perfect. "Will it just be you?"

He gave her a look that was surprisingly wounded. She couldn't help but grin at him, which earned her a smile that looked more...real, somehow. As though what had just passed between them was almost...flirting.

"No. The wedding planner will be joining us—and the seamstress and her assistants, of course."

"Of course." She leaned against the door. Were they flirting? Or was he charming her because that was what all Beaumonts did?

God, he was *so* handsome. He exuded raw power. She had no doubt that whatever he said went.

A man like him would be hard to resist.

"Tomorrow, then," she said.

"I look forward to it." He gave her a tight smile before he turned away. Just as she was shutting the door, he turned back. "Whitney," he said again in that same deep, confident and—she hoped—sincere voice. "It truly is a pleasure to meet you."

Then he was gone.

She shut the door.

Heavens. It was going to be a *very* interesting two weeks.

"So," Whitney began as they passed streetlights decorated like candy canes. The drive had, thus far, been quiet. "Who's on the guest list again?"

"The Beaumonts," Jo said with a sigh. "Hardwick Beaumont's four ex-wives—"

"Four?"

Jo nodded as she tapped on the steering wheel. "All nine of Phillip's siblings and half siblings will be there, although only the four he actually grew up with are in the wedding— Chadwick, Matthew, Frances and Byron."

Whitney whistled. "That's a *lot* of kids." Part of why she'd loved doing the show was that, for the first time, she'd felt as though she'd had a family, one with brothers and sisters and parents who cared about her. Even if it were all just pretend, it was still better than being the only child Jade Maddox focused on with a laserlike intensity.

But ten kids? *Dang.*

"And that doesn't count the illegitimate ones," Jo said in a conspiratorial tone. "Phillip says they know of three, but there could be more. The youngest is…nineteen, I think."

As much as she hated gossip… "Seriously? Did that man not know about condoms?"

"Didn't care," Jo said. "Between you and me, Hardwick Beaumont was an old-fashioned misogynist. Women were solely there for his entertainment. Anything else that happened was their problem, not his."

"Sounds like a real jerk."

"I understand he was a hell of a businessman, but…yeah. On the whole, his kids aren't that bad. Chadwick's a tough nut to crack, but his wife, Serena, balances him out really well. Phillip's… Well, Phillip's Phillip." She grinned one of those private grins that made Whitney blush. "Matthew can come on a bit strong but really, he's a good guy. He's just wound a bit tight. Very concerned with the family's image. It's like…he wants everything to be perfect."

"I noticed." Whitney knew she was talking about the coming-on-strong part, but her brain immediately veered back to when she'd stumbled into his arms. His strong arms.

And then there was the conversation they'd had—the private one. The one that could have been flirting. And the way he'd said her name…

"We're really sorry about last night," Jo repeated for about the fifteenth time.

"No worries," Whitney hurried to say. "He apologized."

"Matthew is…very good at what he does. He just needs to lighten up a little bit. Have some fun."

She wondered at that. Would fun be a part of this? The dinner had said no. But the conversation after? She had no idea. If only she weren't so woefully out of practice at flirting.

"I can still drop out," she said. "If that'll make it simpler."

Jo laughed—not an awkward sound, but one that was

truly humorous. "You're kidding, right? Did I mention the ex-wives? You know who else is going to be here?"

"No…"

"The crown prince of Belgravitas."

"You're kidding, right?" God, she hoped Jo was kidding. She didn't want to make a fool of herself in front of honest-to-God royalty.

"Nope. His wife, the princess Susanna, used to date Phillip."

"Get *out*."

"I'm serious. Drake—the rapper—will be there, as well. He and Phillip are friends. Jay Z and Beyoncé had a scheduling conflict, but—"

"*Seriously?*" It wasn't as though she didn't know that Phillip Beaumont was a famous guy—all those commercials, all those stories about parties he hosted at music festivals—but this was crazy.

"If you drop out," Jo went on, "who on earth am I going to get to replace you? Out of the two hundred people who'll be at the wedding and the six hundred who'll be at the reception, you know how many I invited? My parents, my grandma Lina, my uncle Larry and aunt Penny, and my parents' neighbors. Eleven people. That's it. That's all I have. And you."

Whitney didn't know what to say. She didn't want to do this, not after last night. But Jo was one of her few friends. Someone who didn't care about Whitney Wildz or *Growing Up Wildz* or even that horrible Christmas album she'd put out, *Whitney Wildz Sings Christmas, Yo.*

She didn't want to disappoint her friend.

"Honestly," Jo said, "there's going to be so many egos on display that I doubt people will even realize who you are. Don't take that the wrong way."

"I won't," Whitney said with a smile. She could do this. She could pull off normal for a few weeks. She couldn't compete with that guest list. She was just the maid of honor. Who would notice her, anyway? Besides Matthew, that was…

"And you're right. It won't be like that last fund-raiser."

"Exactly," Jo said, sounding encouraging. "You were the headliner there—of course people were watching you. Matthew only acted like he did because he's a perfectionist. I truly believe you'll be fine." She pulled into a parking lot. "It'll be fine."

"All right," Whitney agreed. She didn't quite believe the sentiment but she couldn't disappoint Jo. "It will be fine."

"Good."

They got out. Whitney stared at the facade of the Bridal Collection. This was it. Once she was in the dress, there was no backing out.

Oh, who was she kidding? There was no backing out anyway. Jo was right. They were the kind of people who didn't have huge social circles or celebrities on speed dial. They were horse people. She and Jo got along only because they both loved animals and they both had changed their ways.

"You're really having a wedding with Grammy winners and crown princes?"

"Yup," Jo said, shaking her head. "Honestly, though, it's not the over-the-top wedding that matters. It's the marriage. Besides," she added as they went inside, "David Guetta is going to be doing the music for the reception. How cool is that?"

"Pretty cool," Whitney agreed. She didn't recognize the name, but then, why would she? She wasn't famous anymore.

Maybe Jo was right. No one would care about her. She'd managed to stay out of the headlines for almost three years, after all—that was a lifetime in today's 24/7 news cycle. In that time, there'd been other former teen stars who'd grabbed much bigger headlines for much more scandalous reasons.

They walked into the boutique to find Matthew pacing between rows of frothy white dresses and decorations that were probably supposed to be Christmas trees but really looked more as though someone had dipped pipe cleaners in glitter. The whole place was so bright it made her eyes hurt.

Matthew—wearing dark gray trousers and a button-up shirt with a red tie under his deep green sweater—was so out of place that she couldn't *not* look at him. She wouldn't have thought it possible, but he looked even better today than he had the other night. As she appreciated all the goodness that was Matthew Beaumont, he looked up from his phone.

Their eyes met, and her breath caught in her throat. The warmth in his eyes, the curve to his lips, the arch in his eyebrow—heat flooded Whitney's cheeks. Was he happy to see her? Or was she misreading the signals?

Then he glanced at Jo. "Ladies," he said in that confident tone of his. It should have seemed wholly out of place in the midst of this many wedding gowns, but on him? "I was just about to call. Jo, they're waiting for you."

"Where's the wedding planner?" Whitney asked. If the planner wasn't here, then she and Jo weren't late. Late was being the last one in.

"Getting Jo's dress ready."

Dang. Whitney tried to give her friend a smile that was more confident than she actually felt. Jo threaded her way back through racks of dresses and disappeared into a room.

Then Whitney and Matthew were alone. Were they still almost flirting? Or were they back to where they'd been at dinner? If only she hadn't fallen into him. If only he hadn't recognized her. If only…

"Is there someone else who can help me try my dress on?"

"Jo's dress requires several people to get her into it," he said. Then he bowed and pointed the way. "Your things are in here."

"Thanks." She held her head high as she walked past him.

"You're welcome." His voice trickled over her skin like a cool stream of water on a too-hot day.

She stepped into a dressing room—thankfully, one with a door. Once she had that door shut, she sagged against it. That voice, that face were even better today than they'd been last night. Last night, he'd been trying to cover his surprise and anger. Today? Today he just looked happy to see her.

She looked at the room she'd essentially locked herself in. It was big enough for a small love seat and a padded ottoman. A raised dais stood in front of a three-way mirror.

And there, next to the mirrors, hung a dress. It was a beautiful dove-gray silk gown—floor length, of course. Sleeveless, with sheer gathered silk forming one strap on the left side. The hemline was flared so that it would flow when she walked down the aisle, no doubt.

It was stunning. Even back when she'd walked the red carpet, she'd never worn a dress as sophisticated as this. When she was still working on *Growing Up Wildz*, she'd had to dress modestly—no strapless, no deep necklines. And when she'd broken free of all the restrictions that had hemmed her in for years, well, "classic" hadn't been on her to-do list. She'd gone for shock value. Short skirts. Shorter skirts. Black. Torn shirts that flashed her chest. Offensive slogans. Safety pins holding things together. Anything she could come up with to show that she wasn't a squeaky-clean kid anymore.

And it'd worked. Maybe too well.

She ran her hands over the silk. It was cool, smooth. If a dress could feel beautiful, this did. A flicker of excitement started to build. Once, before it'd been a chore, she'd liked to play dress-up. Maybe this would be fun. She hoped.

Several pairs of shoes dyed to match were lined up next to the dress—some with four-inch heels. Whitney swallowed hard. There'd be no way she could walk down the aisle in those beauties and not fall flat on her face.

Might as well get this over with. She stripped off her parka and sweater, then the boots and jeans. She caught a glimpse of herself in the three-way mirror—hard not to with those angles. Ugh. The socks had to go. And…

Her bra had straps. The dress did not.

She shucked the socks and, before she could think better about it, the bra. Then she hurried into the dress, trying not to pull on the zipper as the silk slipped over her head with a shushing sound.

The fabric puddled at her feet as she tried to get the zipper pulled up, but her arms wouldn't bend in that direction. "I need help," she called out, praying that an employee or a seamstress or anyone besides Matthew Beaumont was out there.

"Is it safe to come in?" Matthew asked from the other side of the door.

Oh, no. Whitney made another grab at the zipper, but nothing happened except her elbow popped. *Ow.* She checked her appearance. Her breasts were covered. It was just the zipper….

"Yes."

The door opened and Matthew walked in. To his credit, he didn't enter as if he owned the place. He came in with his eyes cast down before he took a cautious glance around. When he spotted her mostly covered, the strangest smile tried to crack his face. "Ah, there you are."

"Here I am," she agreed, wondering where else on earth he thought she could have gotten off to in the ten minutes she'd been in here. "I can't get the zipper up all the way."

She really didn't know what to expect at this point. The majority of her interactions with Matthew ranged from outright rude to surly. But then, just when she was about to write him off as a jerk and nothing more, he'd do something that set her head spinning again.

Like right now. He walked up to her and held out his hand, as if he were asking her to dance.

Even in the cramped dressing room, he was impossibly

handsome. But he'd already muddled her thoughts—mean one moment, sincere the next. She didn't want to let anything physical between them confuse her even further.

When she didn't put her hand in his, he said, "Just to step up on the dais," as if he could read her thoughts.

She took his hand. It was warm and strong, just as his arms had been. He guided her up the small step and then to the middle. "Ah, shoes," he said. Then he let her go.

"No—just the zipper," she told him, but he was already back by the shoes, looking at them.

Lord. She knew what was about to happen. She was all of five-four on a good day. He would pick the four-inch heels in an attempt to get her closer to Jo's height. And then she'd either have to swallow her pride and tell him she couldn't walk in them or risk tripping down the aisle on the big day.

"These should work," he said, picking up the pair of peep-toed shoes with the stacked heel only two inches high. "Try these on."

"If you could just zip me up first. *Please.*" The last thing she wanted to do was wobble in those shoes and lose the grip she had on the front of her dress.

He carried the shoes over to her and set them on the ground. Then he stood.

This time, when his gaze traveled over her, it didn't feel as if he were dismissing her, as he had the first time. Far from it. Instead, this time it was almost as if he was appreciating what he saw.

Maybe.

She felt him grab the edges of the dress and pull them together. Something about this felt...intimate. Almost too intimate. It blew way past possible flirting. She closed her eyes. Then, slowly, the zipper clicked up tooth by tooth.

Heat radiated down her back, warming her from the inside out. She breathed in, then out, feeling the silk move over her bare flesh. Matthew was so close she could smell his cologne—something light, with notes of sandalwood. Heat built low in her back—warm, luxurious heat that made her want to slowly turn in his arms and stop caring whether or not the dress zipped at all.

She could do it. She could hit on the best man and find out what had been behind that little conversation they'd had in private last night. And this time, she wouldn't trip.

Except…except for his first reaction to her—if she hit on him, he might assume she was out to ruin his perfect wedding or something. So she did nothing. Matthew zipped the dress all the way up. Then she felt his hands smoothing down the pleats in the back, then adjusting the sheer shoulder strap.

She stopped breathing as his hands skimmed over her.

This had to be nothing. This was only a control freak obsessively making sure every detail, every single pleat, was perfect. His touch had nothing to do with *her*.

She felt him step around her until he was standing by her side. "Aren't you going to look?" he asked, his voice warm and, if she didn't know any better, inviting.

She could feel him waiting right next to her, the heat from his body contrasting with the cool temperature of the room. So she opened her eyes. What else could she do?

The sight that greeted her caused her to gasp. An elegant, sophisticated woman stood next to a handsome, powerful man. She knew that was her reflection in the mirror, but it didn't look like her.

"Almost perfect," Matthew all but sighed in satisfaction.

Almost. What a horrible word.

"It's amazing." She fought the urge to twirl. Someone as buttoned-up as Matthew probably wouldn't appreciate a good twirl.

The man in the reflection grinned at her—a real grin, one that crinkled the edges of his eyes. "It's too long on you. Let's try the shoes." Then, to her amazement, he knelt down and held out a shoe for her, as if this were some backward version of *Cinderella*.

Whitney lifted up her skirt and gingerly stepped into the shoe. It felt solid and stable—not like the last pair of fancy shoes she'd tried to walk in.

She stepped into the other shoe, trying not to think about how Matthew was essentially face-to-knee or how she was in significant danger of snagging these pretty shoes on the edge of the dais and going down in a blaze of glory.

When she had both shoes firmly on, Matthew sat back. "How do those feel?"

"Not bad," she admitted. She took a preliminary step back. "Pretty good, actually."

"Can you walk in them? Or do you need a ballerina flat?"

She gaped at him. Of all the things he might have asked her, that wasn't even on the list. Then it hit her. "Jo told you I was a klutz, right?"

He grinned again. It did some amazing things to his face, which, in turn, did some amazing things to the way a lazy sort of heat coiled around the base of her spine and began to pulse.

"She might have mentioned it."

Whitney shouldn't have been embarrassed, and if she was, it shouldn't have bothered her anymore. Embarrassment was second nature for her now, as ordinary as breathing oxygen.

But it did. "Because you thought I was drunk."

His Adam's apple bobbed, but he didn't come back with the silky smile he'd pulled out on her last night, the one that made her feel as if she was being managed.

"In the interest of transparency, I also considered the option that you might have been stoned."

Four

Whitney blinked down at him, her delicate features pulled tight. Then, without another word, she turned back to the mirror.

What happened? Matthew stood, letting his gaze travel over her. She was, for lack of a better word, stunning. "The color suits you," he said, hoping a compliment would help.

It didn't. She rolled her eyes.

Transparency had always worked before. He'd thought that his little admission would come out as an ironic joke, something they could both chuckle over while he covertly admired the figure she cut in that dress.

What was it about this woman that had him sticking his foot in his mouth at every available turn?

It was just because she wasn't what he'd been expecting, that was all. He'd been up late last night, digging into the not-sordid-at-all history of Whitney Maddox, trying to get his feet out of his mouth and back under his legs. She *was* a respected horse breeder. Her horses *were* beautiful animals and that one *had* won a gold medal. But there weren't any pictures of Whitney Maddox anywhere—not on her ranch's website, not on any social media. Whitney Maddox was like a ghost—there but not there.

Except the woman before him was very much here. His hands still tingled from zipping her into that dress, from the glimpse of her panties right where the zipper had ended. How he itched to unzip it, to expose the bare skin he'd seen but not touched—slip those panties off her hips.

He needed to focus on what was important here, and that was making sure that this woman—no matter what name she went by—did not pull this wedding off message. That she did not pull *him* off message. That was what he had to think about. Not the way the dress skimmed over her curves or the way her dark hair made her stand out.

Before he knew what he was doing, he said, "You look beautiful in that dress."

This time, she didn't roll her eyes. She gave him the kind of look that made it clear she didn't believe him.

"You can see that, right? You're stunning."

She stared at him for a moment longer. "You're confusing me," she said.

She had a sweet smell to her, something with warm vanilla notes overlaying a deeper spice. Good enough to eat, he thought, suddenly fascinated with the curve of her neck. He could press his lips against her skin and watch her reaction in the mirror. Would she blush? Pull away? Or lean into his touch?

She looked away. "I could change my hair."

"What?"

"I could try to dye it all blond, although," she said with a rueful smile, "it didn't turn out so well the last time I tried it. The white streak won't take dye, for some reason. God knows I've tried to color it over, but it doesn't work. It's blond or nothing."

"Why on God's green earth would you want to dye your hair?"

He couldn't see her as a blonde. It would be wrong on so many levels. It'd take everything that was fine and delicate about her and make it washed-out, like a painting left out in the rain.

"If I'm blonde, no one will recognize me. No one would ever guess that Whitney Wildz is standing up there. That way, if I trip in the shoes or drop my bouquet, people will just think I'm a klutz and not assume I'm stoned. Like they always do."

Shame sucker punched him in the gut. "Don't change your hair." He reached out and brushed the edge of her bangs away from her face.

She didn't lean away from him, but she didn't lean into him, either. He didn't know if that was a good thing or not.

"But…" She swallowed and tried to look tough. She didn't make it. "I look like me. People will *recognize* me. I thought you didn't want that to happen."

"You say that as if looking like yourself is a bad thing."

In the mirror's reflection, her gaze cut to him. "Isn't it?"

He took a step closer to her, close enough that he could slide his fingers from the fringe of her hair down her neck, down her arm. He couldn't help it, which was something outside of his experience entirely. He'd *always* been able to help himself. He'd never allowed himself to get swept up in something as temporary, as fleeting, as emotional attraction. He'd witnessed firsthand what acting on attraction could do, how it could ruin marriages, leave bastard babies behind— leave children forgotten.

With the specter of his father hovering around him, Matthew managed to find some of the restraint that normally came so easy to him. He didn't slide his hand down her bare arm or pull her into his chest. Instead, he held himself to arranging the shoulder of the dress. She watched him in the mirror, her eyes wide. "You are *beautiful*," he said. It came out like something Phillip would say—low and seductive. It didn't sound like Matthew talking at all.

She sucked in a deep breath, which, from his angle, did

enticing things to her chest. He wanted to sweep her into his arms. He wanted to tell her he'd had a crush on her back in the day. He wanted to get her out of that dress and into his bed.

He did none of those things.

Focus, damn it.

He took a step back and tried his hardest to look at her objectively. The heels helped, but the hem of the dress still puddled around her. She'd need it hemmed, but they had to settle on the shoes first.

"Let's see how you walk in those." There. That was something that wasn't a come-on and wasn't a condemnation. Footwear was a safe choice at this point.

She stood for a moment, as if she was trying to decide what his motivations were. So he held out his arm for her. He could do that. She'd walk back down the aisle on his arm after the ceremony. Best they get used to it now.

After a brief pause, she slipped her hand around his elbow and, after gathering her skirts in one hand, stepped off the dais. They moved toward the door, where he opened it for her.

She walked ahead of him, the dress billowing around her legs just as he'd wanted it to. The salon had a bouquet of artificial flowers on a nearby table. He handed them to her. "Slow steps, big smile."

"Right," she said, an odd grin pulling up at the corners of her mouth. "No skipping. Got it."

She walked down the aisle, then turned and came back toward him with a big fake smile on her face. Then, just as she almost reached him, the toe of her shoe caught in the too-long hem of the dress and she stumbled. The bouquet went flying.

He caught her. He had to, right? It wasn't about pulling her into his arms. This was a matter of personal safety.

He had her by her upper arms. "Sorry," she muttered as he pulled her back onto her feet.

"Don't worry about it."

She gave him a hard look, her body rigid under his hands. "I had to worry about it yesterday. You're sure I'm not on anything today?"

Okay, yes, he deserved that. That didn't make it any less sucky to have it thrown back in his face.

Without letting go of her, he leaned down and inhaled deeply. "No trace of alcohol on your breath," he said, staring at her lips.

She gasped.

Then he removed one of his hands from her arm and used it to tilt her head back until she had no choice but to look him in the eyes.

Years of dealing with Phillip while he was drunk had taught Matthew what the signs were. "You're not on anything."

"You...can tell?"

He should let her go. She had her balance back. She didn't need him to hold her up and she certainly didn't need him to keep a hand under her chin.

But he didn't. Instead, he let his fingers glide over her smooth skin. "When you become a Beaumont, you develop certain skills to help you survive."

She blinked at him. "When you *become* a Beaumont? What does that mean? Aren't you a Beaumont?"

Matthew froze. Had he really said that? Out loud? He *never* drew attention to his place in the family, *never* said anything that would cast doubt on his legitimacy. Hell, his whole life had been about proving to the whole world that he was a Beaumont through and through.

What was it about this woman that made him stick his foot into his mouth?

Whitney stared at him. "You're confusing me again,"

she repeated, her voice a whisper that managed to move his heart rate up several notches. Her lips parted as she ever so slightly leaned into his hand.

"You're the one who's confusing me," he whispered back as he stroked his fingertips against her skin. For a woman who was neither here nor there, she was warm and solid and so, *so* soft under his hands.

"Then I guess we're even?" She looked up at him with those pale green eyes. He was going to kiss her. Long. Hard. He was going to taste her sweetness, feel her body as it pressed against his and—

"Whitney? Matthew?"

Jo's voice cut through the insanity he'd been on the brink of committing. He let go of Whitney, only to grab her immediately when she took a step back and stepped on her hem again.

"I've got you," he told her.

"Repeatedly," she said. He couldn't tell if she was amused or not.

Then Jo came around the corner, seamstresses and salon employees trailing her. She pulled up short when she saw the two of them and said, "I need to go," as the wedding planner started unfastening the back of her dress.

"What?" Matthew said.

"Why?" Whitney said at the same time.

"A mare I'm training out on the farm is having a meltdown and Richard is afraid she's going to hurt herself." She looked over her shoulder at the small army of women who were attempting to get her out of her dress. "Can you go any faster?"

There were murmurs of protest from the seamstresses as the wedding planner said, "We can't risk tearing the dress, Ms. Spears."

Jo sighed heavily.

Whitney and Matthew took advantage of the distraction

to separate. "I'll come with you," Whitney said. "I can help. You taught me what to do."

"No, you won't," he said.

It must have come out a little harsher than he meant it to, because every woman in the room—all six of them—stopped and looked at him. "I mean," he added, softening his tone, "we have too much to do. We have to get your dress hemmed, we have an appointment with the stylist this afternoon— everyone is set except you. We *must* keep your schedule."

There was a moment of silence, broken only by the sound of Jo's dress rustling as the seamstresses worked to free her from the elaborate confines.

Whitney wasn't looking at him. She was looking at Jo. She'd do whatever Jo said, he realized. Not what he said. He wasn't used to having his orders questioned. Everyone else in the family had long ago realized that Matthew was always right.

"Matthew is right," Jo said. "Besides, having a new person show up will only freak out Rapunzel. I need to do this alone."

"Oh," Whitney said as if Jo had just condemned her to swing from the gallows. "All right."

"Your dress is amazing," Jo said, clearly trying to smooth over the ruffled feathers.

"Yours, too," Whitney replied. Jo's compliment must have helped, because Whitney already sounded better.

That was another thing Matthew wasn't expecting from Whitney Wildz. A willingness to work? A complete lack of interest in throwing a diva fit when things didn't go her way?

She confused him, all right. He'd never met a woman who turned his head around as fast and as often as Whitney did. Not even the celebrities and socialites he'd known made him dizzy the way she did. Sure, such women made plays for him—he was a Beaumont and a good-looking man. But none of them distracted him from his goal. None of them got him off message.

He tried telling himself it was just because he'd liked her so many years ago. This was merely the lingering effects of a crush run amok. His teenage self was screwing with his adult self. That was all. It didn't matter that Whitney today was a vision in that dress—far more beautiful than anything he'd ever imagined back in the day. He had a job to do—a wedding to pull off, a family image to rescue, his rightful place to secure. His adult self was in charge here.

No matter what the Beaumonts put their minds to, they would always come out on top. That'd been the way Hardwick Beaumont had run his business and his family. He'd amassed a huge personal fortune and a legacy that had permanently reshaped Denver—and, one could argue, America. He expected perfection and got it—or else.

Even though Chadwick had sold the Beaumont Brewery, even though Phillip had crashed and burned in public, Matthew was still standing tall. He'd weathered those storms and he would pull this wedding off.

"There," one of the seamstresses said. "Mind the edge..."

Jo clutched at the front of the dress. "Matthew, if you don't mind."

Right. He turned his back to her so she could step out of the $15,000 dress they'd chosen because it made Jo, the tomboy cowgirl, look like a movie-star goddess, complete with the fishtail bodice and ten-foot-long train. The Beaumonts were about glamour and power. Every single detail of this wedding had to reflect that. Then no one would ever question his place in the family again.

Not even the maid of honor.

He looked down at Whitney out of the corner of his eye. She was right. With her fine bone structure, jet-black hair with the white stripe and those large eyes, he could dress her in a burlap sack and she'd still be instantly recognizable. The dress only made her features stand out that much more.

So why hadn't he agreed that a drastic change to her hair was a good idea?

It'd be like painting pouty ruby-red lips on the *Mona Lisa*. It'd just be wrong.

Still, he felt as if he'd done very little but insult her in the past twenty-four hours, and no matter what his personal feelings about Whitney were, constantly berating a member of the wedding party was not the way to ensure things stayed on message.

"I'll take you to lunch," he offered. "We'll make a day of it."

She gave him the side eye. "You normally spend your day styling women for weddings?"

"No," he said with a grin. "Far from it. I'm just making sure everything is—"

"Perfect."

"Exactly."

She tilted her head to one side and touched her cheek with a single fingertip. "Aren't you going to miss work?"

"This is my job." Again, he got the side eye, so he added, "I do the PR for Percheron Drafts, the beer company Chadwick started after he sold the Beaumont Brewery." He'd convinced Chadwick that the wedding needed to be a showcase event first. It hadn't been that hard. His older brother had learned to trust his instincts in the business world, and Matthew's instincts told him that marrying former playboy bachelor Phillip Beaumont off in a high-profile high-society wedding would pay for itself in good publicity.

Convincing Phillip and Jo that their wedding was going to be over-the-top in every possible regard, however, had been another matter entirely.

"I see," she said in a way that made it pretty clear she

didn't. Then she cleared her throat. "Won't your girlfriend be upset if you take me out to lunch?"

That was what she said. What she meant, though, was something entirely different. To his ears, it sure sounded as though she'd asked if he had really been about to kiss her earlier and whether he might try it again.

He leaned toward her, close enough he caught the scent of vanilla again. "I'm not involved with anyone," he said. What he meant?

Yeah, he might try kissing her again. Preferably someplace where seamstresses wouldn't bust in on them.

He watched the blush warm her skin. Again, his fingers itched to unzip that dress—to touch her. But… "You?"

His web searches last night hadn't turned up anything that suggested she was in a relationship.

She looked down at the floor. "I find it's best if I keep to myself. Less trouble that way."

"Then lunch won't be a problem."

"Are you sure? Or will you need to search my bag for illegal contraband?"

Ouch. Her dig stung all the more because he'd earned it. Really, there was only one way to save face here—throw himself on his sword. If he were lucky, she'd have mercy on him. "I'm sure. I'm done being an ass about things."

She jolted, her mouth curving into a smile that, no matter how hard she tried, she couldn't repress. "Can I have that in writing?"

"I could even get it notarized, if that's what it'd take for you to forgive me."

She looked at him then, her eyes full of wonder. "You already apologized last night. You don't have to do it again."

"Yes, I do. I keep confusing you. It's ungentlemanly."

Her eyebrows jumped up as her mouth opened but behind them, someone cleared her throat. "Mr. Beaumont? We're ready to start on Ms. Maddox's dress."

Whitney's mouth snapped shut as that blush crept over her cheeks. Matthew looked around. Jo and her dress were nowhere to be seen. He and Whitney had been standing by themselves in the middle of the salon for God knows how long, chatting. Flirting.

Right. They had work to do here.

But he was looking forward to lunch.

Five

"I'm sorry, sir, but the only seats we have are the window seats," the hostess said.

Matthew turned to look at Whitney. He hadn't expected Table 6 to be this crowded. He'd thought he was taking her to a quiet restaurant where they could talk. Where he could look at her over a table with only the bare minimum interruption.

But the place was hopping with Christmas shoppers taking a break. Shopping bags crowded the aisle, and there were more than a few people wearing elf hats and reindeer antlers. The hum of conversation was so loud he almost couldn't hear Bing Crosby crooning Christmas carols on the sound system.

"We can go someplace else," he offered to Whitney.

She pulled down her sunglasses and shot him a look, as if he'd dared her to throw a diva fit. "This is fine."

Matthew glanced around the restaurant again. He really didn't want to sit at a bar-high counter next to her. On the other hand, then he could maybe brush against her arm, her thigh.

They took the only two spots left in the whole place. A shaft of sunlight warmed their faces. Whitney took off her sunglasses and her knit hat and turned her face to the light.

She exhaled, a look of serene joy radiating from her. She was so beautiful, so unassuming, that she simply took his breath away.

Then it stopped. She shook back to herself and gave him an embarrassed look. "Sorry," she said, patting her hair back into place. "It's a lot colder here than it is in California. I miss the sun."

"Don't apologize." Her cheeks colored under his gaze. "Let's order. Then tell me about California." She notched a delicate eyebrow at him in challenge. "And I mean more than the basics. I want to know about *you*."

The corners of her mouth curved up as she nodded. But the waitress came, so they turned their attention to the daily specials. She ordered the soup and salad. He picked the steak sandwich. The process seemed relatively painless.

But Matthew noticed the way the waitress's eyes had widened as Whitney had asked about the soup du jour. *Oh, no,* he thought. The woman had recognized her.

Maybe it wouldn't be a problem. The restaurant was busy, after all. The staff had better things to do than wonder why Whitney Wildz had suddenly appeared at the counter, right?

He turned his attention back to Whitney. Which was not easy to do, crammed into the two seats in this window. But he managed to pull it off. "Now," he said, fixing her with what he really hoped wasn't a wolfish gaze, "tell me about you."

She shrugged.

The waitress came back with some waters and their coffee. "Anything else?" she asked with an ultraperky smile.

"No," Matthew said forcefully. "Thank you."

The woman's eyes cut back to Whitney again and she grinned in disbelief as she walked away. Oh, hell.

But Whitney hadn't noticed. She'd unwrapped her straw and was now wrapping the paper around her fingers, over and over.

Matthew got caught up in watching her long fingers bend the wrapper again and again and forgot about the waitress.

"You're confusing me," she said, staring hard at her scrap of paper. "Again."

"How?" She gave him the side eye. "No, seriously—
please tell me. It's not my job here to confuse you."

She seemed to deflate, just a little. But it didn't last.
"You're looking at me like that."

He forced his attention to his own straw. Hopefully, that
would give her the space she needed. "Like how?"

The silence stretched between them like a string pulling
tight. He was afraid he might snap. And he never snapped.
He was unsnappable, for God's sake.

But then his mind flashed back to the bare skin of her
back, how the zipper had ended just at the waistband of her
panties. All he'd seen was a pretty edge of lace. Now he
couldn't get his mind off it.

"I can't decide if you think I'm the biggest pain in the
neck of your life or if you're— If you—" She exhaled, the
words coming out in a rush. "If you like me. And when you
look at me like that, it just…makes it worse."

"I can't help it," he admitted. It was easier to say that without looking at her. Maybe this counter seating wasn't all bad.

Her hands stilled. "Why not?" There was something else
in her voice. That something seemed to match the look she'd
given him last night, the one that craved his approval.

He couldn't tell her why not. Not without telling her…
what? That he'd nursed a boyhood crush on her long after
he'd left boyhood behind? That he'd followed her in the
news? That this very afternoon, she'd been the most beautiful woman he'd ever seen?

"Tell me about you," he said, praying that she'd go along
with the subject change. "Tell me about your life."

He felt her gaze on him. Now it was his turn to blush. "If
I do, will you tell me about you?"

He nodded.

"Okay," she agreed. He expected her to begin twisting
her paper again, but she didn't. She dug out her phone. "This

is Pride and Joy," she said, showing him a horse and rider holding a gold medal.

The picture was her phone's wallpaper. Her pride and joy, indeed. "That was the Games, right?"

"Right." Her tone brightened considerably at his memory. "I'd been getting close to that level but…I wanted him to win, you know? Having bred a horse that could win at that level made me feel legitimate. Real. I wasn't some crazy actress, not anymore. I was a real horse breeder."

She spoke calmly—no hysterics, no bravado. Just someone determined to prove her worth.

Yeah, he knew that feeling, too. Better than he wanted to.

"There are people in this world who don't know about that show," she said, staring at her phone. "People who only know me as Whitney Maddox, the breeder of Pride and Joy. You have no idea how *huge* that is."

"I'm starting to get one." He lifted the phone from her hand and studied the horse. He'd seen a similar shot to this one online. But she wasn't in either one.

She slid her fingertip over the screen and another horse came up. Even he could tell this was a younger one, gangly and awkward looking. "This is Joy's daughter, Ode to Joy. I own her mother, Prettier Than a Picture—Pretty for short. She was a world-champion dressage horse, but her owner got indicted and she was sold at auction. I was able to get her relatively cheap. She's turned out some amazing foals." The love in her voice was unmistakable. Pretty might have been a good business decision, but it was clear that the horse meant much more to Whitney than just a piece of property. "Ode's already been purchased," she went on. "I could keep studding Joy to Pretty for the rest of my life and find buyers."

"Sounds like job security."

"In another year, I'll deliver Ode," she went on. "She's only one right now." She flicked at her screen and another photo came up. "That's Fifi," she told him. "My rescued greyhound."

The sleek dog was sprawled out on a massive cushion on the floor, giving the camera a don't-bother-me look. "A greyhound?"

"I was fostering her and just decided to keep her," Whitney replied. "She'd run and run when she was younger and then suddenly her life stopped. I thought—and I know this sounds silly because she's just a dog—but I thought she understood me in a way that most other living creatures don't."

"Ah." He didn't know what else to say to that. He'd never felt much kinship with animals, not the way Phillip did with his horses. His father had never really loved the horses he'd bought, after all. They'd been only investments for him—investments that might pay off in money or prestige. "You foster dogs?"

She nodded enthusiastically. "The no-kill shelter in Bakersfield never has enough room." Her face darkened briefly. "At first they wouldn't let me take any animals but…" Her slim shoulders moved up and down. Then the cloud over her face was gone. "There's always another animal that needs a place to stay."

He stared at her. It could have been a naked play for pity—poor little celebrity, too notorious to be entrusted with animals no one else wanted. But that was not how it came out. "How many animals have you fostered?"

She shrugged again. "I've lost count." She flicked the screen again and a strange-looking animal appeared.

He held the phone up so he could get a better look, but the squished black-and-white face stayed the same. "What is *that*?"

"That," she replied with a giggle that drew his gaze to her face, "is Gater. He's a pug-terrier-something."

Hands down, that was the ugliest mutt Matthew had ever seen. "How long have you had him?"

"Just over two years. He thinks he rules the house. Oh, you should have seen him when Jo and Betty stayed with me. He was furious!" She laughed again, a sweet, carefree sound that did more to warm him than the sun ever could.

"What happened?"

"He bit Betty on the ankle, and she kicked him halfway across the living room. No broken bones or skin," she hurried to add. "Just a pissed-off dog and donkey. Gater thinks he's the boss, and Fifi doesn't care as long as Gater stays off her cushion."

Whitney leaned over and ran her fingers over the screen again. A photo of some cats popped up, but that was not what held Matthew's attention. Instead, it was the way she was almost leaning her head against his shoulder, almost pressing her body against his arm.

"That's Frankie and Valley, my barn cats."

"Frankie and Valley? Like Frankie Valli, the singer?"

"Yup." Without leaning away, she turned her face up toward his. Inches separated them. "Frankie was a...stray." Her words trailed off as she stared at Matthew's face, his lips. Her eyes sparkled as the blush spread over her cheeks like the sunrise after a long, cold night.

He could lean forward and kiss her. It'd be easy. For years, he'd thought about kissing Whitney Wildz. He'd been young and hormonal and trying so, *so* hard to be the Beaumont that his father wanted him to be. Fantasies about Whitney Wildz were a simple, no-mess way to escape the constant effort to be the son Hardwick Beaumont wanted.

Except he didn't want to kiss that fantasy girl anymore. He wanted to kiss the flesh-and-blood woman sitting next to him. She shouldn't attract him as she did. He should see nothing but a headache to be managed when he looked at her. But he didn't, damn it. He didn't.

Matthew couldn't help himself. He lifted the hand that

wasn't holding her phone and let the tips of his fingers trail down the side of her cheek.

Her breath caught, but she didn't turn away—didn't look away. Her skin was soft and warmed by the sun. He spread his fingers out until the whole of his palm cradled her cheek.

"I didn't realize you were such a fan of Frankie Valli," she said in a breathy voice. Her pupils widened as she took another deep breath. As if she was waiting for him to make his move.

"I'm not." The problem was, Matthew didn't have a move to make. Phillip might have once moved in on a pretty woman without a care in the world about who saw them or how it'd look in the media.

But Matthew cared. He had to. It was how he'd made a place for himself in this family. And he couldn't risk all of that just because he wanted to kiss Whitney Maddox.

So, as much as it hurt, he dropped his hand away from her face and looked back at the screen. Yes. There were cats on the screen. Named after an aging former pop idol.

He could still feel Whitney's skin under his touch, still see her bare back...

Something outside the window caught his eye. He looked up to see two women in their mid-twenties standing on the sidewalk in front of the restaurant. One had her phone pointed in their general direction. When they saw that he'd noticed them, they hurried along, giggling behind their hands.

Dread filled him. Okay, yes, Whitney was recognizable—but she wasn't the only woman in the world with an unusual hair color, for crying out loud. This had to be...a coincidence.

He turned his attention back to the phone, but pictures of cats and dogs and horses barely held his attention. He wanted their food to come so they could eat and get the hell out of here. He wanted to get Whitney to a place where even if people did recognize her, they had the decency not to make a huge deal out of it.

She flicked to the last photo, which was surprisingly *not* of an animal. Instead, it was of a cowgirl wearing a straw hat and tight jeans, one foot kicked up on a fence slat. The sun was angled so that the woman in the picture was bathed in a golden glow—alone. Perfect.

Whitney tried to grab the phone from him, but he held on to it, lifting it just out of her reach. "Is this…you?"

"May I have that back, please?" She sounded tense.

"It *is* you." He studied the photo a little more. "Who took it?"

"Jo did, when she was out last winter." She leaned into him, reaching for the phone. "Please."

He did as the lady asked. "So that's the real Whitney Maddox, then."

She froze, her fingertip hovering over the button that would turn the screen off. She looked down at the picture, a sense of vulnerability on her face. "Yes," she said in a quiet voice. "That's the real me." The screen went black.

He cleared his throat. "I think I like the real you."

Even then she didn't look at him, but he saw the smile that curved up her lips. "So," she said in a bright voice, "your turn."

Hell. What was he supposed to say? He looked away—and right at the same two women he'd seen earlier. Except now there were four of them. "Uh…"

"Oh, don't play coy with me," she said as she slipped her phone back into her jacket pocket. Then she nudged him with her shoulder. "The real you. Go."

This time, when the women outside caught him looking, they didn't hurry off and they sure didn't stop pointing their cameras. One was on her phone.

It was then that he noticed the noise. The restaurant had gone from humming to a hushed whisper. The carols over the sound system were loud and clear. He looked over his shoulder and was stunned to find that a good part of the restaurant was staring at them with wide eyes. Cell phones were out. People were snapping pictures, recording videos.

Oh, hell. This was about to become a PR nightmare. Worse—if people figured out who he was? And put two and two together? Nightmare didn't begin to cut what this was about to become.

"We need to leave."

The women outside were headed inside.

"Are you trying to get…out…?" Whitney saw the women, then glanced around. "Oh." Shame flooded her cheeks. She grabbed her sunglasses out of her bag and shoved them back onto her face. "Yes."

Sadly, the glasses did little to hide who she was. In fact, they gave her an even more glamorous air, totally befitting a big-name star.

Matthew fished a fifty out of his wallet and threw it on the counter, even though they weren't going to eat anything they'd ordered.

As they stood, the small group of women approached. "It's really you," one of the woman said. "It's really Whitney Wildz!"

The quiet bubble that had been building over the restaurant burst and suddenly people were out of their seats, crowding around him and Whitney and shoving camera phones in their faces.

"Is this your boyfriend?" someone demanded.

"Are you pregnant?" someone else shouted.

"Are you ever going to clean up your act?" That insult was shouted by a man.

Matthew was unexpectedly forced into the role of bouncer. He used his long arms to push people out of Whitney's way as they tried to walk the twelve feet to the door. It took several minutes before they were outside, but the crowd moved with them.

He had his arm around her shoulders, trying to shield her as he rushed for his car. With his long legs, he could have left half of these idiots behind, but Whitney was much shorter than he was. He was forced to go slow.

Someone grabbed Whitney's arm, shouting, "Why did you break Drako's heart?"

Matthew shoved and shoved hard. They were at his car, but people were pushing so much that he had trouble getting the passenger door open. "Get back," he snarled as he hip-checked a man trying to grab a lot more than Whitney's arm. "Back off."

He got the door open and basically shoved her inside, away from what had rapidly become a mob. He slammed the door shut, catching someone's finger. There was howling. He was feeling cruel enough that he was tempted to leave the finger in there, but that would be the worst sort of headline—Beaumont Heir Breaks Beer Drinker's Hand. So he opened the door just enough to pull the offending digit out and then slammed it shut again.

Whitney sat in the passenger seat, already buckled up. She stared straight ahead. She'd gotten her hat back on, but it was too late for that. The parts of her face that were visible were tight and blank.

Matthew stormed around to the driver's side. No one grabbed him, but several people were recording him. Great. Just freaking great.

He got in, fired up the engine on his Corvette Stingray and roared off. He was furious with the waitress—she'd probably called her girlfriends to tell them that Whitney Wildz was at her table. He was furious with the rest of the idiots, who'd descended into a mob in mere minutes.

And he was furious with himself. He was the Beaumont who always, always handled the press and the public. Image was everything and he'd just blown his image to hell and back. If those people hadn't recognized him from the get-go, it wouldn't take much online searching before they figured it out.

This was exactly what he hadn't wanted to happen—Whitney Wildz would turn this wedding and his message into a circus of epic proportions. Yeah, he'd been a jerk to her about it last night, but he'd also been right.

Even if she was a cowgirl who fostered puppies and adopted greyhounds, even if she was a respected horse breeder, even if she was *nothing* he'd expected in the best possible ways, it didn't change the perception. The perception was that Whitney Wildz was going to ruin this wedding.

And he wouldn't be able to control it. Any of it. Not the wedding, not the message—and not himself.

He was screwed.

Six

They drove in silence. Matthew took corners as if he were punishing them. Or her. She wasn't sure.

She wished she had the capacity to be surprised by what had happened at the restaurant, but she didn't. Not anymore. That exact scene had played out time and time again, and she couldn't even feel bad about it anymore.

Instead, all she felt was resigned. She'd known this was going to happen, after all. And if she was disappointed by how Matthew had reacted, well, that was merely the by-product of him confusing her.

She'd allowed herself to feel hopeful because, at least some of the time, Matthew liked her.

The real her.

She thought.

She had no idea where they were, where they were going, or if they were going there in a straight line. He might be taking the long way just in case any of those fans had managed to follow them.

"Are you all right?" he growled out as he pointed his sleek car toward what she thought was downtown Denver.

She wouldn't flinch at his angry tone. She'd learned a long time ago that a reaction—any reaction—would be twisted around. Best to be a placid statue. Although that hadn't always worked so well, either.

"I'm fine."

"Are you sure? That one guy—he *grabbed* you."

"Yes." Had that been the same man whose hand had gotten crushed in the door?

Even though she had her gaze locked forward, out of the corner of her eye she could see him turn and give her a look of disbelief. "And that doesn't piss you off?"

This time, she did wince. "No."

"Why the hell not? It pissed me off. People can't grab you like that."

Whitney exhaled carefully through her nose. This was the sort of thing that someone who had never been on the receiving end of the paparazzi might say. Normal people had personal space, personal boundaries that the rest of humanity agreed not to cross. You don't grab my butt, I won't have you arrested.

Those rules hadn't applied to her since the days after her show had been canceled. The day she'd bolted away from her mother's overprotective control.

"It's fine," she insisted again. "It's normal. I'm used to it."

"It's bullshit," he snapped. "And I won't stand by while a bunch of idiots take liberties with you. You're not some plaything for them to grope or insult."

She did turn to look at him then. He had a white-knuckle grip on the steering wheel as he glared at the traffic he was speeding around. He was serious.

She couldn't remember the last time someone hadn't just stood by and watched the media circus take her down.

Like the time she'd flashed the cameras. She hadn't had on any panties because the dress made no allowances for anything, the designer had said. Yeah, she'd been high at the time, but had anyone said, "Gee, Whitney, you might want to close your legs"? Had anyone tried to shield her from the cameras, as Matthew had just done, until she could get her skirt pulled down?

No. Not a single person had said anything. They'd just kept snapping pictures. And that next morning? One of the worst in her life.

He took another corner with squealing tires into a parking spot in front of a tall building. "We're here."

"Are you on my side?" she asked.

He slammed the car into Park, causing her to jerk forward. "What kind of question is that?"

"I mean..." Was he the kind of guy who would have told her she was flashing the cameras? Or the kind who would have gotten out of the way of the shot? "No one's ever tried to defend me from the crowds before."

Now it was his turn to look at her as if she were nuts. "No one?"

This wasn't coming out well. "Look, like you said—in the interest of transparency, I need to know if you're on my side or not. I'm not trying to mess up your message. I mean, you saw how it was." Suddenly, she was pleading. She didn't just want him on her side, watching her back—she *needed* him there. "All I did was take off my hat."

He gave her the strangest look. She didn't have a hope in heck of trying to guess what was going on behind his deep blue eyes.

"That's just the way it is," she told him, her voice dropping to a whisper. Every time she let her guard down—every time she thought she might be able to do something normal people did, like go out to lunch with a man who confused her in the best possible ways—this was always what would happen. "I—I wish it wasn't."

He didn't respond.

She couldn't look at him anymore. Really, she didn't expect anything else of him. He'd made his position clear. His duty was to his family and this wedding. She could respect that. She was nothing but a distraction.

A distraction he'd almost kissed in a crowded restaurant.

So when he reached over and cupped her face in his hand,

lifting it until she had no choice but to look at him, she was completely taken off guard. "I refuse to accept that this is 'just the way it is.' I *refuse* to." His voice—strong and confident and so close—did things to her that she barely recognized. "And you should, too."

Once, she'd tried to fight back, to reclaim her name and her life. She'd tried to lend her celebrity status to animal shelters. It'd gotten her nothing but years of horrible headlines paired with worse pictures. She hadn't done anything public since the last incident, over two years ago.

She looked into his eyes. If only he were on her side… "What I do doesn't matter and we both know it."

He gave her another one of those looks that walked the fine line between anger and disgust. "So what are you going to do about it?"

She glared at him. She couldn't get mad at those people— but him? She could release a little rage on him. After all, he'd been barely better than those people last night. "I'm not going to sit around and fume and mope about how I'm nothing but a *commodity* to people. I'm not going to sit around and feel bad that once upon a time I was young and stupid and crazy. And I'm not going to let anyone else sit around and feel bad for me. I'm not an object of your pity *or* derision. Because that's not who I am anymore."

If he was insulted by her mini tirade, he didn't show it. He didn't even let go of her. Instead, one corner of his mouth curled up into an amused grin.

"Derision, huh?" He was close now, leaning in.

"Yes."

That'd been last night. Right after she'd first fallen into his arms. After she'd dared to hope she might have a little Christmas romance. The memory made her even madder.

"So if you're going to ask me to drop out, just get on with it so I can tell you I already told Jo I would and she begged me not to because *you* invited a bunch of strangers to her wedding and she wants one friend standing next to her. Now, are you on my side or not?"

Because if he wasn't, he needed to stop touching her. She was tired of not knowing where she stood with him.

He blinked. "I won't let anyone treat you like that."

"Because it's bad for your message?"

His fingers pulled against her skin, lifting her face up. Closer to him. "Because you are *not* a commodity to me."

The air seemed to freeze in her lungs, making breathing impossible. He was going to kiss her. God, she wanted him to. Just as she'd wanted him to kiss her in the restaurant.

And see what had happened? She could still feel that man's hand on her butt.

As much as she wanted to kiss Matthew—to be kissed for the real her, not the fake one—she couldn't.

"I'm going to ruin the wedding." It was a simple statement of an unavoidable fact.

It worked. A shadow clouded his face, and he dropped his hand and looked away. "We're going to be late."

"Right." She didn't want to do this anymore, didn't want to be the reason the wedding went off script. She wanted to go back to her ranch—back where dogs and cats and horses and even Donald, the crazy old coot, didn't have any expectations about Whitney Wildz.

Matthew opened her door and held out his hand for her. She'd promised Jo. Until Jo told her she could quit, she couldn't. She wouldn't. That was that.

So she sucked it up, put her hand in Matthew's and stood.

He didn't let go of her, didn't step back. Instead, he held on tighter. "Are you sure you're okay?"

She put on a smile for him. She wouldn't be okay until she was safely back home, acres of land between her and the nearest human. Then she'd put her head down and get back to work. In a while—a few weeks, a few months—this wedding would be superseded by another celebrity or royal doing something "newsworthy." This would pass. She knew that now. She hadn't always known it, though.

"I'm fine," she lied. Then, because she couldn't lie and look at him, she stared up at the white building. "Where are we?" Because the sign said Hotel Monaco.

"The Veda spa is inside the hotel."

He still didn't let her go. He tucked her hand into the crook of his elbow, as if they'd walked out of 1908 or something. When she shot him a look, he said, "Practice."

Ah, yes. That whole walking-down-the-aisle thing.

So she put on her biggest, happiest smile and held an imaginary bouquet in front of her. She'd been an actress once, after all. She could fake it until she made it.

He chuckled in appreciation. "That's the spirit," he said, which made her feel immensely better. He handed his keys to a valet and they strode through the hotel lobby as if they owned the place.

"Mr. Beaumont! How wonderful to see you again." The receptionist at the front desk greeted them with a warm smile. Her gaze flicked over Whitney. "How can I help you today?"

"We're here for the spa, Janice," he said. "Thank you." As he guided Whitney down a hallway, she gave him a look. "What?"

Jealousy spiked through her. "You check into a hotel in your hometown in the middle of day often? So often they know you by name?"

He pulled up right outside the salon door. "The Beaumonts have been using the hotel for a variety of purposes for years. The staff is exceedingly discreet. Chadwick used it for board meetings, but our father was…fond of using it for other purposes." Then he blushed. The pink color seemed out of place on his cheeks.

Ah—the father who sired countless numbers of children. She bit her tongue and said, "Yes?"

"Nothing," he said with more force than she expected. "The Beaumonts have a long business relationship with the hotel, that's all. I personally do not check into the rooms."

He opened the door to the spa. Another receptionist stood to greet them. "Mr. Beaumont," she said with a deferential bow of the head. "And this is—" she checked a tablet "—Ms. Maddox, correct?"

"Yes," Whitney said, feeling her shoulders straighten a bit more. If she could get through this as Ms. Maddox, that'd be great.

"This way. Rachel is ready for you."

They went back to a private room. Whitney hadn't been in a private salon room in a long time. "This is nice," she said as Matthew held the door open for her.

"And it better stay that way. Rachel," he said to the stylist with every color of red in her hair, "can you give me a moment? I have something I need to attend to."

"Of course, Mr. Beaumont." Rachel turned to face her. "Ms. Maddox, it's a delight to meet you."

Whitney tried not to giggle. A delight? Really? Still, this was a good test of her small-talk skills. At the wedding, she would be meeting a lot of people, after all. "A pleasure," she agreed.

She sat in the chair, and Rachel fluffed her hair several times. "Obviously, the bride will have her hair up," Rachel said. "Ms. Frances Beaumont has requested Veronica Lake waves, which will look amazing. Ms. Serena Beaumont will have a classic twist. You…" Her voice trailed off as she fingered Whitney's home-cut pixie.

"Don't have a lot to work with," Whitney said. "I know. I was thinking. Maybe we should take it blond."

Rachel gasped in horror. "What? Why?"

"She's not taking it blond," Matthew announced from the door as he strode in. He didn't look at Whitney—he was too busy scowling at his phone. But the order was explicit.

"Of course not," Rachel hurriedly agreed. "That would be the worst possible thing." She continued fluffing. "We could add in volume and extensions. Blond is out but colored strands are very hot right now."

Whitney cringed. Extensions? Volume? Colored streaks? Why not just put her in a torn T-shirt emblazoned with the *Growing Up Wildz* logo and parade her down the street?

"Absolutely not," Matthew snapped. "We're going for a glamorous, classic look here."

If the stylist was offended by his attitude, she didn't show it. "Well," she said, working her fingers through Whitney's hair, "I can clean up the cut and then we can look at clips? Something bejeweled that matches the dresses?"

"Perfect," Matthew agreed.

"People will recognize me," Whitney reminded him, just because she felt as if she should have some say in her appearance. She glanced at the stylist, who had the decency to not stare. "Just like they did at the restaurant. If you won't let her dye it, at least get me a wig."

"No." But that was all he said as he continued to scowl at his phone.

"Why the heck *not*?"

He looked up at her, his eyes full of nothing but challenge. "Because you are beautiful the way you are. Don't let anyone take that away from you." Then his phone buzzed and he said, "Excuse me," and was gone.

Whitney sat there, stunned, as Rachel cleaned up her pixie cut.

Beautiful?

Was that how he thought of her?

Seven

This was going south on him. Fast. Matthew struggled to keep his cool. He'd learned a long time ago that losing his temper didn't solve anything. But he was getting close to losing it right now.

When the photo of him and Whitney, taken from the sidewalk while they sat inside the restaurant, had popped up on Instagram with the caption OMG WHITNEY WILDZ IN DENVER!?! he'd excused himself from the stylist's room so that he could be mad without upsetting Whitney. She'd had enough of that already.

He'd already reported the photo, but he knew this was just the beginning. And after years of cleaning up the messes his siblings and stepmothers had left behind, he also knew there was no way to stop it.

He was going to make an effort, though. Containment was half the battle. The other half? Distraction.

If he could bury the lead on Whitney under some other scandal…

He scanned the gossip sites, hoping that someone somewhere had done something so spectacularly stupid that no one would care about a former teen star having lunch.

Nothing. Of all the weeks for the rest of the world to be on its best behavior.

In the days of old—when he'd found himself faced with a crowd of paparazzi outside his apartment, demanding a re-action about his second stepmother's accusation that she'd caught Hardwick Beaumont in bed with his mistress in this very hotel—Matthew had relied on distraction.

He'd called Phillip, told him to make a scene and waited for the press to scamper off. It'd worked, too. Bailing Phil-lip out was worth it when Hardwick had called Matthew into his office and told him he'd done a nice job handling the situation.

"You're not mad at Phillip? Or…me?" Matthew had asked, so nervous he'd been on the verge of barfing. The only other times Hardwick had called Matthew into his office had been to demand to know why he couldn't be more like Chadwick.

Hardwick had gotten up and come around his desk to put his hands on Matthew's shoulders. Hardwick had been older then, less than five years from dying in the middle of a board meeting.

"Son," Hardwick had said with a look that could have been described only as fatherly on his face. It'd looked so unnatural on him. "When you control the press, you rule the world—that's how a Beaumont handles it."

Son. Matthew could count on both hands the number of times that Hardwick had used that term of affection. Mat-thew had finally, *finally* done something the old man had no-ticed. For the first time in his life, he'd felt like a Beaumont.

"You just keep looking out for the family," Hardwick had said. "Remember—control the press, rule the world."

Matthew had gotten very good at controlling the press—the traditional press. It was the one thing that *made* him a Beaumont.

But social media was a different beast, a many-headed hydra. You cut off one Instagram photo, another five popped up.

He couldn't rely on Phillip to cause a scene anymore, now that the man was clean and sober. Chadwick was out, as well—he didn't deal with the press beyond the controlled environment of interviews that Matthew prescreened for him.

Matthew stared at his phone. He could call his sister Frances, but she'd want to know why and how and details before she did anything. And once she found out that her former childhood idol Whitney Wildz was involved...

That left him one choice. He dialed his younger brother Byron.

"What'd I do now?" Byron said. He yawned, as if Matthew had woken him up at two in the afternoon.

"Nothing. Yet." There was silence on the other end of the line. "You *are* in Denver, right?"

"Got in this morning." Byron yawned again. "Hope you appreciate this. It's a damn long flight from Madrid."

"I need a favor."

"You mean beyond flying halfway around the world to watch Phillip marry some horse trainer?" Byron laughed.

Matthew gritted his teeth. Byron sounded just like Dad. "Yes. I need you to be newsworthy today."

"What'd Phillip do this time? I thought he was getting married."

"It's not Phillip."

Byron whistled. "What'd you get into?"

Matthew thought back to the photo he'd already reported. Whitney—sitting right next to him. Those people hadn't known who he was, but it wouldn't take long for someone to figure out that Whitney Wildz was "with" a Beaumont. "I just need a distraction. Can you help me out or not?"

This was wrong. All wrong. He was trying to prove that the Beaumont family was back on track, above scandal. He was trying to prove that he had complete control over the situation. And what was he doing?

Asking his brother to make a mess only days before the wedding...to protect Whitney.

What was he thinking?

He was thinking about the way her face had closed down the moment she realized people were staring, the way she sat in his car as if he were driving her to the gallows instead of a posh salon.

He was thinking about the way she kept offering to change her hair—to drop out—so that he could stay on message.

He was thinking how close he'd come to kissing her at that lunch counter.

"How big a distraction?"

"Don't kill anyone."

"Damn," Byron said with a good-natured chuckle. "You'll bail me out?"

"Yeah."

There was a pause that made Matthew worry. "Hey—did you invite Harper to the wedding?"

"Leon Harper, the banker who forced Chadwick to sell the Brewery?"

"Yeah," was the uninformative response. But then Byron added, "Did you invite him?"

"No, I didn't invite the man who hated Dad so much he took it out on all of us. Why?"

"I'll only help you out if you invite the whole Harper family."

"He has a *family*?" Matthew had had the displeasure of meeting Harper only a few times, at board meetings or other official Brewery functions. The man was a shark—no, that was unfair to sharks everywhere. The man was an eel, slippery and slimy and uglier than sin.

Plus, there was that whole thing about hating the Beaumonts enough to force the sale of the family business

"Are you serious? Why on God's green earth would you want Harper there?"

"Do you want me to make headlines for you or not?" Byron snapped.

"They can't come to the wedding—there's no room in the chapel. But I'll invite them to the reception." There would be plenty of room for a few extra people at the Mile High Station. And in a crowd of six hundred guests—many of whom were extremely famous—the odds of Harper running into a Beaumont, much less picking a fight with one, were slim. Matthew could risk it.

"Done. Don't worry, big brother—I've got a bone or two to pick now that I'm Stateside." Byron chuckled. "Can't believe you want me to stir up trouble. You, of all people."

"I have my reasons. Just try not to get a black eye," Matthew told him. "It'll look bad in the photos."

"Yeah? This reason got a name?"

The back of Matthew's neck burned. "Sure. And does the reason you ran off to Europe for a year have a name?"

"I was working," Byron snapped.

"That's what I'm doing here. Don't kill anyone."

"And no black eyes. Got it." Byron hung up.

Matthew sagged in relief. Byron had been in Europe for over a year. He claimed he'd been working in restaurants, but really—who could tell? All that Matthew knew was that Byron had caused one hell of a scene at a restaurant before winding up in Europe. There he'd kept his head down long enough to stay the heck out of the headlines. That'd been good enough for Matthew. One less mess he had to clean up.

This would work. He'd send out a short, boring press release announcing that Whitney Maddox, former star of *Growing Up Wildz* and close friend of the bride, was in Denver for the Beaumont wedding. The Beaumonts were pleased she would be in the wedding party. He'd leave it at that.

Then tonight Byron would go off the rails. Matthew was reasonably sure that his little brother wouldn't actually kill anyone, but he'd put the odds of a black eye at two to one. Either way, he was confident that Byron would do something that washed Whitney right out of the press's mind. Who cared about a former child star when the prodigal Beaumont had returned to raise hell at his brother's wedding?

"Mr. Beaumont?" Rachel, the stylist, opened the door and popped her head out. "We're ready for the big reveal."

"How'd she turn out?" Now that he had his distraction lined up, he could turn his attention back to Whitney. *All* of his attention.

Rachel winked at him. "I think you'll be pleased with the results."

Matthew walked into the private room. Whitney's back was to him. Her hair wasn't noticeably shorter, but it was shaped and sleek and soft-looking. A large rhinestone clip was fastened on one side, right over her white streak. He walked around to the front. Her eyes were closed. She hadn't seen yet.

God, she was beautiful. *Stunning.* The makeup artist had played up her porcelain complexion by going easy on the blush and heavy on the red lips. Instead of the smoky eye that Frances and Serena were going to wear, the artist had gone with a cat's-eye look.

"Whoa," he heard himself say. How could people look at this woman and only see Whitney Wildz?

Because the woman sitting in the chair in front of him was so much *more* than Whitney Wildz had ever been.

Whitney's nose wrinkled at him, but there was no missing the sweet little smile that curved up the corners of her mouth.

He was *going* to kiss her. Just as soon as they didn't have hairstylists and makeup artists hanging around, he was going to muss up that hair and smudge that lipstick and he wasn't going to feel bad about it at all.

"Ready, Ms. Maddox?" Rachel said. She spun Whitney's chair around and said, "Ta-da!"

Whitney blinked at her reflection, her pale eyes wide with shock.

Rachel's smile tensed. "Of course, it'll look better with the dress. And if you don't like it…"

"No, it's perfect," Matthew interrupted. "Exactly how I want her to look. Great job."

Whitney swallowed. "Perfect?" It came out as a whisper. He noticed her chest was rising and falling with increasing speed.

He knew what was happening. His sister Frances had always done the same thing when she'd been busted for sneaking around with the hired help. The shallow, fast breathing meant only one thing.

Whitney was about to freak out.

"If you could give us a moment," he said to the stylist.

"Is everything—?" Rachel asked, throwing a worried look back at Whitney as Matthew hurried the woman out of the room.

"It's perfect," Matthew reassured her as he shut the door in her face. Then he turned back to Whitney.

She'd come up out of the chair and was leaning into the mirror now. His mind put her back in her dress. "You're going to look amazing."

She started, as if she'd forgotten he was still there. Meeting his gaze in the mirror's reflection, she gave him a nervous grin. "I don't look like…*her* too much?"

Like Whitney Wildz.

He couldn't see anything of that ghost of the past in the woman before him—anything beyond a distinctive hair color. She *wasn't* Whitney Wildz—not to him. She was someone else—someone better.

Someone he liked.

Someone he'd defend, no matter what the cost.

He couldn't help it. He closed the distance between them and brushed the careful edge of her hairstyle away from her cheek. Then he tilted her head back to face him.

"You look like *you*," he assured her.

Her gaze searched his. The desperation was undisguised this time. He wanted to make her feel better, to let her know that he'd take care of her. He wouldn't throw her to the wolves or leave her hanging.

His lips brushed hers. Just a simple, reassuring kiss. A friendly kiss.

Yeah, right.

Except…she didn't close her eyes. He knew this because he didn't, either. She watched him kiss her. She didn't throw her arms around his neck and she didn't kiss him back. She just…watched.

So he stopped.

She was even paler now, practically a ghost with red lips as she stared at him with those huge eyes of hers.

Damn it. For once he'd let his emotions do the thinking for him and he'd screwed up.

"Whitney…"

"Knock-knock!" Rachel said in a perky voice as the door opened. "What did we decide?"

He ran the back of his hand over his mouth and then looked at Whitney. "I think she's perfect."

Eight

Matthew had been right. The staff at the hotel and spa were exceedingly discreet. There were no cameras or phones pointed at her when she walked out of the hotel. No one yelled her name as the valet pulled up with Matthew's car. Not a single person tried to grab her while the doorman opened her door and waited for her to get seated.

But Matthew had kissed her. Somehow, that made everything worse. And better.

She didn't know which. All she knew was that when he'd touched her—when he'd looked at her—and said she looked like herself, she'd wanted to kiss him and not kiss him and demand to know which "you" she looked like.

Which Whitney he thought he was kissing.

God, her brain was a muddled mess. She knew what to expect from the crowd at the restaurant. She did not know what to expect from Matthew Beaumont.

Except that he was probably going to keep confusing her.

Which he did almost immediately.

"I have the situation under control," he told her as they drove off for what she hoped was Jo and Phillip's farm. She couldn't take any more of this gadding about town. "I've done a press release announcing your involvement in the wedding."

"You're *announcing* I'm here? I thought that's what you wanted to avoid." She was feeling better now. Ridiculous, yes. But the sight of her in that mirror, looking like...well, like a Hollywood movie star, but a classic one, had short-circuited her brain. And then he'd kissed her.

"Trust me—after what happened at the restaurant, everyone knows you're here. There's no putting that genie back in the bottle."

"This does not make me feel better." She ran her hand over her hair. It felt much smoother than normal. She didn't feel normal right now.

"As I was saying," Matthew went on with a tense voice, "I've sent out a short, hopefully boring press release announcing that we're happy you're here. Then tonight my younger brother Byron will do something excessive and highly Beaumont-like."

"Wait, what?"

He didn't look at her—traffic was picking up—but his grin was hard to miss. "Byron's going to bury the lead. That's you."

"I—I don't understand. I thought you wanted the Beaumonts to stay *out* of the headlines." She was sure that he'd said something to that effect yesterday.

"I do. Byron was going to be newsworthy anyway. He flew off to Europe over a year ago and even I don't know why. This is just...building on that buzz."

She gave him a look. Was he serious?

He was.

"And it's the kind of situation I'm used to dealing with," he went on. "I can control this kind of press. I'm not going to let people manhandle you." He said it in such a serious tone that she was momentarily stunned.

"Why?"

"Why what?"

She swallowed, hoping she wouldn't trip over her words.

At least she was safely buckled in a car. The chances of her tripping over her feet were almost zero. "Why are you doing this for me?"

"Because it's the right thing to do."

She wanted to believe that. Desperately. But… "You're going to throw a Beaumont under the bus for me? You don't even know me."

"That's not true. And it's not throwing Byron under the bus if he willingly agrees. The situation is under control," he said again, as if it was a mantra.

She wasn't sure she believed that, no matter how many times he said it. "You don't even *know* me," she repeated. "Yesterday you wouldn't have just thrown me under the bus to stay on message—you would have backed the bus over me a few times for good measure."

"I know you breed award-winning horses, rescue dogs, name your cats after aging pop singers and will do anything for your friends, even if it puts you in the line of fire." He glanced over at her. "I know you prefer jeans and boots but that you can wear a dress as well as any woman I've ever seen. I know that once you were a rock star but now you're not."

Her cheeks warmed at the compliments, but then she realized what he'd said. Rock star? She'd played a rock star on television. Most people considered her an actress first—if they considered her a musician at all.

Unless… There was something going on here, something that she had to figure out right now. "You recognized me. Right away."

He didn't respond immediately, but she saw him grip the steering wheel even tighter. "Everyone recognizes you. You saw what happened at lunch today."

"Women recognize me," she clarified. "Who watched the show when they were kids."

"I'm sure they do." Did he sound tense? He did.

She was getting closer to that *something*. "Did you watch my show?"

"Frances did." He sounded as if he was talking through gritted teeth. "My younger sister."

"Did you watch it with her?"

The moment stretched long enough that he really didn't have to answer. He used to watch the show. He used to watch *her*. "Did you see me in concert? Is that why you called me a rock star?"

In response, he honked the horn and jerked the car across two lanes. "Stupid drivers," he muttered.

Normally, she wouldn't want to know. She didn't want people's version of her past to project onto her present. But she needed to know—was this the reason why he'd run so hot and cold with her?

"Matthew."

"Yes, okay? I used to watch your show with Frances and Byron. Frances, especially, was a huge fan. We never missed an episode. It was the only time when I could *make* time for them, make sure they didn't feel forgotten by the family. Our father had already moved on to another wife, another set of new children and another mistress. He never had time for them, for any of us. And I didn't want my brother and sister to grow up like I had. So I watched the show with them. Every single one of them. And then your concert tour came through Denver the week before their fifteenth birthday, so I got them front-row tickets and took them. Our father had forgotten it was their birthday, but I didn't."

She sat there, flabbergasted. Jo had said Hardwick Beaumont was a bastard of a man, but to not even remember your own kids' birthdays?

"And…and you were amazing, all right? I'd always wondered if you really did the singing and guitar on the show or if it was dubbed. But it was all you up on that stage. You put on a hell of a show." His voice trailed off, as if he was lost in the memory, impressed with her musical talents all over again. "I'd always…" He sighed heavily.

"What? You'd always *what*?"

"I'd always had a crush on you." His voice was quiet, as if he couldn't believe he was saying the words out loud. "Seeing you in person—seeing how talented you really were—only made it worse. But then the show got canceled and you went off the rails and I felt…stupid. Like I'd fallen for a lie. I'd let myself be tricked because you were so pretty and talented. I was in college by then—it really wasn't cool to crush on a teen star. And the headlines—every time you made headlines, I felt tricked all over again."

Okay, so how was she supposed to reply to *that*? *Gosh, I'm sorry I destroyed a part of your childhood? That I never had a childhood?*

She'd had people tell her they loved her before—had it shouted at her on sidewalks. Love letters that came through her agent—he forwarded them to her with the quarterly royalty checks. And she'd had more than a few people tell her how disappointed they were that she wasn't a proper role model, that she wasn't really a squeaky-clean rock star.

That she wasn't what they wanted her to be.

"You weren't— Last night…you weren't mad at me?"

He chuckled. It was not a happy sound. "No. I was mad at myself."

Why hadn't she seen it earlier? He'd had a crush on her. He might have even fancied himself in love with her.

No, not with her. With Whitney Wildz.

"But *you* kissed *me*."

True, it hadn't been a let's-get-naked kind of kiss, but that didn't change the basic facts. He'd told her she was beautiful at several important points throughout the day, gone out of his way to reassure her, listened to her talk about her pets and…kissed her anyway.

He scrubbed a hand through his hair, then took an exit off

the highway. It was several minutes before he spoke. "I did." He said it as though he still didn't believe it. "My apologies."

"You're apologizing? For the kiss? Was it that bad?"

Yeah, he'd sort of taken her by surprise—she'd been in a state of shock about her face—but that wasn't going to be *it*, was it? One strike and she was out of luck?

"You didn't kiss me back."

"Because I didn't know who you thought you were kissing." Point of fact, despite all the illuminating personal details he'd just revealed, she *still* didn't know who he'd thought he was kissing.

"You," he said simply. "I was kissing you."

She opened her mouth to ask, *Who?*

This was not the time for ambiguous personal pronouns. This was the time for clarity, by God. Because if he still thought he was kissing a rock star or an actress, she couldn't kiss him back. She just couldn't.

But if he was kissing a klutz who rescued puppies...

She didn't get the chance to ask for that vital clarification, because suddenly they were at the guard gate for Beaumont Farms. "Mr. Beaumont, Ms. Maddox," the guard said, waving them through.

Matthew took the road back to the house at what felt like a reckless speed. They whipped around corners so fast she had to hold on to the door handle. Then they were screeching to a halt in front of Phillip and Jo's house. The place was dark.

Whitney's head was spinning from more than just his driving. She couldn't look at him, so she stared at the empty-looking house. "Who am I? Who am I to you?"

Out of the corner of her eye, she saw his hands flex around the steering wheel. After today she wouldn't be surprised if he'd permanently bent it out of shape, what with all the white-knuckle gripping he'd been doing.

He didn't answer the question. Instead, he said, "Can I walk you inside?"

"All right."

They got out of the car. Matthew opened the door to the house for her and then stood to the side so she could enter first. She had to stop—it was dark and she didn't know where the light switches were located.

"Here." Matthew's voice was close to her ear as he reached around her. She stepped back—back into the wall.

He flipped the light on but he didn't move away from her. Instead, he stood there, staring down at her with something that looked a heck of a lot like hunger.

What did people do in this situation?

To hell with what other people did. What did *she* want to do?

She still wanted the same thing she'd wanted when she'd shown up here—a little Christmas fling to dip her toes back into the water of dating and relationships. She still wanted to feel sexy and pretty and, yes, graceful.

But the way that Matthew was looking down at her…there was something else there, something more than just a casual attraction that might lead to some really nice casual sex.

It scared her.

"I don't think they're home," he said, his voice husky.

"That's a shame," she replied. He'd made her feel pretty today, but right now? That hunger in his eyes?

She felt sexy. Desirable.

He wanted her.

She wanted to be wanted.

Just a Christmas fling. The maid of honor and the best man. Something that'd be short and sweet and so, *so* satisfying.

He hesitated. "Is it?"

"No." She turned until her back was against the wall.

His other arm came up beside her, trapping her in between them. "I'll stop. If you want me to."

She touched one of his cheeks. His eyelashes fluttered. But he hadn't answered her question.

He seemed to realize it. "I don't know what you are to me," he told her, the words coming out almost harsh. He leaned down and touched his forehead to hers. "But I know *who* you are."

This time, she knew the kiss wouldn't be the soft, gentle thing he'd pressed against her lips before. This time, it would be a kiss that consumed her.

She wanted to be consumed.

But he hadn't clarified anything, damn it. She put her hands on his chest and pushed just hard enough to stop him. Not hard enough to push him away. "Tell me, Matthew. Tell me who you're going to kiss."

Now both of his hands were cradling her face—pulling her up to him. "Whitney," he whispered. The length of his body pressed her back against the wall, strong and hard and everything she wanted it to be. "Whitney Maddox."

She didn't wait for him to kiss her. She kissed him first. She dug her fingers into the front of his sweater and hauled him down so she could take possession of his mouth, so she could offer up her own for him.

He groaned into her as she nipped at his lower lip. Then he took control of the kiss. His tongue swept into hers as his hands trailed down her cheeks, onto her neck and down her shoulders. Then he picked her up. The sudden change in altitude caused her to gasp.

"You need to be taller," he told her as he kissed along her cheek to her neck, her ear. His hands were flat against her bottom, boosting her to make up for the eight-inch height difference between them. Then he squeezed.

She had no choice. Her legs went around his waist, pulling him into her. She could feel his erection straining against his pants, pressing against her. She trembled, suddenly filled with a longing she couldn't ignore for a single second more.

Then his hips moved, rocking into hers. The pressure was intense—*he* was intense. Even though she had on jeans, she could feel the pads of his fingertips through the denim, squeezing her, pulling her apart.

His body rocked against hers, hitting the spot that sent the pressure spiraling up. She wanted to touch him, wanted to feel all the muscles that were holding her up as if she weighed nothing at all, but suddenly she had to hold on to him for dear life as he ground against her.

Her head fell back and bounced off the wall, but she didn't care—and she cared a whole lot less when Matthew started nipping at her neck, her collarbone. His hips flexed, driving him against her center again and again.

"Oh," she gasped. "Oh, Matthew."

"Do you like it," he growled against her chest.

"Yes."

"Louder." He thrust harder.

"Yes—*Oh!*" She gasped again—he was— She was going to—

He rocked against her again, in time with his teeth finding the spot between her shoulder and neck. He bit down and rubbed and—and—

"Oh yes, oh yes, *oh yes!*" she cried out as he pinned her back against the wall and held her up as she climaxed.

"Kiss me back," he told her, his forehead resting against hers. He was still cupping her bottom in his hands, but instead of the possessive squeezing, he was now massaging her. The sensation was just right. *He* was just right. "Always kiss me back."

So she kissed him, even as the climax ebbed and her body sagged in his arms. She kissed him with everything she had, everything she wanted.

Because she wanted everything. Especially a man who put her first.

"Tell me what you want," he said. Already his hips were

moving again, the pressure between her legs building. "I want this to be perfect for you. Tell me everything you want."

She cupped his cheeks in her hands. "Perfect?"

He gave her a look that started out as embarrassed but quickly became wicked. "Do you doubt me?"

After that orgasm? For heaven's sake, they were still fully clothed! What was he capable of when they were naked?

She grinned at him, feeling wicked in her own right. "Prove it."

Nine

"Oh, I'll prove it," Matthew told her. He hefted her up again. Then they were moving. He carried her through the house. He knew where they were going—his old room. If he didn't get all these clothes off them and bury himself in her body soon, he might just explode.

She wasn't helping. True, she didn't weigh very much and, since he was carrying her, she didn't trip or stumble into him. But the way she busied herself by scraping her teeth over his earlobe? He was going to lose it. Him, who was always in control of the situation. Of himself.

She'd stripped that control away from him the moment she'd walked into his life.

"This is my old room," he told her when they got to her door. He managed to get the door open. Then he kicked it shut.

Then he laid her out on the bed. Normally, he took his time with women. He was able to keep a part of himself back—keep a certain distance from what he was doing, what they were trying to do to him. Oh, they enjoyed it—he did, as well—but that level of emotional detachment was important somehow. He didn't know why. It just was.

Besides, being detached made it easier to make sure the women he was with were getting what they wanted from him.

But seeing Whitney on his old bed? Her hair was mussed now, her red lipstick smudged. She was no longer the perfect beauty he'd tentatively—yes, detachedly—kissed in the salon.

She was, however, his. His for right now. And he couldn't hold back.

He stripped off his coat while she tried to wriggle out of her jeans. Then, just as he had his sweater over his head, she kicked him in the stomach.

"Oof," he got out through clenched teeth. He stepped out of range and jerked the sweater the rest of the way off.

"Sorry! Oh, my gosh, I'm so sorry." Whitney lay on her back. She had one leg halfway out of her jeans, the other stuck around the ankle. "I didn't— I wasn't trying to— Oh, *damn*."

He caught the jeans, now practically inside out, and yanked them off her. Then he climbed onto the bed. Her blush was anything but pale or demure. An embarrassing red scorched her cheeks.

"I'm sorry," she whispered, looking as if she might start crying.

He straddled her bare legs as he pinned her wrists by her head. "None of that," he scolded her. "Nervous?"

She dropped her gaze and gave him a noncommittal shrug.

"Look at me," he told her. "Do you still want to do this?"

She didn't look. "I'm such a klutz. I'm sorry I kicked you."

"*Look* at me, Whitney," he ordered. When she didn't, he slid her wrists over her head so he could hold them with one hand and then he took her by the jaw and turned her face to his.

There was so much going on under the surface. She was trying to hide it by not looking at him, but he wasn't having any of it. "Apology accepted. Now forget it happened."

"But—"

He cut her off with a kiss, his hand sliding down her neck. "One of the things I like about you is that you get clumsy when you're nervous. It's cute."

Defiance flashed over her face. Good. "I don't want to be cute."

"What do you want?"

She sucked in a tiny breath—and was silent.

Oh, no, you don't, he thought. He snaked his hand down her front and then up under her sweater until he found her breast.

God, what a breast. Full and heavy and warm—and so responsive. Even through her bra, her nipple went to a stiff point as he teased her. "Is that what you want?"

She didn't answer. Not in words. But her breathing was faster now, and she'd tucked her lower lip into her mouth.

What control he had regained when she'd kicked him started to fray like a rope. He rolled her nipple between his finger and thumb. Her back arched into him, so he did it again, harder. "Is that what you want?"

She nodded.

"Say it," he told her. "Say it or I will tie you to this bed and *make* you say it."

The moment the words left his mouth, he wondered where they'd come from. He didn't just randomly tie people up. He wasn't into that kinky stuff. And when he'd dreamed of making it with Whitney Wildz, well, hell, back then, he hadn't even known people did that sort of thing.

But she didn't reply. Her eyes got huge and she was practically panting, but she didn't utter a word.

Then she licked her lips. And he lost his head.

Challenge accepted.

He let go of her breast and pulled her up, then peeled her sweater off her. The bra followed. She said nothing as he tore her clothes off, but when he kissed the side of her breast, when he let his tongue trace over her now-bare shoulder, she shuddered into him.

He couldn't stop whatever this was he'd started. He'd made her cry out in the entry hall. He'd make her do it again. He wrenched his tie off, then looped it around her wrists. Not tight—he didn't want to hurt her. But knowing her, she'd hit him in the nose with her elbow and nothing ruined some really hot sex like a bloody nose.

The tie secure around her wrists, he loosely knotted it to the headboard. Then he got off the bed.

Whitney Maddox was nude except for a thin pair of pale pink panties that looked so good against her skin. Her breasts were amazing—he wanted to bury his face in them and lick them until she cried his name over and over.

And she was tied to his bed.

Because she'd let him do that. Because she'd *wanted* him to do that.

He'd never been so excited in his life.

He stripped fast, pausing only long enough to get the condom out of his wallet. He rolled it on and then went to her. "I want to see all of you," he said, pulling her panties down. She started to lift her legs so he could get them off her ankles, but he held her feet down. "I'm in charge here, Whitney."

He trailed a finger down between her breasts, watching her shiver at his touch. Finally, *finally*, she spoke.

"I expect perfection."

"And that's what you'll get."

He climbed between her legs and stroked her body. She moaned, her head thrashing from side to side as he touched her.

He couldn't wait much longer. "You okay?" he asked. He wanted to be sure. They could play this little game about making her say it, but he also didn't want to hurt her. "If it's not okay, you tell me."

"This is okay. This is…" She tried to shift her hips closer to his dick. "Am I…am I sexy?"

"Oh, babe," he said. But he couldn't answer her, not in words. So he fit his body to hers and thrust in.

"Matthew!" she gasped in the same breathless way she'd cried his name in the hall.

"Yeah, louder," he ground out as he drove in harder.

"Matthew!" she cried again. Her legs tried to come off the bed, and she almost kneed him in the ribs.

"Oh, no, you don't," he told her as he grabbed her legs and tucked them up under his arms. Then he leaned down into her.

She was completely open to him, and he took advantage of that in every way he knew how—and a few he didn't even know he knew.

"Is this what you want?" he demanded over and over.

"Yes." Always, she said yes.

"Say it louder," he ordered her, riding her harder.

"Yes! Oh, Matthew—*yes*!"

There was nothing else but the moment between when he slid out of her body and drove back in. No thoughts of family or message or public image. Nothing but the woman beneath him, crying out his name again and again.

Suddenly her body tensed up around his. "Kiss me," she demanded. "Kiss me!"

"Kiss me back," he told her before he lowered his lips to hers.

Everything about her went tight as she kissed him. Then she fell back, panting heavily.

Matthew surrendered himself to her body. He couldn't fight it anymore.

Then he collapsed onto her chest. Her legs slid down his, holding him close. He knew he needed to get up—he didn't want to lose the condom—but there was something about holding her after what he'd done to her…

Jesus—had he really tied her up? Made her cry out his name? That was…something his father would have done.

"Can you untie me now?" she asked, sounding breathless and happy.

Focus, he told himself. So he sat back and undid the tie from the headboard. He'd really liked that tie, too, but he doubted it'd ever be the same.

He started to get out of bed to get cleaned up and dressed, but she sat up and tackle-hugged him so hard it almost hurt. But not quite. After he got over his momentary shock, he wrapped his arms around her.

"Thank you," she whispered. "It was…"

"Perfect?" He hoped so, for her sake.

At that, she leaned back and gave him the most suggestive smile he'd ever seen. He could take her again. He had another condom. He could loop his demolished tie back through the headboard and…

"I'm not sure. We might have to do it again later. Just to have a point of comparison, you understand." Then a shadow of doubt crossed her face. "If you wanted to," she hurried to add.

He pulled her back into his arms. "I'd like that. I'd like that a lot. You were amazing. Except for the kicking part."

She giggled, her chin tucked in the crook of his neck. He grabbed one of her wrists and kissed where he'd had it bound.

Then, from the floor, his phone chimed Phillip's text message chime.

And the weight of what he was supposed to be doing came crushing back down on him.

Why was he lolling away the afternoon in bed with Whitney? This was not the time to be tying people up, for crying out loud. He had a wedding to pull off—a family image to save.

An image that was going to be a whole hell of a lot harder to save when Byron got done with it.

Matthew had to keep the wheels from falling off. He had

to take care of the family. He had to prove he was one of them. A Beaumont.

Then Whitney kissed his jaw. "Do you need to go?"

"Yeah."

He didn't want to. He wanted to stay here, wrapped up with her. He wanted to say to hell with the wedding, the message—he didn't care. He'd done the best he could.

He cared about Whitney. He shouldn't—her old image was going to keep making headaches for him and it'd been only twenty-four hours since he'd met her.

But that didn't change things.

And yet it changed everything.

The phone chimed again. And again. Different chimes. It sounded as though Byron had pulled his stunt.

"I've got to go bail out Byron," he told her. "But I'll see you soon." He got off the bed, trashed the condom and got dressed as fast as he could. By now his phone sounded like a bell choir.

"When?" She sat on the bed, her knees tucked up under her chin. Except for the part where she was completely nude—or maybe because of it—there was an air of vulnerability about her.

"Lunch, tomorrow. You've got to choose where you want to have the bachelorette party. I'll take you to all the places I've scouted out." He picked up his phone. Jeez, that was a lot of messages in less than five minutes. "What a mess," he muttered at his phone. "I'll get you at eleven—that'll give you time with Jo and it'll give me time to fix this."

He leaned down and gave her a quick, hard kiss. Then he was out the door.

He knew he shouldn't be surprised that Phillip was standing in the living room—this was his house, after all—but the last thing Matthew needed right now was to be confronted by his brother.

Phillip looked at him with a raised eyebrow. But instead

of asking about Whitney, he said, "Byron got picked up. He said to tell you he's sorry, but the black eye was unavoidable."

Matthew's shoulders sagged. His little brother had done exactly what he wanted him to—but damned if it didn't feel as though Matthew was suddenly right back at the bottom of the very big mountain he was doomed to be constantly climbing—Mount Beaumont. "What'd he do?"

"He went to a restaurant, ordered dinner, asked to see the chef and proceeded to get into a fistfight with the man."

Matthew rubbed the bridge of his nose. "And?"

"The media is reporting he ordered the salmon."

"Ha-ha. Very funny. I'll get him."

He was halfway to the door when Phillip said, "Everything okay with Whitney?"

"Fine," he shot back as he picked up the pace. He had to get out of here, fast.

But Phillip was faster. He caught up to Matthew at the door. "Better than yesterday?"

"Yes. Now, if you'll excuse me…"

Phillip grinned. "Never thought you had it in you, man. You always went for such…boring women."

"I don't know what you're talking about."

Denial—whether it was to the press or his family—came easily to Matthew. He had years of practice, after all.

"Right, right." He gave Matthew the smile that Matthew had long ago learned to hate—the one that said *I'm better than you are.* "Just a tip, though—from one Beaumont to another—always wipe the lipstick off *before* you leave the bedroom."

Matthew froze. Then he scrubbed the back of his hand across his mouth. It came away bright red.

Whitney's lipstick.

"Uh…this isn't what it looks like."

"Really? Because it looks like you spent the afternoon sleeping with the maid of honor." Matthew's fists curled, but

Phillip threw up his hands in self-defense. "Whatever, man. I'm not about to throw stones at your glass house. Say," he went on in a too-casual voice, "this wouldn't have anything to do with Byron telling me he'd done what you asked him to, would it? Except for the black eye, of course."

Matthew moved before he realized what he was doing. He grabbed Phillip by the front of his shirt. "Do. Not. Give. Her. Crap."

"Dude!" Phillip said, trying to peel Matthew's hands away from his shirt. "Down, boy—down!"

"Promise me, Phillip. After all the messes I cleaned up for you—all the times I saved your ass—*promise me* that you won't torture that woman. Or Byron won't be the only one with a black eye at this wedding."

"Easy, man—I'm not going to do anything."

Matthew let go of his brother. "Sorry."

"No, you're not. Go." Phillip pushed him toward the door. "Bail Byron out so we can all line up for your perfect family wedding. That's what you want, isn't it?"

As Matthew drove off, his mind was a jumble of wedding stuff and family stuff and Whitney. Zipping Whitney into the bridesmaid dress. Stripping her out of her clothes. Admiring her perfectly done hair. Messing her hair up.

He had to pull this wedding off. He had to stay on message. He had to prove he belonged up there with the other Beaumonts, standing by Phillip's side.

That was what Matthew wanted.

Wasn't it?

Ten

She checked her watch. Three to eleven. She'd gotten up at her regular time and gone out with Jo to look at the young mare she was working with. Jo hadn't pressed her about Matthew, except to say, "You and Matthew…" there'd been a rather long pause, but Whitney hadn't jumped into the breach "…do all right yesterday?" Jo had finally finished.

"Yeah. I think you were right about him—he seems like a good guy who's wound a bit too tight."

Which *had* to be the explanation as to why he'd tied her to the bed with a necktie.

Which did nothing to explain why she'd let him do it and explained even less why she'd enjoyed it.

And now? Now she was going to spend the afternoon with him again. Which was great—because it'd been so long since she'd had sex with another person and Matthew wasn't just up to the task—he was easily the best lover she'd ever had.

But it was also nerve-racking. After all, he'd tied her to the bed and made her climax several times. How was she supposed to look him in the eye after that? Yes, she'd slept around a lot when she'd been an out-of-control teenager trying to prove she was an adult. Yes, she'd had some crazy sex. The gossips never let her forget that.

But she'd never had that kind of sex clean and sober. She'd never had any kind of sex sober. She'd never looked a lover in the eye without some sort of chemical aid to cover up her anxiety at what she'd done, what she might still do.

And now, as she adjusted her hat and sunglasses, she was going to have to do just that. She had no idea what to do next. At least she had Betty—the small donkey's ears were soft, and rubbing them helped Whitney keep some sort of hold on her anxiety. It would be fine, she kept telling herself as she petted Betty. *It* will *be fine*.

At exactly eleven, Matthew walked through the door at Phillip and Jo's house, cupped her face in his hands and made her forget everything except the way she'd felt beneath his hands, his body. Beautiful. Sexy.

Alive.

"Hi," he breathed as he rested his forehead against hers.

Maybe this wouldn't be complicated. It hadn't seemed complicated when he'd pinned her to the wall yesterday. Maybe it would be…easy. She grinned, slipping her arms around his waist. "Hi." Then she looked at him. "You're wearing a tie?"

Color touched his cheeks, but he didn't look embarrassed. If anything, he looked the way he had yesterday—hungry for more. Hungry for her.

"I usually wear ties." Heat flushed down her back and pooled low. But instead of pulling that tie off, he added, "Are you ready?"

She nodded, unable to push back against the anxiety. This time, at least, it didn't have anything to do with him. "We have to go, right?"

He leaned back and adjusted her hat, making sure her hair was fully tucked under it. "We'll just look at the places. And after yesterday, I cut a couple of the other options off the list, so it's only four places. We'll park, go in, look at the menu and come back out. Okay?"

"What about lunch?" Because the going-in part hadn't been the problem yesterday.

"I decided we'll have lunch at my apartment."

She looked at him in surprise. "You decided, huh?"

Thus far, she hadn't actually managed to successfully make it through a meal with him. If they were alone at his place, would they eat or...?

He ran his thumb over her lower lip. "I did." Then Betty butted against his legs, demanding that he pet her, too. "You getting ready to walk down the aisle, girl?" he asked as he checked his phone. "We need to get going."

Despite the kiss that followed this statement—how was she going to make it to lunch without ripping his clothes off?—by the time they got into the car and were heading off the farm, she was back to feeling uneasy. She didn't normally fall into bed with a man she'd known for a day. Not since she'd started over.

Matthew had said he knew she was Whitney Maddox... but had he, really? He'd admitted having a huge crush on her back in the day.

"You're nervous," he announced when they were back on the highway, heading toward Denver.

She couldn't deny it. At least she'd made it into the car without stepping on him or anything. But she couldn't bring herself to admit that she was nervous about him. So she went with the other thing that was bothering her. "How's your brother—Byron?"

Matthew exhaled heavily. "He's fine. I got him bailed out. Our lawyers are working to get the charges dropped. But his black eye won't be gone by the wedding, so I had to add him to the makeup artist's list."

"Oh." He sounded extremely put out by this situation, but she was pretty sure he'd told his brother to do something dramatic. To bury her lead. She couldn't help but feel that, at the heart of it, this was her fault.

"The media took the bait, though. You didn't even make the website for the *Denver Post*. Who could pass up the chance to dig up dirt on the Beaumont Prodigal Son Returned? That's the headline the *Post* went with this morning. It's already been picked up by *Gawker* and *TMZ*."

She felt even worse. That wasn't the message Matthew wanted. She was sure that this was exactly what he'd wanted to avoid.

"You're quiet again," he said. He reached over and rubbed her thigh. "This isn't your fault."

The touch was reassuring. "But you're off message. Byron getting arrested isn't rehabilitating the Beaumont family image."

"I know." He exhaled heavily again. "But I can fix this. It's what I do. There's no such thing as bad PR."

Okay, that was another question that she didn't have an answer to. "Why? Why is *that* what you do?"

Matthew pulled his hand back and started drumming his fingers against the steering wheel. "How much do you know about the Beaumonts?"

"Um…well, you guys were a family beer company until recently. And Jo told me your father had a bunch of different children with four different wives and he had a lot of mistresses. And he forgot about your sister and brother's birthday."

"Did Jo say anything else?"

"Just that you'd threatened all the ex-wives to be on their best behavior."

"I did, you know." He chuckled again, but there was at least a little humor in it this time. "I told them if they caused a scene, I'd make an example out of them. No one's hands are clean in this family. I've buried too many scandals." He shot her an all-knowing grin. "They won't risk pissing me off. They know what I could do to them."

She let that series of ominous statements sink in. Suddenly, she felt as if she was facing the man who'd caught her the first night—the man who'd bury her if he got the chance.

But that wasn't the man who'd made love to her last night—was it? Had he offered his brother up as bait to protect her…or because that was still an easier mess to clean up than the one she'd make?

"Are your hands clean?"

"What?"

"You said no one's hands in your family are clean. Does that include you?"

His jaw tensed, and he looked at her again. He didn't say it, but she could tell what he was thinking. Not anymore. Not since he tied her to the bed.

Just then his phone chimed. He glanced down at the screen before announcing, "We need to keep to the schedule."

Right. They weren't going to talk about him right now.

He obviously knew a great deal about her past, but what did she know about him? He was a Beaumont, but he was behind the scenes, keeping everyone on message and burying leads.

"We're here," he announced after a few more minutes of driving. She nodded and braced herself for the worst.

The restaurant seemed overdone—white walls, white chairs, white carpet and what was probably supposed to be avant-garde art done in shades of black on the wall. A white tree with white ornaments stood near the front. It was the most depressing Christmas tree Whitney had ever seen. If a restaurant was capable of trying too hard, this one was. Whitney knew that Jo would be miserable in a place like this.

"Seriously?" she whispered to Matthew after reading the menu. Most of it was in French. She had no idea what kind of food they served here, only that it would be snooty.

"One of the best restaurants in the state," he assured her.

Then they went to a smaller restaurant with only six tables

that had a menu full of locally grown microgreens and other items that Whitney wasn't entirely sure qualified as food. Honest to God, one of the items touted a kind of tree bark.

"How well do you even know Jo?" she asked Matthew as they sped away from the hipster spot. "I mean, really. She's a cowgirl, for crying out loud. She likes burgers and fries."

"It's a nice restaurant," he defended. "I've taken dates there."

"Oh? And you're still seeing those women, are you?"

Matthew shot her a comically mean look.

She giggled at him. This was nice. Comfortable. Plus, she hadn't had to take her hat or sunglasses off, so no one had even looked twice at her. "Gosh, maybe it was your pretentious taste in dining, huh?"

"Careful," he said, trying to sound serious. The grin, however, completely undermined him. "Or I'll get my revenge on you later."

All that glorious heat wrapped around the base of her spine, radiating outward. What was he offering? And more to the point—would she take him up on it this time?

Still, she didn't want to come off as naive. "Promises, promises. Do either of the remaining places serve real food?"

"One." His phone chimed again. "Hang on." He answered it. "Yes? Yes, we're on our way. Yes. That's correct. Thanks."

"*We're* on our way?"

That got her another grin, but this one was less humorous, hungrier. "You'll see."

After a few more minutes, they arrived at their destination. It wasn't so much a restaurant but a pub. Actually, that was its name—the Pub. Instead of the prissiness of the first two places, this was all warm wood and polished brass. "A bar?"

"A pub," he corrected her. "I know Jo doesn't drink, so I was trying to avoid places that had a bar feel to them. But if I left it up to Frances, she'd have you all down at a male strip club, shoving twenties into G-strings."

Realization smacked her upside the head. This wasn't about her or even Jo—this whole search for a place to have a bachelorette party was about managing his sister's image. "You were trying to put us in places that would look good in the society page."

His mouth opened, but then he shut it with a sheepish look. "You're right."

The hostess came forward. "Mr. Beaumont, one moment and I'll get your order."

"Wait, what?"

He turned to her and grinned. "I promised you lunch." He handed her a menu. "Here you go."

"But…you already ordered."

"For the bachelorette party," he said, tipping the menu toward her.

She looked it over. There were a few oddities—microgreens, again!—but although the burgers were touted as being locally raised and organic, they were still burgers. With fries.

"In the back," Matthew explained while they were waiting, "they have a more private room." He leaned down so that his mouth was right by her ear. "It's perfect, don't you think?"

Heat flushed her neck. She certainly hadn't expected Denver at Christmas to be this…warming. "You knew I was going to pick this place, didn't you?"

"Actually, I reserved rooms in all four restaurants. There'll be people looking to stalk the wedding party no matter what. And since we've been seen going over the menu at three of the places, they won't know where to start. This will throw them off the trail."

She gaped at him. *That* was what covering your bases looked like. She'd never been able to plan like that. Which was why she was never ready for the press.

"Really? I can't decide if that's the most paranoid thing I've ever heard or the most brilliant."

He grinned, brushing his fingers over her cheek. "You can't be too careful."

He was going to kiss her. In public. She, more than anyone, knew what a bad idea that was. But she was powerless to stop him, to pull away. Something about this man destroyed her common sense.

The hostess saved Whitney from herself. "Your order, Mr. Beaumont."

"Thank you. And we have the private room for Friday night?"

"Yes, Mr. Beaumont."

Matthew grabbed the bagged food. "Come on. My place isn't too far away."

Matthew pulled into the underground parking lot at the Acoma apartments. He'd guessed right about the Pub, which was a good feeling. And after Whitney's observations about burgers and fries, he felt even better about ordering her that for lunch.

But best of all was the feeling of taking Whitney to his apartment. He didn't bring women home very often. He'd had a couple of dates that turned out to be looking for a story to tell—and sell. Keeping his address private was an excellent way to make sure that he wouldn't get up in the morning and find paparazzi parked outside the building, ready to catch his date leaving his place in the same outfit she'd had on the night before.

He wasn't worried about that happening with Whitney. First off, he had no plans of keeping her here all night long—although that realization left him feeling strangely disappointed. But second?

As far as he could tell, no one had made him as the man sitting next to Whitney Wildz the other day. Frankly, he couldn't believe it—it wasn't as if he were an unknown quantity. He talked to the press and his face was more than recognizable as a Beaumont.

Still, it was a bit of grace he was willing to use as he led Whitney to the elevator that went up to the penthouse apartment.

Inside, he pressed her back against the wall and kissed her hungrily. Lunch could wait, right?

Then she moaned into his mouth, and his body responded. He'd wanted to do this since he'd walked into Phillip's house this morning—show her that he could be spontaneous, that he could give her more than just one afternoon. He wanted to show her that there was more to him than the Beaumont name.

Even as the thought crossed his mind, the unfamiliarity of it struck him as…wrong. Hadn't it *always* been about the Beaumont name?

"Oh, Matthew," she whispered against his skin.

Yeah, lunch could wait.

Then the doors opened. "Come on," he said, pulling her out of the elevator and into his penthouse.

He wanted to go directly to the bedroom—but Whitney pulled up short. "Wow. This is…perfect."

"Thanks." He let go of her long enough to set the lunch bag down on a counter. But before he could wrap his arms around her again, she'd walked farther in—not toward the floor-to-ceiling windows but toward the far side of the sitting room.

The one with his pictures.

As Whitney stared at the Wall of Accomplishments, as he thought of it, something Phillip had said last night came back to him. *You always went for such boring women.*

They hadn't been boring. They'd been *safe*. On paper, at least, they'd been perfect. Businesswomen who had no interest in marrying into the Beaumont fortune because they had their own money. Quiet women who had no interest in scoring an invite to the latest Beaumont Brewery blowout because they didn't drink beer.

Women who wouldn't make a splash in the society pages.

Whitney? She was already making waves in his life—waves he couldn't control. And he was enjoying it. Craving more. Craving *her*.

"This…" Whitney said, leaning up on her tiptoes to look at the large framed photo that was at the center of the Wall of Accomplishments. "This is a wedding photo."

Eleven

"Yes. That's my parents' wedding."

The tension in his voice was unmistakable.

"But you're in the picture. That's you, right? And the boy you're standing next to—that's Phillip? Is the other one Chadwick?" The confusion pushed back at the desire that was licking through her veins. She couldn't make sense out of what she was looking at.

"That's correct." He sounded as if he were confirming a news story.

"But…you're, like, five or something? You're a kid!"

A tight silence followed this statement. She might have crossed some line, but she didn't care. She was busy staring at the photo.

A man—Hardwick Beaumont—was in a very nice tuxedo. He stood next to a woman in an exceptionally poofy white dress that practically dripped crystals and pearls. She had giant teased red hair that wasn't contained at all by the headband that came to a V-point in the middle of her forehead. The look spoke volumes about the high style of the early '80s.

In front of them stood three boys, all in matching tuxedos. Hardwick had his hand on Chadwick's shoulder. Next to Chadwick stood a smaller boy with blond hair. He wore a wicked grin, like a sprite out to stir up trouble. And standing in front of the woman was Matthew. She had her hand on his shoulder as she beamed at the camera, but Matthew looked as though someone were jabbing him with a hatpin.

When he did speak, he asked, "You didn't know that I wasn't born a Beaumont?"

She turned to stare at him. "What? No—what does that mean?"

He nodded, nearly the same look on his face now that little-kid Matthew had worn for that picture. "Phillip is only six months older than I am."

"Really?"

He came to stand next to her, one arm around her waist. She leaned into him, enjoying this comfortable touch. Enjoying that he wasn't holding himself apart from her.

"It was a huge scandal at the time—even by Beaumont standards. My mother was his mistress while he was still married to Eliza—that's Phillip and Chadwick's mother." He paused, as if he were steeling himself to the truth. "Eliza didn't divorce him for another four years. I was born Matthew Billings."

"Wait—you didn't grow up with your dad?"

"Not until I was almost five. Eliza found out about me and divorced Hardwick. He kept custody of Chadwick and Phillip, married my mom and moved us into the Beaumont mansion."

She stared at him, then back at the small boy in the photo. *Matthew Billings.* "But you and Phillip seem so close. You're planning his wedding. I just thought…"

"That we'd grown up together? No." He laughed, a joyless noise. "I remember her telling me how I'd have my daddy and he'd love me, and I'd have some brothers who'd play with me, so I shouldn't be sad that we were leaving everything behind. She told me it was going to be perfect. Just…perfect."

The way he said it made it pretty clear that it wasn't. Was this why everything had to be *just so*? He'd spent his life chasing a dream of perfection?

"What happened?"

He snorted. "What do you think? Chadwick hated me—deeply and completely. Sometimes Phillip was nice to me because he was lonely, too." He pointed at the wedding photo. "Sometimes he and Chadwick would gang up on me because I wasn't a real Beaumont. Plus, my mom got pregnant with Frances and Byron almost immediately and once they were born...well, they were Beaumonts without question." He sighed.

His dad had forgotten about him. That was basically what Jo had said Hardwick Beaumont did—all those wives, mistresses and so many children that they didn't even know how many there were. What a legacy. "So how did you wind up as the one who takes care of everyone else?"

He moved, stepping back and wrapping both arms around her. "I had to prove I belonged—that I was a legitimate Beaumont, not a Billings." He lowered his head so that his lips rested against the base of her neck.

She would not let him distract her with something as simple, as perfect, as a kiss. Not when the key to understanding *why* was right in front of her.

"How did you do that?"

His arms were strong and warm around her as they pulled her back into his chest. All of his muscles pressed against her. and for a moment she wondered if he was going to push her against the wall and make her cry out his name again, just to avoid answering the question.

But then he said, "I copied Chadwick. I got all As, just like Chadwick did. I went to the same college, got the same MBA. I got a job at the Brewery, just like Chadwick. He was the perfect Beaumont—still is, in a lot of ways. I thought—It sounds stupid now, but I thought if I could just *be* the perfect Beaumont, my mom would stop crying in her closet and we'd be a happy family."

"Did it work?" Although she already knew the answer to that one.

"Not really." His arms tightened around her, and he splayed his fingers over her ribs in an intimate touch. She leaned into him, as if she could tell him that she was here for him. That he didn't have to be perfect for her.

"When Frances and Byron were four, my parents got divorced. Mom tried to get custody of us, but without Beaumont money, she had nothing and Hardwick's lawyers were ruthless. I was ten."

"Do you still see her?"

"Of course. She's my mother, after all. She works in a library now. It doesn't pay all of her bills, but she enjoys it. I take care of everything else." He sighed against her skin, his hands skimming over her waist. "She apologized once. Said she was sorry she'd ruined my life by marrying my father."

"Do you feel the same way?"

He made a big show of looking around his stunning apartment. "I don't really think this qualifies as 'ruined,' do you?"

"It looks perfect," she agreed. But then, so did the wedding photo. One big happy family.

"Yeah, well, if there's one thing being a Beaumont has taught me, it's that looks are everything. Like when a jealous husband caught Dad with his wife. There was a scene—well, that's putting it mildly. I was in college and walked out of my apartment one morning and into this throng of reporters and photographers and they were demanding a good reaction quote from me—they wanted something juicy, you know?"

"I know." God, it was like reliving her own personal hell all over again. She could see the paparazzi jostling for position, shouting horrible things.

"I didn't know anything about what had happened, so I just started…making stuff up." He sounded as if he still didn't believe he'd done that. "The photos had been doctored. People would do anything for attention, including lay a trap for the richest man in Denver—and we would be suing for libel. The family would support Hardwick because he was right. And the press—they took the bait. Swallowed it hook, line and sinker. I saved his image." His voice trailed off. "He was proud of me. He told me, 'That's how a Beaumont handles it.' Told me to keep taking care of the family and it'd be just fine."

"Was it?"

"Of course not. His third wife left him—but he bought her off. He always bought them off and kept custody of the kids because it was good for his image as a devoted family man who just had really lousy luck when it came to women. But I'd handled myself so well that when a position in the Brewery public relations department opened up, I got the job."

He'd gone to work for his brother after that unhappy childhood. She wasn't sure she could be that big of a person. "Do your brothers still hate you?"

He laughed. "Hell, no. I'm too valuable to them. I've gotten Phillip out of more trouble than he even remembers and Chadwick counts me as one of his most trusted advisors. I'm…" He swallowed. "I'm one of them now. A legitimate Beaumont—the brother of honor at the wedding, even. Not a bastard that married into the family five years too late." He nuzzled at the base of her neck. "I just… I wish I'd known it would all work out when I was a kid, you know?"

She knew. She still wished she knew it would all work out. Somehow. "You know what I was doing when I was five?"

"What?"

"Auditions. My mother was dragging me to tryouts for commercials," she whispered into the silence. "I didn't care about acting. I just wanted to ride horses and color, but she wanted me to be famous. *She* wanted to be famous."

She'd never understood what Jade Maddox got out of it,

putting Whitney in front of all those people so she could pretend she was someone else. Hadn't just being herself been enough for her mother?

But the answer had been no. Always no. "My first real part was on *Larry the Llama*—remember that show? I was Lulu."

Behind her, Matthew stilled. Then, suddenly, he was laughing. The joy spilled out of him and surrounded her, making her smile with him. "You were on the llama show? That show was terrible!"

"Oh, I know it. Llamas are *weird*. Apparently everyone agreed because it was canceled about six months later. I'd hoped that was the end of my mother's ambitions. But it wasn't. I *dreamed* about having brothers or sisters. I didn't even meet my dad until I became famous, and then he just asked for money. Jade's the one who pushed me to audition for *Growing Up Wildz*, who pushed them to make the character's name Whitney."

His eyebrows jumped. "It wasn't supposed to be Whitney?"

"Wendy." She gave him a little grin. "It was supposed to be Wendy Wildz."

"Wow. That's just…" he chuckled. "That's just wrong. Sorry."

"It is. And I went along with it. I thought it'd be cool to have the same name as the character. I had no idea then it'd be the biggest mistake of my life—that I'd never be able to get away from Whitney Wildz."

He spun her around and gazed into her eyes. "That's not who you are to me. You know that, right?"

She did know. She was pretty sure, anyway. "Yes."

But then his mouth crooked back into a smile. "But… Lulu?"

"Hey, it was a great show about a talking llama!" she shot

back, unable to fight back the giggle. "Are you criticizing quality children's programming written by adults on drugs?"

"What was it ol' Larry used to say? 'It's Llama Time!' And then he'd spit?" He tried to tickle her.

She grabbed his hands. "Are you mocking llamas? They're majestic animals!"

He tested her grip, but she didn't let go. Suddenly, he wasn't laughing anymore and she wasn't, either.

She found herself staring at his tie. It was light purple today, with lime-green paisley amoebas swimming around on it. Somehow, it looked good with the bright blue shirt he was wearing. Maybe that was because he was wearing it.

He leaned down, letting his lips brush over her forehead, her cheek. "What are you going to do?" he asked, his voice husky. "Tie me up? For making fun of a llama?"

Could she *do* that? It'd been one thing to let him bind her wrists in a silk necktie yesterday. He'd been in control then—because she'd wanted him to be. She'd wanted him to make the decisions. She'd wanted to be consumed.

But today was different. She didn't want to be consumed. She wanted to do the consuming.

She pushed him back and grabbed his tie, then hauled his face down to hers. "I won't stand for you disparaging llamas."

"We could sit." He nodded toward a huge dining-room table, complete with twelve very available chairs surrounding it. The chairs had high backs and latticed slats. But he didn't pull his tie away from her hand, didn't try to touch her. "If you want to."

"Oh, I want to, mister. No one gets away with trash-talking *Larry the Llama*." She jerked on his tie and led him toward the closest chair.

"Larry was ridiculous," Matthew said as she pushed him down.

"You're going to regret saying that." She yanked his tie

off. It still had the knot in it, but she didn't want to stop to undo it. She didn't want to stop and think about what she was doing.

"Will I?" He held his hands behind his back.

"Oh, you will." She had no idea how to tie a man up in the best of times. So she looped the tie around his wrists and tried to tie it to the slat that was at the correct height. "There. That'll teach you."

"Will it?" Matthew replied. "Llamas look like they borrowed their necks from gira—"

She kissed him, hard. He shifted, as if he wanted to touch her, but she'd tied him to a chair.

She could do whatever she wanted, and he couldn't stop her.

Sexy. Beautiful. Desirable. That was what she wanted.

She stepped away from him and began to strip. Not like yesterday, when she'd been trying to get out of her clothes so fast she'd kicked him. No, this time—at a safe distance—she began to remove her clothing slowly.

First she peeled her sweater over her head, then she started undoing the buttons on her denim shirt—slowly. One at a time.

Matthew didn't say anything, not even to disparage llamas.

Instead, Matthew's gaze was fastened to Whitney's fingertips as one button after another gave.

A look of disappointment blotted out the desire when he saw the plain white tank top underneath.

"It's cold here," she told him. "You're supposed to dress in layers when it's cold."

"Did the llamas tell you that? They lie. You should be naked. Right now."

She was halfway through removing her tank top when he said that. She went ahead and pulled it the rest of the way off, but said, "Just for that, I'm not going to get naked."

His eyes widened in shock. "What?"

She stuck her hands on her hips, which had the handy effect of thrusting her breasts forward. "And you can't touch me, because you're tied up." Just saying it out loud gave her a little thrill of power.

For too damn long, she'd felt powerless. The only way she'd been able to control her own life was to become a hermit, basically—just her and the animals and crazy Donald up the valley. People took what they wanted from her—including deciding who she was—and they never gave her any say in the matter.

Not Matthew. He'd let her do whatever she wanted—be whoever she wanted.

She could be herself—klutzy and concerned about her animals—and he still looked at her with that hunger in his eyes.

She kicked off her boots and undid her jeans. Miracle of miracles, she managed to slide them off without tipping over and falling onto the floor.

Matthew's eyes lit up with want. With *need*. She could see him breathing faster now, leaning forward as if he could touch her. Heat flooded her body—almost enough to make up for the near-nudity. She felt sexy. Except for the socks.

Well, she'd already told him she wasn't going to get naked. Although she was having a little trouble remembering why, exactly.

Plus, he was sitting there fully clothed. And she didn't know where any condoms were. "Condoms?" They were required. She'd been accused of being falsely pregnant far too many times to actually risk a real pregnancy. The last thing she needed in her life were more headlines asking, Wildz Baby Daddy?

"Wallet." The tension in his voice set her pulse racing. "Left side."

"You just want me to touch you, don't you?"

He grinned. "That is the general idea. Since you won't let me touch you."

"I stand for llama solidarity," she replied as she walked toward him. "And until you can see reason..."

"Oh, I can't. No reason at all. Llamas are nature's mistake."

"Then you'll just have to stay tied up." She straddled him, but she didn't rest her weight on his obvious erection. Instead, she slid her hands over his waist and down around to his backside until she felt his wallet. She fished it out, dropped it onto the table and then ran her hands over him again. "I didn't really get to feel all of this last time," she told him.

"You were a little tied up."

She ran her hands over his shoulders, down his pecs, feeling the muscles that were barely contained by the button-down shirt and cashmere sweater. Then she leaned back so she could slide her hands down and feel what was behind those tweed slacks.

Matthew sucked in a breath so hot she felt it scorch her cheek as she touched the length of his erection. He leaned forward and tried to kiss her, but she pulled away, keeping just out of his reach. "Llama hater," she hissed at him.

"You're killing me," he ground out as he tried to thrust against her hand.

"Ah-ah-ah," she scolded. This was...*amazing.* She knew that, if he wanted to, he could probably get out of the tie and wrap her in his arms and take what she was teasing him with. And she'd let him because, all silliness aside, she wanted him *so* much.

But he wasn't. He wouldn't, because she was in control. She had all the power here.

Tension coiled around the base of her spine, tightening her muscles beyond a level that was comfortable. She let her body fall against his, let the contact between them grow.

"Woman," Matthew groaned.

She tsked him as she slid off. "You act like you've never been tied up before."

"I haven't." His gaze was fastened to her body again. She felt bold enough to strike a pose, which drew another low groan from him.

"You...haven't?"

"No. Never tied anyone up before, either." He managed to drag his gaze up to her face. "Have you?"

"No." She looked at him, trying to keep her cool. He hadn't done this before? But he'd seemed so sure of himself last night. It wasn't as though she expected a man as hot and skilled as he was to be virginal, but there was something about being the first woman he'd wrapped his necktie around—something about her being the first woman he'd let tie him to a chair—that changed things.

No. No! This was just a little fling! Just her dipping her sexual toes back in the sexy waters! This was not about developing new, deeper feelings for Matthew Beaumont!

She snagged the condom off the table. "I demand an apology on behalf of Larry the Llama and llamas everywhere." Then—just because she could—she dropped the condom and bent over to pick it up.

He sucked in another breath at the sight she was giving him. "I beg of your forgiveness, Ms. Maddox." She shifted. *"Please,"* he added, sounding desperate. "Please forgive me. I'll never impugn the honor of llamas again."

Ms. Maddox.

She needed him. Now.

She slid her panties off but kept the bra on. She undid his trousers and got them down far enough that she could roll the condom on. Then, unable to wait any longer, she let her body fall onto his.

She grabbed his face and held it so she could look into his eyes. "Matthew..."

But he was driving up into her and she was grinding down onto him and there wasn't time for more words. They had so very little time to begin with.

"Want to…kiss you," Matthew got out, each word punctuated with another thrust.

His clothing was rubbing against her, warming her bare skin. Warming everything. "Kiss me back?" she asked, knowing what the answer would be.

"Always," he replied as she lowered her lips to his. "Always."

Always. Not just right now but always.

She came apart when their lips met, and he came with her.

She lay on top of him, feeling the climax ebb from her body. It was then that she wished she hadn't tied him up, because she wanted him to hold her.

"I had no idea that llamas got you so worked up," he told her as his lips trailed over her bare shoulder. "I'll make a mental note of it."

She leaned back and grinned at him. "Was that okay? I didn't hurt you or anything—? Oh! I should untie you!"

"Uh—wait—" he said, but she was already at the back of the chair.

The tie lay in a heap on the ground. Not around his wrists. Not tied to the chair. She blinked at the puddle of bright fabric. Confusion swamped her. "When— Wait—if you weren't tied up, why didn't you touch me?"

He stood and adjusted his pants before turning around. He was, for all intents and purposes, the same as he'd been before, minus one necktie. And she was standing here in her socks and a bra. She couldn't even tie a man up.

"Why didn't you touch me?" she asked again.

He came to her then, wrapping his arms around her and holding her tight to him. "Because," he said, his lips pressing against her forehead, "you tied me up. It was kind of like…making a promise, that you were in charge. I keep my promises."

"Oh," she breathed. People didn't often keep promises, not to her. Her mother hadn't protected her, hadn't managed

her money. Her former fiancé hadn't kept a single promise to her.

She had crazy Donald, who didn't know who she was, and…Jo, who'd promised that she wouldn't tell anyone about the months she'd spent with Whitney, wouldn't tell a living soul where Whitney lived.

And now Matthew was promising to follow her wishes.

She didn't know what to make of this.

From somewhere far away, his phone chimed. "Our lunch is probably ice-cold," he said without letting her go or answering his phone.

At the mention of the word *cold*, she shivered. She was mostly naked, after all. "We haven't had a successful meal yet."

The phone chimed again. It seemed louder—more insistent. "I need to deal with some things. But if you want to hang out for a bit, I can take you home and we can try to have dinner out at the farm?"

"I'd like that."

"Yeah," he agreed, brushing his lips over hers as his phone chimed again and again. "So would I."

Twelve

It was a hell of a mess. And what made it worse was that it was self-inflicted. He'd made this bed. Now he had to lie in it.

Matthew tried to focus on defusing the situation—which wasn't easy, given that Whitney was exploring his apartment. Normally, he didn't mind showing off his place. It was opulent by any normal standard—truly befitting a Beaumont.

But now? What would she see when she looked at his custom decorating scheme? Would she see the very best that money could buy or…would she see something else?

None of the other women he'd brought back here had ever focused on his parents' wedding picture. They might have made a passing comment about how cute he was as a kid, but the other women always wanted to know what it was like being Phillip's brother or meeting this actor or that singer. They wanted to know how awesome it was to be one of the famous Beaumont men.

Not Whitney. She already knew what fame felt like. And she'd walked away from it. She didn't need it. She didn't need other people's approval.

What must she think of him, that he *did* need it? That he had to have the trappings of wealth and power—that he had to prove he was not just *a* Beaumont but the best one?

Focus. He had a job to do—a job that paid for the apartment and the cars and, yes, the ties. Matthew didn't know why Byron had gone after that chef. His gut told him there was a history there, but he didn't know what it was and Byron wasn't talking.

So Matthew did what he always did. He massaged the truth.

He lied.

The other guy had swung first. All Byron had done was complain about an underdone salmon steak, and the chef took it personally. Byron was merely defending himself. So what if that wasn't what the police report said? As long as Matthew kept repeating his version of events—and questioning the motives of anyone who disagreed with him—sooner or later, his reality would replace the true events.

"What's in here?" Whitney called out. Normally, he didn't like people in general and women in particular to explore his space on their own. He kept his apartment spotless, so it wasn't that. He liked to explain how he'd decided on the decorating scheme, why the Italian marble was really the only choice, how a television that large was really worth it. He liked to manage the message of his apartment.

He liked to manage the people in his apartment.

However, Whitney was being so damned adorable he couldn't help but smile.

"Where?" he shouted back.

"Here— Oh! That's a *really* big TV!"

He chuckled. "You're in the theater room!"

"Wow…" Her voice trailed off.

He knew that in another five minutes they'd have almost the exact same conversation all over again.

Matthew realized he was humming as he gave his official Beaumont response to the "unfortunate" situation again and again. Byron was merely noting his displeasure with an undercooked dish. The Beaumonts were glad the cops were called so they could get this mess straightened out. They would have their day in court.

Then a new email popped up—this one wasn't from a journalist but from Harper, his father's nemesis.

"Thank you for inviting us to the reception of Phillip Beaumont and bride at the last second, but sadly, no one in the Harper family has the least interest in celebrating such an occasion."

The old goat hadn't even bothered to sign the kiss-off. Nice.

Normally, it would have bothered Matthew. Maybe it did, a little. But then Whitney called out, "You have your own gym? Really?"

And just like that, Matthew didn't care about Harper.

"Really!" he called back. He sent off a short reply stating how very much Harper would be missed—Hardwick Beaumont had always counted him as a friend. Which was another bold-faced lie—the two men had hated each other from the moment Hardwick had seduced Harper's first wife less than a month after Harper had married her. But Harper wasn't the only one who could write a kiss-off.

Speaking of kissing...Matthew checked the weather, closed his computer and went looking for Whitney. She was standing in his bathroom, of all places, staring at the wide-open shower and the in-set tub. "It's just you, right? Even the bathroom is monster huge!"

"Just me. You need to make a decision."

Her eyes grew wide. "About what?"

He brushed his fingers through her hair. It'd gotten mussed up when she'd stripped for him. He liked it better that way. "The weather might turn later tonight. If you want to go back to the farm, we'll need to leave soon."

One corner of her mouth curved up. "*If*? What's the other option?"

"You are more than welcome to stay here with me." He looked around his bathroom. "I have plenty of room. And

then I could show you how the shower works. And the bath."
He'd like to see that—her body wet as he soaped her up.

She gave him a look that was part innocence, part sheer
seduction. A look that said she might like to be soaped up—
but the thought scared her, as well. "I don't have any of my
things…"

He nodded in agreement. Besides, he tried to reason with
himself, just because there hadn't been paparazzi waiting for
them when they got to the building didn't mean that there
wouldn't be people out there in the morning. And the last
thing he needed right now was someone to see him and the
former Whitney Wildz doing the walk of shame.

"Besides," she went on, looking surprisingly stern, "it's
Christmas—almost, anyway—and you don't even have a
tree. Why don't you have a tree? I mean, this place is amazing—but no tree? Not a single decoration? Really?"

He brushed his fingertips over her cheeks again. He didn't
normally celebrate Christmas here. "I spend Christmas night
with my mom. If they're in town, Frances and Byron come
by. She always has stockings filled with cheesy gifts like
yo-yos and mixes for party dips. She has a small tree and
a roasted turkey breast and boxed mashed potatoes—not
high cuisine by any stretch." He wouldn't dare admit that
to anyone else.

Christmas night was the one night of the year when he
didn't feel like Matthew Beaumont. Back in Mom's small
apartment, cluttered with photos of him and her and Frances and Byron—but never Hardwick Beaumont—Matthew
felt almost as if he were still Matthew Billings.

It was a glimpse into the past—one that he occasionally let himself get nostalgic about, but it never lasted very
long. Then, after he gave his mother the present he'd picked
out for her—something that she could use but a nicer version than she could afford herself—he'd kiss her goodbye
and come back to this world. His world. The world where
he would never admit to being Matthew Billings. Not even
for an afternoon.

Except he'd just admitted it to Whitney. And instead of the clawing defensiveness he usually felt whenever anyone brought up the Billings name, he felt...lighter.

Whitney gave him a scolding look. "It sounds lovely. I watch *It's a Wonderful Life* and share a ham with Gater and Fifi. I usually bring carrots to the horses, that sort of thing." She sighed, leaning into his arms. "I miss having someone to celebrate with. That's why I came to this wedding. I mean, I came for Jo, but..."

"Tell you what—we'll head back to the farm now, because it looks all Christmassy, and then—" his mouth was moving before he realized what he was saying "—then after the wedding, maybe we can spend part of Christmas together before you go home?"

"I'd like that." Her cheeks flushed with warmth. "But I don't have a present for you."

He couldn't resist. "You are the only present I want. Maybe even tied up with a bow...." He gathered her into his arms and pressed her back against the tiled wall with a rather heated kiss.

Several minutes passed before she was able to ask, "Are you done with your work?"

"For now, yes." Later he'd have to log back in and launch another round of damage control. But he could take a few hours to focus on Whitney. "Let me take you home."

She giggled. "I don't think I have much of a choice in that, do I? My truck's still out on the farm." A look of concern crossed her face. "Can you drive your car in the snow?"

"I'm a Beaumont," he said, his words echoing off the tiled walls of the bathroom. "I have more than one vehicle."

After a comfortable drive out to the farm in his Jeep, Whitney asked him if he'd stay for dinner. Jo had already set a place for him at the table and Phillip said, "Hang out, dude."

So, after a quick check of his messages to make sure that

nothing else had blown up, Matthew sat down to dinner—homemade fried chicken and mashed potatoes. Finally, over easy conversation about horses and celebrities, he and Whitney managed to successfully eat a meal together.

Then Jo said, "We're going to watch *Elf*, if you want to join us."

"I auditioned for that movie," Whitney said, leaning into him. "But I was, um, under the influence at the time and blew it pretty badly, so Zooey Deschanel got the part. It's still a really funny movie. I watch it every year."

Matthew looked at Phillip, who was pointedly not smiling at the way Matthew had wrapped his arm around Whitney's waist. "Sure," Matthew heard himself say. "It sounds like fun."

As the women popped popcorn and made hot chocolate, of all things, Phillip pulled him aside under the pretense of discussing the sound for the movie. "Who are you," he said under his breath, "and what have you done with my brother Matthew?"

"Shove it," Matthew whispered back. He didn't want to have this conversation. Not even with Phillip.

His brother did no such shoving. "Correct me if I'm wrong," he went on, "but weren't you on the verge of personally throwing her out of the wedding a few nights ago?"

"Shove. It."

"And yesterday—well, she's an attractive woman. I can't fault you for sleeping with her. But today?" Phillip shook his head, clearly enjoying himself. "Man, I don't think I've ever seen you be so…lovey-dovey."

Matthew sighed. He wanted to deck Phillip so badly, but the wedding was in a matter of days. "Lovey-dovey?"

"Affectionate. I can't remember the last time I've seen you touch a woman, outside of handshakes and photo ops. And you *never* just sit around and watch a movie. You're always working."

"I'll have to log back on in a few hours. I'm still working."

Phillip looked at him out of the corner of his eye. "You can't keep your hands off her."

Matthew shrugged, hoping he looked noncommittal. He touched women. He took lovers. He was a Beaumont—having affairs was his birthright.

Boring women, he remembered Phillip calling them yesterday. Women he took to stuffy restaurants and to their own place to bed them so no one would see that he'd had a guest overnight.

It wasn't that he wasn't affectionate. It was that he was careful. He had to be.

He wished Jo and Whitney would hurry the hell up with that popcorn. "I like her."

"Which her? The fallen star or the horse breeder?"

"The horse breeder. I like her."

Phillip clapped him on the shoulder. "Good answer, man. Good answer. The movie is ready, ladies," he added as Jo and Whitney made their way over to them.

Matthew hurried to take the full mugs of cocoa—complete with marshmallows—from Whitney. Then Jo produced blankets. She and Phillip curled up on one couch with the donkey sitting at their feet as they munched popcorn and laughed at the movie.

Which left him and Whitney with the other couch. He didn't give a rat's ass for the popcorn. He set his cocoa down where he could reach it, then patted the couch next to him. Whitney curled up against his side and pulled the blankets over them.

"Do you watch a lot of movies?" he asked in a quiet voice, his mouth against her ear.

"I do. I get up really early when it's warm—farmer's hours—and I'm pretty tired at night. Sometimes I read—I like romances." He could see the blush over her face when she said that, as if he'd begrudge her a happy ending. "It took a while before I could watch things like this and not think a bunch of what-ifs, you know?"

He wrapped his arms around her waist and lifted her onto his lap. Maybe Phillip was right. Maybe he wasn't normally affectionate with the women who came into his life. But he *had* to touch Whitney.

They watched the movie. Whitney and Jo had clearly watched it together before. They laughed and quoted the lines at each other and had little inside jokes. Matthew's phone buzzed a few times during the show, but he ignored it.

Phillip was right about one thing—when was the last time he'd taken a night off and just hung out? It'd been a while. Matthew tried to think—had he planned on taking a couple of days off after the wedding? No, not really. The wedding was the unofficial launch of Percheron Drafts, Chadwick's new craft beer. Matthew had a 30 percent stake in the company. They were building up to a big launch just in time for the Big Game in February. The push was going to be hard.

He'd made plans to have dinner with his mother. That was all the time he'd originally allotted for the holiday. But now? He could take a few days off. He didn't know when Whitney was heading back to California, but if she wanted to stick around, he would make time for her.

By the time the movie ended, he and Whitney were lying down, spooning under their blankets. He hadn't had any popcorn, and the cocoa was cold, but he didn't care. With her backside pressed against him, he was having a hard time thinking. Other things were also getting hard.

But there was a closeness that he hadn't anticipated. He liked just holding her.

"I should go," he said in her ear.

She sighed. "I wish you didn't have to."

Phillip and Jo managed to get untangled from their covers first. "Uh, Matthew?"

"Yeah?" He managed to push himself up into a sitting position without dumping Whitney on the floor.

"Icy."

"You see what?"

"No, icy—as in ice. On your car. And the driveways."

"Damn, really?" He waited long enough for Whitney to sit up. Then he walked to a window. Phillip was right. A glaze of ice coated everything. "The weather said snow. Not ice. Damn. I should have…"

"You're stuck out here, man." Phillip gave him a playful punch in the shoulder. "I know it'll be a real hardship, but you can't drive home on ice."

Matthew looked at Whitney. She'd come to stand next to him. "Ice…wow," she said in the same tone she'd used when she'd been exploring his apartment. "We don't get ice out in California. Not like this!" She slipped her hand into his and squeezed.

He could stay the night. One night wrapped up in Whitney and then he could fall asleep with her in his arms. Wake up with her there, too. He didn't do that often. Okay, he didn't ever do that.

Only one problem. "I didn't bring anything."

"We have guest supplies," Jo called out.

Phillip stood up straight and looked Matthew over. "Yeah, we probably still wear the same size."

"Stay," Whitney said in a voice that was meant only for him. "Stay with me. Just for the night. Call it…an early Christmas present."

It really wasn't an argument. He couldn't drive home on ice and honestly? He didn't want to. Suddenly he understood why Phillip had always preferred the farmhouse. It was warm and lived-in. If Matthew went back to his apartment—monster huge, as Whitney had noted, and completely devoid of holiday cheer—and Whitney wasn't there with him, the place would feel…empty.

Lonely.

It'd never bothered him before. But tonight he knew it would.

"I'll need to log on," he told everyone. "We still have a wedding to deal with."

"Of course," Jo said. She was smiling, but not at him. At Whitney. "You do what you need to do."

Matthew spent an hour answering the messages he'd ignored. Whitney had gone up to read so she wouldn't distract him from his work. He knew he was rushing, but the thought of her in his room again—well, that was enough to make a man hurry the hell up.

When he opened his door, the fire was blazing in the hearth, and Whitney was in bed. She looked…perfect. He couldn't even see Whitney Wildz when he looked at her anymore. She was just Whitney.

The woman he wanted. "I was waiting for you," she told him.

"I'll make it worth the wait." Then she lifted up the covers and he saw that she was nude.

Thank God for ice.

Thirteen

The day of the bachelorette party came fast. Whitney got to stay on the farm for a couple of days, which should have made her happy. She was able to work with Jo and some of the many horses on the farm—Appaloosas, Percherons and Sun, the Akhal-Teke. Phillip treated her like a close friend and the staff on the farm was the definition of discreet and polite at all times. They made cookies and watched holiday shows. Even the farm manager, an old hand named Richard, took to calling her Whit.

By all rights, it should have been everything she wanted. Quiet. Peaceful. Just her and a few friends and a bunch of horses. No cameras, no gossips, no anything having to do with Whitney Wildz. Except...

She missed Matthew.

And that wasn't like her. She didn't miss people. She didn't get close enough to people to miss them when they went.

Well, that wasn't true. She'd missed the easy friendship with Jo when Jo had hitched her trailer back up to her truck and driven on to the next job.

But now, after only two days without him, she missed Matthew. And she shouldn't. She just shouldn't. So he'd made love to her that night, rolling her onto her stomach to do things to her that *still* made her shiver with desire when she thought about them. And so she'd woken up in his arms the next morning and they'd made love so sweetly that she still couldn't believe she hadn't dreamed the whole thing.

How long had it been since she'd woken up with a man in bed? A long time. Even longer since the man in question had made love to her. Told her how beautiful she was, how good she was. How glad he was that he'd stayed with her.

It was a problem. A huge one. This was still a temporary thing, a Christmas fling that would end with the toss of the bridal bouquet. If she were lucky, she'd get Christmas morning with him. And that'd be it. If she missed Matthew now, after just a couple of good days, how bad off would she be when she went home? When she wouldn't have to wait another day to see him?

How much would she miss him when she wasn't going to see him again?

It'd hurt to watch him get into his car and slowly drive away. He'd offered to let her come with him, but she'd refused. She was here for Jo and, anyway, Matthew had things he needed to do. Weddings to manage, PR debacles to control. Just another reminder of how far apart their lives really were.

To her credit, Jo hadn't said much about the sudden relationship. Just, "Are you having a good time with Matthew?"

"I am," Whitney had said truthfully. Although *fun* seemed as if it wasn't strong enough of a word. Fun was a lovely day at an amusement park. Being with Matthew? It was amazing. That was all there was to it. He was *amazing*.

"Good." That was all Jo said about it.

Now, however, Whitney and Jo were driving in to the Pub to meet the other women in the wedding party. Matthew would be out with Phillip and all their brothers—bowling, of all things. Although Whitney wasn't sure if that was one of those fake activities Matthew had planned to keep the paparazzi guessing.

Whitney kept her hat on as the hostess showed them back to the private room. There were already several other women there, as well as a small buffet laid out with salads, burgers and fries. *Matthew*, Whitney thought with a smile as she took off her hat and sunglasses. Maybe he did know Jo better than she thought.

"Hi, all," Jo said. "Let me introduce—"

"*Oh, my God*, it's really you! You're Whitney Wildz!" A young woman with bright red hair came rushing up to Whitney. In the brief second before she grabbed Whitney by the shoulders, Whitney could see the unmistakable resemblance to both Matthew and Phillip—but especially Matthew. The red hair helped.

"You really *are* here! And you know Jo! *How* do you know Jo? I'm Frances Beaumont, by the way."

"Hi," Whitney tried out. She'd known this was going to happen—and today was certainly a more controlled situation than normal. She had Jo and there were only a few women in the room. But she'd never really mastered the proper response to rabid fans.

"Yes, as I was saying," Jo said in a firm voice as she pried Frances's hands off Whitney's shoulders, "this is Whitney Maddox. She's a horse breeder. I know her because we've worked horses together." She tried to steer Frances away from Whitney, but it didn't work.

"You're really *here*. Oh, my God, I know you probably have this happen all the time, but I was your *biggest* fan. I loved your show *so* much and one time Matthew took me to see you in concert." Before Whitney could dodge out of the way, Frances threw her arms around her and pulled Whitney into a massive hug. "I'm *so* glad to meet you. You have no idea."

"Um…" was all Whitney could get out as her lungs were crushed. Frances was surprisingly strong for her size. "I'm getting one."

"Frances," Jo said, the warning in her voice unmistakable. "Could you at least let Whitney get her coat off before you embarrass yourself and go all fangirl?"

"Right, right! Sorry!" Frances finally let go. "I'm just so excited!" She pulled out her cell phone. "Can I get a picture? Please?"

"Um..." Whitney looked around, but she found no help. Jo looked pissed and the other women were waiting for her to make a decision. She was on her own here. What would Matthew do? He'd manage the message.

"If you promise not to post it on social media until after the wedding." She smiled at how in control that sounded.

"Of course! I don't have to post it at all—this is just for me. You have *no* idea how awesome this is." She slung her arm around Whitney's shoulders and held the camera up overhead before snapping the selfie. "That is so awesome," she repeated as she approved the picture. "Can I send it to Byron and Matthew? We always used to watch your show together."

"I've already met him. Matthew, that is." Suddenly, she was blushing in an entirely different way. And there was no hiding from it, since everyone in the room was staring at her.

Another woman stood up. "You'll have to excuse Frannie," this woman said with a warm smile. She looked nothing like a Beaumont, but beyond that, she was holding a small baby that couldn't be more than a month old. "She's easily excitable. I'm Serena Beaumont, Chadwick's wife. It's delightful to meet you." She shifted the baby onto her shoulder and held out a hand.

"Whitney." She didn't have a lot of experience dealing with babies, but it had to be safer than another hug attack from Frances. "How old is your baby?"

"Six weeks." Serena smiled. She turned so that Jo and Whitney could see the tiny baby's face. "This is Catherine Beaumont."

"She's adorable." She was actually kind of wrinkly and still asleep, but Whitney had no other points of reference, so the baby was adorable by default.

"Her being pregnant made getting the bridesmaids' dresses a mess," Frances said with a dramatic roll of her eyes. "Such a pain."

"Said the woman who is not now, nor has ever been, pregnant," Serena said. But instead of backbiting, the whole conversation was one of gentle teasing. The women were clearly comfortable with each other.

Whitney was introduced to the rest of the women in attendance. There was Lucy Beaumont, a young woman with white-blond hair who did not seem exactly thrilled to be at the party. She left shortly after the introductions, claiming she had a migraine.

Whitney also met Toni Beaumont, who seemed almost as nervous as Whitney felt. "Toni's going to be singing a song at the wedding," Jo explained. "She's got a beautiful voice."

Toni blushed, looking even more awkward. She was considerably younger than the other Beaumonts Whitney had met. Whitney had to wonder if she was one of Hardwick Beaumont's last children? If so, did that make her…maybe twenty? She didn't get the chance to find out. Toni, too, bailed on the proceedings pretty quickly.

Then it was just Jo, Frances, Serena and Whitney—and a baby who was sleeping through the whole thing. "They seem…nice," Whitney ventured.

"Lucy doesn't really like us," Frances explained over the lip of her beer. She was the only one drinking. "Which happens in this family. Every time Dad married a new wife, the new one would bad-mouth the others. That's why Toni isn't comfortable around us, either. Her mom told her we were all out to get her."

"And," Serena added, giving Frances a sharp look, "if I understand correctly, you *were* out to get her when you were a kid."

Frances laughed. "Maybe," she said with a twinkle in her eye. "There might have been some incidents. But that was more between Lucy and Toni. I was too old to play with *babies* by that point. Besides, do you know how much crap Phillip used to give me? I swear, he'd put me on the meanest horse he could find just to watch me get bucked off and cry. But I showed him," she told Whitney. "I learned how to stay on and I don't cry."

Serena rolled her eyes and looked at Whitney. "It's a strange family."

Whitney nodded and smiled as if it were all good fun, but she remembered Matthew telling her how his older brothers used to blame him for, well, *everything*.

"Okay, yeah," Frances protested. "So we're all a little nuts. I mean, I'm never going to get married, not after having *that* many evil stepmothers. Never going to happen. But that's the legacy we were born into as Beaumonts—all except Matthew. He's the only one who was ever nice to all of us. That's why Lucy and Toni were here today—he asked them to come. Said it was important to the family, so they came. The only person who doesn't listen to him is Eliza, Chadwick and Phillip's mom. Everyone else does what he says. And seriously? That man not only wouldn't let me take you guys to the hottest club, but he wouldn't even let me hire a stripper." She scoffed while rolling her eyes, a practiced gesture of frustration. "He can be such a control freak. He probably even picked out your shoes or something."

There was a pause, and then both Frances and Serena turned to look at Whitney.

Heat flooded Whitney's cheeks. Matthew had, in fact, picked out her shoes. And her hairstyle. And her lipstick. Right before he'd mussed them all up. She wasn't about to argue the control-freak part. But then, he'd also let her tie him up. He'd kept up the illusion even though her knot hadn't held. Just so she could be in control.

"So," Frances said in a too-bright tone. "You *have* met Matthew."

"Yes." The one word seemed safer. She wasn't used to kissing and telling. Heck, she was still getting used to the kissing thing. She was absolutely not going to tell anyone about it.

"And?" Frances looked as if she were a lioness about to pounce on a wounded wildebeest.

Whitney hated being the wildebeest. "We're just working to make sure that the wedding goes smoothly. No distractions." She thought it best not to mention the shoes. Or the ties.

Serena nodded in appreciation, but Frances made a face of exasperation. "Seriously? He's had a huge crush on you for, like, forever! I bet he can barely keep his hands off you. And frankly, that man could stand to get distracted."

"Frannie!" Jo and Serena said at the same time. The baby startled and began to mew in tiny-baby cries.

"Sorry," Serena said, draping a blanket over her shoulder so she could nurse, Whitney guessed.

"Well, it's true! He's been driving us all nuts with this wedding, insisting it has to be perfect. Honestly," Frances said, turning her attention back to Whitney, "I'm not sure he ever just does something for fun. It'd be good for him, you know?"

Whitney was so warm she was on the verge of sweating. She thought of the way he'd ignored his phone while they cuddled on the couch, watching a Christmas movie. Was that fun?

"He had a crush on Whitney Wildz," she explained, hoping her face wasn't achieving a near-fatal level of blush. "That's not who I am."

They'd cleared that up before the clothes had started to come off. He knew that she was Whitney Maddox. He liked her for being her, not because she'd once played someone famous. End of discussion.

Except…Matthew was, in fact, having trouble keeping his hands off her. Off *her*, right? Not Whitney Wildz?

She didn't want the doubt that crept in with Frances's knowing smile. But there it was anyway. She couldn't be 100 percent sure that Matthew wasn't sleeping with Whitney Wildz, could she? Just because he'd called her Ms. Maddox a few times—was that really all the proof she needed?

"Sure," Frances said with a dismissive wave of her hand. "Of course."

"You're being obnoxious," Serena said. Then she added to Whitney, "Frances is good at that."

"I'm just being honest. Matthew's way too focused on making sure we all do what he thinks we should. This is a rare opportunity for him to do something for himself. Lord knows the man needs more fun in his life. You two should go out." She paused, a smile that looked way too familiar on her face. "If you haven't already."

This was it. After all these years, all those headlines and horrible pictures and vicious, untrue rumors, Whitney was finally going to die of actual embarrassment. She'd have thought she couldn't feel it this much anymore—that she was immune to it—but no. All it took was one affair with a Beaumont and an "honest" conversation with his little sister and *boom*. It was all over.

Jo sighed. "Are you done?"

"Maybe," Frances replied, looking quite pleased with herself.

"Because you know what Matthew's going to do to you when he finds out you're treating my best friend like this, don't you?"

At that, a look of concern managed to blot out Frances's satisfied smile. "Well…hey, I've been on my best behavior ever since you guys decided to get married. No headlines, no trouble. I leave that to Byron."

And Byron had gotten into trouble only because Matthew had asked him to. For her. There was a moment of silence, during which Whitney considered getting her coat and going. Except she couldn't leave without Jo. Damn it.

Then the silence was broken. "But what about—?" Serena said, joining the fray.

"Or the one time when you—" added Jo.

"Hey!" Frances yelped, her cheeks turning almost as red as her hair. "That's not fair!"

"We're just being honest," Serena said with a grin that bordered on mean.

Jo nodded in agreement, giving Whitney an encouraging grin. "What did Phillip tell me about that one guy? What did he call you? His Little Red—"

Frances's phone chimed. "Sorry, can't listen to you make fun of me. Must answer this very important text!" She read her message. "Byron says he can't believe that's really Whitney Wildz." She began to type a reply.

"What are you going to tell him?" Whitney asked.

"What do you think?" Frances winked at her. "That your name is Whitney Maddox."

"Is that…Whitney Wildz?" Byron held his phone up to his good eye. "Seriously?"

"What?" Matthew grabbed the phone away from his brother. "Jesus." It was, in fact, Whitney, standing next to Frances, smiling for the camera. She looked good. A little worried but that was probably because Frances had a death grip on her shoulders.

He was going to kill both of them. Why would Whitney let anyone take her picture? And hadn't he warned Frances not to do anything stupid? And didn't taking a picture of Whitney and plastering it all over the internet count as stupid?

The phone chimed as another message popped up.

Tell Matthew that she made me promise to only send it to you. No social media.

Matthew exhaled in relief. That was a smart compromise. He could only hope Frances would hold up her end of that promise. He handed the phone back over, hoping he appeared nonchalant. "That was a character she played," he said in his most diplomatic tone. "Her name is Whitney Maddox." He shot a look at Phillip, who was enjoying a cigar on Matthew's private deck.

Phillip gave him his best innocent face, then mimed locking his lips and throwing away the key.

The guys had managed to arrive at Matthew's place without notice. It was just the five of them. Byron didn't get along with their other half brothers David and Johnny at all and Mark was off at college. Matthew had decided to keep the guest list to the wedding party. Just the four Beaumont men who could tolerate each other. Most of the time.

Plus the sober coach, Dale. When Phillip was out on the farm, he was fine, but he'd been sober for only seven months now and with the pressure of the wedding, no one wanted a relapse. Hands down, that would be the worst thing to happen to the wedding. There would be no recovering from that blow to the Beaumont image and there would be no burying that lead. It would be game over.

Matthew and Phillip had made sure that Dale would be available for any event that took place away from the farm. Currently, Dale was sitting next to Phillip, talking horses. This was what the Beaumont men had come to—soda and cigars on a Saturday night. So this was what getting old was like.

"Who?" Chadwick asked, taking the phone.

"Whitney Wildz." Byron was studying the picture. "She was this squeaky-clean girl who starred in a rock-and-roll update of *The Partridge Family* called *Growing Up Wildz*. Man," he went on, "she looks *amazing*. Do you know if she's—?"

"She's not available," Matthew said before he could stop himself. But Byron was a Beaumont. There was no way Matthew wanted his little brother to get it into his head that Whitney was fair game.

All three of his brothers gave him a surprised look. Well, Chadwick and Byron gave him a look. Phillip was trying too hard not to laugh, the rat bastard. "I mean, if anyone tried to hit on her, it'd be a media firestorm. Hands off."

"Wait," Chadwick said, studying the picture again. "Isn't this the woman who's always stoned or flashing the camera?"

"She's not like that," Matthew snapped.

"What Matthew means to say," Phillip added, "is that in real life, Whitney raises prize-winning horses and lives a fairly quiet life. She's definitely *not* a fame monster."

"*This* is the woman who's the maid of honor?" Chadwick's voice was getting louder as he glared at the phone. "How is this Whitney Wild person not going to make this wedding into a spectacle? You know this is the soft opening for Percheron Drafts, Matthew. We can't afford to have anything compromise the reception."

"Hey—easy, now, Chad." Chadwick flinched at Phillip's nickname for him. Which Phillip used only when he was trying to piss off the oldest Beaumont. Yeah, this little bachelor party was going downhill, fast. "It's going to be fine. She's a friend of Jo's and she's not going to make a spectacle of anything. She's perfectly fine. Matthew was worried, too, but he's seen that she's just a regular woman. Right?" He turned to Matthew. "Back me up here."

"Phillip's correct. Whitney will be able to fulfill her role in the wedding with class and style." *And*, he added mentally, *with a little luck, some grace*. He hoped he'd put her in the right shoes. "She won't be a distraction. She'll help demonstrate that the Beaumonts are back on top."

Funny how a few days ago he'd been right where Chadwick was—convinced that a former star would take advantage of the limelight that went with a Beaumont Christmas wedding and burn them all. Now all Matthew was worried about was Whitney getting down the aisle without tripping.

He glanced up to see Byron staring at him. "What?"

It was Chadwick who spoke first. "We can't afford any *more* distractions," he said, half punching Byron on the arm. "I'm serious."

"Fine, fine. I prefer to eat my own cooking anyway." Byron walked off to lean against the railing on the balcony. Then he looked back at Matthew.

Matthew knew what that meant. Byron wanted to talk. So he joined his little brother. Then he waited. It was only when Phillip distracted Chadwick by asking about his baby daughter that Matthew said, "Yes?"

"Did you ask Harper?" Byron kept his voice low. Yeah, there was no need to let Chadwick in on this conversation. If Chadwick knew that they'd asked his nemesis to the wedding… Well, Matthew hated bailing people out.

"I did. He refused. The Harpers will not be joining us at the reception."

"Not even…?" Byron swallowed, staring out at the mountains cloaked in darkness. "Not even his family? His daughter?"

Suddenly, Matthew understood. "No. Is she the reason you've got a black eye?"

Byron didn't answer. Instead, he said, "Is Whitney Wildz *your* reason?"

"Her name," Matthew said with more force than he probably needed, "is Whitney Maddox. Don't you forget it."

Byron gave him the look—the same look all the brothers shared. The Beaumont smile. "Exactly how 'not available' is she, anyway?"

Deep down, Matthew had to admire how well his little brother was handling himself. In less than a minute, he'd completely redirected the conversation away from Harper's daughter and back to Matthew and Whitney. "Completely not available."

"Well," Phillip announced behind them, "this has been

lovely and dull, but I've got a bride-to-be waiting for me who's a lot more entertaining than you lot."

"And I've got to get home to Serena and Catherine," Chadwick added.

"I swear," Byron said, "I leave for one lousy year and I don't even know you guys anymore. Chadwick, not working? Phillip, sober and monogamous? And you?" He shot Matthew a sidelong glance. "Hooking up with Whitney Wild—"

"Maddox," Matthew corrected.

Byron gave him another Beaumont smile and Matthew realized what he'd just done—tacitly agreed that he was, in fact, hooking up with Whitney. "Right. You hooking up with anyone. Next thing you know, Frances will announce she's joining a nunnery or something."

"We can only hope," Chadwick grumbled before he turned to Phillip and Dale. "You okay to get home?"

Dale spoke. "You're going straight home to the farm?"

"Yeah," Phillip replied, slapping the man on the shoulder. "Jo's waiting on me. Thanks for—"

Matthew cut him off. "I'll see that he gets home."

"What—" Phillip demanded. He sounded pissed.

Matthew didn't look at him. He focused on Dale and Chadwick. "There's been a lot of pressure with this wedding. We can't be too careful."

"—the hell," Phillip finished, giving him a mean look.

Matthew refused to flinch even as he wondered what he was doing. At no point during the wedding planning had Phillip been teetering on the brink of dependency. Why was Matthew implying that he suddenly needed a babysitter?

Because. He wanted to see Whitney.

"Good plan," Chadwick said. "Dale, is that okay with you?"

"Yeah. See you tomorrow at the rehearsal dinner." Dale took off.

When it was just the four brothers, there was a moment of

awkward silence. Then the awkwardness veered into painful. What was Matthew doing? He could see the question on each man's face. Byron's black eye. Casting doubts on Phillip's sobriety. That wasn't who Matthew was. He was the one who did the opposite—who tried to make the family sound better, look better than it really was. He put the family name first. Not his selfish desire to see a woman who was nothing but a PR headache waiting to happen.

Phillip glared at him. Yeah, Matthew had earned that. "Can we go? Or do you need to take a potshot at Chadwick, too?"

Chadwick paused. He'd already headed for the door. "Problem?"

"No. Nothing I can't handle," Matthew hurried to say before Byron and Phillip could tattle on him.

He could handle this. His attraction to Whitney? A minor inconvenience. A totally amazing, mind-blowing inconvenience, but a minor one. He could keep it together. He had to. That was what he did.

Chadwick nodded. That he was taking Matthew at his word was something that should have made Matthew happy. He'd earned that measure of trust the hard way. It was a victory.

But that didn't change the fact that he was, at this exact moment, undermining that trust, as well.

Yeah, he could handle this.

He hoped like hell.

Fourteen

The drive out to the farm was fast and tense.

"After this wedding," Phillip finally said as he fumed in the passenger seat, "you and I are going to have words."

"Fine." Matthew had earned it, he knew.

"I don't get you," Phillip went on, clearly deciding to get those words out of the way now. Matthew thought that it'd be better if they could just fight and get it over with. "If you wanted to come out to the farm and see her, you could have just come. Why'd you have to make it sound like I had my finger on the trigger of a bottle? Because I don't."

"Because."

"What the hell kind of answer is that?"

Matthew could feel Phillip staring at him. He ignored him. Yeah, he'd bent the truth. That was what he did. Besides, he'd covered up for Phillip so many times they'd both lost count.

"You don't have to hide her. Not from us. And certainly not from me. I already know what's going on."

The statement rankled him. The fact that it was the truth? That only made it worse. "I'm not hiding."

"Like hell you're not. What else would you call that little show you put on back there? Why else does Byron have a black eye? You can dress it up as you're protecting her because that's what you do but damn, man. There's nothing wrong with you liking the woman and wanting to spend time with her. You think I'd hold that against you?"

"You would have. In the past."

"Oh, for crying out loud." Phillip actually threw his hands up. "There's your problem right there. You're so damn concerned with what happened last year, five years ago—thirty-five years ago—that you're missing out on the *now*. Things change. People change. I'd have thought that hanging out with Whitney would have shown you that."

Matthew didn't have a comeback to that. He didn't have one to any of it.

Phillip moved in for the kill. Matthew wasn't entirely used to the new, improved, changed Phillip being this right and certainly not right about Matthew. "Even Chadwick would understand if you've got to do something for *you*. You don't have to manage the family's image every single minute of your life. Figure out who you are if you're not a Beaumont."

Matthew let out a bark of laughter. "That's rich, coming from you."

If he wasn't a Beaumont? Not happening. He'd fought too hard to earn his place at the Beaumont table. He wasn't going to toss all that hard work to "figure out" who he was. He already knew.

He was Matthew Beaumont. End of discussion.

"Whatever, man. But the next time you want to cover your tracks, don't use me as a human shield. I don't play these games anymore."

"Fine."

"Good."

The rest of the drive was silent.

Matthew was mad. He was mad at Phillip—but he wasn't sure why. Because the man had spoken what felt uncomfortably like the truth? And Byron—he'd gotten that damn black eye. Because Matthew had asked him to do something dramatic.

And he was—he was mad at Whitney. That was what this little verbal skirmish was about, wasn't it? Whitney Maddox.

Why did she have to be so—so—so *not* Whitney Wildz? Why couldn't she be the kind of self-absorbed celebrity he knew how to manage—that he knew how to keep himself distant from? Why did she have to be someone soft and gentle and—yeah, he was gonna say it—innocent? She shouldn't be so innocent. She should be jaded and hard and bitter. That way he wouldn't be able to love her.

They pulled up at the farmhouse. Matthew didn't want to deal with Phillip anymore. Didn't want to deal with any of it. He was not hiding her, damn it.

He strode into the house as if he owned the thing, which he didn't. Not really. But it was Beaumont Farms and he was a Beaumont, so to hell with it.

He found Jo and Whitney on the sofas, watching what looked like *Rudolph the Red-Nosed Reindeer*, the one he'd watched back when he was a kid. Whitney was already in her pajamas. Jo's ridiculous donkey, Betty, was curled up next to Whitney. She was petting Betty's ears as if it were a normal everyday thing.

Why didn't he feel normal anymore? Why had he let her get close enough to change him?

"Hi," she said in surprise when she looked up. "Is everything—?"

"I need to talk to you." He didn't wait for a response. Hell, he couldn't even wait for her to get up. He scooted Betty out of the way and pulled Whitney to her feet.

"Are you—*whoa*!"

Matthew swept her legs up and, without bothering to look back at where Phillip was no doubt staring daggers at him—hell, to where the donkey was probably staring daggers at him—he carried Whitney up the stairs.

She threw her arms around his neck as he took the steps two at a time. "Are you okay?"

"Fine. Just fine." Even as he said it, he knew it wasn't true. He wasn't fine and she was the reason.

But she was the only way he knew how to make things fine again.

"Bachelor party went okay?" she asked as he kicked open the door to her room.

"Yeah. Fine." He threw her down on the bed and wrenched off his tie.

Her eyes went wide. "Matthew?"

"I—I missed you, okay? I missed you." Why did saying it feel like such a failure? He didn't miss people. He didn't miss women. He didn't let himself care enough to miss them.

But in two damn days, he'd missed her. And it made him feel weak. He wrapped the tie around his knuckles and pulled, letting the bite of silk against his skin pull him back. Pull him away from her.

She clambered up to her knees, which brought her face almost level with his. "I missed you, too."

"You did?"

She nodded. Then she touched his face. "I…I missed waking up with you."

At her touch—soft and gentle and innocent, damn it all—something in him snapped. "I don't want to talk."

She was the reason he was the mess he was. He had to—he didn't know. He had to put her in her place. He *had* to keep himself distanced from her, for his own sanity. And he couldn't do that while she was touching him so sweetly, while she was telling him she missed him.

One eyebrow notched up. Too late, he remembered announcing that the whole reason he was sweeping her off her feet was to talk to her.

But she didn't say anything. Instead, she pushed herself up onto her feet and stripped her pajama top off. Then, still standing on the bed—not tipping over, not accidentally kicking him—she shimmied out of her bottoms, which was fine because it was damnably hard to think the lustful thoughts he was thinking about someone who was wearing pink pants covered with dogs in bow ties. Then she sank back down to her knees in front of him.

No talking. No touching. He would keep a part of himself from her, just as he did with everyone else. No one would know what she meant to him. Not even him.

Then he had her on her back, but that was still too much. He couldn't look into her eyes, pale and wide and waiting for him. He couldn't see what he meant to her. He couldn't risk letting her see what she meant to him. So he rolled her onto her belly and, after getting the condom, buried himself in her.

She didn't say a word, not even when her back arched and her body tightened down on his and she grabbed the headboard as the climax rolled her body. She was silent as he grabbed her hips and drove in deep and hard until he had nothing left to give her.

They fell onto the bed together, panting and slick with sweat. He'd done what he needed to—what a Beaumont would. This was his birthright, wasn't it? White-hot affairs that didn't involve feelings. His father had specialized in them. He'd never cared about anyone.

Matthew needed to get up. He needed to walk away from Whitney. He needed to stay a Beaumont.

Then she rolled, looped her arms over his neck and held him. No words. Just her touch. Just her not letting him go.

How weak was he? He couldn't even pull himself away from her. He let her hold him. Damn it all, he held her back.

It was some time before she spoke. "After the wedding… after Christmas morning…"

He winced. "Yes?" But it was surprisingly hard to sound as if he didn't care when his face was buried in the crook of her neck.

"I mean," she hurried on, her arms tightening around his neck, "that'll be... We'll be..."

It. That'll be it. *We'll be* done. That was what she was trying to say. Then—and only then—did he manage to push himself up. But he couldn't push himself away from her. "My life is here in Denver, and you..." He swallowed, wishing he were stronger. That he could be stronger for her. "You need the sun."

She smiled—he could see her trying—but at the same time, her eyes began to shine and the corners of her mouth pulled down. She was trying not to cry. "Right."

He couldn't watch her, not like this. So he buried his face back against her neck.

"Right," he agreed. *Fine,* he thought, knowing it wasn't. At least that would be clean. At least there wouldn't be a scene that he'd have to contain. He should have been relieved.

"Anytime you want to ride the Trakehners," she managed to get out, "you just let me know."

Then—just because she made him so weak—he kissed her. Because no matter how hard he tried, he couldn't hold himself back. Not around her.

Fifteen

They spent the next morning looking over the carriage that would pull Phillip and Jo from the chapel to the reception. The whole thing was bedecked with ribbons and bows of red-and-green velvet, which stood out against the deep gray paint of the carriage. Whitney wasn't sure she'd ever really grasped what the word *bedecked* meant, but after seeing the Beaumont carriage, she understood completely. "It's a beautiful rig."

"You like it?" Matthew said. He'd been quiet all morning, but he'd held her hand as they walked around the farm together. In fact, he had hardly stopped touching her since they'd woken up. His foot had been rubbing against her calf during their breakfast; his hands had been around her waist or on her shoulders whenever possible.

Whitney had been worried after last night. Okay, more than worried. She'd originally thought that he was mad at her because of the picture with Frances, but there'd been something else going on.

After the intense sex—and the part where he'd agreed that this relationship was short-term—she had decided that it wasn't her place to figure out what that "something else" was. If he wanted to tell her, he would. She would make no other claims to him.

She would try not to, anyway.

"I do." She looked at the carriage, well and truly bedecked. "It's going to look amazing. And with Jo's dress? *Wow.*"

He trailed his hand down her arm. She leaned into his touch. "Do you have a carriage like this?"

She grinned at him. He really didn't know a whole lot about horses, but he was trying. For her. "Trakehners aren't team horses, so no."

He brushed his gloved fingertips over her cheek. She could feel the heat of his touch despite the fabric. "Want to go for a ride?"

She pulled up short. "What?"

"I'll have Richard hook up the team. Someone can drive us around."

"But…it's for the wedding."

"I know. You're here *now*." Then he was off, hunting up a hired hand to take them on a carriage ride around Beaumont Farms.

Now. Now was all they had. Matthew gallantly handed her up into the carriage and tucked the red-and-green-plaid blankets around her, then wrapped his arm around her shoulder and pulled her into him. Then they were off, riding over the snow-covered hills of the farm. It was…magical.

She tried not to overthink what was happening between them—or, more to the point, what wasn't going to happen in a few days. What was the point of dwelling on how she was going to go back to her solitary existence, with only her animals and crazy Don to break up the monotony?

This was what she wanted—a brief, hot Christmas-vacation romance with a gorgeous, talented man. A man who would make her feel as if Whitney Maddox was a woman who didn't have to hide anymore, who could take lovers and have relationships. This was getting her out of the safety of her rut.

This time with Matthew was a gift, plain and simple. She couldn't have dreamed up a better man, a better time. He was, for lack of a better word, *perfect*.

That had to be why she clung to him extra hard as they rode over the ice-kissed hills, the trees shimmering under the winter sun. This was, hands down, the most romantic thing she'd ever done—even though she knew the score. She had him now. She didn't want to miss any of that.

So when it was time to go to the rehearsal, she went early with Matthew. They were supposed to eat lunch, but they wound up at his palatial apartment, tangled up in the sheets of his massive bed, and missed lunch entirely. Which was fine. She could eat when she was alone. And the dinner after the rehearsal would be five-star, Matthew promised.

They made it to the chapel for the rehearsal almost an hour ahead of everyone else—of course they did. The place was stunning. The pews were decorated with red-and-gray bows that matched the ones on the carriage perfectly atop pine garlands, making the whole place smell like a Christmas tree. The light ceilings had dark buttresses and the walls were lined with stained-glass windows.

"We're going to have spotlights outside the windows so the lights shine at dark," Matthew explained. "The rest of the ceremony will be candlelit."

"Wow," Whitney breathed as she studied the chapel. "How many people will be here for the wedding?"

"Two hundred," he said. "But it's still an intimate space. I've been working with the videographers to make sure they don't overtake the space. We don't want anything to distract from the happy couple."

She took a deep breath as she held an imaginary bouquet in front of her. "I should practice, then," she said as she took measured steps down the aisle. "Should have brought my shoes."

Matthew skirted around her and hurried to the altar. Then he waited for her. Her cheeks flushed warm as an image of her doing this not in a dove-gray gown but a long white one forced its way across her mind.

Now, she thought, trying not to get ahead of herself. *Stay in the now.*

That got harder to do when she made it up to the altar, where Matthew was waiting. He took her hands in his and, looking down into her eyes, he smiled. Just a simple curve of the lips. It wasn't rakish; it wasn't predatory—heavens, it wasn't even overtly sexual.

"Ms. Maddox," he said in a voice that was as close to reverent as she'd ever heard him use.

"Mr. Beaumont," she replied because it seemed like the thing to do. Because she couldn't come up with anything else, not when his gaze was deepening in its intensity.

It was almost as if, standing here with Matthew, in this holy place…

No. She would not hope, no matter how intense his gaze was, no matter how much his smile, his touch affected her. She would not hope, because it was pointless. She had three more days before she left for California. Tonight, Christmas Eve and maybe Christmas morning. That was it. No point in thinking about something a little more permanent with him.

He leaned forward. "Whitney…"

Say something, she thought. *Something to give me hope.*

"Hello? Matthew?"

To his credit, he didn't drop Whitney's hands. He did lean back and tuck her fingers into the crook of his arm. "Here," he called down the aisle as the wedding planner came through the doors. Then, to Whitney, he said, "Shall we practice a few times before everyone gets here?"

"Yes, let's." Which were not words of hope.

That was fine. She didn't want any.

Really.

* * *

Against his will, Matthew sent Whitney home with Jo and took Phillip back to his place. Even though they were going to shoot photos before the ceremony, Jo had decided that she wanted to at least get ready without Phillip in the house.

Phillip wasn't exactly talking to Matthew, which was fine. Matthew had things to do anyway. The press was lining up, and Matthew had to make sure he was available for them before they wandered off and started sniffing around.

This was his job, his place in this world. He had to present the very best side of the Beaumonts, contain any scandals before they did real damage and...

His mind drifted back to the carriage ride across the farm with Whitney—to the way she'd looked standing hand in hand with him at the altar.

For such a short time, it hadn't mattered. Not the wedding, not the public image—not even the soft launch of Percheron Drafts. His showroom-ready apartment, his fancy cars—none of that mattered.

What had mattered was holding a beautiful woman tight and knowing that she was there for him. Not for the family name, the fortune, the things.

Just him.

And now that time was over and he was back to managing the message. The good news was that Byron's little brawl had done exactly what Matthew had intended it to—no one was asking about Whitney Wildz.

He checked the social media sites again. Whitney had insisted on keeping her hat on during the rehearsal and the following dinner and had only talked with the embedded press representatives when absolutely required. He knew he should be thankful that she was keeping her profile as low as possible, but he hated that she felt as if she had to hide.

All was as calm as could be expected. As far as he could tell, no one in attendance had connected the quiet maid of honor with Whitney Wildz. Plus, the sudden influx of famous people eating in restaurants and partying at clubs was good press, reinforcing how valuable the Beaumont name was without Matthew being directly responsible for their actions.

It wouldn't last, he knew. He sent out the final instructions to the photographer and videographer, which was semipointless. Whitney was in the wedding party, after all. And he hadn't let her change her hair. They'd have to take pictures of her. But reminding the people on his payroll what he expected made him feel better anyway.

They just had to get through the wedding. Whitney had to make it up the aisle and back down without incident.

Just as she'd done today. She'd been downright cute, miming the action in a sweater and jeans and that hat, of course. But tomorrow?

Tomorrow she'd be in a gown, polished and proper and befitting a Beaumont wedding. Tomorrow she'd look perfect.

He could take a few days after the wedding, couldn't he? Even just two days off. This thing had swallowed his life for the past few months. He'd earned some time. Once he got Phillip and Jo safely off on their honeymoon and his siblings and stepmothers back to their respective corners, once he had Christmas dinner with his mom, he could...

He could go see Whitney. See her in the sun. Ride her horses and meet her weird-looking dogs and her pop-singer cats.

This didn't change things, he told himself as he began to rearrange his schedule. This was not the beginning of something else, something *more*. Far from it. They'd agreed that after the wedding, they were...done.

Except the word felt wrong. Matthew had never had a problem walking away from his lady friends before. When it was over, it was over. There were no regrets, no looking back and absolutely no taking time off to spend a long weekend together.

It was close to midnight when he found himself sending her a text. What are you doing? But even as he hit Send, he knew he was being foolish. She was probably in bed. He was probably waking her up. But he couldn't help himself. It'd been a long day, longer without her. He just wanted... Well, he just wanted her.

A minute later, his phone pinged and there was a blurry photo of Whitney with a tiny donkey in her lap. He could just see the silly dogs in bow ties on her pajama pants. Jo had leaned over to grin into the frame, but there was no missing Whitney's big smile. Watching Love Actually and eating popcorn, came the reply.

Good. Great. She was keeping a low profile and having fun at the same time.

Then his phone pinged again.

Miss you.

He could take a couple of days. Maybe a week. Chadwick would understand. As long as they made it through the wedding with no big scandals—as long as all the Beaumonts stayed out of the news while he was gone—he could spend the time with Whitney.

Miss you, too, he wrote back. Because he did.

He was pretty sure he'd never missed anyone else in his life.

The day of the wedding flew by in a blur. Manicures, pedicures, hairstylists, makeup artists—they all attacked Whitney and the rest of the wedding party with the efficiency of a long-planned military campaign. Whitney couldn't tell if that was because Matthew had everything on a second-by-second schedule or if this was just what happened when you had the best of the best working for you.

She finally met Byron Beaumont, as he was next in the makeup artist's chair after they finished painting Whitney's lips scarlet-red. She winced as she looked at the bruise around his face that was settling into purples and blues like a sunset with an attitude.

"Ms. Maddox," he said with an almost formal bow. But he didn't touch her and he certainly didn't hug her, not as Frances had. Heck, he didn't even call her Whitney Wildz. "It's an honor."

"I'm sorry about your eye," she heard herself say, as if she were personally responsible for the bruising. Byron looked a great deal like Matthew. Maybe a few inches shorter, and his eyes were lighter, almost gray. Byron's hair was almost the same deep auburn color as Matthew's, but his hair was longer with a wave to it.

Byron grinned at her then—almost the exact same grin that Matthew had and that Phillip had. "Anything in the service of a lady," he replied as he settled into the chair, as if he had his makeup done all the time.

By four that afternoon, the ladies were nibbling on fruit slices with the greatest of care to sustain them through the rest of the evening. "We don't want anyone to pass out," the wedding planner said as she stuck straws into water bottles and passed them around.

Then they were at the chapel, posing for an endless series of photos. She stood next to Jo, then next to Frances, then between Frances and Serena. They took shots with Jo's parents, her grandmother, her aunt and uncle. Since Toni Beaumont was singing a song during the wedding, they had to have every permutation of who stood where with her, too.

Then the doors to the chapel opened, and Whitney heard Matthew say, "We're here." The men strode down the aisle as if they owned the joint. At first she couldn't see them clearly. The chapel wasn't well lit and the sunlight streaming in behind them was almost blinding. But then, suddenly, Matthew was leading the Beaumont men down the aisle.

She gasped at them. At him. His tuxedo was exquisitely cut. He could have been walking a red carpet, for all the confidence and sensuality he exuded.

"We're keeping to the schedule, right, people?" he demanded. Then their gazes met and the rest of the world—the stylists and wedding planner chatting, the photographer bossing people around—all of it fell away.

"Perfect," he said.

"You, too," she murmured. Beside her, Frances snickered. Oh, right—they weren't alone. Half the Beaumont family was watching them. She dropped her gaze to her bouquet, which was suddenly very interesting.

Matthew turned his attention to the larger crowd. "Phillip's ready for the reveal."

"Everyone out," the photographer announced. "I want to get the bride and groom seeing each other for the first time. Joey," he said to Jo. He'd been calling her that for half an hour now. Whitney was pretty sure it wouldn't be much longer before Jo cracked and beat the man senseless with his own camera. "You go back around and walk down the aisle."

Jo glanced at Whitney and rolled her eyes, which made them both giggle. Whitney gathered up Jo's train, and they hurried down the aisle as fast as they could in these dresses. It was only when they had themselves tucked away that Frances gave the all clear.

Whitney and Frances peeked as Jo made her way up the aisle to where Phillip was waiting for his bride. "I don't know if I've ever seen him that happy," Frances whispered as Phillip blinked tears of joy out of his eyes. "I hope it lasts."

"I think it will," Whitney decided.

"I just…" Frances sighed. "I just wish we could all stop

living in our father's shadow, you know? I wish I could believe in love. Even if it's just for them."

"Your time will come," Whitney whispered as she looked at Frances. "If you want it to."

"I don't. I'm never getting married," Frances announced. Then, standing up straighter, she added, "But if you want to marry Matthew, can I be your bridesmaid?"

Whitney opened her mouth and then closed it because as much as she wanted to tell Frances her head was in the clouds and that after tonight Whitney and Matthew were going their separate ways, she couldn't dismiss the image of him standing with her at the very same altar where Jo and Phillip now stood. For that brief moment—when she'd wanted him to say something that would give her hope that they weren't done after this. When she'd thought he was going to do just that. And then they'd been interrupted.

Finally, she got her mouth to work. "I'm not going to marry Matthew."

"Pity," Frances sniffed. "I saw how he looked at you. Trust me, Matthew doesn't look at other people like that."

So everyone had seen that look. Whitney sighed. But before she could respond, a deep voice behind them said, "Like what?"

The women spun around at Matthew's voice. Whitney teetered in her shoes, but Matthew caught her before she could tip forward. Then his arms were around her waist, and he was almost holding her. But not quite. They managed to keep a glimmer of space between them.

"Hi," Whitney breathed. She wanted to tell him how much she'd missed him. She wanted to ask if they could spend this last night together, after the reception, so that their Christmas morning could start off right. She wanted to tell him that he was the most handsome man she'd ever seen.

She didn't get the chance.

"Like that," Frances said with obvious glee.

"Frannie." Matthew's voice was as clear a warning as Whitney had heard since that very first night, when he'd realized who she'd once been. The space between him and Whitney widened ever so slightly. "Go make sure Byron stays out of trouble, please."

Frances rolled her eyes. "Fine. I'm going, I'm going. But he's not the one I'm worried about right now." Then, with a rustle of silk, she was gone.

And they were alone in the vestibule. "You look amazing," she managed to get out.

"So do you," he said as his arms tightened around her.

"I'd kiss you, but…"

"Lipstick," he agreed. "We're going to have to go out for more photos soon."

A quick moment. That was all they had. But she wanted more. She at least wanted tonight. One more night in his arms. Then, somehow, she'd find a way to let him go. "Matthew…" she said.

At the same time, he said, "Whitney…"

They paused, then laughed. But before she could ask for what she wanted, the photographer called out, "The best man and maid of honor? Where are you, people?"

"Tonight," Matthew said as he looped his arm through hers. "We'll talk at the reception, all right?"

All she could do was nod as they walked down the aisle together, toward the happy couple and the bossy photographer.

Whitney didn't trip.

Sixteen

Everything went according to plan. After they finished the photos in the chapel—including a series of shots with Betty in her flower-girl-slash-ring-bearer harness—the whole party went to a nearby park and took shots with snow-covered trees and ground as the backdrop. They also did the shots of Jo and Phillip getting into and out of the carriage.

Then, just because everything was going so smoothly, Matthew asked the photographer to take pictures of each of the couples with the carriage, just so he and Whitney could have a photo of the two of them with the Percheron team. So they'd have something to remember this week by.

Serena and Chadwick didn't mind, but Frances and Byron clearly thought he was nuts and Matthew didn't miss the look Phillip gave him.

He wasn't hiding how he felt about Whitney, okay? He *wasn't*. That wasn't why he had the photographer take extra shots of all the couples by themselves. He reasoned that Chadwick and Serena had had a small ceremony—absolutely no pomp and circumstance had been allowed. True, Serena had been about seven months pregnant and, yes, Chadwick had already had a big wedding for his first marriage. Serena's parents had walked her down the aisle while Phillip,

Matthew and Frances stood as witnesses. Cell phone photos didn't count. So Matthew was really doing this for Chadwick and Serena, so they'd have beautiful photos of them at their very best. And if Matthew and Whitney got some memories out of it, so much the better.

And because he was not hiding how he felt about her, he had his arms on her while the photographer snapped away. An arm around her waist when they leaned underneath the evergreen tree, its branches heavy with glistening snow. Handing her up into the carriage. Tucking her against his waist.

For their part, his family was…okay with it. Byron had slapped him on the back and said, "Some women are worth the bruises, huh?" Matthew had ignored his baby brother.

Chadwick's big comment was, "The situation is under control, correct?"

To which Matthew had replied, "Correct." Because it was.

For the moment, anyway.

"You doing okay?" Matthew whispered to Phillip as they stood at the front of the chapel. He could see that Phillip had started to fidget.

"Why is everything going so slow?" Phillip whispered back as Frances did the "step, pause, step, pause" walk down the aisle to Pachelbel's *Canon in D.* "I want Jo."

"Suck it up and smile. Remember, the cameras are rolling."

Matthew looked out over the full house in the chapel. Phillip's mother had a place of honor in the front, although she had chosen not to sit with Jo's family. Which didn't surprise Matthew a bit. Eliza Beaumont was not a huge fan of anything that had to do with the Beaumont family, a list that started with Matthew and went on for miles.

But Phillip had wanted his mother at his wedding and Matthew had the means to make it happen, so the woman was sitting in the front row, looking as relaxed as a prisoner before a firing squad and pointedly ignoring everyone.

Serena was headed down the aisle now, although she was moving at a slightly faster clip than Frances had been. "Beautiful," Chadwick whispered from the other side of Matthew. "I have to say, I'm impressed you pulled this off."

"Don't jinx it, man," Matthew hissed through his smile.

Then Serena was standing next to Frances and everyone waited.

Matthew could see Whitney, standing just inside the doors. *Come on, babe,* he thought. *One foot in front of the other. You can do it. It'll be fine.*

Then the music swelled and she took the first step. Paused. Second step. Paused. Each foot hit the ground squarely. She didn't wobble and she didn't trip on her hem. She *glided* down the aisle as if she'd been born with a bouquet in her hand and a smile on her face. The whole time, she kept her gaze fastened on him. As though she was walking not just to him but *for* him.

God, she was *so* beautiful. Simply perfect. But then, the woman in her doggy pajamas had been perfect, too. Even when she was klutzy and nervous and totally, completely Whitney, she was absolutely perfect.

How was he going to let her go?

She reached the altar and took her place. He could see how pleased she was with herself, and frankly, he was pretty damn happy, too.

Then there was a moment that should have been silent as the music changed to the wedding march and Jo made her big entrance.

Except it wasn't silent. A murmur ran through the crowd—the highest of Denver's high society, musicians and actors and people who were famous merely for being famous.

Then he heard it. "...Whitney Wildz?" Which was followed by "...that hair!" More murmurs followed. Then a click. The click of a cell phone snapping a picture.

He looked at Whitney. She was still smiling, but it wasn't

the same natural, luminous thing it'd been earlier. Her face was frozen in something that was a mockery of joy.

It'll be okay, he wanted to tell her. He wanted to believe it.

Then the music swelled up, drowning out the whispers and the clicks. Everyone stood and turned to the entrance. Betty tottered down the aisle as the daughter of one of the brewery's employees tossed rose petals onto the ground. Betty should have held everyone's attention.

But she didn't. Not even a mini donkey wearing a basket and a crown of flowers over her floppy ears could distract from Whitney Wildz. People were holding their devices high to get the best shot of her.

Jo came down the aisle on the arms of her parents. Matthew took advantage of this to get the wedding rings untied from the small pillow on Betty's back, and then the farm manager, Richard—looking hilariously uncomfortable in a suit—led the small animal off before she started munching on the floral arrangements.

When he stood back up, Matthew caught Whitney's eye as Jo took her place at the altar. He gave her an encouraging nod, hoping that she'd get the message. *Ignore them. Don't let them win.*

When the music stopped this time, the murmuring was even louder. The preacher took his place before the happy couple. Jo handed Whitney her bouquet.

The murmuring was getting louder. People weren't even trying to whisper now. Matthew wanted to shout at the crowd, *This is a wedding, for God's sake! Have some decency!* But he'd long since learned that you didn't feed the fire like that. Ignoring the excited whispers was the only way to make it through this.

"Matthew," Chadwick said in the quietest of whispers, and Matthew knew what his older brother was thinking. This was having the situation under control? *This* was handling it?

The preacher began to talk about vows and love, but he had to stop and pitch his voice up in volume to be heard.

Matthew kept his attention on the happy couple—and on Whitney. She was blinking too fast, but her smile was locked. Her face looked as if it were going to crack in half. She didn't look at him, but she didn't need to. He could read her well enough.

This was just like the restaurant all over again. She'd done nothing—not even tripped, much less fallen, and yet she was setting off a media firestorm. He had the sinking feeling that if he got out his phone and checked social media, Whitney would already be trending.

Then, out of the corner of his eye, he saw it. Movement, in the aisle. As best he could without turning and staring, he looked.

Oh, hell. People were getting up and exiting the pews—coming into the aisles. Phones and cameras were raised. They were jostling—yes, jostling—for a better shot. Of Whitney. Of someone they thought was Whitney Wildz.

"If I may," the preacher said in a tone better suited for a fire-and-brimstone Sunday sermon than a Christmas Eve wedding. "If I may have *silence*, please."

That was when Whitney turned her stricken face to his. He saw the tears gathering, saw how fast she was breathing. "I'm sorry," she said, although he couldn't hear her over the crowd. He read her lips, though. That was enough.

"No," he said, but she didn't hear him. She was already turning to hand Jo's bouquet to Serena and then she was running down the aisle, arms stiffly at her side.

Gone.

Oh, hell.

"Ms. Maddox?"

Whitney realized that she was outside.

The horse-drawn carriage was parked in front of the chapel, waiting for the happy couple. The happy couple whose wedding she'd just ruined. She vaguely recognized the driver as one of the farmhands, but he wasn't wearing jeans and flannel. "Is everything okay?"

"Um…" No. Nothing was okay. And worse? She didn't know when it would start being okay again. The chapel was on a college campus. She had to walk…that way to get to a main road?

Snow began to fall on her bare shoulders. She hadn't even managed to snag her cape, but who cared. She wasn't going back in there. She was going…

Home. That was where she was headed. Back to her solitary ranch where she could live out her solitary life. That was where she belonged. Where she wouldn't embarrass herself, which was bad enough. She was used to that.

She'd ruined Jo's wedding. Her best friend—hell, her only friend—and Whitney had ruined the wedding. She hadn't fallen, hadn't even dropped her bouquet.

She'd just been herself.

Why had she ever thought she could do that?

She wrapped her arms around her waist to try and keep warm as she walked away from the carriage and the driver. She didn't really have a plan at this point, but she knew she couldn't take off in the wedding carriage. The very carriage she'd ridden in yesterday, snuggled in Matthew's arms. She'd already messed up the wedding. She drew the line at stealing the carriage.

"Ms. Maddox?" the driver called behind her, but she ignored him. She needed to get back to the farm so she could get her things and go—and there was no way the horse and carriage could get her there.

She'd walk to the main road and catch a taxi. Taxis could get her to the farm and from there, she could leave. There. That was a plan.

The snow was coming down thick and fast, each flake

biting into her bare shoulders with what felt like teeth. It felt as if it were trying to punish her, which was fine. She deserved it.

She'd tried. She'd tried *so* hard. She'd offered to step aside. She'd tried to convince Matthew to let her change her hair. And she damn well had on panties today. Industrial-strength Spanx in opaque black, just to be extra sure.

But it wasn't enough. It would never be enough. She would *always* be Whitney Wildz. And every time she got it into her foolish little head that she wasn't—that she could be whoever she wanted to be—well, this was what would happen. If she didn't hurt herself, she'd hurt the people she cared for. People like Jo.

People like Matthew.

God, she couldn't even think of him without pain. She'd *told* him she was going to ruin the wedding, but the man had decided that through the sheer force of his will alone, she wouldn't. He'd been bound and determined—literally—to have the perfect Beaumont wedding. He was a man who was used to getting what he wanted. He'd given her a chance to show him—to show everyone—that she was Whitney Maddox. For a beautiful moment—a too-short moment—she'd thought they had succeeded.

But that'd been just an illusion and they were both the poorer for indulging in it. He had to hate her now. She was living proof that he couldn't control everything. He'd never be able to look at her and see anything but imperfection.

She slipped but managed not to fall. The sidewalks were getting slicker by the second and these shoes weren't suited for anything other than plush carpeting. She could hear the sounds of traffic getting closer, and she trudged on. Good. The farther she could get from the wedding, the better.

Her stomach turned again. She hoped Jo and Phillip were still *able* to get married. What if the whole thing had devolved into a brawl or something? What if the preacher decided Whitney's running was a sign from God that Jo and Phillip shouldn't be married? It was on her head. All of it.

She'd just come upon the main street when she heard "Whitney?" from behind her.

Matthew. No, God, please—not him. She couldn't look at him and see his failure and know it was hers.

She waved her hands, hoping there was a taxi somewhere. Anywhere. And if there wasn't, she'd keep walking until she found one.

"Whitney, wait! Babe," she heard him shout. Damn it, he was getting closer.

She tried to hurry, but her foot slipped. Stupid heels on the stupid snow. The whole universe was out to get her. She thought she would keep her balance but she hit another slick spot and started to fall. Of course. Maybe someone would get a picture of it. It'd make a great headline.

Instead of falling, though, she was in his arms. The warmth of his body pushed back against the biting cold as he held her tight. It was everything she wanted and nothing she deserved. "Let me go," she said, shoving against him.

"Babe," he said, pointedly not releasing her from his grip. If anything, he held on tighter. "You're going to freeze. You don't even have your cape."

"What does it matter, Matthew? I ruined the wedding. You saw how it was. You and I both knew it was going to happen and...and we let it." The tears she'd been trying not to cry since the first whisper had hit her ears threatened to move up again. "Why did I let it happen?"

He came around to her front and forced her to look at him. He was not gentle about it. "Because you're Whitney Maddox, damn it. And I don't care about Whitney Wildz. You're enough for me."

"But I'm not and we both know it. I'm not even enough for me. I can never be the perfect woman you need. I can never be perfect." The tears stung at her eyes almost as much as the snow stung against her skin. And that, more than any-thing else, hurt the most.

"You *are*," he said with more force. "And you didn't ruin the wedding. Those people—they did. This is on them. Not you."

She shook her head, but before she could deny it—because Matthew had never been more wrong in his life—shouts of "Whitney? Whitney!" began to filter through the snow.

A taxi pulled up next to them and the cabbie shouted, "You need a cab, lady?"

Matthew got a fierce look on his face. "Let me handle them," he said as he stripped off his tuxedo jacket and wrapped it around her shoulders. "Follow my lead. I can fix this."

She wanted to believe it. She wanted him to protect her, to save her from herself.

But she couldn't. She couldn't let him throw away every-thing he'd worked for because of her. She wasn't worth it.

"Don't you see? I can't be another mess you have to clean up. I just can't." She ducked under his arm and managed to get the taxi door open on the second try. "It has to be this way," she told him.

Before the press could swarm, she got in the taxi and slammed the door. Matthew stood there, looking as if she'd stabbed him somewhere important. It hurt to look, so she focused on the cabbie.

"Where to, lady?" he asked.

"Can you take me to the Beaumont Farms? Outside the city?"

The cabbie stared at her dress, then at Matthew and the press, complete with flashing cameras and shouting. "You can pay?"

"Yes."

The fare would be huge, but what did it matter?

This evening had already cost her everything else.

Seventeen

Matthew was going to punch something. Someone. Several someones.

Hard.

Whitney's taxi sped off, its wheels spinning for traction on the newly slick streets. Then the press—the press *he* had invited to the wedding—was upon him like hungry dogs fighting over the last table scrap.

"Matthew, tell us about Whitney!"

"Matthew! Did you see Whitney Wildz drinking before the wedding? Can you confirm that Whitney Wildz was drunk?"

"Was she on drugs?"

"Is there something going on, Matthew? Are you involved with Whitney Wildz?"

"Did Whitney have a baby bump, Matthew? Who's the father?"

"Is Byron the father? Is that why he has a black eye? Did you two fight over her?"

The snow picked up speed, driving into his face. It felt good, the pain. It distracted him from the gut-wrenching agony of Whitney's face right before she ran down the aisle. Right before she got into the taxi.

"Ladies and gentlemen," he said in his meanest sneer. There were no such people before him. Just dogs with cameras.

No one blinked. The sarcasm was lost on them entirely. They just crowded closer, microphones in his face, cameras rolling. For a moment, he felt as if he were back in college and, at any second, someone was going to ask him what he thought about those photos of his father with his pants around his ankles.

Panic clawed at him. No one had ever asked if he wanted to manage the Beaumont public image. It was just something he'd fallen into and, because he was good at it, he'd stuck with it. Because it earned him a place in the family. Because defending his father, his brothers, his stepmothers—that was what made him a Beaumont.

Figure out who you are if you're not a Beaumont.

Phillip's comment came back to Matthew, insidious little words that Matthew had thought were Phillip's attempt at chipping away at Matthew's hard-won privilege.

But if being a Beaumont meant he had to throw Whitney to the dogs...could he do that? Did he want to?

No. That was not what he wanted. It'd never been, he realized. Hadn't he asked Byron to generate some press? Hadn't that been putting Whitney first?

Who am I? Her voice whispered in his ear. *Who am I to you?*

She'd said those words to him in the front seat of his car, right before he'd tied her to the bed.

She was Whitney Maddox. And she was Whitney Wildz. She was both at the same time.

Just as he was Matthew Beaumont and Matthew Billings. He'd never stopped being Matthew Billings. That lost little boy had always been standing right behind Matthew, threatening to make him a nobody again.

Because if he wasn't a Beaumont, who was he? He'd always thought the answer was a nobody. But now?

Who was *he* to *her*?

Who was he?

He was Matthew Beaumont. And being a Beaumont was saying to hell with what people thought of you—to hell with even what your family thought of you. It was not giving a rat's ass what the media said.

Being a Beaumont was about doing what you wanted, whenever you wanted to do it. Wasn't that what was behind all of those scandals he'd swept under the rug for all these years? No one else in his family ever stopped to think. They just *did*. Whatever—whoever—they wanted.

He looked at the cameras still rolling, the reporters all jostling for position to hear what juicy gossip he was going to come up with. The headlines tomorrow would be vicious—but for the first time in his life, he didn't care.

"Ladies and gentlemen," he began again, "I have no comment."

Dead silence. Matthew smirked. He'd truly managed to stun the lot of them into silence.

Then he turned and hailed a cab. Mercifully, one pulled right up to the curb.

"Where to, buddy?" the cabbie asked as Matthew shut the door on the gaping faces of the press.

Who was he? What did he want?

Whitney.

He had to get her. "The Beaumont Farms, south of the city."

The cab driver whistled. "That's gonna cost you."

"Doesn't matter." Then, with a smile, he added, "I'm a Beaumont."

Eighteen

"Ms. Maddox?" The guard stepped out of the gate when Whitney climbed out of the taxi. "Is everything all right?"

She really wished people would stop asking that question. Wasn't the answer obvious? "I…I need to pay him and I don't have any money. On me. I have some cash in the house…" She shivered. The cabbie had turned the heat on full blast for her, but it hadn't helped. Matthew's jacket wasn't enough to fend off the elements. The snow was coming down thick and fast and the cabbie was none too happy about the prospect of making it home in this weather.

The guard stared at her with obvious concern. Then he ushered her into the guard house. "I'll pay the driver and then get a truck and take you to the house. Don't move."

He said it as if he was afraid she might go somewhere, but she didn't want to. There was heat in this little building.

Plus, she was almost back to the farmhouse. This nice guard would take her the rest of the way. She'd get out of this dress and back into her own clothes. She didn't have much. She could be packed within twenty minutes. And then…

If she left immediately, she could be home by tomorrow afternoon. Back to the warmth and the sun and her animals and crazy Donald, none of whom would ever care that she'd ruined the Beaumont Christmas wedding. Yes. Back to the safety of solitude.

The guard came back with a truck and helped her into the passenger seat. He didn't tell her how much it had cost to get the cabbie to drive away. She'd pay it back, of course. She'd use the money from the royalty checks for *Whitney Wildz Sings Christmas, Yo*. Fitting.

"I'm going home," she told him when he pulled up in front of the house and got out to unlock the front door for her. "Tonight."

"Ms. Maddox, the snow is going to continue for some time," he said, the worry in his voice obvious. "I don't think—"

"I can drive on snow," she lied. She couldn't stay here. That much she knew.

"But—"

Whitney didn't listen. She said, "Thank you very much," and shut the door in the man's face. Which was a diva thing to do, but it couldn't be helped.

She didn't get lost on her way back to what had been her room and Matthew's room. Their room. Well, it wasn't that anymore.

She changed and started throwing things into her bags. She'd have time when she got home to shake out the wrinkles. She didn't have that time now.

The dress…it lay in a heap on the floor, as if she'd wounded it in the line of duty. She'd felt beautiful in the dress. Matthew had thought so. She'd felt…

She'd felt like the woman she was supposed to be when she'd worn it. Glamorous and confident and sexy and worthy. And not scandalous. Not even a little.

She picked it up, shook it out and laid it on the bed. Then she did the same with his tuxedo jacket. In her mind's eye, she saw the two of them this afternoon, having their pictures taken in a park, in a carriage bedecked in Christmas bows.

They hadn't even gotten to walk down the aisle together. She'd ruined that, too.

Her bags were heavy and, because she hadn't packed carefully, extra bulky. Getting them both out of the door and down the hall was bad enough. She was navigating the stairs one at a time when she heard the front door slam open.

"Whitney?"

Matthew. *Oh, no.* That was all that registered before she lost her grip on one of her bags. It tangled with her feet and suddenly she was falling down the last few stairs.

And right into his arms. He caught her just as he had before—just as he was always doing.

Then, before she could tell him she was sorry or that she was leaving and she'd pay back the cab fare, he was kissing her. His hair was wet and his shirt was wet and he was lifting her up to him, sliding his hands around her waist and holding her.

And he was kissing her. She was so stunned by this that she couldn't do anything but stare at him.

He pulled away, but he didn't let her go. Hell, he didn't even set her on her feet. He just held her as though his life depended on it.

She needed to get out of his arms so she could go back to being invisible Whitney Maddox. But she couldn't. Was it wrong to want just a few more minutes of being someone special? Was it wrong to want that hope, even if she was going to get knocked down for daring to hope almost immediately?

Matthew spoke. "*Always* kiss me back," he said, as if this were just another wild Tuesday night and not the ruination of everything. Then her bags—which had come crashing down after her—seemed to register with him. "Where are you going?"

"Home," she told him. She would not cry. Crying solved

nothing. And really, this was everything she'd expected. "I don't belong here. I never did."

"That's not true."

Oh, so they were just going to deny reality? Fine. She could do that. "Why are *you* here? Why aren't you at the wedding?" Then, because she couldn't help herself—because she might never get another chance to have him in her arms—she placed her palm on his cheek.

He leaned into her touch. "I had this revelation," he said as he touched his forehead to hers. "It turns out that I'm not a very good Beaumont."

"What?" she gasped. She'd heard him say how hard it was to earn his place at the table—at the altar. Why would he say that about himself? "But you're an amazing man— you take care of people and you took your sister and brother to my concert and the whole wedding was *amazing*, right until I ruined it!"

His grin was sad and happy and tired, all at the same time. Her feet touched the ground, but he didn't let her go.

"A Beaumont," he said with quiet conviction, "wouldn't care what anyone else thought. They wouldn't care how it played in the media. A Beaumont would do whatever he wanted, whenever he wanted, consequences be damned. That's what makes a Beaumont. And I've never done that. Not once." He paused, lifting her up even closer. "Not until I met you."

Hope. It was small and felt foreign in her mind—so foreign that she almost didn't recognize it for what it was. "Me?"

"You. For the first time in my life, I did something because I wanted to, regardless of how it'd play in the press." He touched her hair, where the bejeweled clip still held her stubborn white streak in place. "I fell in love with you."

Her heart stopped. Everything stopped. Had he just said... that he'd fallen in love with her? "I—" But she didn't have anything else.

Then, to her horror, she heard herself ask, "Who am I to you?"

He gave her a little grin, as if he'd known she was going to ask the question but had hoped she wouldn't. "You're a kind, thoughtful, intelligent woman who can get clumsy when you're nervous. You'd do anything for your friends, even if it puts you in the line of fire."

"But—"

He lifted her face so she had to look at him. "And," he went on, "you're beautiful and sexy and I can't hold myself back when I'm around you. I can't let you go just because of how it'll look in a headline."

"But the press—tomorrow—" She shuddered. The headlines would be cruel. Possibly the worst in her life, and that was saying something. The Beaumont public image would be in tatters, thanks to her. "Your family... I ruined *everything*," she whispered. Why couldn't he see that?

His grin this time was much less sweet, much more the look of a man who could bend the press to his will. "You merely generated some PR, that's all. And there's no such thing as bad PR."

"That's not— What?"

"Don't let the guessing games that complete strangers play hold you back, Whitney. Don't let a manufactured scandal keep us apart."

"But—but—but your life is here. And I need the sun. You said so yourself."

"The Beaumonts are here," he corrected her. "And we've already established that I'm not a very good Beaumont."

The thing that was hope began to grow inside of her until it was pulsing through her veins, spreading farther with each heartbeat. "What are you saying?"

"Who am I?" His voice was low and serious. It sent a chill up her spine that had nothing to do with his wet shirt. "If I'm not a Beaumont, who am I to you?"

"You're Matthew." He swallowed, his Adam's apple bobbing nervously. "It never mattered to me what your name is—Billings, Beaumont—I don't care. I came here thinking it'd be nice to meet a man who could look at me without thinking about Whitney Wildz or all the headlines. A man who could make me feel sexy and wanted, who could give me the confidence to maybe start dating. Who could show me it was even possible."

He cupped her face in his hands, his thumbs stroking her cheeks. "And?"

"And…that man was you. Eventually," she added with an embarrassed smile, remembering the first time she'd fallen into his arms. "But now the wedding's over. And I—" Her voice caught. "I can't be another mess you have to manage, Matthew. And I can't ever be perfect. You know I can't."

"I know." For the briefest of seconds, it felt like a book being slammed shut. "But," he added, "I don't want perfection. Because I'll never get it. I can try and try to be the perfect Beaumont until I lie down and die and I'll never make it. That's what you've shown me."

A little choked sob escaped her lips. No matter what she did, she'd never be perfect, either. Not even to him. "Great. Glad to help."

"Be *not* perfect with me, Whitney. Let me be a part of your life. Let me catch you when you fall—and hold me up when I stumble."

"But…the press—the headlines—"

"They don't matter. All that matters is what you and I know. And this is what I know. I have never *let* myself fall in love before, because I've been afraid that loving someone else will take something away from me. Make me less of a man, less of a Beaumont. And you make me more than that. More than my name. You make me whole."

The impact of his words hit her hard. Suddenly, those tears that she hadn't allowed herself to cry because the disappointment and shame were always to be expected—suddenly, those tears were spilling down her cheeks. "I didn't expect to find you. I didn't expect to fall in love with you. I don't—I don't know how to do this. I don't want to mess this up. More than I already have."

"You won't," he said, brushing his lips over hers. "And if you try, I'll tie you to the bed." She giggled, and he laughed with her. "We will make this work because I'm not going to let you go. You will always be my Whitney. Although," he added with a wicked grin, "I was thinking—you might want to try out a new last name. Maybe something that starts with a *B*."

"What are you saying?"

"Marry me. Let me be there for you, *with* you."

"Yes. Oh, God—*Matthew*." She threw her arms around his neck. The tears were coming faster now, but she couldn't hold them back. It was messy and not perfect but then, so was life. "You see me as I really am. That's all I ever wanted."

"I *love* you as you really are." He swept her feet out from underneath her and began to climb the stairs back to his room. Their room. "Love me back?"

"Always," she told him. "Always."

* * * * *

MILLS & BOON®

Want to get more from Mills & Boon?

Here's what's available to you if you join the exclusive **Mills & Boon eBook Club** today:

✦ *Convenience – choose your books each month*
✦ *Exclusive – receive your books a month before anywhere else*
✦ *Flexibility – change your subscription at any time*
✦ *Variety – gain access to eBook-only series*
✦ *Value – subscriptions from just £1.99 a month*

So visit **www.millsandboon.co.uk/esubs** today to be a part of this exclusive eBook Club!

MILLS & BOON®

Sparkling Christmas Regencies!

A seasonal delight for Regency fans everywhere!

Warm up those cold winter nights with this charming seasonal duo of two full-length Regency romances. A fantastic festive delight from much-loved Historical authors. Treat yourself to the perfect gift this Christmas.

Get your copy today at www.millsandboon.co.uk/Xmasreg

Also available on eBook